In
Case
of
Emergency

In Case of Emergency

Poorna Bell

CENTURY

1 3 5 7 9 10 8 6 4 2

Century
20 Vauxhall Bridge Road
London SW1V 2SA

Century is part of the Penguin Random House group of companies whose
addresses can be found at global.penguinrandomhouse.com.

First published in the UK by Century in 2022

www.penguin.co.uk

A CIP catalogue record for this book is available from the British Library.

ISBN 978-1-529-13574-9 (Hardback)
ISBN 978-1-529-13575-6 (Trade paperback)

Poop by Mourad Mokrane from NounProject.com
Pray by AliWijaya from NounProject.com
Tear by Kaleo from NounProject.com

Set in 11.4/16.25 pt Palatino LT Pro
Typeset by Jouve (UK), Milton Keynes
Printed and bound in Great Britain by Clays Ltd, Elcograf S.p.A.

The authorised representative in the EEA is
Penguin Random House Ireland, Morrison Chambers,
32 Nassau Street, Dublin DO2 YH68.

www.greenpenguin.co.uk

For Mal. You came with me to the ends of the earth, always know that I will do the same for you.

Prologue

1999

Some moments in life are nothing like you expect they will be.

Seeing the Mona Lisa. (Way smaller than the knock-off poster sold in Dartford Market of her smoking a massive spliff.) The first day of your first period. (Not magical and followed by the realisation that you're locked into a thirty-year contract once a month.) Running away from home. (You quite like having regular food and access to a familiar toilet.)

But occasionally a significant thing happens that is different from whatever you imagined because it is so much more. And while it may be as rare as the sighting of a Great Comet, sometimes that moment is a First, illuminated with such brightness in recollection that the memory of it burns for an entire lifetime.

I wanted my first kiss to be like Angela Chase kissing Jordan Catalano from *My So-Called Life*, all chapped lips and goofy smiles in the school boiler room, but I think deep down I believed it would be a bit crap. My friends had all experienced terrible first kisses – toothy, submerged in dribble, and almost always shared with someone who just happened to be there and willing. At sixteen, time was running out for me.

It almost happened with Skateboard Steve. I'd had a crush on him ever since I'd seen him in a Nirvana T-shirt, mooching around the town centre with a dog chain around his neck and a skateboard in one hand. We were both at the school disco in the local community centre to mark the end of term. The DJ, also the owner of the local hardware store, Hard Nutz, was trying to jolly along a bunch of sullen teenagers who had peeled off into segregated groups of boys and girls pasted to the walls.

A bunch of us were trying to escape the bad pop music, sitting outside by some scrubby grass and a Pin Bin. Squinting through thick eyeliner, we attempted to look subversive and cool with our bottles of Coke and 7Up mixed with whatever we'd managed to steal from our parents' drinks cabinets.

As Backstreet Boys' 'I Want It That Way' began playing, Steve started leaning in. *It's happening!* I thought. *Finally!* But then he stopped, went the colour of a lettuce and vomited melon liqueur all over his jeans.

As a fairly unremarkable-looking Indian girl in a predominantly white suburban town, I hadn't expected an opportunity for a first kiss to come around again quite so soon. My parents were stricter than those of my English classmates and I wasn't usually the type of girl boys fawned over. Brown women back then weren't even seen as desirable; the Dartford W. H. Smith had yet to stock the *Kama Sutra* and dodgy online Indian auntie porn wasn't yet a thing.

But then, my best friends and I went on our first holiday sans parents, to Cornwall. And there, someone had finally seen me for who I was.

It was like something from a movie, but better. Because in a movie, there'd be someone cheesy like Shania Twain playing as our lips came together, but in real life, it was Smashing Pumpkins' 'Today.' Possibly the most perfect song, for a perfect kiss.

Everything felt like it was beginning. Everything felt like it was ending – just like that point before a river meets the sea. The taste of him on my lips, the feeling of knowing someone in a way I had never known anyone before, the sense of freedom and power over my own body, the softness of it all, carried through to a wave of emotion that felt like it would burst right out of me.

'Shall I go get us some drinks?' I asked, extricating myself from underneath the old, scratchy blankets that smelled slightly of dog. He placed another kiss on my lips in silent affirmation and picked up his guitar. I pulled on my jacket as scattered notes trailed behind me like confetti.

The sharp air jolted me out of that warm place. Overhead, the sky had transformed from a piercing blue to an expanse of black shot through with diamonds. I looked up at the stars as they shone, ancient and powerful, as if to

remind me that the world is beautiful. Even for an unremarkable Indian girl.

I picked out two semi-cold cans of beer from the booze
bucket by my friends, all clustered and wrapped in a tangle
around the bonfire, whistling and cheering as I returned. I
loved them and knew I could count on them for anything.

'Dicks,' I mouthed at them, unable to stop a smile so
wide, it threatened to glue the corners of my lips to my
ears permanently. Walking back to the shed, I sang along
to the lyrics booming out.

But as I reached for the handle, the sound of the guitar
stopped. I heard two voices. One belonged to the beautiful boy I had just kissed. The other belonged to a person
I had sat next to at lunch for the best part of three years,
exchanged letters with almost daily at the school gates,
who had stayed at my house countless times, eaten my
mother's food and sat with me on my sofa as we debated
which one of the Hanson brothers we'd shag, marry or
kill. I paused to hear what nice things she might be saying
about me. But as I listened, I realised that what she was
saying wasn't nice at all.

I was unable to believe this was happening. The
euphoria I'd felt turned to ash in my mouth. Imagine: the
worst things you think about yourself, being said by someone you thought would always love and protect you.

We all have expectations of those big moments in life.
First kisses, first loves. We even have expectations of the
less nice moments, like heartbreak. I always thought my
first proper heartbreak would be the result of a great love,

and I'd play The Cure and Air Supply so loud my mum would bang on the door and then make me a ham and cheese toastie to cheer me up.

But I never expected in a million years that my first heartbreak would follow so soon after my first kiss. Or that the first person to break my heart wouldn't be a boy, but one of my best friends.

1

'You saw the Chelsea match, yeah?' said David from Commercial Partnerships. I inwardly groaned. My male colleagues started talking excitedly about players and penalties and how 'they were robbed, mate'. One of the more kindly ones – and it was usually one of the dads who had a daughter – took a look at me and asked: 'Do you watch football, Bel?'

I shook my head and the rueful expression on his face confirmed what he thought he knew: *girl, not interested in football.* Which, if he'd ever met my older sister Devi or my niece Karen, he would know was an outdated stereotype.

Instead, I fiddled with the cable connecting my laptop to the main screen of the boardroom we had all gathered in for our quarterly directors' meeting. As head of New Creative, I was expected to give the first presentation. As was always the case when I was the only woman in a room, I was made to default to the role of mummy, only stopping short of burping them. It was expected that I'd oversee all the extra stuff, from double-checking the assistant had made enough coffee to making sure the tech had been set up. I hated doing it but had learned the hard way that if I didn't, no one would, and I'd be the one left without coffee.

A full-bodied hush rippled through the room, which meant our CEO Crispin had arrived. I took my pre-assigned seat near the top of the table, which had real front-of-the-bus vibes, but at least I wasn't seated anywhere near Tristan. Like me, he was one of the youngest directors in the advertising agency. Unlike me, he was a man whose unique brand of arrogance had no doubt been fermented at private school, matured as he stepped from one plum opportunity to the next with minimal effort, and distilled into the person I knew today. That is, a bozo who wielded his good looks for evil ends and, if rumours were true, had a penchant for charming new female interns then ghosting them to the brink of madness.

I focused instead on Crispin, who was as always neat and beautifully dressed. He was vocal about maintaining his lean figure with daily cardio and strict food rules. At client lunches he would only eat white fish or vegetarian food. Cheese, he said, was the Devil's smegma, and he'd stopped eating bread in 1998. This meticulousness did not, however, extend to alcohol and other substances. His age was rumoured to be anywhere between sixty and seventy-five, indeterminate because of light brushstrokes of Botox and fillers.

There was one highlight to being in this meeting. Although he wasn't in town often, when he was, Crispin favoured me, and not in a creepy way. His ex-wife was Indian, and although she turned out to be 'a Satanic bitch viper who stole half his money', he doted on their daughter Tamara. I think I reminded him of her even though we looked nothing alike – she was tall and looked like an Instagram model with latte-coloured skin, while I was short, a rich shade of walnut with bodily proportions that would have been fashionable in an ancient Hindu text circa 400 BC. Sturdy forearms, robust breasts, a melon bottom all condensed in slightly too small a space. But perhaps it was also because he didn't scare me, and I didn't simper around him, that I had won favour. Just as he treated me like a proxy daughter, I treated him like a proxy father and my lighthearted nagging was always in his best interests.

'Good to see you all, gang,' he said, standing at the head of the table. 'Much to discuss. Is it too early for whisky?' It was 9.30 a.m. The men puffed out their chests like pigeons swaggering on the cornices of Trafalgar Square and murmurs of 'it's five o'clock somewhere', 'whisky breakfast' and 'never too early', filled the air. But their expressions said otherwise. Most of them were entering their forties or fifties and simply wanted to make it through the day and get home in time to put their kids to bed.

'No, Crispin, we're not having whisky,' I said. 'Most of us haven't even had a coffee yet.' He looked at me and then at his assistant Jane, who also shook her head. 'Oh, boo,' he replied. 'Fine, we'll wait until lunch. Fun sponge.'

I could sense the relief rippling through the room and some of the directors gave me a grateful smile, looking at me properly for the first time that day. I'd been a director for two years, and still some of them seemed surprised when I turned up to a meeting. At 36, I wasn't that much younger than some of them, but because I looked younger, I had to constantly reinforce that I wasn't some fresh-faced newbie who'd been hired to fill a seat. There was often a momentary delay as they registered how I was dressed and spoke, during which they had to reconfigure their mental Rolodex of reference points for people who looked like me: corner shop owner's daughter, demure, frigid onion-chopper, garlic-masher, terrorist's wife.

'I'll get us started, shall I?' I said and stood up confidently, inside feeling as if any moment, the woven cream carpet would give way to molten lava. Crispin smiled in silent approval. There was no sign of the hurricane clamped behind his teeth that would very soon begin the sequence of events that up-ended everything.

*

We were over halfway through the morning. Aside from the fact that this was one of the most important meetings of the year – a quarterly update on each department – time with Crispin was limited because he was mostly based in Monaco. It was the ultimate cliché, but he had vast sums of disposable income and took every opportunity to sunbathe, eat lobster and drink champagne for as long as he was able. Leopard, our agency, was one of many in his portfolio of businesses, but as he had built the agency from the ground up himself, he took more of an interest in what we did. And he liked to get involved.

Unlike other big bosses who sat in an open-plan office with their employees in an attempt to convince their teams they were 'just one of the gang' (while the actual gang liberated company stationery and toilet paper because they didn't get bonuses or six-figure salaries), Crispin had no interest in dissolving the hierarchy. As much as I knew I had a seat at the boardroom table because I had earned it, there was a part of me that never felt fully in my own skin here, always misty-eyed with regret for the dream I had relinquished of working at a small, independent agency to make money and a name for myself.

Working at a smaller company might have been less toxic for the soul, but I also knew that I liked £4 hipster coffees and not having to worry about paying my bills, or what I spent on nights out. Maybe playing a part and wearing a cape dress that made me look like a flying squirrel – even though the shop assistant had assured me I'd feel powerful in it – weren't the worst things in the world.

Along with everyone else, I needed to overegg my successes and spin failures into candyfloss, sweetened with promises of how we'd do better. This meeting would determine our budget for next year. We had brief, high-pressure windows to impress Crispin. Those who didn't invariably found their department restructured. Tristan,

Head of New Media, was in the middle of his presentation and people were discreetly checking their phones as the clock inched towards lunch. Crispin cut him off midway, which was never a good sign.

'This is great, Tristan, but I have a question for you – what the fuck happened with Lightning? That's your area, right?'

Tristan's face froze. 'Lightning?' I'd never seen him rattled before. I liked it.

'Yes,' said Crispin. 'The Oseni fuck-up.'

Everyone put their phones down, sensing that at any moment things could explode. By now Tristan had rearranged his face into a mask of self-assurance.

'Well,' he said, 'it was an easy mistake to make, and I'd say that it was a team failure, not just New Media's.' It wasn't an easy mistake to make, and worse, I had the feeling that some of us were about to be fed to the furnace of Crispin's wrath.

'Yes,' said Crispin, 'but it also cost us a lot of money. I don't care whether it was a hard or an easy mistake to make: how the fuck did this happen?'

The Oseni Fuck-Up, as it was referred to, was related to a campaign that we'd put together for Lightning, an emerging, cutting-edge sports brand, who wanted a prominent Black personality to lead it. The client was spending a lot of money and wanted the Premier League footballer Edward Oseni, who'd just won the BBC's Sports Personality of the Year Award but was known as much for his philanthropy as for his sporting skill. In one of the early meetings, we'd had a big discussion about maybe instead going for someone like the up-and-coming rapper Eric O, whose star was on the rise and who had already been seen wearing their clothes. Eventually, Lightning went for Oseni, though, and on the day of the meeting to celebrate the partnership, our social media manager had sent his intern to fill in for him and take notes because he was off on annual leave.

Maybe the intern was hungover from the night before or maybe, like most people in the company, he was some little snotnose who got the gig because of nepotism and didn't actually care about being there. But whatever the reason, when he put out tweets about the campaign, he used a picture of Eric O, but captioned it with Edward Oseni's name. And because that team had zero Black people in it, no one noticed for about six hours. The ensuing outrage from media outlets and influencers was tremendous. Memes were created and Lightning pulled the campaign.

Crispin looked pointedly at Tristan, who quickly said: 'I mean, yes, there are definitely people in my team accountable, but we all help out across each other's campaigns. I'm surprised Bel of all people didn't catch it sooner, to be honest.'

I started in my chair at the sound of my name. The rest of the earthworms around the table were blind to the undercurrent of what was really happening here. New Creative and New Media worked quite closely together, so they assumed I was being dragged into it because of my role. But I knew Tristan wasn't that stupid. I'd heard him making 'jokes' about diversity hires.

And now it seemed it wasn't enough that the company trotted me out whenever they needed to show a flash of diversity; apparently I was meant by default to be the race monitor *just because I wasn't white*?

I looked at Tristan poisonously. 'Why should *I* of all people have caught it?'

He shrugged and smiled. 'Because I know how much you care about D&I.'

D&I: Diversity and Inclusion. Everyone knew that it was the hot topic of discussion at industry events, with actual change being far off because the only people who took it seriously were those most impacted by it but with the least power. And the people who ran companies, sat on boards and chose leadership teams, continued to hide behind the 'best person for the job' rationale, and it remained a mystery or perhaps sheer coincidence how the 'best' people just happened to look and behave exactly like them.

Catching a hint of suppressed fury in the air, Crispin said: 'Well, look, let's move on. We'll discuss it later, Tristan. Dan, you're next . . .'

As Dan, Head of Research, launched into his presentation, I sat in my chair feeling incandescent with fury. I needed an outlet before I exploded. But who to text? Certainly not Devi – she'd probably be packing my niece's school lunch or running around after her husband. And my friend Katrina wouldn't get it because while she talked about being half Greek *a lot*, if she'd been at that boardroom table she'd have been as clueless as the rest. I needed some-one who understood.

I scrolled through my phone and on impulse texted Ranvir, a colleague who wasn't as senior as me. I'd worked with her a few times. She and I always said we 'must go for drinks' and never did, but we had a camaraderie when we saw each other in meetings and moaned about the lack of Black and brown people in the business. I was saved in her phone as Becky and she was saved in mine as Barry, for a joke.

The diversity in this company is RIDIC – you won't believe the racist piece of shit I just had to deal with.

She wasn't online, so I put my phone back down and looked up, wondering why everyone had gone quiet. I looked at the main screen. There was my message to 'Barry', for everyone to see, in stark black and white. I had completely forgotten that my laptop, which was synced to my phone, was still plugged in.

Even the freshly baked jammy doughnut, flecked with sugar crystals that sparkled in the midday sun, couldn't soothe the knot of nerves building in my stomach. My assistant Maggie, who had placed it wordlessly on my desk as if sensing the anxiety radiating through the glass doors of my office, was one of my few sources of joy at Leopard. Immaculately dressed and British Ghanaian, she reflected the unshakable confidence of Gen Y in the straight set of her shoulders and the way she never, ever seemed flustered.

In contrast, I sat hunched at my desk, cape dress bunched around me like a depressed Bond villain, replaying the scene over and over again. Crispin saying, 'We'll talk about this later,' in a clipped tone devoid of warmth. Tristan hadn't smirked for once but actually looked . . . shocked. I guess no one likes being called racist, not even him.

I knew how lucky I was to have my own office, with an assistant who didn't spend all her time on TikTok. And offices with windows in Marylebone – the expensive patch behind Oxford Circus, with stucco-faced terraces of Georgian buildings – were even rarer, even if mine did overlook the local STD clinic tucked away in a dripping, damp archway of Victorian brick, like something from a Dickens novel. But the burning question now was: had I jeopardised my career?

I picked up the doughnut just as my phone buzzed in my hand, which resulted in a rogue squirt of jam onto my dress. I dabbed at it with water and realised the second-worst thing about white cape dresses: even if you could pull them off, you could definitely *only* pull them off when they were pristine.

Rather than the text I'd expected from my friend Katrina with her ETA for lunch, it was just an Instagram notification. Two swipes took me to a photo of my sister Devi with my sixteen-year-old niece. It seemed Karen had just got into the under-18s county football team. Devi beamed out from under a black beanie hat, her glossy curly hair and beautiful heart-shaped face pressed proudly to her daughter's.

For a moment I envied Devi's life back in the sub-urbs, where most of her daily challenges seemed to centre around the supermarket shop and Karen's A-level choices. I debated whether to text congratulations, but when I saw that the last WhatsApp from her had been sent two weeks ago, and realised she'd chosen to share this news on Insta-gram rather than telling me directly, I popped my phone in my bag. It wasn't out of spite, more that I didn't know if a text from me would mean anything to her, and she was likely already celebrating with Karen and Mum and Dad anyway.

Besides, hopefully Katrina was waiting for me at the restaurant, and I needed to talk to someone about what had just happened. Even if she wouldn't properly under-stand, it was better than nothing. Despite the warmth of the day, I draped a black scarf over the jam stain and headed out.

*

Dirty Joe's Pizza was possibly the worst choice for a stress-free lunch, given that it was no-reservations, they were always packed and got testy if your guest hadn't shown up within five minutes.

But it was Katrina's favourite, and it was her turn to choose where we ate. We had known each other for about a year, after meeting each other at a military fitness class in the park. She had thrown up behind a tree after a round of burpees and I'd handed her a tissue, which she accepted gratefully while the instructor yelled, 'Puke is for the weak! Get back in, no excuses!' By chance, I then bumped into her a few weeks later at an industry awards ceremony. We both burst into laughter at the memory of the instructor – neither of us had gone back since – and she told me she worked as a publicist. Our offices were only a ten-minute walk apart and we fell into an easy friendship.

She always had invites to great parties that she let me tag along to, and she was usually available at a minute's notice. She was also always late. And now, it appeared, wasn't answering her phone. The waiter had already approached me twice in fifteen minutes.

'We really need the table,' he said on his third pass.

'Travis,' I snapped, looking at his name tag, 'I am having the mother of days. *Please* cut me some slack.'

Travis pushed his oversized Prada glasses onto the bridge of his nose and pointed at the queue. One man in his thirties was tapping at his watch as if he was about to miss an event of utmost importance as opposed to ordering a Semi Hard and Hot nine-inch Pepperoni. I looked at my phone again. No response from Katrina to my last three **Where are you**!!! messages. Travis coughed.

'For fuck's sake,' I muttered under my breath. 'You know what? Release the table. I'll just go eat a falafel wrap while hunched on a bench that hopefully isn't spattered with pigeon poop.'

'Sounds wonderful!' He beamed fleetingly at me then

turned the full wattage of his charm onto the next couple in line, ushering them to my now-vacated table as if welcoming the Queen into the royal box.

*

June in London can be a trying time. It lulls you into open-toed sandals and possibly even shedding that extra cardigan you carry around with you just because it's England. On the other hand, it can descend into days of unending rain, that fogs up the windows, slides damp little fingers down the small of the back, pulls wisps of hair into frizzy curls.

Although it was humid, the temporary reprieve from rain meant that the streets were filled with people wanting to be anywhere but their stagnant, temperature-controlled offices. I was dying to escape the sad fate of the desk lunch and being interrupted with *Ooh, sorry, are you eating?* just as your food is inches away from your mouth. I stormed past a group of men who'd loosened their ties while laughing about something or other as they queued for burritos, a woman heading purposefully towards Oliver Bonas with a returns bag in her hand, a bunch of students in flannel shirts and oversized glasses arranging themselves over a bench.

I was worried about Crispin and Tristan, I was upset at Katrina who still hadn't texted. I was hangry because I still hadn't eaten. There *had* to be someone else I could call.

I scrolled on my phone while walking, flipping the

scarf over my shoulder angrily as it loosened and came half-undone. With my head still brimming with a thousand different thoughts, the scarf yet again unravelled and I yanked it once more.

All of this meant that I didn't notice the open trapdoor leading to a pub cellar, yawning like a mouth directly in my path. I didn't notice the hazard cones placed around it, warning pedestrians to beware. I stepped past these with the confidence of a person whose feet would automatically encounter paving stones, but was quickly forced to adjust to the reality of empty space and a ten-foot drop.

The brain is a highly sophisticated organ, with over 120 billion neurons, and inside it, information can travel at speeds of up to 268 miles per hour. But still, when faced with certain situations, there is only one word in the universal language that adequately conveys the complexity of what is happening.

'Arrrgggggggggggggghhhhhhhhh!'

Time stretched into infinity as I hit my head and dark unconsciousness smothered out the light.

2

The last time I'd experienced unconsciousness was as a teenager. I'd been submerged in a bath so hot it felt as if it was cooking the outer edges of my toes. Unable to withstand any more lobstering, I pulled the plug and quickly stood up. The sudden transition from heat to cold made me faint, and the next thing I knew, I was lying facedown, bum exposed to the elements, attempting to breathe through the vanishing Matey bubbles while water gurgled down the plug hole.

Emerging from that place – the black cosmos that the brain keeps like a storage locker adjacent to your consciousness – was even more disconcerting as an adult. The lack of input between my last memory of being on the sunny streets of Marylebone and my current reality of lying on a hospital bed, was jarring. And it was definitely not a dream, because dreams were not accompanied by smells. Specifically, an olfactory bouquet of overcooked mashed potato and bleach. Thin blue curtains had been pulled shut either side to afford some shred of privacy from the five other beds in the room.

I tried to get up, but there was a shooting pain in my head. I touched the side of my skull to find that there was a bandage wound around it. Panic flashed through me. *What if I'd broken my brain?!* I lifted the blanket draped across me and looked down to see that I was still wearing the cape dress, but if I thought it looked bad with a solitary jam stain on it before, there were no words for what it looked like now, covered in crud.

'Hello?' I said with a croak.

'She's awake, nurse!' a voice yelled from the other side of the curtain. I gingerly reached over to pull it back and saw a twenty-something South Asian woman with extremely dilated pupils smiling at me from the next bed.

'Salma,' she said.

'Bel,' I replied, lying back on the pillow, exhausted by that small movement.

'What are you in for?' she asked.

'I have no idea,' I said. 'I think I fell down a hole.' A hole? That sounded like something a cartoon character would say.

'Weird. Is that why your dress looks like that?'

Thankfully, at that exact moment, a doctor came in carrying a clipboard, and yanked the curtain back to its closed position. 'I'm Doctor Dave,' she said, sitting on the edge of the bed. 'And you are . . . Beryl Kumar, is that correct?'

'BERYL?!' I heard a squawk from the other side of the curtain.

'Ms Malik, please stop that or we'll have to get you

moved. I don't want to have to say it again,' Doctor Dave said firmly. Despite her businesslike tone, I knew what was coming.

'Beryl?' she said, looking at me with a smile twitching at the corners of her mouth, trying to fight it like the pull of a magnet.

'It's Sanskrit,' I said tightly, as I'd had to explain pretty much my entire life, to people who wondered why I had the same name as an old lady who lived in the Wirral and liked to eat Hobnobs. 'It's the name of a gemstone – one that my dad gave to my mum when they met, and it was all he could afford.'

'Ah. Well, it's an unusual name,' she said.

'Yes,' I said. 'And so is Doctor Dave, wouldn't you say?'

'Fair enough,' she said good-naturedly. 'Although it's actually Davé – my husband is Indian. His surname, you see. I just say Dave because it's easier. Also, I like to see the looks on people's faces when they expect someone who looks like Phil Mitchell, and they get, well, me.'

'Call me Bel,' I said, hoping that this wouldn't be an opportunity for the other person to tell me how much they liked Indian food or how they'd once holidayed on the trains there and wasn't it amazing? My parents hadn't thought it was important for Devi or me to visit India when we were younger, and it was often disconcerting to have a place I knew little about being described to me in such fanatic detail by someone who meant well, but whose ancestors had probably ruled over mine within the last hundred years.

My head was aching; my entire body felt as if it was filled with rust and fur. I wanted to get this over with and go home.

'Okay, Bel, so what do you remember?'

I remembered that brief, terrifying moment of falling down into the cellar, and the next thing I knew I was here, I told her. 'Nothing else?' she asked. I shook my head and immediately regretted the movement as a crackle of what felt like lightning shot across my temple.

Dr Dave nodded. 'Let me tell you what happened, then. Firstly, you're an extremely lucky woman,' she said. 'It might not feel like that now, but you fell feet-first into a pub cellar, a distance of ten feet, and somehow you have no broken bones. You did hit your head, however, and there was some external bleeding hence the bandage, but we've run some scans and there isn't any internal bleeding or damage to the skull.'

She talked about concussion, things to look out for, how to monitor the bleeding. She told me not to text and walk at the same time, and that I wouldn't believe how many accidents were caused by people not paying attention. When she was done, she looked expectantly at me. While I was relieved that I hadn't snapped my neck, I was still hungry, my clothes were filthy and my head hurt. I just wanted to go home.

'At any rate,' she said, eventually realising that protestations about me learning the error of my ways were not going to happen, 'you're free to go home. We've notified your emergency contact who should be arriving any moment.'

In Case of Emergency

'Wait, how did you know who to contact?'

'Your work pass was round your neck. We contacted them, and they notified your loved one. I've got rounds to do, but I'll check in with you before you're discharged.' She gave me a quick smile and walked off purposefully towards another section of the ward.

My bag had been placed on the bedside table with my pass poking out of it. I needed to let Maggie know what had happened and find out who she'd called. I fished about for my phone only to see that the screen was smashed to bits. It definitely wouldn't have been Mum or Devi I'd named, but maybe my last flatmate, Roger? I hoped not – we hadn't parted on the best of terms due to his tendency to microwave fish and broccoli at the same time.

I heard the gentle scrape of a curtain hook. 'Yes, Salma?' I said, still staring up at the ceiling.

'Want to know what I'm in here for?' she said, with the mad look in her eyes of a seagull staking out a cone of chips.

'Listen,' I said, 'I hope you don't mind, but I'm really tired so I'm going to . . .' I pulled the curtain back again. Closing my eyes, I breathed deep. All I needed was a few moments of peace and quiet to figure out what to do next.

'Hello, Bel,' a deep voice said.

My eyes flew open. I saw the figure at the foot of my bed and realised there was no statute of limitations on how many times a day you can say *argh*.

*

Shortly after my thirtieth birthday back in 2013, I went through a crisis of sorts.

As much as I considered myself to be an independent free-thinker, determined not to follow the path of my older sister Devi who'd married her university sweetheart, Nikhil, and had settled five minutes away from our parents in Kent, I wasn't immune to the world story of What A Woman Should Have Achieved By 30. 'World stories' was my term for certain narratives spun over and over again until they become self-fulfilling and inescapable because the joists of them are nailed down into books, TV shows and films. They become part of the small talk you engage in with taxi drivers or at the supermarket ('I don't think I've seen a sadder sight than a woman buying herself flowers') and of interactions at weddings and family gatherings. ('When is it going to be your turn?')

I'm not saying men aren't pressured around marriage and kids, but as I explained to my friend Anthony, who was wigging out after his fiancée broke up with him, we aren't on an even playing field. While men may be judged more harshly if they don't attain economic success, the same is true for a woman around domestic success no matter how much she has achieved in her career. We weren't even allowed to have our own mortgages or credit cards until the 1970s, I told him. (And possibly shouldn't have said any of this so soon after the break-up that the Save the Date announcement was still stuck to his fridge.)

World stories might make cute rom-coms but they are

not conducive to aiding life decisions. Think about the number of people who settled for an ill-suited partner because turning thirty and being single is a frightening prospect, a superhighway to dying alone.

After I hit thirty, try as I might, I couldn't shake the feeling that I should be building something more permanent in my personal life.

Work was fine but it was hardly dazzling. I focused that wild excess of energy into my love life and tried online dating. This was in the pre-dating-apps era when you had to use a laptop to go onto Match.com and pray that a serial killer didn't lurk behind the GSOH and 'likes to travel'.

A few mediocre dates later, I met Gregor Jamieson in a large, airy pub in the banking district, an area I hated because the atmosphere was soulless and everyone dressed like sad storm clouds. Although his deep voice and Scottish accent conveyed strength of character and confidence, I could tell he was nervous from the way he tugged at his sleeves and the pearling of sweat above his upper lip. I don't think he was intimidated, I simply think I was better-looking than he thought I'd be, and could see him nervously calculating whether he was as good-looking as I expected him to be. I didn't get The Flutter, that initial snap and fizz of hormones and chemistry that, for me, was less about soulmate potential and more about whether I'd be comfortable being naked in front of him and seeing/touching his penis. It didn't help that he kept on blinking.

Was it a nervous tic? Drugs? Frantic Morse Code via his

eyelids to a friend sitting behind me that he needed help? He kept talking in a monologue. How his family lived in a small town near Edinburgh. He'd been living in Finchley for the past five years but was moving out because he was convinced his flatmate was growing cannabis in a cupboard. How he just wanted to meet someone normal so they could eat takeaway while watching TV and was that too much to ask? Then my patience snapped and I said: 'WHY ARE YOU BLINKING?' He looked stunned, then laughed and said he was wearing contact lenses, which were uncomfortable because he usually wore glasses but was trying to impress me. That made me laugh, I felt mildly flattered at the effort he'd made, and suddenly that first-date awkwardness vanished in a whoosh.

One date turned into two, then three, which led to that comfortable, easy moment on the sofa where it was just the two of us being restful in each other's company. Fetching a glass of water for the other, unbidden. Homemade dinners slowly forming a collection of favourite meals used as a balm of kindness and care when the other was having a bad day. The sex was not the best and my mind would drift off at times, wondering, *What time does Homebase open*? And, *Did I send that email to HR or is it in drafts?* But the intimacy of finding home within another person was wonderful. I felt less alone, not just because I was in a couple, but because there was someone who cared about me, made me feel safe, into whom I could pour my worries and needs and find words of comfort or the physicality of an embrace throughout it all. When my mother asked me how dating was going, I felt good because I had an answer. After a year of this, friends at dinner parties started asking us if we'd thought about marriage, and while I hadn't, the idea took root within Gregor and soon that was all we talked about.

I wallpapered over my reluctance by distracting him with meeting my parents, Devi and Nikhil. Mum cooked, Dad gave him the grand tour of his workshop in the garage, and everyone was polite and friendly. I had expected at least one embarrassing childhood story but instead, they asked Gregor questions about his family and mostly talked about work. Although Devi was occupied with Karen who was about to start secondary school, she didn't tease or make a single joke. In a way, the restrained pleasantness was worse. I asked them what they thought of him and the feedback was 'nice'.

His parents were a different story. His mother, Celia, was a ball of nervous energy and announced she'd ordered Indian takeaway for dinner as soon as we arrived. Despite my feminist credentials, I was shocked to find myself judging her. Not for the takeaway thing – I'd encountered a few people who assumed I was unable to contend with a roast potato despite being born and brought up in Britain. But the whole ordering food from outside thing. In Indian homes, my mother's generation would never serve food from outside rather than making it themselves, unless it was for a large gathering. And certainly not for a prospective daughter-in-law.

But also, most Indian takeaway tasted like a joke

perpetrated by brown folks upon unsuspecting white folk. It tasted nothing like the food we made at home. Once, Gregor and I had gone to the Balti Bazaar near Finchley station, where the food somehow managed to taste of everything and nothing. We'd been dating for long enough that I could be honest about why I didn't like eating Indian food out, citing many reasons, from the fact that the most popular dishes were actually British Raj introductions, such as chicken tikka masala and jalfrezis, to my doubts that it was actually cooked by Indians. But Gregor's white man confidence got the better of him. He started chatting to the waiter, who a) revealed he was actually Bangladeshi, and b) confirmed that his mother would throw a shoe at him if he offered her the food they were serving us.

Two years into our relationship, Gregor grew impatient with my inability to give him a firm answer about settling down. After many heated debates we agreed to buy a place together in Tooting. Due to a combination of a then mid-level salary and my ability to piss it away down the pub on a Friday night, as well as on holidays I couldn't afford, I had no money to contribute to the deposit.

Whenever I wavered and thought about calling it off, I remembered when he'd washed my hair while I was ill. How he'd bring me breakfast in bed every Sunday. That he uncomplainingly listened to my rants about being underappreciated at work. I pretended so well, not just to Gregor but to myself, that this was the right decision, the responsible move, the first step to settling down with the sensible lawyer, that when it came to the day of exchanging contracts, my body pulled the emergency handbrake.

Minutes away from the estate agent's office, I found myself throwing up in the bushes by Tooting Bec station. I knew I wasn't pregnant. This was my body making a final attempt to talk to my mind, which had previously blocked out all such attempts to communicate doubt, from racing heartbeats to churning guts.

I hailed a taxi and went back to my flat, hiding under the covers, crying. After many calls and texts from Gregor, I finally faced him a couple of days later and told him how I was feeling. He was furious and said he never wanted to see me again. *You've broken my heart.* I could have handled it differently. But I guess I wanted the idea of a partner more than I actually wanted him.

He removed me from his life with meticulous precision, from cancelling our joint gym membership to notifying people whose weddings we'd jointly RSVP-ed to. But in all of it, I'd forgotten about the brief conversation we'd had while still tying parts of our lives together. A couple of months before we'd broken up, I had started a new job, moving to Leopard. I spent most of my time at Gregor's house as, unlike me, he no longer had flatmates, his furniture was far more comfortable and he had more space. Sitting on his West Elm bed filling out paperwork for my new employees, I'd turned to him, frowning. 'They've asked for a person to call in case of emergency. Should I put my mum? Isn't that what people are supposed to do?'

He'd looked up from the case file he was reading and

said: 'You don't really see your parents that much, do you? And if there was an emergency, how quickly would they be able to come up from Kent? Just put me down.'

I'd looked conflicted but he rubbed my knee and said affectionately: 'Don't worry, B, I'm not going anywhere.'

The memory had slid away, like ice cream through a grate, and I'd completely forgotten to update my record because of all the hurt and guilt that followed soon after.

*

'Did you actually just say "argh", after I've come all this way?' Gregor said.

'Yes, but only because I haven't seen you in forever.'

'Four years,' he said primly, as if it was my fault we hadn't spoken, not him saying: *'Never, ever, ever call me again.'*

'Um . . . thank you for coming. I don't mean that sarcastically, I promise.' I felt myself tripping over my words.

Wasn't it tragic that the minute a relationship ended, the territory of your body and mind and theirs were no longer places either of you had permission to enter?

I had no idea where Gregor's borders had shifted to, and he had little idea of mine. What could we still joke about? The awkwardness of navigating that space was made worse by both of us speaking at the same time.

'I'm sorry—'

'Are you ok—'

I was about to say 'you look well' but that would have been a lie. While his voice sounded the same – like a soothing whisky commercial – he looked like he'd aged in dog years. Then the penny dropped: I'd bet he was now a father.

In addition to the old guilt, fresh remorse arose at the thought of dragging him away from work and family. 'I'm sorry,' I said. 'I completely forgot that you were on file as my emergency contact.'

'Don't worry.' He sighed. 'When they called, I thought it might be something serious, but also that you weren't likely to have called your family. So . . . here we are.'

'You have kids?'

'Yes,' he said, looking surprised at the question, then concerned as to what about his appearance had given it away. 'My fiancée Emma and I have twins. We're expecting a third.'

'Congratulations,' I said, never knowing what to say to people whose children I felt indifferent about. I took in his worn appearance, marked the disintegration of his sex appeal, and felt sorry for him.

The awkwardness returned, a heavy silence that curdled between the beep of monitors and the murmuring of nurses in the distance. Gregor cleared his throat and fiddled with his glasses. 'Well, you seem okay, shall I go?'

'Yeah, sorry – I didn't mean to hold you up. I'm sure you've got to get back to work. I'll be fine, honest.' I tried to smile brightly and make the words seem convincing, but there was a limit to the number of times you could say *I'm fine* when inside you were crumbling into loneliness, so far from fine that your throat closed up. I didn't want Gregor there, but I also knew that when he left, there would be no one.

'Hey,' he said gently, sitting on the furthest edge of the bed, 'maybe you should call your parents? Or at least Devi?'

'No. They'll just fuss and then I'll be concerned about their concern. It's just . . . I can't.' The emotional weight of what had happened was starting to grow heavier as it met the physical after-effects that made me feel so reduced and visceral.

As I finally sought release in crying, Gregor shuttled his hand back and forth in micro movements across the bed, uncertain of whether to come closer. An arm shot out from Salma's side of the curtain and handed me a tissue, which I gratefully took. Why did men never know how to comfort women when they cried? They were mostly busy trying to manage their own discomfort, either because it reminded them of their own crying mothers or because they felt some deeply programmed need to fix whatever was wrong, but couldn't.

'They might like to know something serious has happened to you,' Gregor said, once the crying had diminished a little in volume. 'This is a big deal.'

'This isn't a big deal,' I said sharply, blowing my nose for what I hoped was the final time. 'I'm fine, I've been discharged.'

He creased his brow, irritated. Maybe he'd come here expecting some kind of atonement from me. 'I could've done without having to come here,' he said, 'because now

I've got to work late, and I might miss bath time with Oliver and Stevie.'

I stared at him. While I felt bad and embarrassed that he'd been called to the hospital, I remembered why I had broken up with him. He liked to save up his moments of self-sacrifice, hoard them like a greedy little dragon, then drip-feed them passive- aggressively over the ensuing days and weeks.

'I don't plan on falling into a cellar again anytime soon, I promise,' I said tightly.

He picked up his coat and hesitated. 'We're not going to talk about it then? Any of it?'

'Do you want to?'

'I don't know,' he replied. 'Maybe this isn't the right time or place.'

'If this were a film, Gregor, I'd say: "What do you want me to say?" And you'd say . . .' I paused, waiting for him to speak.

He stared at me. 'This isn't a game, Bel.'

'And you'd say?' I prompted, still hoping we could leave things on a pleasant note rather than cutting ourselves on jagged pieces of old arguments.

He let out an irritated grunt. 'And I'd say, "I want you to say sorry." And that you made a mistake by breaking up with me. And not because I want us to get back together – my life with Emma and the kids is great. But because I want to know that it hurt you too. And that your life has never been the same.'

Finding kindness and common ground after a

break-up was hard because you both knew where the grenades were kept. But I was taken aback by the meanness of this. It had been four years, and he still wanted to punish me.

'I can't say that because it isn't true.'

'But you didn't ask for what was true. You asked me what I wanted you to say.'

'And that would make you feel better?'

'No. Or maybe, yes.'

'Why are you here, Gregor?'

'I feel sorry for you. And because you don't have anyone else.'

'How would you know that?'

He shrugged, and at that small movement I knew he had Googled me or looked at my social media to see what was happening in my life.

'I do have people,' I said, 'and I don't need your pity. I already said I was sorry. So if what you're looking for here is suffering and remorse, honestly, you can go fuck yourself.'

He pressed his lips together. 'I didn't mean it like that . . .' I closed my eyes, and when I heard a rustle of movement, I opened them and he was gone. I let out a big sigh of relief.

'Bloody hell,' Salma said, her voice floating through the thin curtain. 'I thought that dickhead would never leave.'

*

With my phone smashed, an Uber ride home was not an option. I hailed a black cab, readying myself for the usual chattiness a journey entailed. I was surprised to find my driver was a woman, her brows arching in concern as I gave her the address of my flat in Battersea.

'Are you okay, love?' she said craning her neck to look at me after I'd clambered in. 'It's just that normally when people look like you do now, they get someone to pick them up. Like a family member.'

Please make her stop talking to me, I silently implored the universe.

Eventually we arrived and I slowly creaked out of the car, my body growing stiffer with each passing minute. A fresh dose of medication bubble-wrapped me from the worst of the pain. Internally I felt numb. My perspective shrank to the smallest increments of time: making a cup of tea, consigning the cape dress to the bin.

A warm shower showed me the places I'd been hurt the most, where even the softness of water was unbearable. I looked down at my body, covered in the dark petals of bruises that hadn't fully blossomed yet. I turned off the shower and changed into my M&S pyjamas. Soon after that, I was buried deep within a mound of blankets on the huge, pillowy, L-shaped sofa that took up most of my living room. A double cheeseburger and fries were en route according to my takeaway app, and the coffee table was covered with Diet Coke, orange juice and a big bottle of sparkling water.

Although the sunlight was a shade softer now, by 5 p.m.

it was still bright enough that I partially drew the curtains. On a normal day I loved sitting on the tiny balcony bathed in light, watching people walk along the sweeping curve of the Thames. But this was not a normal day.

Although the Becky/Barry racism debacle had made me vow to unsync my phone from my laptop, I was glad for it now that said phone was smashed to pieces. I pulled out my home laptop and started messaging people. Maggie had been frantically trying to get hold of me. Apparently falling into a pit and not breaking every bone in my body was enough to make Crispin completely overlook the events of the morning too. He'd sent me a lovely email, telling me to take all the time I needed and promised that a gift was on its way. 'I picked it out myself,' he wrote. Which for him was a big deal since usually he got Jane to buy everything including birthday presents for his daughter.

Katrina had sent a string of grovelling messages saying that she'd been on a shoot with Dua Lipa and had been horribly delayed hence her no-show at lunch.

Dua Lipa, I couldn't say no! 😢 🙏

But she'd called Maggie, and heard what happened, and was extremely sorry, and did I want her to come over? (I didn't, because as much as I liked Katrina, it would become about her guilt, and my head ached even at the prospect of it.)

There was a part of me, I'm ashamed to admit, that

wanted to be fussed over. I scrolled through the first ten chats on my WhatsApp and texted a few people.

No one messaged back. A sense of dejection crept in, but, I reasoned, they were probably still at work. I went a bit further down the list and messaged the next five. My friend Anthony, who had rallied from his failed engagement and now had a baby with a wonderful woman he'd met on Tinder of all places. And Amy, the only lasting friend I'd made through Gregor. I hovered uncertainly over Ranvir's name and decided not to text her.

Waiting for them to reply was agony. I closed the laptop and went back to watching *The Matchmaker*. I'd got as far as two people being introduced via a woman who looked like an unhappy raisin, with a sour expression, like she was chewing on tamarind. When I couldn't bear it any longer, I flipped the lid to see a constellation of blue ticks, but only a couple of replies. Anthony said **OMG!** And that he hoped I was okay, and his daughter Elliot was a handful. My brunch friends said **let me know if you need anything** and **wow you're so lucky you weren't hurt.**

I realised that most of these people had no intention of prolonging the exchange. There was no way they'd pass up on bath time or work calls or dinner dates, to come all the way to Battersea. These were stock phrases that once might have rung true, but the older I got, the less certain I was that anyone really meant what they said.

My laptop pinged with a message from my mother.

Mum: Bel, you haven't texted your father in ages. He is
  worried.

Like many immigrant mothers, mine struggled to convey
her emotions unless they were projected through someone else. Like a sock puppet in a therapy session, she used
my father to tell me how she really felt about things. My
'father' was worried I wouldn't meet anyone romantically,
my 'father' was upset that I hadn't called on her birthday,
and my 'father' was wondering if I wanted him to buy me
some socks he saw on sale in Marks and Spencer because
he'd observed on my last visit that mine had holes in them.

Me: My phone's not working Mum – is everything
  okay?
Mum: Is everything okay? Are you okay? What
  happened to your phone?

This was why I hadn't called them. If a broken phone
could prompt a reaction worthy of a daytime soap, what
on earth would she say about an accident that had landed
me in hospital?

Me: Yes, fine. I just dropped it and the screen smashed.
Mum: You should be more careful – phones aren't cheap.
  Anyway, some great news. Karen got into the under-
  18s county football team! I'm such a proud Naani.

I wanted to type 'I KNOW' and inject as much bitterness
into it as possible. But then she would ask how I knew, and
I'd have to say Instagram. And then I'd have to explain what

Instagram was. If I lied and said Devi told me, she'd ask my sister about it, Devi would then text me out of embarrassment and it would become a whole complicated thing.

Normally I would have brushed this off, gone into a work meeting or drinks or a Barry's Bootcamp. But the only thing that stretched ahead of me was hours alone with my thoughts. Had mine and Devi's relationship crumbled to the point where she didn't think she needed to tell me news that was important to her and Karen? And wasn't it extremely messed up that my *mother* knew things about her life that I didn't, and somehow that had become a very normal thing?

But maybe it wasn't unusual. When I thought about the last time I was home, I realised with a jolt that it was *two and a half months ago*. It was at most a thirty-five-minute train journey from Waterloo. Suddenly I missed my family with an intensity that I hadn't felt in years.

Usually my mother was the one who'd text: **Your FATHER is wondering when you are coming to visit**. And I'd sigh, and make a plan to get in and out of the house as quickly as possible. But maybe going to see them now wouldn't be the worst thing.

> **Me: That's great Mum. Devi must be so pleased. Listen, I was thinking of coming to visit next weekend. Are you home?**

She took her time replying, but eventually responded.

> **Mum: Bel. Are you sure you are okay?**

Jesus wept.

> Me: Yes, Mum.
> Mum: Then your father will be so pleased. Devi will
>   come.

*

Devi will come, my mother had written. It sounded off-key. When I visited my parents, Devi always made an appearance, but it was never overtly stated that she would be coming over. It was a given she'd be there, but also that she wouldn't stay long. She always had something to dash off to, whether it was picking up Karen from a friend's house or running an errand for Nikhil.

On impulse, I pulled out the ragged and worn photo album that I kept on the under layer of my coffee table. I blew away the dust and opened it up to a page where there was a photograph of Devi holding me as a baby.

How had I not realised before that most of my friends were in actual fact work acquaintances? None of them had ever met my parents, nor did they even know the name of the town I came from. How had my life become this disconnected?

When Gregor and I got together, I was happy to let him become my life. When we broke up, work became my life. I'd tried reconnecting with my friends who had children, but like salmon on the migration run, they'd followed the pattern of moving further out to the sub-urbs. Organising social events was difficult, especially while juggling a busy new job. I should have been more empathetic and generous with my time, but the combination of my not wanting to be around happy families after my break-up, combined with their disinclination to put themselves out, meant that things fizzled out. They hadn't needed me, and the feeling was mutual. Until now.

As I worked my way through the album, baby Bel (a nickname that was only permissible to a select few) morphed into a little girl with knobbly knees and a big smile. Devi was in most of the photos until I was about eleven. Around that time the smile gave way to a long-suffering scowl as I entered my teens.

Give or take a few kilograms, I hadn't changed much. Very long hair, round eyes and a broad mouth. Then the sharp jolt I always felt while looking at photos of my old school friends, my wolf pack. Ama, Marina, Ling and me. Sixteen. On the beach in Cornwall. The first holiday we'd ever been on without our parents. Our faces looked so feline and beautiful. I don't ever remember feeling that beautiful. I could almost breathe in the unmarked years on our faces, the decisions we had yet to make, the infinite potential of our futures.

I measured the line between how much I had loved all of them at the time, and how dark and silent our connection was now. Ama was the only one I had tried to make an effort to see after our big falling out, but we'd gradually grown apart and then the distance became too wide to bridge. I kept tabs on her occasionally; knew she'd qualified as a nurse, and that her mother still lived in the same flat where we'd spent countless hours together as teenagers. On impulse, I looked to see if she was on Instagram and there she was.

Of course, I'd thought of messaging her over the years. Never Marina and Ling, only her.

I'd thought about reaching out before, but always stopped short once I played out how it would go. In the end, my paranoia that she'd be angry at me or, worse, not bother to reply, always won out. What did I have to lose now? If she told me to go away, it would hurt my feelings, but the absence of her would still be felt. I started typing a direct message.

> Hi Ama, long time no see.
> Hi Ama, wow it's been ages!
> YO! Bet you didn't think you'd hear from me.
> Hey Ama, I'm sure you hate me but . . .
> Hi Ama, I fell into a pub cellar and didn't break my neck. How's life been treating you?

I deleted each one, and then distracted myself with foraging for a Twix. Then rearranged the photos in the album. Then I needed to pee. After that there was making a cup of tea and sorting out the nest of blankets on the sofa. When I ran out of tasks and the silence of my WhatsApp crushed me, I took a deep breath and started a new message.

Ama, I know it must be a complete shock hearing
from me, and I completely understand if you want to
ignore this, or you don't want me to contact you again.
But I came across an old photo of us, that one from
Cornwall? It made me smile and remember. I've missed
you. More than words, as Nuno Mendes Bettencourt
would say. I hope you are happy and well.

I took a picture of the photo using my laptop camera. I
sent it. Then screamed. Then closed my laptop. And then
opened it again. I saw the three dots of doom. A sign
that she'd seen the message and was typing a response. I
screamed again.

Babybel! It is so good to hear from you, what a
beautiful, wonderful surprise. I just had a squizz at
your photos and see that you are as stunning as ever.
Nuno Mendes B . . . what an absolute blast from the
past. How are you? Tell me everything.

I couldn't believe what I was reading. She wasn't angry.
She'd used my nickname. She wanted to know how I
was. I typed out **I'm fine** and then deleted it. I couldn't do
that. Not with her.

Life is mostly good but . . . today not so much. I had
a freak accident – literally fell into a pub cellar while
texting in the street (not a joke) and ended up in
hospital. I've been discharged and I'm okay. Sorry, I
know I shouldn't dump this on you in literally the
second message we've exchanged.

I saw her start to type and then pause. It felt like it went on for an eternity. I regretted oversharing. Ama didn't need me dumping on her life after I had spent so long contributing precisely nothing to it. But it seemed she didn't mind.

> I'm so sorry to hear you've experienced that, and I am glad you are okay. As for texting while walking . . . you always were TERRIBLE at multi-tasking – remember when you were singing the chorus of 'When I Come Around' while eating chips and you choked on one and then I had to give you the Heimlich? In all seriousness though . . . I'm so glad you reached out. It makes complete sense that you're shocked and upset. It's a big, traumatic thing to have happened. But also, I know you, and I hope you have support around you and aren't just trying to deal with this alone. Are you with anyone at the moment?

No one else had asked me that. No one had asked if I felt alone in all the years since I had built a life for myself. A successful one, I thought. At the age of thirty-six, I lived in a pretty flat in Battersea, had a good job, a decent wardrobe. I had friends and family. My love life was probably best described as interesting, but not dire. I exercised. Occasionally, to declutter my brain, I'd go and see a play or visit an art gallery. I looked and seemed like a whole person. But it turned out that, no matter how hard I tried to fill it, a tiny chunk was missing from my heart. Would always be missing.

I read Ama's words again.

**I know you, and I hope you have support around you
and aren't just trying to deal with this alone.**

There are many parallels between romantic relationships and close friendships. Certainly when they break
up, they look the same. The pain, the anguish, the hurt, the
void. But the perfect knowledge of someone that comes
only after a long-established friendship, the familiarity of
who they really are, is something that never truly vanishes.

I texted Ama back, starting with a joke about how she
might never have become a nurse if not for knowing someone as accident-prone as me, and found myself smiling for
the first time that day.

3

Tabla, the Indian restaurant at the back of Tottenham Court Road, was packed on a Tuesday lunchtime, but Katrina had called ahead and managed to get us a table outside.

I'd groaned when she'd told me where we were going. There were some good South Asian restaurants in central London (though none of them held a candle to the basic-but-brilliant places in Southall and East Ham) but Tabla was one of several flycatcher venues designed to lure in customers from the theatres nearby.

To coincide with my week of recuperation, spring had made an early exit, dropping its blossom stickily on the pavements to make way for summer. Which was delightful when all I had to do was drink beer in my shorts and sit on my balcony, but not so great when it meant hopping on the Tube and keeping a cool head so I could get my work done.

'Wheeew, it's baking,' Katrina said, fanning herself as she sat down. According to BBC Weather, we were in the middle of a mini heatwave. I plucked at my shirt around the armpits in a futile attempt to evade sweat patches.

I'd always been paranoid about sweating after Bethany Barratt at school told me frankly: 'You smell of B.O.' I'd spent the rest of the year in a cloud of Impulse O2 spray so thick it was almost visible. A lady next to us was surreptitiously rolling down her 80-denier tights under the flimsy plastic table.

As she studied the menu, Katrina said: 'I know eating Indian food in hot weather is mad, but I *really* fancy a jalfrezi.' Of course she did. Disregarding the fact that billions of Indians eat Indian food in hot weather every day and so it could hardly be 'mad', I felt irritation rise in me. Katrina hadn't thought to ask if I wanted curry in 30-degree heat. Being in her company was bringing out this passive-aggressive voice in me that hadn't been there before.

Perhaps the accident had affected a part of my brain that meant I could no longer deal calmly with petty annoyances. Or perhaps it was Katrina who was particularly annoying. As I heard her ask the waiter if the poppadoms were organic, I realised something had shaken loose in me since the accident. Nothing that would show up on a brain scan, perhaps more a loosening of the internal framework I'd painstaking built to separate the different parts of my life.

It had begun with Ama and the fact that I'd been ordered to have a few days off and not reply to emails. There was only so much Netflix a person could watch, and the pain from my injuries kept me up at night. *Great,* I thought at 3 a.m. while moonlight streamed obstinately around my blackout curtains, *more thinking time.* During one of these spells, when my mind strayed inexorably towards Devi and whether I should text her, my phone pinged with a message. Ama. It was nothing serious, a nineties meme that she sent after finishing her shift at the hospital. I wasn't so naïve as to expect a few messages to repair everything between us, but they cast a warm glow in the blackness.

I felt as if I'd opened a door to a part of myself I hadn't seen in years. I told her about the job I did, seasoning it with self-deprecation about selling my soul. She texted in response: **But does it allow you to lead the life you want to live?** It did, I admitted. But the more we texted, the more our exchange shone a light over areas I hadn't fully considered before, and the truth was that I didn't know if this was the life I wanted to live. She asked me about Devi and that hurt. Not because of the enquiry but because I'd realised how much I wanted to reach out to my sister. And yet, felt unable to.

You could just text her, an irritating little voice said in my head. *Isn't it weird that you haven't told her what happened?*

Coming back to work, to a bunch of flowers on my desk and a big hug from Maggie, had felt like a mild reprieve. 'I don't normally hug people,' she said, 'but . . . you know.' The glow faded quickly when I went to the canteen and was asked by Barry the research assistant, with all the sensitivity of someone craning their neck as they drove past a car crash: 'So what happened then?'

Lunch with Katrina was meant to be a way of easing myself back in on my first day. Just as the waiter asked me what I wanted to order, my phone pinged. I'd half-hoped it was Ama, but instead it was a work email. Jane. I couldn't ignore it. Apparently, Crispin was flying out later that evening and wanted a meeting with me before he left. Maybe I *hadn't* escaped the whole calling-Tristan-a-racist incident. Just as I finished typing a reply confirming my attendance, Katrina said: 'No phones, we've got lots to talk about. I'm worried about you.'

My spine straightened as I steeled myself for gruesome questions about my accident. 'So . . . what's happening on the dating front?' she asked, pouting.

Oh.

She leaped into the silence to tell her own story, about how she'd met some incredible guy named Chris with a six-pack you could eat sushi off. He was a property developer but also collected vintage vinyl and drove a Tesla, and although he hadn't texted after they'd shagged last night, she was sure, *sure*, he'd call. 'I mean,' she said with shining eyes, 'he made me *toast*, Bel.'

I listened to her story feeling mildly stunned, glad to be wearing sunglasses so that my expression didn't give anything away. While I hadn't wanted to talk about the accident, it was somehow worse not to be asked about it at all. Was it because I looked okay? The bandage on my head had been removed so there was no outward sign I'd been injured but . . . I couldn't imagine meeting up with a friend and not even asking: 'Are you okay after falling ten feet into a black hole?'

While it was great that I had a single, child-free friend

to hang out with, I was beginning to suspect that if we didn't work in industries that overlapped, and at offices so close together, Katrina and I wouldn't be friends. Our main topic of discussion was men, and she wasn't a great influence in terms of meeting someone remotely normal who didn't send dick pics, pose with guns, or have a collection of cats' teeth. She loved dating apps, and especially loved the stories that came with them. Half the time I didn't know if I went on dates because I wanted an interesting story to tell her by the end of it or because I actually wanted to meet someone decent. Often we'd meet up and compare war stories and Katrina would make sympathetic noises or howl with laughter, but I didn't know how to tell her it wasn't an even playing field.

While I struggled to avoid the swamp of self-pity, Katrina was effortlessly cool – the type of person who could wear several prints at a time without looking like the inside of a magician's pocket. She was also four years younger than me and everyone who used dating apps knew that once you hit your thirties, human years automatically converted to dog years. Plus, she was white. I could never say this to her because she wouldn't understand it, and then we'd just descend into a frustrating conversation with her reiterating how hard it was for her *too*, and then I'd just be left with a sick feeling that would turn in my stomach like a peach pit refusing to be digested. But I knew that it was harder being brown. In the same way that I knew it was much harder for Black women than it was for me, and for Asian guys who were viewed as overly effeminate.

'So,' she said, as a plate of tandoori chicken was placed in front of me, 'what's going on with you? I mean, obviously you fell in a pit and survived,' she joked, 'but love life? Dating? Come on, hit me. What happened to that guy at work – Alex?' She shovelled a spoon of jalfrezi into her mouth and looked at me expectantly.

'Nothing is going on with Alex,' I said, wanting to change the subject immediately as the familiar prickle of guilt ran down my neck. Alex was a hot nerd who worked in IT. He had the unhealthy pallor of someone who spent way too much time at a screen, but at last year's Christmas party I saw potential in his blue eyes and square jaw. After many free drinks, I dragged him back to mine, and afterwards he asked if I wanted to go out with him. I blame it on *Love Actually* and mulled wine, but there was romance in the air, and a part of me that wanted to see where it could lead.

We went out three times; the first to a Chinese restaurant, the second to a craft brewery, and the third was dinner at his flat in Bethnal Green. But as he nuzzled my hair in the morning, I realised this wasn't what I wanted. Thinking back, it was Gregor all over again. Also, he was too keen. Way too keen. So I did the mature thing and ghosted him. I avoided the canteen, ignored his texts. I wasn't proud of it, but I didn't know how to explain to a perfectly normal guy who texted on time and was kind, that I just wasn't into him. Six months later, I was still one of the people most hated by the IT department.

'You know jalfrezi isn't actually an Indian dish, right?'

I said, unable to stop myself. 'It was invented by cooks during the British Raj to give them something to do with leftover cooked meat.'

'What's that got to do with getting you some man aubergine?' said Katrina with her mouth full. 'Come on. We've got to get you back in the game.'

Before I could say anything, she'd already opened Tinder on her phone and was now scrolling through profiles in an attempt to entice me to download the app on mine.

'Here,' Katrina said, 'this guy looks hot! And he's kind of your type – looks like he has a bit of an edge. Want me to send you his profile?' I took her phone and almost dropped it as if it could give me herpes. It was Tristan.

'No. No! Not my type,' I said, signalling to the waiter for the bill.

'I'll swipe on him then. Ah! We've matched!' Of course Katrina was his type. She was a size 8, had long shiny brown hair and bright blue eyes. Even if she ate a loaf of bread, I was sure she'd still have a flat stomach.

'Ooh, okay, I've found a guy for you but . . . hmm . . . you probably won't date him because he's Asian.'

'Sorry, why wouldn't I date him?' I took a long slurp of my Coke.

'Because you don't want to get married and all of that, right?'

I laughed. 'Kat, just because he's Asian doesn't mean we're automatically going to get married. You know that's not how it works, right?'

54

'Yes, of course,' she laughed, but her smile didn't quite meet her eyes. The faintest blush bloomed on her cheeks.

'Cut your losses. I'm hopeless,' I said to ease the tension as the waiter came back with the card machine. 'Maybe I'm not destined to meet anyone special. It's okay. I'm fine with being on my own.'

'Don't say that! You know what? I've got just the thing. Hang on.' I waited patiently while she fished about in her bag, thinking maybe she was looking for the business card of someone she might want to set me up with. 'Aha!' she said triumphantly, pulling out a small piece of pale pink crystal. I was mystified. 'Rose quartz,' she said knowingly. 'It'll sort everything out, trust me.'

I looked at the crystal in her outstretched hand. She looked so confident that there didn't seem to be anything else to do but accept her gift. 'Thank you. I don't know what to say.' And I really didn't. What did it do? What was I supposed to do with it? Did I put it in my handbag or my vagina? How was this going to fix my love life? I kissed her goodbye, slightly relieved to be leaving.

*

In the lift going up to Crispin's floor, I Googled Katrina's gift to me.

'Rose quartz is the stone of universal love. It purifies and opens the heart at all levels . . .'

You could wear it in necklaces, bracelets, pendants; you could carry it with you. There were even dildos made of the stuff. *So it's not just about opening your heart,* I thought, and cackled out loud just as the lift doors opened.

'Something funny, Bel?'

I looked up to see Tristan standing in the reception area. *What was he doing here? And, oh, god, was he going to ask me about my accident?*

I cleared my throat and locked my phone. 'Just a meme someone sent. Are you here to see Crispin?'

'Yeah, he called a meeting with Lightning. Both you and I have been summoned,' he said, rolling his eyes and trying to draw me into a mood of camaraderie.

You must think I was born yesterday, you dog, I thought. *I'm not giving you any ammunition to use against me.*

A heads-up from Crispin that this wasn't just a meeting between the two of us would have been nice. But then again, while being close to the CEO had its perks, the downside was that he expected me to a) automatically know what was in his brain, and b) adapt to any situation he threw me into, like a corporate version of Ninja Warrior. As we sat side by side, I felt Tristan fidget, the tension building in him as he struggled to formulate a question. Eventually he coughed and said: 'Are you well, otherwise?'

I knew this was his way of asking me about the accident, but I also knew it was a brand of English gentility and politeness that I simply didn't have the time or the energy for. You could be sitting impaled on a metal railing and they would avert their eyes, cough politely and ask was everything alright?

It made me question my decision not to tell my family about the accident. I hadn't wanted to bother them because I didn't want to deal with the daily messages checking to see if I was still alive, or the endless 'be careful' texts every time I stepped outside the front door, but that was starting to seem a better option than politely underplaying an incident that could have had serious consequences.

Usually we'd be greeted by Jane, so we both looked up in surprise when Crispin emerged from the boardroom in person. 'Bel,' he said, giving me a kiss on both cheeks. 'I am so glad to see you doing well after your horrible accident.'

Before I could reply, he continued: 'It got me thinking, after that unfortunate texting incident in the quarterly meeting.'

'I'm sor—' I began, but he waved me to silence.

'It was a wake-up call. I didn't particularly care for the language you used but I know Tristan felt bad about it too.' Tristan didn't look as if he felt remotely bad about it. 'So I decided to take action. You know how I feel about innovation and getting ahead of a problem, yes?'

Before I could answer, he ushered us both into the boardroom, where I saw three people from Lightning, two men and a woman, all in their early thirties. 'Ah,' Crispin boomed, 'here are my two top hitters! New Creative and New Media. Tristan and Bel, meet Ola, Tobi and David.'

Despite Crispin's cheery demeanour and the polite smiles from the Lightning team, the tension created by whatever they'd been discussing before we arrived was palpable. We had to make amends for the Oseni situation and they weren't going to be fobbed off. Ola was the shorter, rounded man with a neat moustache and printed shirt, while Tobi sported a perfectly fluffed Afro and wore an exquisitely tailored pink suit and red shirt. David looked like a male supermodel but was actually an ex-Olympian – tall with a sculpted chest just about contained under a green jumper.

Crispin went into a big overture about how sorry we were regarding the Oseni campaign. Ola, Tobi and David's faces tightened as he talked, and I wondered what Crispin had promised them in order to secure this meeting.

'As I alluded to in my email,' he said, 'this isn't just about saying sorry or offering financial compensation. I want Lightning to be at the heart of our Diversity and Inclusion innovation here.'

David raised an eyebrow. 'What innovation?' he said. 'I've seen the leadership team on your website – there isn't a single Black employee there.'

Crispin looked triumphant and my heart sank. 'That's exactly what we want to change.'

'You're going to change your leadership team?' Tobi said with barely concealed disbelief.

'Not quite,' Crispin said. 'We've got a lot of people locked into full-time contracts and that will be hard to change. But I am going to set up a new department, which among other things will look at funding and growing Black-owned brands and talent. We can also include Asian creatives – that's the whole of Asia, by the way – as well as people from the disabled community, the neurodiverse . . . that sort of thing. The people in charge of recruitment and getting it set up will be Tristan and Bel, here.'

The phrase *that sort of thing* just hung in the air. Basically, in lieu of any real change, Crispin was setting up a separate department, which would negate any initiative for change in other parts of the business, as well as completely boxing in and othering talent by placing them in a 'special' category.

The three Lightning representatives were stunned. I had a thousand questions, none of which I could voice in front of them. In no particular order of importance: the prospect of working with Tristan on anything, particularly something as sensitive as this, filled me with horror. But I also knew that any general, catch-all Diversity & Inclusion project was almost always useless because people danced around what they thought diversity was, and nothing real was ever achieved. Just when I thought the visitors might walk out, Crispin unleashed his nuke.

'As an incentive for Lightning's support we'd waive your fees for three months. We'd do all your campaigns and pay your ad spend.' It was a huge sum to write off.

'Six months,' Tobi said, to allow him to say no, and for them to exit gracefully.

'Done,' he replied. Tobi looked shocked, but they were still seated. I didn't blame them. Six months of fee-free work – for a small sports brand like theirs, it was an offer that would allow them to expand in a way they would never have been able to afford. All of us silently hated that this was the way the world worked, and that we would have to compromise our values until we were in a position to run things better ourselves.

*

Ranvir texted to ask if I wanted to go for a drink after work in the local pub, the Rat and Parrot, a place steeped in the regrets of work dalliances, purveyor of a piss-poor wine list. Its only redeeming quality was that it was two doors down from the office. I politely declined. While I liked her, we'd never done a solo outing and I didn't have the mental Polyfilla for polite conversation. Plus, I knew it would never be 'just one'. With so much brewing inside my head, I didn't want to end up lost inside a bottle.

After I'd texted back: **Barry, another time, I promise**, she'd asked me how I was. **I'm fine**, I replied. When I sat and thought about it for longer than a minute, though, I knew I wasn't fine. My mind would melt into the blackness of it, that terror of falling, which couldn't have lasted more than a few seconds. And not just the falling. What had followed it too. Gregor. Coming home alone. Looking at a list of contacts and realising the only space they occupied was in my phone. Another part of me said brusquely: *But you WERE fine. Stop wallowing. You barely had any injuries. You've got a great job. Love life is tbc but that's okay. What's the point of thinking about it?*

Sitting on my balcony, staring at a blood-orange sun

criss-crossed by white contrails, I kept turning over today's meeting in my mind.

Working in a corporate environment exacted a price. Which was: that even if you didn't like things, *especially* if you didn't like things, you glued a smile to your discontent and carried on anyway. Noting Ola, David and Tobi's aghast expressions, Crispin had said: 'Bel is one of my best, and she'll make sure we do a great job with it.'

'What exactly will this new department *do*?' Ola asked.

'Well, it will focus on bringing in talented Black executives and creatives,' Crispin countered, 'that will be a big part of it. But it will also look at other areas of diversity and expanding our client roster.'

It sounded wishy-washy because it was. But also the question on everyone's lips including my own was: how can you create a department with Black talent in it, if the people doing the hiring aren't Black? I was well aware that Asians had long since been used by companies to make it look as if they were diverse, and been happy to go along with it because some opportunity was better than none at all. We all knew I'd just been trotted out as the token brown to make Crispin's venture more legitimate.

'Bel can handle anything,' he'd said. 'She literally fell into a ten-foot hole a week ago and emerged without a scratch! Mad, isn't it?'

Everyone laughed nervously, except for Tobi who registered a dark expression flit across my face momentarily. 'That must have been awful,' she said. 'Are you okay?'

She was the only one apart from Ama and Maggie who'd responded in a way that hadn't been a joke.

Fuming about work felt out of sync with such a perfect summer evening. But I couldn't stop myself. Why didn't I say anything? Because I had been blind-sided, but also because it had felt uncomfortable, something dark and bitter flowing from a familiar place. To sugar the pill, Crispin took me aside afterwards to say that my salary would be increased by ten per cent in recognition of the extra work. The money was meaningless when my soul felt dirty. But I said thank you and hated myself for it.

I would have kept brooding had my phone not pinged with a text. 'Mum, I swear to god . . .' I started muttering under my breath. But it wasn't Mum, it was Ama.

In our last exchange of messages, she'd asked me if I was seeing anyone, a question that didn't spark the usual defensive reaction. I said I wasn't and asked her if she was seeing anyone, and she'd said yes but that it was a conversation best held in person. She was about to start her shift and told me she'd text later.

> Ama: I don't want to jump the gun and I know you
> might not want to/it might be too soon but . . .
> I wanted to know if you'd like to come over for
> dinner Friday evening? I know it's short notice and
> you probably have plans, but I would love to catch
> up and for you to meet my partner.

I didn't know how to interpret the word 'partner' – maybe it was the woman who featured so heavily on Ama's

Instagram? If so, then this was a big deal for her because when we'd last been in touch regularly, she was straight. Or so I'd thought. But that wasn't the most important part of the message. Ama wanted to meet up with me. More than that, it felt significant that she was inviting me to her home, to meet someone who was important to her. Unless, of course, her partner was there as a buffer in case things got weird and intense.

Although dinner sounded high-pressure and terrifying (mainly because I was worried about sabotaging it by being discordant or irritating), the only plans I'd made were with my sofa and a TV show called *My Indian Bae*. It followed the lives of various couples, one partner Indian, the other not, and told their stories through the lens of them encountering and coming to terms with Indian mindsets and traditions. Although it sounded like the premise from hell, it was actually surprisingly sweet.

Yes, Shola, I texted back using her nickname based on the RnB singer Shola Ama. **I'll be there.**

Ama: Oy! None of that in front of B, please. I'll text you the address tomorrow.

4

I was utterly terrified when I turned up on her doorstep. The address Ama had texted was in Streatham – barely a ten-minute train journey from where I lived in Battersea. She had been there all this time, and I hadn't known. It was also not far from Tooting, where Gregor and I had planned to live. When I got off the train, I was seized by a massive panic. This was a terrible idea. What had possessed me to say yes? We would have nothing to talk about, or worse, we would talk about the past. Her partner would hate me, Ama would hate me – my anxiety went on and on.

I was so deep in a spiral that I almost didn't notice I'd reached her house. Number 52 Lavender Lane. It sounded beautiful and fragrant, a place of warm summer breezes and people skipping along. In reality it was just another London street with some pretty brick Victorian buildings and a hodgepodge infill of flat conversions and 1970s houses.

I rang the doorbell of a purpose-built maisonette. B turned out to be Bronwyn who was Bron, the rosy-cheeked platinum-blonde woman from Ama's Instagram. Bron had close-cropped hair and quadriceps that warranted worship, her well-muscled legs stuffed into sliders and shorts. She opened the door like a Viking guarding the entrance to Valhalla; she had the same solid, no-nonsense look about her. Not gruff, but the kind of person you'd feel safer for having around.

'You must be Bel,' she said. And on seeing my face fall because I'd expected Ama to answer the door, added: 'Ama's just getting changed – a baby pooped on her at work.'

'Ah, gross,' I said, stepping across the threshold.

'Exactly,' Bron answered.

'BEL!' Ama yelled from upstairs. 'I'm so sorry! This isn't how I wanted us to meet after so long but I'm covered in baby shit! Bron will take care of you, I promise. Won't you, B?'

The immediate informality of it put me at ease, and a wave of relief washed through me. 'Hi! Don't worry, take your time!' I yelled back, smiling.

'BRON, TAKE CARE OF BEL!' the disembodied voice continued.

'Jesus Christ,' Bron bellowed. 'What do you think I'm going to do to her? Interrogate her?' There was silence.

'WELL, NOW I DO!' Ama shouted. 'AND TELL LUKE TO BE NICE!'

Luke? Who was Luke? My anxiety returned. I'd already been unsure about whether it was a compliment to meet her partner or if her partner had been asked to be there in case it got awkward, but now this seemed to confirm my worst suspicions. I'd thought this would be a chance for me to reconnect with Ama, which seemed unlikely if she'd invited over other people too.

'Just get ready, will you?' Bron yelled back before gesturing me towards the kitchen.

Bron worked as a fire fighter, she said, but had taken a few days off to get some DIY work done around the house. She apologised for the mess and said a work friend of hers, Luke, was helping. 'He won't be here long,' she added, which quietened my nerves. Luke was nowhere to be seen, so Bron offered to give me the tour.

Although it wasn't as pretty as the Victorian houses on the road, she said they didn't have the issues that those particular buildings were notorious for. The heating worked and there wasn't any damp. The living room was unremarkable – TV, worn velvet sofa and a couple of bookcases – but the kitchen was something else. It was huge, with a marble-topped breakfast bar so that one person could talk and relax at it while the other cooked. An entire wall of cookbooks and state-of-the-art appliances overlooked a generously sized garden (by London standards) with a tiny greenhouse at the far end.

Catching the impressed look on my face, Bron said: 'We love food, and we're trying to grow more of our own produce. Ama is a better cook but she was working today and I wasn't – so my apologies, it's my talents you'll be subjected to tonight.' She pulled a bottle of cold Pinot Gris out of the packed fridge, handed me a glass. After filling it, she moved to the kitchen worktop and started chopping onions.

I felt as if I'd been in this type of home many times before. It was warm, familiar; reminded me of the old Ama. Back then, she'd lived closest to our school, and her mum Tina was a working single mother, which meant we frequently had the place to ourselves. They'd lived in a compact council flat on a forgotten bit of road just behind the Safeway's near Dartford High Street.

It wasn't fancily furnished, but unlike our house, which was larger but filled with clutter, it was spotless. There were photos everywhere, Blu-Tacked to the fridge, in the frames clustered on every surface. Some were a window into their life in Sri Lanka before they came to England: the view from their house in Colombo fringed in coco-nut trees, or Ama picking the first ripe mango that grew in their garden. Others were tinged with a sweet sadness, like the photos of her father who had died when she was ten: a kind-looking man with a broom-like moustache, who loved to carry her on his shoulders. He looked so much like my own dad that the first time I saw his photo, I almost cried.

We'd barrel in, still in our school clothes, which by then were honking with sweat and dust, pulling plastic boxes of Mrs Sendhil's food from the fridge, *kottu roti* and fish cut-lets. Ama's mother filled the hole where a father should be with a constant supply of food, and there was never a time when we came home and a full meal wasn't waiting for us in the fridge. In my house, by comparison, it depended on the mood of the matriarch. If she was in an 'I'm not a servant, you can all make your own meals' rage, then we knew it was frozen-food time. At other times there was plenty in the fridge – a fraught and inconsistent approach to feeding a family.

As Bron cooked, we made small talk. I was in the middle of explaining *My Indian Bae* after she'd asked me if I'd seen any good shows lately. 'So they have to embark on new experiences connected to their partner's homeland, and learn a new skill by the end of the show?'

'Yes.' I nodded. 'They're judged by a panel of aunties, and there's a cash reward at the end of it for whoever puts in the most effort.'

'LUKE!' she yelled all of a sudden. 'Would you put your fucking T-shirt on!'

I turned around and almost died right there on the spot as the wine left my body and spluttered into the air. Emerging out of the hallway like the world's grumpiest Strippergram was a man in his early thirties, with dark shaved hair, muscles and tattoos. Bare-chested and tanned, he was wearing baggy workmen's trousers and carrying a toolbox. As they both stared at my reaction, I felt I had to explain.

'I'm sorry,' I said, trying not to laugh, 'but you look as if you've just turned up for someone's hen do.'

Bron laughed as Luke angled his head and said in a soft and deadly tone: 'And what role would I play at this hen do?'

I couldn't start the evening by making a bad impression. 'You know what? Never mind. It's great to meet you, Luke.' He stared silently back at me – not in a hostile manner, but as if I was a new species he'd encountered, which instantly made me feel foolish and embarrassed.

'Wash your hands, dickhead,' Bron said, 'and then I'll give you a beer.' He nodded curtly. 'This is Ama's friend Bel, by the way. Be nice.' He grunted and walked towards the kitchen sink.

Even after he'd washed his hands and put on a T-shirt, when he stood next to me the scent around him reminded me of the river: as if muddy, skittery things that once had fins and tendrils, had been ground into dust and pressed into his skin. He drank his beer silently while Bron stirred something heavenly in a saucepan.

'Ama told me about your accident by the way,' she said. 'Are you okay?'

'Oh, yeah, I'm fine,' I replied. I didn't want to discuss it with Bron, whom I'd only just met.

'What happened?' Luke asked, taking a sip of his beer. 'If you don't mind me asking.'

'It's okay,' I said to Bron, indicating that she could tell him. I was irritated he was there, and found his standoffish manner a bit try-hard, but at least he'd had the decency to ask. By the time she was finished, he whistled and said: 'You were very lucky. I had a call out like that last year and . . . the person didn't make it.'

They both bowed their heads in unison for a moment, a brief gesture of respect to wherever in the universe that person's soul had gone. I felt the blackness of the cellar rushing towards me, the parallel dimension of a more fatal outcome brushing bony fingers against the nape of my neck. I stood up quickly and walked over to the wall of pictures to distract myself.

There were Ama and Bron's individual baby pictures; photos of them on holiday together, beaming at the camera with sweaty, happy faces on the beach; pictures from a festival of Ama holding a turnip shaped like Jesus. I smiled when I saw the photo of us from Cornwall, but I also saw pictures of Ling and Marina grown up, smiling with Ama. That queasy, oily feeling that rose within me was replaced by the sensation of all the air leaving my body. In my Googling of Ama, I hadn't wanted to look them up. But also I hadn't considered that just because our lives as four friends had abruptly combusted and ended then, it didn't mean that the friendship was over for the others. I had spent years thinking about what had happened during that holiday in Cornwall, had flinched whenever I walked around Dartford and came across our old haunts, until eventually I just stopped going back. But clearly they hadn't been marked by events in the same way.

I had pored over Ama's photos on Instagram, trying to absorb the changes in her, every wrinkle, every extra pound of flesh, every bone, and now I found myself doing the same with Ling and Marina. I pored over Ling's jewellery including her wedding band, and Marina's expensive Chanel jacket. It was too much; it was not nearly enough. I wanted to ask Ama about them, but I also . . . didn't. I wasn't sure how heavy it would make my heart, how much regret would puddle at my feet.

Who was Ling married to? How much food did Marina not eat to keep her body that thin? How could Ama still be friends with those people after the way they'd behaved?

I turned my attention back to the room and re-focused. I didn't have the right. Whatever had happened, I couldn't bring that here. Not today. Not if I wanted to see Ama again. No matter how teenage I felt, I had to remember I wasn't that person anymore.

'It might be worth chatting to someone about it, Bel,' I could hear Bron saying but her voice sounded distant, as if I was far down below the surface, trying to bring together thoughts that were being pulled in different directions by the current. 'People often feel quite traumatised by this stuff.' I dragged my gaze back to her, busily chopping vegetables, then to Luke who was staring at his beer.

Before I could say I was fine again, I heard footsteps thundering down the stairs like a baby elephant. I remembered how it used to drive her mother mad; at least that side of Ama hadn't changed.

'BERYL THE PERIL!' a voice yelled and there she was, all five foot eight inches of her, older but still as beautiful as when I last saw her. I felt relief, and the warmth of her burned away my nervousness.

She was Ama, but also she wasn't. She was always a head-turner but now she looked more comfortable in her body, as if it finally fitted her. I hadn't been around for the years in which she'd learned confidence on the bodies of lovers, or in the lives she helped save. But, tightly pressed against what I didn't know about her were parts that were familiar. Ama had impossibly long legs and arms, bronze-coloured skin and almond-shaped eyes, one green and one light brown due to a genetic condition called heterochromia. Her long, mermaid hair was tied up in a big bun on top of her head. She was still the only person I knew who could make dungarees and a plaid shirt look sexy.

'You still look amazing,' she said to me, and scooped me into a hug. 'Look at all this hair, this booty, these boobs, this skin.'

'Me?' I said. 'What about you. Look at YOU. How do you always look like you've just stepped out of an issue of *Vogue*?'

She snorted. '*Vogue*? Please tell that to the elderly patient whose bedpan I emptied not three hours ago.

'Oh, yeah,' she said, as my eyes widened, 'lots to catch up on.' She pointed to Bron. 'I'm gay.'

'Yeah, I gathered that,' I said with a smile.

'And we're getting married,' she said, putting her arms around Bron, who gently kissed the inside of her wrist.

'Congratulations to you both,' I said, lifting my glass, and saw that Luke silently did the same with his. I was there, celebrating with Ama, but a small part of me mourned for the past, the moment she'd got engaged and had called all her friends to let them know the good news. If I could have gone back in time and spoken to my sixteen-year-old self, she would have said: '*What? In what universe does Ama get engaged and you don't know about it? And you don't even know if you're invited to the wedding? How did you turn into such a dickhead!*'

I wondered if Ling and Marina were invited. When we were all friends, the thought of the four of us not celebrating together would have been inconceivable.

'You don't seem shocked,' Ama replied, looking at me sideways. She searched my face in a way that told me that perhaps this conversation hadn't gone quite as easily with some of the other people in her life.

'It kind of makes sense,' I shrugged. 'I mean, you presented as straight, but you never really seemed that into boys when we were kids. And when we were in Cornwall, you and India seemed to have this chemistry. But we were also kids in the nineties and everyone kissed everyone else then, so I never really thought about it much.'

'Oh, India and me totally hooked up on that holiday,' she said mischievously.

'AHEM,' Bron said.

'Honey, India was Marina's cousin,' Ama said, smiling sweetly at her, 'and now she's married to a man and has two kids. And has not aged well. Okay?'

'Fine,' Bron grumbled.

Looking at the warm, funny woman Ama had become, she felt as familiar to me as my own family members. And yet there were parts of her that were unknown, that required me to feel around the edges and learn where the new joins were.

'It's been . . .' I started to say, my voice unexpectedly catching on a surge of emotion.

'A long time, I know,' she finished. 'But it's good to see you.' I noticed the inflection.

'I didn't mean to say but,' she caught herself. 'I mean, it's fucking good to see you, pal.' She squeezed my shoulders for emphasis. Ama had always been like that, I remembered. On the face of it, bright, light and chatty, which made people underestimate her, but she had always been able to see and feel more deeply than most. Maybe because she'd experienced losing her dad so young.

'Luke,' she said sweetly, 'I love you, and appreciate you, but isn't it time you got back to your boat?'

'Wow,' he said, rolling his eyes, 'message received. I only installed a new bathroom for you, but you know, whatever.'

'I'm sorry, I'm sorry,' she said, scooping him into a hug, 'but I haven't seen Bel in years, and we need to catch up.'

'Fine,' he grumbled, 'I'm going. But you both owe me dinner.' He waved goodbye and downed his beer, before grabbing his toolbox and leaving. I'd never encountered someone so good-looking with such an impregnable personality. It wasn't even arrogance but rather a distilled version of a doomsday survivalist. Indifferent. Detached.

When she was sure the door had closed, Ama said: 'He's beautiful, isn't he?'

'I mean, he is but he seems . . . you know.'

'Difficult? Yeah – he comes across like that at first but he's actually a real softie. When B first introduced us at her birthday party, he didn't talk to me for the whole night. But he's an interesting guy. Left home at fifteen, lives on a boat, cultivates this whole river hermit vibe.'

'*That's* why he smells like the Thames!' I exclaimed.

'You were *smelling* him?' Ama said, winking.

'Oh, god, not like that,' I groaned.

'Stop teasing her, Ama,' Bron said, gently laughing, and went back to chopping.

Ama walked over to fill Bron's glass and placed a kiss softly on the back of her head. Bron rubbed her hand against Ama's arm in appreciation.

'How did you two meet?' I asked.

At that, both of their faces were lit by the glow of the fully loved, the ones who know that when they come home, it is to someone who is their equal and who sees it all, wants it all, the good and the bad about them. As they started to speak, their voices twined together to summon the shape and size of that love.

They met in hospital. *I was training to be a nurse, she was training to be a fire fighter,* Ama said. Bron came into A&E with a young man who had been attacked with a nail gun. I had to admire a couple who could retain dreamy looks on their faces while describing such grisliness. Despite Ama looking like Sweeney Todd, the demon barber of Fleet Street, because the guy had spurted blood all over her uniform, she was 'the most beautiful person' Bron had ever seen. She wanted to ask Ama out but an invitation to coffee seemed too insignificant for what Bron felt. As she stuffed her hands in her pockets nervously, her fingers brushed against the ridge of the concert tickets in her pocket. Her promise to give one to a colleague had drowned in the pool of Ama's eyes.

'Bel,' Ama burst out before Bron could say it, 'she actually said: "*Listen, I know this sounds silly but I have tickets to see this band tomorrow night, and you probably haven't heard of them, but they're this nineties rock band . . .*" And guess which band it was, Bel?' But I was merely a bystander as both of them were lost in each other and their story, as if they were the only two people in the room. 'The Smashing Pumpkins,' Ama sighed happily.

She knew I would understand the importance of that, and I did. They were one of our favourite bands when we were teenagers – we competed to see who was the first to buy a copy of *Mellon Collie and The Infinite Sadness*. We listened to it repeatedly, scrawling fragments of lyrics on school notebooks. The band always held a special place in my heart after becoming the soundtrack to my first kiss.

Ama's phone buzzed and Bron said: 'No phones, Ama, they can handle things without you.' By way of explanation, she turned to me and said: 'This happens a lot. We'll be having a nice evening and then Ama gets some upsetting update on what's happening with a patient.'

'Ahem!' Ama said. 'You do too, you know. Fire fighting isn't exactly picking daisies.' Bron stuck out her tongue. 'I thought of you today, by the way, Bel,' Ama said, switching to a serious tone. 'We had a patient come in who'd had a seriously bad fall – not the same as yours but similar. Wasn't so lucky as you though, needs brain surgery.'

'We told her she was lucky,' said Bron.

A flash of irritation took me by surprise. Why were they making such a big deal of it?

'I'm glad you're doing okay and that the scans came back fine. But how are you doing really?' Ama said.

'I mean, I'm fine, it's no big deal,' I said, a bit too sharply judging by the bruised look in Ama's eyes. She stared back at me and said: 'It is a big deal, though, Bel. You might be fine physically but mentally it can be a lot.' It felt jarring. The Ama I knew had never been this serious. Then again, the Ama I knew had never been a nurse either, or done grown-up things like own a car or get engaged. I suddenly felt overwhelmed by how much I didn't know about her. 'Have you processed it?' she pushed. 'Really thought about what happened?'

I knew Ama, but I didn't know Ama, I realised. I wanted to tell her that the night of the accident, I couldn't sleep. That the sensation of being swallowed by a blackness so terrifying and all-consuming jolted me awake. I wanted to tell her that when I eventually did get to sleep, I felt as if I was hallucinating. I had entire conversations with Devi which had never taken place. I stood in front of Marina and Ling, and they finally said sorry to me.

I wanted to tell her that I didn't know what was real. That her texts had kept me anchored to the here and now but that on certain days, that darkness I encountered at the bottom of the cellar spooled around me everywhere I went. I knew what I was truly afraid of: being alone. But that I was even more afraid of reaching out and being turned away. I wanted to tell her that when daylight came, I locked these thoughts away because they felt like madness.

'I haven't processed it,' I said quietly. 'And I didn't mean to snap. It's just . . . you're the first person who has properly asked me how I feel about it. And I do want to answer you only I don't have the words right now.'

'That's okay,' she said, and took my hand.

We were interrupted by a cough from Bron. 'Wine?'

*

A bottle later, we were holed up in the conservatory, which I learned they used as a dining area in the warmer months. We'd navigated small talk successfully and were moving into deeper waters. Ama frowned when I said I hadn't told my parents or Devi about the accident. I fobbed her off by telling her I'd be going to Kent soon and would tell them then.

'It's weird that you haven't told them,' Ama said plainly.

'Well,' I changed the subject, 'working out whether to tell them is the least of my problems.'

I then went into how embarrassing it was that Gregor turned up as my emergency contact. And because neither of them knew who he was, I went into a rundown of our relationship and how things ended between us.

They both shared a look. 'What?' I asked.

'I mean, I don't tell my parents things, Bel,' said Bron, 'but that's because I have other friends and family who understand me a bit better. I wouldn't be able to deal with something like this alone.'

Ama looked at me so gently I almost couldn't bear it. I could see the words forming as she slightly angled her head: *Is that why you reached out?*

'I mean . . . I'm not alone.' Even I couldn't continue under the weight of that lie. Some of my so-called friends hadn't replied to my WhatsApp messages days after the accident. Sensing that perhaps I'd open up a bit more if she wasn't there, Bron excused herself by saying she had to check on the food. Then, Ama and I were left together in that rapidly thickening soup of emotions.

'I didn't reach out to you because I was alone or desperate,' I said, unable to look at her. A lie. 'And if you had said you never wanted to hear from me, that would have been fine.' Another lie. 'When all of this shit happened, I reached back for something or someone who would feel like home and realised . . . there was nothing. Just an empty space. And I thought about you, and how long it had been, and how the reasons for why we stopped being friends just didn't seem as important anymore.'

Ama's expression was impossible to read.

'I don't mean they weren't important at the time,' I said quickly, not wanting her to think I was trivialising things.

I saw Ama mentally sorting through her thoughts. Deciding what to say, how much to bring up. 'Do you remember the last time we saw each other?' she said. 'That awful bar?' I nodded.

We were twenty-one and I was working for my first-ever agency, which rewarded its employees with free drinks for the first hour on a Friday evening at the bar opposite. The catch was that it was only beer or house wine, but at that age we didn't care so long as it had an alcohol percentage. Technically I wasn't allowed to invite friends, but I managed to sneak drinks to Ama, and my colleagues played along.

On the third occasion we did this, we got blindingly drunk. I remember Ama heading off home back to Dartford while I managed to crawl back to the hole I lived in with four other flatmates in Mile End. I invited her out again, but she never seemed to be free – at the time she hadn't decided on nursing and was working a couple of different jobs. At first, I chalked it down to her being busy but as time went on and she'd either not reply or send me a curt **Can't, thanks**, I started to get angry. I set her a test: I waited to see if she'd contact me, ask me out. But she didn't. Months went past without her sending me a message, and with each passing month my upset grew bigger until it coalesced into a mindset of *fuck you, I don't need you anyway*. I had already experienced an interruption in our friendship after the Cornwall trip, though I had thought we had managed to create our own separate dynamic after that. Clearly I'd been wrong.

Over the years I had managed to convince myself that it was for the best, we had grown too far apart, but that photo of Marina, Ling and Ama stuck in my throat like a fishbone.

'You stopped messaging me,' I said, slightly reproachfully. 'And I never knew why. And I was too afraid to find out that maybe you just didn't like me anymore. Sorry.

Hearing this come out of my mouth, it sounds so . . . child-ish. But it was easier to stay away than actually ask you what was going on.'

She let out a big sigh. 'I didn't mean to make you feel like you needed to stay away. I just . . .' More silence, but a different kind. As if she was treading water, feeling how much space and fluidity was around her before stretching out her limbs. This time, I didn't try to fill it, but allowed it to rest gently between us.

'After I saw you,' she said, 'I came out properly about six months later. I'd been struggling with it for a long time, and I'd always planned to tell you, but that night was kind of the last straw. Your work friends were awful, Bel. They would do coke in the toilets and come out totally obnox-ious. And I saw you changing as you worked there. When you were around them, you were a different person.'

'How do you mean?'

She hesitated. 'That night, I think one of them made some joke about Ellen – I think there was something in the news about her dating Portia de Rossi – and one of them called her a dyke. And I remember this because it was at a time when I was pretty sure I was gay, like gay gay, and was going to come out to you. But I remember you *laughed*. And you'd never been . . . I don't know, the type of person who'd just laugh along to fit in. At least, I never thought so. I wasn't mad at you, but I felt like our lives were going in different directions.'

I was mortified. 'Ama, I wish . . . why didn't you tell me?'

'Because I'm not perfect,' she said. 'I've made a ton of

mistakes too. And I was twenty-one, still figuring out my own identity, and decided I needed to protect that more than anything. And I had a lot on my plate thinking about nursing school and so on. Maybe it was selfish but that was what I needed to focus on at the time. It wasn't you – you didn't do anything wrong. It was how things were and maybe needed to be at the time.'

'Incoming!' Bron yelled, bringing in plates of steaming spaghetti Bolognese and plonking them in front of us. 'Oh, I forgot the parmesan.' And she rushed out again.

While it was hard to be instantly contrite because that required an abrupt adjustment of a reality I'd believed in, and had built an entire narrative around, I knew it was necessary to say something real. To drop the mask and be true in that moment. To say what I really meant. Or else this precious feeling, this spark between Ama and me, might disappear forever. And next time, even if I fell into a sink hole the size of Hackney, I might not have the chance to reach out to her again.

'Ama, I'm sorry,' I said, looking directly into her eyes. Because that felt important too. And because I was surprised to realise that while I told myself I would be fine if we never saw each other again, the thought of it upset me so much, I wanted to hold onto her, fight for a space in her life. 'I really am. I've missed you. A lot. More than you'll ever know.' There was a lot still left unsaid, and a lot I needed and wanted an answer to. But that could come later.

Her eyes were shining with tears. 'There's nothing to forgive,' she said. 'I've missed you more than you know too.' Now I was crying. We hugged each other, bawling our eyes out.

Bron came back into the room. 'Christ! Is the Bolognese really that bad?'

5

For proof of the balance that exists in the world, Kent is the perfect microcosm. The beauty of the 'garden county' is reflected in cradles of hanging baskets, rolling hills and fields of bright yellow rapeseed, walls of rhododendrons reaching skywards heavy with blooms, and farmland filled with the sweet scent of crushed cherries. But this is no utopia.

Besides the sleepy, rural landscape, there is acre upon acre of pebbledash, dual carriageways and scrubby bits of high street. The train journey almost always elicits gasps and sighs of approval from first-time visitors as greenery begins to burst through the urban sprawl. But the carriages are mostly populated by groups of middle-aged men, beer curling their mouths into the habitual sourness that emboldens them to utter profanities outside their own homes; baby-faced teenagers as feral as bin foxes. The presence of these groups charges the atmosphere because it's not a matter of *if* but *when* the most unstable of them will identify a victim, and either say something rude, throw a chip, fart loudly, start chanting, play their music on speakerphone . . . and you have to pray to all the gods in your shrine that their target won't be you.

Hangover sweat speckled on my forehead, and I hoped I gave off enough of a *don't fuck with me* vibe to be left alone. I was already sliding into the familiar tyre tracks of behaviour that marked A Trip Back Home, ticking off things in a silent Bingo that included being mildly hungover, a text from my mother reminding me to 'come early', a battle with the ticket machine that meant I'd had to run to catch my train, a chicken and bacon sandwich from Pret, a bottle of full-fat Coke, and a sullen longing to be back on my own sofa, staring vacantly at Saturday morning TV. I wondered whether my dad would be late coming to pick me up.

Reconnecting with Ama, and our conversation about how differently we'd interpreted the breaking of our friendship all those years ago, had made me run an inventory on my relationship with my family. I realised that on average I saw them about eight times a year, and that included birthdays. It wasn't a generous eight either. I'd come up on the train after work on a Friday and be back in London to go out Saturday evening. Or I'd ooze onto the train on Saturday afternoon, usually hungover, and leave the moment I woke up Sunday morning. I had been doing this for so long, I couldn't remember if I'd created this regime to protect myself from being irritated by my parents and Devi or if they'd pushed me away. Regardless, it was with some shock and dismay that I realised we had somehow created two different households, in different locations, that happened to overlap from time to time, but co-existed quite independently of each other.

It made me reconsider things. For instance, it was a bugbear that Devi would always talk about how busy she was being a mum, making me feel like I was encroaching on time she could have spent with Karen and Nikhil. But maybe she projected that because I hadn't been either dependable or even around.

I tried talking to Gregor when we were together about how awkward I felt with my own family. He said I was being dramatic; some people had families that were far worse. Of course that must be true, but it hadn't occurred to me before that perhaps if I visited more often, it wouldn't feel so much like re-entering the Earth's atmosphere each time I did go home.

As the train shunted to a halt, I could see the familiar sight of my mother's red Nissan Micra and wondered why my dad hadn't come to pick me up instead in his VW. *She's going to make me go to the supermarket with her instead of going straight home.* I groaned inwardly.

She was waving from the car park wearing her gardening clothes – oversized chinos and a T-shirt stained brown with her own compost mix.

'Bel!' she said, giving me a big hug. She smelled faintly of cloves and frying onions. People often said I looked like my mother because we both had deep-set eyes, similar-shaped noses and thick, long hair, but where she was small-boned like a bird due to her Bengali genes, my father's South Indian genes had taken over in my case to give me a build that a creepy Tinder date 'once likened to a statue of a fertility goddess'.

'We just need to stop at the supermarket . . .' Mum said. Another box ticked on homecoming Bingo.

*

Mum's blueprint for being an adult came from the pieces of other women's lives, donated by aunts and older female cousins when they occasionally remembered the orphan girl whose mother had died when she was eight.

Her father had died not long after her birth, and his family had cut ties with her mother because of some perceived slight not long after that, which meant there was no one to fill in the memory of him. She lived in the enormous extended family home, several buildings on one plot of land in Kolkata, and spent her childhood locked into survival mode. She had no chance of inheriting any of the family wealth because she was so far down the pecking order, with no real guardians to look after her interests apart from a few cousins to whom she was close. In consequence my mother's parenting style was fitful and inconsistent; sometimes suffocating, other times remote. She wanted to give us everything she hadn't had, and yet her inner child wanted to punish us for what she'd missed out on.

At five foot tall she was petite and, by Western standards, beautiful. A button nose. Luminous eyes. But her skin was the colour of mahogany – by Indian standards, too dark to be considered attractive. No surprise then that when my father came along, with his thick head of hair and owlish glasses, radiating all the serenity and confidence of a second child who'd grown up with a loving if slightly interfering family, she agreed to marry him despite only being nineteen at the time.

It'd be unfair to say that she levelled disapproval at me for the way I lived, and the choices I made – I think she had no way of understanding it. Many immigrant parents fail to understand that by making a better life for their children, they automatically give us more choices. Yet the narrow world view resulting from their own upbringing, with worries about scarcity, or the need to protect their own heritage against things like fish fingers and the Kardashians, means they expect us to make the same choices as they did.

My childhood was a good one in the sense that life was so boring and staid in suburbia, I frequently invented my own drama. I never had to worry about food or shelter. But when I became an adult, I heard the ticking of the clock, as if my life and Mum's were now taking place on opposite sides of a chessboard. And each time I made a move that didn't mirror the decisions she had taken at the age I was currently, I could see the disappointment rising from her like steam. It was never lost on me that whereas I spent my twenty-first birthday in The End nightclub downing shots of Sambuca, my mother spent hers giving birth to Devi.

In contrast to me then, Devi was the ultimate package when it came to daughters. She met Nikhil when she was twenty-one, got married at twenty-four and had Karen at twenty-six.

*

'How are things, Mum, everyone okay?' I looked out of the window at the old haunts that were once so familiar to me. From the number 477 bus stop where I'd pray to Christ/ Allah/Vishnu/Arriva that my bus would arrive on time so I wouldn't miss curfew, to the little record shop where Ama, Ling, Marina and I would meet outside every Saturday, year-round.

'Everything is fine. I've gone down to working three days a week, your dad is also cutting back on his hours. Karen got into her football team! Did you hear? I also went to House of Fraser and you'll never guess how much I got this pair of jogging bottoms for . . .' She rattled off all of the happenings of the last two months, according to the list of priorities in her head, which included outsmarting a shop assistant into giving her twenty per cent off some sweaters to a patient in the surgery who'd been rude to her. Mum worked as the office manager in Dad's dental practice.

Although she was still a few years off retirement age, they'd saved enough to cut back and enjoy life a bit more. I approved because rarely did they make choices that were kind to themselves.

'And how's Devi, she okay?' I asked, half-immersed in thought. I'd decided to tell my parents about the accident when we got home and was already dress-rehearsing their reactions. Mum was a terrible driver at the best of times, but at this she banked a kerb and almost ran a red light. She ignored my question and kept talking about the savings she made in Lidl, while continuing to drive erratically. My hangover was barking in protest at the sharp stops and unexpected swerves. 'Mum,' I said abruptly. 'What's going on?'

'I've just told you!' she yelled, about to take her hands off the wheel again, making me wonder whether it was possible for a person to have two near-death experiences in a fortnight.

'I'm not talking about the five pence you saved on a pair of socks! Why are you avoiding my question about Devi?'

'Oh,' she said, sadly. '*That*. Well, not my place to say. Yet.' And with that, she punched a few buttons on the car stereo and, appropriately, Phil Collins' 'Something in the Air Tonight' started playing loudly.

*

Like many first-generation Asians, my parents had at some point in the past, stood at a crossroads marked 'America' and 'England', and instead of going for Hollywood, giant refrigerators, good music and sunshine, they chose the small soggy island that was home to the Queen, Marks and Spencer knickers, fish and chips. Frequently as a teenager, watching TV shows that depicted American high-school life, boozy house parties and boys who didn't have chins like an under-cooked knuckle of lamb, I wondered how much more shiny and exciting my life would be if they'd only chosen differently. Correction, if Dad had been allowed to do what he wanted. He'd always been in love with America and its big houses, but Mum insisted that they had to move to England because her cousin Padmini lived there. Padmini was one of a handful of relatives from the big Kolkata compound who she'd liked.

Although Dad had given up on his American dream, he hadn't given up on the big house. When I was about to go to secondary school, they finally saved up enough to buy a home with a decent plot of land. The house itself had been a small three-bedroom affair, but over the years they had knocked down walls, expanded and almost rebuilt the entire thing so that now it had much more space where they could indulge in their separate hobbies. Dad loved building things, and the garage had been lengthened to include a separate area for his carpentry projects.

Although I still had a bed in my old room, the rest of it had been turned into Mum's yoga studio. Devi's bedroom had no bed at all, presumably because she lived only a ten-minute drive away, and was now a sewing room/ supply closet for all the 'bargains' Mum found in the sales.

Dad's areas of the house were denoted by scraps of wood and bits of machinery, while Mum's displayed plants and baskets of fabric and embroidery. Like a lot of people who arrived in Britain without much money in the seventies, their approach to interior design had not evolved much beyond inherited pieces, ranging from

Indian nesting tables to a cast-off leather sofa. When I was growing up, it used to drive me mad that the furniture made no sense, but as an adult I'd say that the house looked comfortable and happy.

Mum was making me a cup of tea when Dad arrived, a bit breathless. 'Oh, Baloo, it's good to see you,' he said, kissing the top of my head. A limited number of people were allowed to call me Beryl, but an even smaller number – one person, specifically – was allowed to call me Baloo. But even as he said my nickname, his eyes were faraway and he looked pained, as if he'd been dealing with something uncomfortable. They exchanged small talk about needing a pint of milk and some eggs, then there was a heavy, uncomfortable pause.

Although I'd finally been prepared to talk to them about what had happened and my visit to the hospital, I had a horrible feeling it was about to be trumped by something more serious.

'Let's sit in the dining room, shall we?' Dad said solemnly. The dining room was where we'd entertain guests but would never eat ourselves on a normal day.

The car journey with Mum had exhausted my patience. 'Why can't you tell me here? The anticipation is worse than whatever it is you're going to say. Just tell me!' I heard my voice rising to a high pitch, hated this shrill, exaggerated version of myself that I worked so hard to soften when I wasn't with them.

'Come on,' he said, jostling me to the dining room. As we sat down, they shared a look. Clearly they'd rehearsed this. Mum was the first to speak. 'Bel, this isn't easy to say,' and she looked away, 'but Devi and Nikhil are getting divorced.' Dad took his glasses off and rubbed his eyes.

'What?' I said, shocked. 'What do you mean? They've been together for years. What happened?'

'She can talk to you about that herself,' Mum said, trying not to cry, 'but we wanted to tell you first. I don't know why this bad thing happened to us, I thought they were happy . . .' She put her head in her hands.

'Anju . . .' Dad said, wrapping his arms around her, and I felt something leave my mother as she let go of the brave face she'd been putting on. She started crying in earnest and he held her more tightly. They had been together for decades, had lived more years together than they had apart. I wanted that for myself so badly.

But Devi and Nikhil . . . the news of their impending divorce was shocking. Not because it signified the end of their marriage and all the mess that would follow for the two of them, Karen and my parents, but because it immediately rewrote the script I'd imagined for Devi, the 'good, obedient daughter'. It overturned the way I had envisaged her life, given that divorces didn't just happen overnight. Clearly they must have been unhappy for some time, and I'd had no idea. But there was a deep poignancy in Mum assuming that Devi would talk to me about it because we were sisters, and I felt the loss and the lack within that. In every film I'd watched, it was sisters first, parents second. It wasn't meant to be the other way around. I should have been the first person Devi had told, and it said so much about our relationship that I was one of the last.

'How do you feel about it, Bel?' Dad said quietly.

'I feel bad for Devi. And Karen, of course.' I thought about Ama and the glow of the joy she felt about getting married, the future with Bron she was already sketching out while stepping through a doorway that had now closed for my sister.

'At her age,' Mum wailed, 'I just don't know if she'll ever meet anyone again.' Dad kissed her head. 'It'll be okay,' he said. 'Anju, she'll be fine.'

My mother's melodrama snapped me out of the thoughts swirling in my head. 'Devi isn't exactly a goblin, Mum. Maybe let the dust settle on this relationship before lining her up for the next one.'

'Ayy, Bel,' Dad said reproachfully, 'your mother is only worried. We all are.'

'I know but . . .' I trailed off, exasperated. I could hardly say that Devi and I were best mates, but even I knew that the last thing on her mind would be her dating prospects. She was probably feeling really sad and worrying how the split might affect Karen. A colleague of mine I once found sobbing in the toilets after her marriage ended had told me that you expect divorce to be just another break-up, and think you'll be okay because you've experienced break-ups before. But nothing really prepares you for the depth of sadness, the death by a million cuts of your old wedding photos or a painting you bought together on holiday, the disintegration of a whole joint future.

I took a breath and remembered something Ama said about parenting the night before, in the context of coming out to her mother. It was about the moment you realise as an adult that they don't have all the answers, that they never did, that half of what we thought was parenting was a game of smoke and mirrors and guesswork. It's irreversible, she said, and you see in that moment their fragility and fallibility.

'I'm sorry, Mum,' I said, ticking yet another box on the Bingo card. This one: apologising to my mother for losing my temper. 'Tell me what I can do.'

*

A six-year age gap is tough to navigate in the sibling world. Four years, and you could just about bridge the divide to become friends and confidantes. Anything more, and you found yourself awkwardly at very different stages of childhood. When I was seven, Devi was entering her teens. And by the time I was a teenager, she was exiting them. Perhaps it might have been recoverable if the older sibling was a Peter Pan type, but Devi had always seemed sensible and staid.

Before I started secondary school, I loved the fact that she looked after me like a second mother. It made me feel adored and safe, and it filled in the gaps when my own mother was in one of her moods or disappeared to India to visit her family, sometimes for a couple of months at a time. Devi would be the one to make me corned beef sandwiches for my packed lunch, or pick me up from dance class, even though she would have been at an age when other girls were pushing the boundaries of their independence and having fun.

By my mid-teens I'd largely outgrown my own mother, and definitely had no need for two. What I needed most was a sister: someone who would guide me through the world, give me advice without judgement and go into battle for me. But Devi didn't know how to stop mothering me and eventually I stopped telling her things. It was probably why I leaned so much on my school friends, and why it hurt so deeply when things turned out the way they did.

We were proof that siblings could have the same upbringing and emerge like Danny DeVito and Arnold Schwarzenegger from *Twins*. When I was pining over long-haired white boys named Steve and Brandon, she had married her brown university sweetheart. There was the big Indian wedding held in the local golf club, and on their first anniversary holiday in Thailand, she conceived Karen.

Much to Nikhil's dismay, she told him that the pregnancy news meant they'd have to postpone moving to London and be nearer one of their sets of parents. Given that he was starting work as a first-year doctor, which took him to hospitals all over the country, she chose our parents. Although she'd planned to start her own business after Karen went into nursery, she melted into the life of a suburban mum, working as a part-time office manager. It was the life I didn't want for myself but had assumed my sister was fulfilled by.

In all the time I had mourned the relationship I felt we should have had, I hadn't thought about being a good sister to her. I clearly hadn't been, given that I was only hearing about her divorce second-hand. I saw a choice looming: I could remain resentful that I hadn't been told, continue to keep myself at a distance and let Devi figure it out on her own. Or I could do the hard thing, as I had done with Ama, and think about what Devi really needed, which at this moment was very much what I needed too. We each needed a sister.

*

For someone apparently bereft following the news of her oldest child's divorce, my mother had been remarkably industrious.

Several stuffed bin bags stood in the middle of Devi's old bedroom, which was decorated in greys and whites, a defunct NKOTB clock with the whole gang keeping silent watch from the corner and the sun flooding through gauze curtains. The bags contained letters, memorabilia and my old school shirt signed with signatures from everyone in my class.

'I wouldn't normally ask,' Mum said, looking slightly sheepish, 'but your dad and I were thinking of clearing some space. I want to give Devi and Karen the option of staying here.'

Devi lived a ten-minute drive away from Mum and Dad, and while a big part of that had been to ensure they'd be there to help her with Karen, being geographically nearby was a very different beast from being under the same roof as them.

'Why on earth would a grown forty-two-year-old woman with a teenager want to do that?'

'What do you mean?' Mum said, offended. 'Why wouldn't she?'

It doesn't matter how old you are, or how successful in your career, South Asian parents will always treat you like a child who is incompetent at managing your own life without their constant meddling, supervision and guidance. Being an immigrant parent was like rearing your chick in the Sahara when you had been raised in the Antarctic. You didn't know the threats so you saw them everywhere, and believed that if you could only keep your offspring close and micro-manage them, they'd be better off.

I tried a different approach.

'Mum, have you asked Devi if she wants to move in with you?' I said gently.

'No,' she said slowly, 'but she won't be married anymore.'

'I'm not married and I've managed just fine,' I replied.

'But you're different, Bel, you're used to doing things on your own. Devi is used to having someone around to manage things.'

'Mum, you do remember she is married to Nikhil, one of the most useless potatoes on the planet?'

'Bel,' my mother said exasperatedly, 'I don't want to have an argument about this. I want to give Devi and

Karen the option. Could you *please* decide what you want to throw out, so I can make room for them *if* they want to stay?'

'Yes, of course,' I sighed.

My phone pinged.

Have you told them yet?

Ama. She wanted to know if I'd told my parents about my accident. On the current list of priorities, it had fallen right off.

No, you pest. It's not the right time.
Rigggggghht. And when is the right time?
Don't you have better things to do like looking for frilly wedding dresses?

She responded with the middle-finger emoji, which made me laugh out loud. The morning after we'd had dinner, she sent me a message saying: **Bron and I would love you to have this.** It was a Save the Date for her wedding. I discovered it was possible to feel elation and a sense of dread at the same time. Being invited to the ceremony meant she wanted me back in her life, but it also meant facing up to the ticking time bomb of when I'd see Marina and Ling again.

'Who's that?' Mum said with interest. 'A boy?'

I snorted. 'No, it most definitely isn't a boy. It's Ama – you remember her, from school? Tall girl, Sri Lankan?'

'Oh, yes, I remember! Her mother was a nurse at Darenth, I think?'

'Well done, Mum.'

'What happened to your other friends? I never really liked the English girl . . .'

'Marina?' Once someone was in Mum's grudge book, they stayed there decades after.

'Yaa, she seemed like trouble. Always wore short skirts. But the other girl I really liked. Always so polite and helpful. She was Chinese, I think?'

'Half-Chinese,' I said, keen to change subject. 'Anyway, shoo! Let me get through all of this.'

*

In the distance, I could hear Dad playing Sam Cooke in his little workshop while Mum pottered about in the garden. A breeze outside shook the trees with a sound like the rustle of skirts and a gentle, restful quiet settled in. Funny how now it felt peaceful when back in my teenage years it seemed oppressive.

I tipped out the contents of a worn, cream cloth bag that had been customised with band names. A waterfall of tightly folded notes and cards fell to the floor. Among the paper was an unfinished tube of Black Cherry lipstick and a small statue of Ganesh that Mum had brought back for me from her trip to India when I was eleven. I picked up a postcard with worn edges, smiling brown women waving as they stood in the middle of a tea plantation, wicker baskets on their backs. *Welcome to Sri Lanka!*

I turned it over and saw Ama's familiar writing. I ran

my fingers over the indentations she had made with her ballpoint pen, a little spark of connection travelling down the corridor of time between past and present. Even though I had only seen her a couple of days previously, I was already looking forward to when I could see her again, to re-experiencing the purity of that excitement at being around someone you love as a friend. The postcard had been sent during a trip to see her family, the same summer that my mother was having one of her 'my family takes me for granted so I'm not going to do anything including cooking or cleaning' periods. I hadn't realised just how much time I'd spent at Ama's place until then, and how, unlike Ling and Marina's houses, it felt like an extension of my own home, somewhere I could be myself.

I thought of that last summer we had all spent together. I'd always had such a clear understanding of what had taken place – or at least I thought I had until I was reunited with Ama. After our holiday in Cornwall, I'd locked away all the troubling memories I had around the girls and what followed.

But afterwards it seemed Ama had still maintained a friendship with Ling and Marina. Had there been something I'd missed?

Although I found the past painful to revisit, it seemed vital to look back at it in order to figure a few things out.

6

A month before we broke up for the school holidays, the four of us – Marina, Ama, Ling and me – were sitting on the floor of Ama's living room consulting The Universe. We wanted to know about our love lives, whether we'd pass our GCSEs and if we'd be able to go on holiday together for the first time ever. It was usually a calm, zen experience except Marina had designated herself as the tarot reader *du jour*.

'Give it – GIVE IT HERE,' she bellowed, wrestling the pack of cards from my hands. 'You bums are doing this all wrong.'

The unnatural orange light from Ama's lava lamp cast shifting shadows over the wall. The smell of sandalwood filled the room from incense I'd nicked from the Gods' shrine at home.

Bags of Haribo lay open and we had a few hours before we'd be expected back home. Enough time for some tarot, music and possibly mooching along to the local Our Price to see if we might stumble across any other indie kids. In the background, 'Hedonism' by Skunk Anansie was playing on Tina Sendhil's record player, which had belonged to her late husband, shipped over especially so she could play his favourite records when his memory weighed heavy. On the anniversary of his death, Donny Osmond's 'I Love You More Than You'll Ever Know' would fill every room, along with the scent of saffron, chilli and lemon as she cooked his favourite dishes. Although between us we all had Sony Walkmans and CD players, we all agreed that vinyl was a lot cooler. Periodically Ama would buy a record if it was on sale in the local music shop, and the rest of us added to the collection.

Ama's was our favourite place to hang out after school. Mine was never on offer because one of my parents was usually at home. Ling's house felt like a museum. We weren't allowed to make noise, bring in dirt, and her parents always seemed slightly irritated we were there at all.

In contrast, Marina's home looked like it should be featured on *MTV Cribs*. Her mother Delilah was the booze mum – the one who'd turn a blind eye and buy us illicit bottles of alcohol even though we were underage. She lived out in the countryside. Fine for a sleepover, but Ama's was in the centre of town, and it was unsupervised. Tina's parenting style was less hands-on than I was used to, but it worked – even when we were being naughty, Ama was always the most sensible. Maybe because she had less to rebel against.

'Marina,' Ling said, 'calm down, man.' She shook out

her long black hair and took a sip of her Coke. 'Tell Bel what she needs to do rather than screeching at her.'

Although Marina was a full-time member of our quartet, she had only joined us in the fourth year from a private school. She refused to elaborate on it, but despite the big house she lived in, and the fancy cars her parents drove, some sort of financial disaster meant that they could no longer afford the fees for St Dunstable's so West Hill Grammar it was. It wasn't a problem for the three of us who had known each other since Year 7, but she remained eternally paranoid that her late arrival meant it was only a matter of time before we kicked her out of the group.

Marina seemingly had a perfect life – the house, the money, the freedom – and when I saw her being ungrateful about it, it irked me. I'll *maybe* admit part of the irritation stemmed from jealousy. Take her hair. Marina's hair changed almost monthly. Presently it was bright red, streaked with blonde. I once brought up the topic of dyeing my hair with my mum, and she looked at me as if I had announced that I was pregnant with the local Londis manager's baby. Marina's wardrobe seemed limitless. Whatever she wanted and asked for, she got. An electric guitar that she never used. Tickets to Reading Festival. The latest Doc Martens.

The only thing we had in common was that we liked Black Cherry lipstick. Except I could never shake the fact that it looked cooler against her paler skin, and I'd always have to rub mine off on the bus home, given that my mother would have shat a slipper at the sight of me wearing make-up.

And when Marina explained things, as she was doing right now, there was a *tone*. A mixture of exasperation and superiority that let you know she knew something you didn't.

Marina held the cards aloft. 'Okay. Let's try this one more time. You shuffle the cards like this.'

'Dude,' I cut her off, 'I know how fucking tarot works.'

'Why aren't you doing it properly then?'

'Because I can't decide what question to ask!'

'I can't help you with that!'

'I KNOW!' I yelled. We both glared at each other.

'Ahhh, Babybel,' Ling said, squeezing my shoulder, 'don't stress it. Look, you want to know about Steve, right?'

'Yes,' I said, a bit less hotly, 'but we've only got another four weeks left of school and I want to know about the summer and—'

'One thing at a time, Bel,' Ama soothed, while braiding a little plait at the front of my long hair. 'Let The Universe tell you about Steve and then we can discuss what to do for the summer.'

Ama always knew how to calm me down. We had met in the first year of secondary school, when she arrived halfway through the year. She had only just arrived here from Colombo and was still adapting to English life. Until she joined, I felt as if I didn't quite fit in and no one really understood me, which was not something I could ever have shared with Ling.

She and I were already friends by the time Ama came along, but it was mostly out of necessity. I'd had to join two weeks into the new term due to a broken leg and even a slightly late start meant that other girls had already formed their little cliques. I was left to sift for friends among the rejects, and these included Ling. Back then, she was eerily quiet and refused to talk to any other students apart from me, which meant any opportunity to expand my social circle was closed down. When Ama came along, though, we were drawn to each other when we realised we both liked Nirvana and Body Shop bath pearls. We absorbed Ling into our fold, and slowly she opened up a bit more.

'I'm sorry,' I said, looking at Marina, 'I know you're trying to help. This Steve situation is stressing me out. Let's try again.'

Steve, or Skateboard Steve as he was known to his mates, was the most beautiful boy in the entire world. He had blue eyes, freckles and a curtain of brown hair. I felt as if I would die if he didn't become mine soon; that longing grew into an ache that I carried around all the time. Even though I knew about SEX, I didn't actually know what would happen once I got him. We were a roomful of virgins, barring Ling who had given Trevor Chow a handjob at Sunday School a few months before. But I knew that when I finally got Steve, everything would become clear and I would feel complete.

The only problem was: how was it going to happen? Apart from having parents who weren't super strict but definitely strict enough to cockblock me, Steve and I didn't exactly run in the same circles. We weren't as cool as Steve and his friends, and that was mainly because we still had curfews, homes with boring, stable parents, and we didn't smoke or drink all the time.

I shuffled the cards while Ama put Radiohead's 'Creep' on the record player. As it always did when that song started playing, the air shifted as everyone stepped inside themselves a little.

I opened my eyes and brought myself back from that soft boundary between dreaming and being. I divided the deck into three equal stacks.

Marina turned the first card, which apparently indicated my past. 'Interesting,' she breathed. 'The Fool Card indicates a risk taken but the start of a great adventure. It means positivity, love, and might involve travelling. If you're single, this might be the first steps taken towards a romantic relationship.'

'Lucky bitch. That sounds amazing,' Ling said. In theory, yes, but the only great adventure I had on the horizon for the summer holidays was getting up late and watching *Looney Tunes* while eating chips for lunch. Every. Day. Marina turned the second card, which indicated my present.

'The Five of Cups,' she read. 'This may affect matters of the heart and signifies following what you desire. Listen to your intuition and take action.'

'There you go,' said Ling. 'Ask Steve out. Sorted.'

I chewed my lip. I was pretty sure Steve didn't know

I was alive, never mind fancying me back. I took a deep breath and turned the third card.

'The Tower,' said Marina. 'Ah.'

'That doesn't look great,' I said, pointing at the card. 'Two people jumping from a burning building?'

'Not necessarily,' she said, peering at her Tarot Explainer book. 'It could mean a time of turmoil, but it could also mean the clearing out of old things for something new. It can seem scary because the change is sudden and can be life-changing, but . . .' Her brow scrunched in concentration. 'Aha. Sometimes that change can be a good thing!' she exclaimed.

'Do I ask Steve out or not?'

Marina frowned and looked at the cards. 'I'm no expert—'

'No shit!'

She shot me a dirty look. 'Maybe this reading isn't about Steve.'

'Great.' I sighed and lay down on the floor, looking up at the yellowing ceiling. 'I'll just die alone.'

'Don't be so dramatic,' Ama said and threw a cushion at my face. 'Now that you've spoken to The Universe, let's discuss the summer holiday. And my sixteenth birthday.'

'I think we should all go to Cornwall,' she said, as if it was the most straightforward thing in the world.

The only obstacle between me and the holiday of a lifetime were my parents and Devi.

*

'BEL!' my sister shouted from downstairs. 'Nikhil will be here any minute – are you ready?'

Fucking Nikhil. I'd never met the guy and already I hated him. Since Devi had come home from university for the weekend, she'd talked of nothing else, obsessing over the food Mum was making for his first Meet the Parents lunch. According to Devi, he couldn't have anything too spicy, he only drank Lilt, and he was Gujarati so could we possibly not serve meat? Dad put his foot down at the last one and said, 'No one messes with my lamb curry. I'm sorry, Devi, but he will have to respect how we do things in this house.'

His refusal to budge had sent her spinning off into the foulest mood. Saturday was lamb curry day as it had been every week previously, and Dad would wake up early to grind the masala. I could hear stomping, slamming, yelling *WHY HASN'T THIS BEEN IRONED?* and other tirades that I'd escaped from using the excuse of homework.

'Homework' was actually the Cornwall pros and cons list. I'd have to carry this scrap of paper into battle with me when I finally mustered up the courage to talk to my parents.

'It's my sixteenth birthday in August as you all know,' Ama had said, 'and I'd like to do something special. I talked to Marina and her aunt and uncle have a big house in Cornwall, in Newquay. She said we can stay with them. I checked the dates, and there's a massive Surfing Festival. We can drink on the beach, listen to music – there'll be bands playing . . .'

As she talked, each of us went into our own fantasy of what this holiday would be like. Finally, we'd be cool. Finally, we'd get to live our dreams of American TV teenage life – drinking beer by a bonfire, kissing boys, partying and making memories that weren't limited to a damp English park. It sounded magical, with just one snag. There was no way my parents would agree to let me go.

'Okay, I've thought of that, don't worry,' Ama said. 'Your parents LOVE me and if they know my mum has agreed to let me go, then they'll be fine with it.'

'Has your mum agreed?' I asked.

'No, of course not! But I'll tell her your parents agreed and that will make her say yes – it's the old smoke and mirrors trick. Your auntie lives in Plymouth, right? We'll agree to go and visit her halfway through the trip, to reassure them, and it'll be fine. And tell them Ling's dad agrees, and I'm sure they'll be okay.'

At this, Marina looked mortally offended. 'Hang on,' she said, 'you guys would be staying at MY family's house – why don't I get a mention?'

Ama looked at her kindly, like a wayward toddler that needed placating with a lollipop. Then hit her with the truth like a brick-filled sack. People tended to forget that Ama was a proper brown person, and as such didn't dance behind British politeness. 'Because you're white, Marina. You represent all those teenagers on TV having underage sex, telling their parents to fuck off and stealing the family car to go to secret house parties. We're downplaying your involvement as much as possible.'

In Case of Emergency

The look on Marina's face made me laugh so much I almost snorted Cherry Coke through my nose. But I knew my parents would say no. Sure, they weren't strict like other brown parents. They let me go for sleepovers, mostly let me wear what I liked and didn't drag me around to other people's houses, or go to the temple, but they were still worried about drinking, sex, smoking, predators, bad influences, and kidnapping. Still, I promised Ama I would ask, and I'd need a list to help me with my mother's inevitable questioning.

Pros
Invaluable lesson of independence
Could visit educational sights such as the Eden project,
    the Newquay Heritage Museum
One week of peace for them
It'd be really cheap
I really want to go
Ama's 16th and she has a dead dad so we should be
    nice to her

Counter-resistance
I'll call every day
We'll be staying with Marina's family
I won't talk to boys
I won't do drugs
I'll visit Padmini Auntie
Ama's mum already said yes
Ling's dad already said yes

*

When I asked Mum why there was such a big age gap between my sister and me, she told me it was planned. But I overheard her telling Padmini Auntie that the condom had split. The idea of my parents having sex, let alone using condoms, made me feel ill for days. Still, I'd always thought sisters were supposed to be best pals, swapping clothes, talking about boys and covering for each other, like Tia and Tamera in *Sister Sister*. But that wasn't me and Devi.

When I was little, I'm embarrassed to say, I viewed her as a god and demonstrated this worship by hanging around all the time, scribbling notes on her schoolbooks and listening in to her conversations on the phone. Meanwhile she was a teenager, stressed out about GCSEs, then A-levels. Just before I became a teenager, she was out the door and off to university in Durham, and a combination of studies and distance meant she only visited every six weeks. The only exception was when I was eleven and she came to stay with me and Dad while Mum was in India. That was the time I broke my leg. But she left just before Mum returned home and afterwards things had been weird between us. Forget asking her for advice about boys – she just turned into a more irritating extension of my parents by disapproving of my friends and questioning any decision Mum and Dad made to let me go out. It wasn't cool.

When Devi barged in, then, while making my list, I wasn't best pleased. But then I saw her face, and it was red. Her eyes puffy from crying.

Though I was sure I would hate Nikhil, and Devi's incessant mentioning of him over the past year had done nothing to soften that, she was my sister. Even if she had ratted me out to Mum about wearing lipstick and more than once scuppered my plans to go loafing with my friends. Maybe if things worked out with her and Nikhil, she'd just calm down a bit and be a bit happier. My list-making could wait.

'Mum and Dad are driving me mad,' she gulped. She didn't often come to me to moan about our parents, but when she did, it made her seem more human. And made me more inclined to help her.

'I tell you what,' I said, 'Nikhil's going to be here in a couple of hours. You have a shower and I'll go down-stairs. I'll check that things are tidy, and Mum isn't doing her usual thing of getting worked up before guests come over, and Dad isn't starting some kind of carpentry pro-ject in the garage. Okay?' She didn't say anything but hung her head.

'You put so much pressure on yourself, Devi,' I said trying to peer behind her wall of hair. 'Mum and Dad are hard work but they're not so bad that they can't be normal for a few hours. It'll be fine, I promise.'

I couldn't really promise such a thing at all – our par-ents were a force unto themselves – but it seemed like the kind of thing that calmed people down. And it seemed to be working. Devi looked at my Guns N' Roses T-shirt which had a naked woman on it. 'Are you going to be wearing *that*?' she said.

'There's the sister I know and love,' I said, rolling my eyes.

*

Dad had made the lamb curry first thing in the morning, but Mum made everything else to accompany it, including the rice, beans fry, dal, a sambar, a chickpea curry and a coconut chicken dish despite the fact that Nikhil was a veggie. 'Chicken isn't really a meat,' she said dismissively.

This much cooking sent her into a mad, frazzled mess – partly because I think it reminded her of the days when she'd had to help cook enormous amounts of food for the extended family back in Kolkata. Meanwhile Dad, having no concept of time, and considering his work done with the one curry he had made, had indeed started a new carpentry project. I told him to stop what he was doing and soothed Mum by cleaning up the living room and the kitchen. I asked both of them to shower and get ready. By the time Nikhil arrived, things seemed normal.

He turned up dressed in a gingham shirt and chinos. He was around five foot nine, the same height as Dad, studying medicine, and to my surprise came from a liberal family with three siblings, all brothers. His dad even went clubbing with them, apparently. Devi wore a rictus grin throughout this conversation. When she spoke, her voice was high and pitchy; out of solidarity she didn't eat any meat.

When lunch was served, Nikhil rolled up his shirt

sleeves and proceeded to eat with his hands, which earned him top marks from Dad, who beamed and said: 'You're alright, for a vegetarian.'

As with most gatherings that involved our family and their friends, I was mostly ignored because I was the youngest. Which usually was fine – it allowed me to slink off and watch TV upstairs or listen to music. Feeling like an outsider in my own family wasn't unusual but usually it was my choice, either through the clothes I wore or the music I listened to. But this time, there was a strange power shift when my parents started talking about meeting Nikhil's parents, and asked Devi and him what their plans would be in terms of getting married. For the first time, I felt pushed aside. As if I had nothing of value to contribute. The four of them were a unit, and I wasn't quite sure where I fitted into that. I wanted Devi to be happy, but it dawned on me that her getting married to Nikhil would only take her further away from us.

My father made a gentle comment that I was unusually quiet. I didn't know how to answer him, so in the gap of waiting for me to reply, Nikhil said: 'Bel, Devi tells me it's the summer before you start your A-levels – I remember that being a big one. Any plans?'

Before I could say anything, Devi laughed and said: 'Let me guess, getting up at noon, eating a cheese toastie and watching TV?'

All of those things were my favourite activities, but the way she spoke, it was like I was some saddo with nothing better to do. Not all of us could be at university drinking shots and dancing at foam parties. Not that I cared about Nikhil's opinion, but it triggered me enough to say: 'Actually I do have something big I'd like to do, but I haven't asked my parents yet.' Aha! Maybe if I asked in front of a stranger, they'd feel less inclined to say no.

Mum and Dad looked very interested.

I told them about the Cornwall plan, emphasising Ama's birthday and that her mum Tina had already agreed. They looked very serious and Dad said: 'We'll have to think about it, Bel, I'm not sure. Maybe . . .'

I don't know what madness seized Devi, but she said: 'Come on! You can't seriously be considering it? Bel's only just turned sixteen!'

Devi owed me big time for straightening out the house and our parents before Nikhil arrived. But apparently she didn't think so. I didn't want her to die but I did want to smother her with a pillow until her legs kicked in protest.

To my surprise, Nikhil stepped in and said: 'I went on my first holiday with my friends when I was sixteen. It was really important to me to do it – A-levels were so full on. We went to Cyprus. It made me more independent. And it was loads of fun.'

Mum looked pensive and said: 'I think we'll chat about it later, okay, Bel?' I nodded.

'Mum, I don't think this is a good idea . . .' Devi began.

I couldn't keep quiet any longer. I knew it would jeopardise my chances of being allowed on the trip but this was the last straw. 'Devi, what is your PROBLEM!' I yelled. She looked at me, stunned. I'd never shouted at her before. 'You're not my mum, alright? What kind of sister are you!'

'Bel, don't talk to your sister like that,' Mum said. The unfairness was searing, it melted my entire core. Devi was being a dick, and I was getting scolded for calling it out?

'I'm only looking out for you, Bel,' Devi said.

'Are you?' I said incredulously. 'Are you really? Because it doesn't feel like it. Most sisters would *help* in a scenario like this, not make it harder.'

'When I was your age, I didn't have the luxury of being able to go on a girls' holiday, okay? You don't know how lucky you are,' she snapped. My mum looked down at the table.

'Right, that's enough, girls,' my dad said, which was unusual because he never usually got involved.

'Fine by me,' I fumed. If we were an English family, one of us would have stomped off and sworn. But we were a brown family, and even after raised voices, no one was allowed to storm off. We sat uncomfortably at the table, all that heightened emotion just hanging in the air, until Nikhil complimented my mother on her sambar and the conversation drifted into small talk when it was safe for me to leave the table.

7

2019

When I was a teenager, I never felt as if Devi and I were on the same team. Everything was carved into such stark, dividing lines between 'them' and 'me'. Then, when she met Nikhil, it felt as if she was gone forever. Suddenly she had other priorities, and it seemed pointless to try and fix things or get closer to her, because to what end?

But now, for the first time since we were adults, we were both single. Karen was getting older, and soon enough she would leave for university. Dinner with Ama the night before – something I'd never thought would be possible – had crystallised my desire for change. But also, I felt an unexpected and huge wave of empathy for my sister. I knew what it was like to be on the outside, and to worry that people judged your choices. It sharpened my need to reconcile with her.

But I had no idea where to start, or whether it would blow up in my face. Only that where there was stubbornness before, now there was willingness at least to try.

While Mum thought I was upstairs sorting through my things, I Googled: 'How to reconnect with your sibling'. I came across an article by one Maureen Crumble writing for *Cumbria Weekly*, who said: *Step one: remove the baggage. Rid yourself of existing tension. Step two: break the ice. Make a joke or start talking so it isn't awkward. Step three: analyse what went wrong and why. Step four: deal with any jealousy – especially if you find yourself unable to be happy for your sibling. Step five: don't give up. If your sibling won't change, think about how you can change.*

It was deeply unhelpful. But the overall message seemed to be that trying was better than not trying, and even if the sister behaved like a knob, to overlook it.

The time lapse between the first crunch of tyres against gravel, indicating Devi's arrival, and the moment she stepped through the door felt like eons. I was strangely nervous, wiping sweating palms against my jeans. Mum and Dad crowded in the hallway, trying to be the first to greet her. I held back slightly. Not because I didn't want to see her but I didn't want her to feel overwhelmed.

'Naani!' I heard Karen say, and my mother looked at her with a tenderness that we'd never received. 'Auntie!' my niece said as soon as she saw me, making Devi look up. I gave her a small smile.

'She doesn't do hugs at the moment,' Devi said, earning herself a glare from her daughter who launched herself at me and pulled me into an embrace. Even if she was being bratty and trying to prove her mother wrong, I was grateful for it. Something about my proximity to Karen, and being held that close, made the emotion I'd felt on seeing Mum this morning resurface. Ama and Bron's words about the accident echoed in my head: *You know you were lucky?*

'What have you brought me?' she demanded.

'Karen!' I heard Devi say as she looked at me apologetically. 'That's not polite!'

'Well, I heard someone got into the under-eighteens . . . I think that warrants a special something,' I said. Karen beamed, but before she could drag me to the living room, I took in Devi's appearance. Still beautiful, but clearly tired to her soul.

Step one: remove the baggage. I cleared my throat. 'Mum and Dad, would you mind if we all had tea?'

They looked at each other. 'Sure, we'll go and make it,' Dad said. 'Biscuits?'

I nodded and looked at Devi. The old me would have said something snide like: 'I can't believe I had to find out about your divorce from Mum and Dad.' The new me, or at least the me that was trying not to be an arsehole, wanted to let her know that I was here for her. The only problem was, I didn't quite know how to do that without it coming across as patronising and mawkish.

We hugged and she said: 'Don't look at me like that.'

'Like what?'

'Like I'm a baby giraffe about to collapse. I'm fine, honest.'

I wanted to say that I was sorry, not just for the divorce but for not knowing about it. For not noticing that Nikhil hadn't come to the last few family gatherings. I also wanted to say: *The reason I'm looking at you like this isn't out of pity but because I need you.* But just because I wanted a different relationship with Devi didn't mean she'd feel the same. And that was scary.

I brushed the thought away and handed Karen her present. She screamed so loudly it made me laugh. They were special-edition Nikes with a mint green tick and a red sole – a freebie from a campaign we'd worked on. 'Auntie, it's good to see you. You've been away for ages,' she said.

'You're only saying that so I give you more presents,' I replied.

I remembered holding Karen the day she was born, in the maternity ward of Darenth Valley Hospital. It was in the depths of winter, a day that stole the warmth from your mouth almost before you breathed out. In Devi's little cubicle with paper-thin blue curtains, however, summer had arrived with this little sunbeam, currently fast asleep, tiny mouth pouting, so freshly minted that the glow of creation was still on her.

Nikhil was AWOL. He was on his younger brother's stag do in Riga and we had been trying to get hold of him for twelve hours. Mum, Dad and I swept up Devi and got her through it. 'I'm going to kill him when I get hold of him, he's such a lad,' she joked, but I wondered why she was not angrier about it. She lost her shit if a waiter forgot her request to put salad dressing on the side, or if someone cut in front of her while boarding a plane.

I don't think I appreciated at the time that she had to joke about it because, regardless of Karen's week-early arrival, the truth was that Nikhil was probably having his penis taped to a lamp-pole when he should have been at home. And perhaps some truths are too hard to take on, especially when so much of your energy has been sapped by giving life to a precious child.

Also, she was probably tired from dealing with badly timed questions from Mum.

'Why have you called her Karen?'

'Because I like the name.'

'But it doesn't mean anything – it's not Indian.'

'It means something to me. I named her after Karen Carpenter.'

'But it's not Indian!'

'So? Being Indian isn't all it's cracked up to be. Do you know how many people mispronounce my name?'

As they argued in the background, I held Karen and loved my niece immediately. Unconditionally. I knew that there was a little part of me that lived on in her, as it did in Mum and Dad, as it did in Devi. But at the time, I was only twenty and my sister already seemed so much older and wiser at twenty-six. My love for Karen was a deep thing but while she was growing teeth and then getting them knocked out at football, performing in school plays and having her first sleepover, I was busy being a twenty-something in London, staying up until 5 a.m. drinking bottles of £3 wine.

I loved Karen, but I found it harder and harder to be at home. So I saw her at birthdays and family celebrations, and when I was visiting Mum and Dad, but we didn't do sleepovers or auntie shopping days. As more time went by, I had no idea who her friends were. I knew she did well academically and, unlike Devi and I, attended a private school, but I had no idea what questions even to ask her about the rest of her life. *What kind of music do you like?* sounded pathetic, and my knowledge of anything football-related made me sound like an undercover cop trying to sniff out drugs in a school. I didn't know if she liked boys (and/or girls), I didn't even know if liking people romantically was cool anymore – I did know that boasting about drinking and getting wasted definitely was not. And how do you even begin to broach those topics without sounding like some nosy, judgemental old person?

The older Karen got, the more she tunnelled into her phone or was out with friends when we'd have family dinners. When I last saw her, at a fairly tense dinner at my parents' with Devi bickering with Nikhil on the phone in the next room, there were parts of her that seemed so familiar: the angle of her nose was just like mine, and the way she'd stand with her hands clasped behind her back was like Dad. While my niece was always affectionate, she didn't look to me for stability or comfort. There was a part of me that yearned for that – not for motherhood, but to be a person she saw as home.

But the bond between her and her mother shone so brightly, it seemed impossible to me that Karen would need anyone else. Or that her mother might need me.

*

While Mum was upstairs showing Devi the space I had started clearing out, I decided to have a proper conversation with Karen.

'Niece?' I said to her.

'Mmmph?' she said, not looking away from her phone.

'Are you okay?'

She looked up, confused. 'How do you mean?'

I pointed upstairs. 'You know, all the divorce stuff. Can't be easy.'

She shrugged. 'It's not great, but it's not been great for years. At least now it's a bit more peaceful.'

'It's not been great for *years*?' I said. Why hadn't I picked up on it? *Because you haven't been around, dickhead.* I wasn't a fan of this interior voice of mine that seemed to have got a bit louder since my fall, but it had a point.

Suddenly, we heard Mum and Devi yelling upstairs. We looked at each other. Footsteps thundered down. Devi came in first, followed by Mum. Devi, red in the face, was saying, 'Let's eat, I've got to get Karen home.'

*

Over dinner, Mum's currified interpretation of shepherd's pie, things were eerily quiet and tense. Whatever Mum and Devi had argued about still hung heavily in the air. It was an odd recalibration of what I thought family life was like when I wasn't around, because usually they never argued, and I always pictured them laughing and joking around the table. Devi asked me how work was going.

Finally! *Step two: break the ice.* I told her about the Oseni situation to try and lighten the mood, but she seemed distracted. Then Karen asked me if I had a boyfriend, and when I said no, asked if I had a girlfriend. At that Dad choked on his food and she glared at him.

'Is there a problem, Ajja?'

'Well . . .' he said, catching her steely expression, which she had definitely inherited from the women in our family. 'No, no problem.'

The elephant in the room was Devi's divorce, but no one seemed to want to discuss that. No one knew there was also a rhinoceros in the room: my accident. I felt the pressure every time someone asked me a question about how I was doing. The need to tell them was building, but it never seemed like the right time.

'Bel,' Mum finally said gloomily during dessert, 'don't worry about clearing out your things. Apparently our place isn't good enough for Devi, so she won't be needing the space.'

Devi rolled her eyes. 'Mum, that is NOT what I said.'

'No? Did you not say that moving in with us would be taking a step backwards?'

'Yes, but that's not what I—'

'It's fine, Devi, honestly,' Mum said, aggressively spooning more chocolate ice cream into her bowl. 'You do whatever you want. After all, you're a grown woman, with a child. Who am I? Only your mother.'

I could see both sides so clearly. Mum's heart was breaking for her child and she wanted to fix things for her. Devi could see her life crumbling around her and moving back to Mum and Dad's would be admitting to failure. Dad looked defeated – clearly some iteration of this conversation had happened before. Karen sat next to me, checking her phone under the table, her ice cream melting to the point of being inedible. 'This happens a lot,' she murmured.

As Mum and Devi continued to argue, I realised there would never be a good time to tell them all about the accident. So why not now?

'Actually,' I said, clearing my throat, 'I'm sorry to interrupt, but something has happened to me that you probably should know about.'

They all looked up expectantly. My family were terrible with this kind of news. They had a long history of over-reactions to any kind of medical diagnosis, accidents, even a questionable-looking mole.

I coughed. 'Recently I, er, had an accident. I was walking down the street and I fell, um, a fair distance through a trapdoor into a cellar.'

Even Karen stopped scrolling. They all stared at me.

'Ah . . . an ambulance was called and I woke up in hospital. But I'm all fine, according to the doctors. I'm sorry, I should have told you sooner, but it never seemed like the right time.'

'*What?*' Mum said, putting her spoon down.

'Don't worry, I'm fine,' I said, trying not to look any of them in the eye as the upset and anger that I hadn't told them was starting to ignite at different levels of intensity, with Karen at one end of the scale and Devi at the other. 'I was really lucky and fell on a crate – nothing worse than a few bruises.'

'Bel,' said Devi, almost shaking, 'when did this happen? Why didn't you tell us?'

'A few days ago,' I lied because some sense of self-preservation told me that if I said two weeks ago, one of us wouldn't be leaving this dinner table alive. 'It wasn't a big deal, honestly. Or I would have told you sooner.'

To my surprise, Devi's eyes welled up. 'Bel, you should have told us at once! Did you have someone with you? *How* could you not tell us?!'

'This is why I didn't say anything.' I was trying really hard not to raise my voice but already I could feel the strings of family history pulling us into the same tired performance. 'There's always this song and dance made about stuff like this and it's not a big deal. And I wasn't alone. Gregor came.'

That was definitely the wrong thing to say, in retrospect. 'GREGOR?!' Devi yelled. I knew the yelling wasn't a hundred per cent at me but more to get out her frustration at Mum, Nikhil, The Universe. 'That soggy damp PUDDING MAN? Didn't you guys break up, like four years ago?'

'But I'm fine, honest. And look, you're going through a . . . lot.'

'So what? Because I'm going through a divorce you don't tell us what's going on with you? Things have been bad with Nikhil for a while, Bel, it's not news to anyone who's been around. Do you know how long it has been since you visited? What if that was the last time we'd seen you, Bel? You don't think about anyone but yourself.'

I was taken aback by how upset Devi was but she'd crossed the line. I didn't expect a great reaction but I didn't expect to be treated as if I'd done something wrong when the entire experience had been horrendous.

'Hey,' I said angrily, 'I get that you're upset, but this was something that happened to me, and it was difficult to tell you all. And I know I haven't been around but you could have talked to me. It's fucking weird to find out about your sister's divorce from your parents.'

'BERYL!' Mum said in a tone that back in the day would have had Devi and me writing our Wills. 'Don't use that word.'

'Which word, Mum?' I snapped. 'F—'

'WELL!' Dad said. 'I think we could all use a breather. Cool our heads. Baloo, why don't you come out with me to the garage?'

Mum was already hurrying round the table to comfort Devi, their argument replaced by ours. I had wanted to fix this for her and felt sick that I'd made things worse. But my anger was still too hot to allow me to apologise immediately, and she seemed like she wanted to be left alone. As she and Mum headed out of the dining room and into the kitchen, I saw that Karen was surreptitiously filming us. I spoke at a low volume only she could hear. 'Karen, if that makes its way onto TikTok, I'm going to tell all of your mates you still sleep with your teddy bear.' I followed Dad out to the garage.

*

The big project he wanted help with was attaching a panel to a desk he was making from scratch. He sold the pieces online and donated the profit to a cancer research centre. An old, quiet homage to a mother-in-law he had never met, whose life had been cut short by cervical cancer. When Mum found out what he was doing, she had cried more than I had ever seen before. When I was younger, right before I slipped away from him into my cranky teenage years, he would show me how to use some of the tools in his garage. I learned basic carpentry, a little bit of electrics and tinkering around with the car. I don't think I ever thanked him for it, but it made me really popular in university because I was the only one who a) had a toolbox (that he made me take with me), and b) knew what to do with it.

'Did I ever tell you about what your mother was like, when we first met?' he said.

'Yeah, Dad, I've heard the story of how you met a thousand times.' I wasn't in the mood for one of his Mr Miyagi talks.

'Not *how* we met, smart-arse,' he said, handing me a flat head screwdriver, 'what she was like *when* we met.'

'No,' I said sullenly.

He rolled up his sleeves and put on a tennis sweatband

to hold back his hair. It was the height of embarrassment when I was a teenager. Now I was just impressed he still had so much of it.

'What I loved about your mother was her independence,' he said. I snorted. 'It may seem strange to you because she's your mother,' he continued, 'and she worries and wants to keep you safe, and cooks for all of us, and you think that's the furthest thing from being independent. But independence, I think, is knowing what you want and going for it. Her family didn't want her to marry me given that she was only nineteen, but she knew she wanted to start a new life and build a family. So that's what she did. Hand me the sandpaper, would you?'

Outside, the evening air was cooling down, the final rays of light carrying with it the last few notes of birdsong. In the distance, the engine of Devi's car started with a sputter. Leaving without saying goodbye to me. The hurt of that was vinegar over old wounds. *Step three: analyse what went wrong.* Maybe our relationship was too broken to repair.

'Thanks,' Dad said, taking the sandpaper from me. 'Your choices are not Devi's choices. Devi's choices are not the ones you've made. Your mother's choices do not have to be your choices. You can live different lives *and* respect each other for it.'

The whisper of sanding filled the silence between us, but I could tell he had more to say. He stopped and rested his hand against the wood. 'We never wanted to pressure you into coming here. We wanted you to feel like you had time for your career, and that you'd want to visit.

But maybe we went too far the other way . . . It's okay to need us, Bel. It is not a weakness, you understand, it's a strength.'

The heat of the argument at dinner had blown out of me, and what settled in my stomach was queasy regret. And Mum's shepherd's pie. 'Yes, Dad, I understand,' I said quietly.

'Ultimately, Bel, only you have to live with the consequences of your life. Even if it's a choice that your mother or I don't understand, as long as it doesn't hurt anyone, you have to remember that and own the decisions you make. Be proud of them. Got it?'

'Yes, Dad,' I said, feeling more morose by the minute.

He emerged from underneath the desk to look at me. His face was kindly and wise, proof that a person's deeds were reflected in their eyes. But Dad still had that flash of steel in him that patients saw when their mouths were wide open and he was sternly assessing their cavities. It came through now.

'But if you ever, *ever* fall into a hole again, and end up in hospital, and don't tell your family . . . I will personally boot you back into it, understand? This is what family does, Bel – be there for each other. You are not an optional add-on, you *are* this family, got it?'

*

Step five: don't give up. (I skipped step four because I wasn't jealous of Devi's life as it stood.)

Devi forgets there was a time when we were comrades. That's what was helping to keep a little flame of hope alive in me. When I was twelve and she was eighteen, our parents had taken us to visit a family friend's house in Leeds. That's what holidays were back then before budget flights became a thing. You'd go to someone's house in a different county, not see any sights, play with their children who usually couldn't give a lukewarm shit about you. Meanwhile your parents drank whisky and gin in the living room; later you all convened for home-cooked Indian food, and then if you were lucky you got your own bed; if you were at the lower end of the pecking order, you'd have the floor and a blanket. Then you drive back and – presto! That was your holiday.

This particular visit had been to see a Bengali lady named Mina Basu. The whole thing was strange from start to finish. She was the friend of a friend of one of Mum's cousins back home. Dad had a dentists' conference so it was just the three of us, and Mina Auntie had no children so we were left to ourselves while she and Mum chatted. With the stress of her A-levels over, Devi was more relaxed than she'd been in a while. I didn't seem to irritate her as much. We were convinced the house was haunted – it had a creepy well in the back garden. We called ourselves Sherlockinder and Holmes-jeet, and pretended to be two detectives trying to figure out who Mina had murdered. We shared the same room, and while we were eating Jammie Dodgers stolen from Mina's biscuit tin, I asked my sister how she felt about going away to uni. She said she was scared but excited, and that she couldn't wait to live in a new city.

I was just happy to share the same space as my big sister. Being able to talk to her in that way felt familiar, but also the start of something new. Then she went away to university and things changed.

The explosiveness of our family dinner had rattled me because I rarely argued with people or got into conflict, but it had also revealed a few things I now had to confront. The first was that Devi was not doing okay, and maybe she had mates who would help her with all this divorce stuff but I was still her sister. Only I could protect her within our own family, not her mum friends. The second was that apparently when you have a near-death experience, your family get really, really pissed off if you don't tell them. And when I had a chance to think about it, I realised that if something similar had happened to them, and they hadn't told me, I'd feel betrayed and angry.

I texted Ama and Katrina before I went to sleep with a summary of everything that had happened. Katrina's response was: **Ugh, so sorry to hear that babe. Sounds like a mare. You have nothing to apologise for! Don't worry – you'll be back in London soon enough. Don't forget to rub the crystal I gave you! Xxxxx**

It wasn't a competition, but Ama's response was far more helpful.

Ama: It sounds like she was worried and upset and it all came out wrong. I remember your sis from

back in the day, and she loves you, Bel. Remember
when you were talking about how Stacey Kendall
made fun of your metalhead boots to me and Devi
overheard? She threatened to flaming dog poop
Stacey's doorstep?

Me: But what do I do? Text her? Leave her alone? It
doesn't seem like she wants me around at the
moment.

Ama: It's like that whole thorn and lion's paw story,
right? Like the lion is angry and roaring and
everyone's like SHIT I'm going to stay away. But
what the lion really needs is for someone to see
past it and take out the thorn and go 'there, there
Mufasa, it'll be okay'. I know it's hard, but you need
to say unconditionally you're there for her, and let
her feel that love a little bit.

Ama's text was why I told Mum that I wasn't going
back on the Sunday morning train (she was surprised but
delighted), and that I was going to pop over to Devi's. Dad
had already left for his men's walking club outing as he
did every Sunday. 'Do you want me to drop you off?' Mum
asked while yanking things out of the freezer for lunch.

'No, I'll just walk,' I said and grabbed my coat.

'Take these,' she said, pushing a packet of Jammie
Dodgers into my hands.

I'd expected to be back in my apartment before noon
on Sunday. Instead I found myself clutching biscuits outside Devi's house, a smart three-bedroom semi-detached

house with mint green plantation shutters and a neat front garden.

Karen answered the door in an oversized sweatshirt, looking at me with huge hazel eyes like a forlorn puppy. 'You okay, kid?' I said and stepped through.

'I'm not a kid,' she huffed, and slid away upstairs.

'Okay,' I called after her, 'I'll just find your mum through my psychic powers, yeah?' Devi's house was modern and immaculate. It also felt empty. I walked through to the back. On a sunny Sunday morning, she'd probably be gardening, I thought, and I was right. Devi was kneeling over a tub of petunias.

'Hey, sis,' I said. She looked up, tightened her lips and went back to digging. 'Can we talk?'

'I don't know that we have much to talk about,' she said, stabbing at the soil with a trowel. *Step five, step five.*

'I'll make you a cup of tea and give you one of these if you give me a chance,' I said, waggling the Jammie Dodgers. The corners of her mouth went up ever so slightly. Mum, the crafty fox, knew they were her favourite. 'You know, those things aren't very healthy,' she said squinting at me.

'Who the fuck eats a Jammie Dodger as a health option?' I said, reaching out my hand to help her up.

*

Devi's kitchen resembled the ones in big American family homes, the kind we'd grown up watching on TV. Warmly lit, wall-to-wall wooden cupboards, the fridge covered with pieces of paper and funny magnets. A big colourful arrangement of flowers; overflowing bowls of fruit. The gentle hum of a massive fridge; a cardigan draped over a chair. It was the homeliest space in her house.

A pot of tea and a plate of Jammie Dodgers were arranged between us. Devi couldn't help herself and had also put out some hummus and carrot sticks as a healthier option.

'I'm sorry,' I said, after a few moments of awkward silence.

'It's fine,' Devi replied opaquely before I could even launch into an explanation. And it could have ended there. We would have continued being aloof and distant, seeing each other on special occasions but never getting beneath the surface. But something in me had changed since my accident. I realised that if ever I was in that situation again, I did not want my moany ex-boyfriend to be the one the doctors called. I wanted it to be someone I genuinely cared about, a person who felt like home, and the fact that I couldn't clearly work out who that would be, troubled me.

'I'm not just saying it because I have to, Devi,' I pressed. 'I genuinely mean it.'

She pulled apart the Jammie Dodger methodically. 'Do you know what you're apologising for?' she said before neatly scooping out the jam. She'd eat it, then dunk the rest of the biscuit in her tea. The whole process was an abomination.

'Well, all of it,' I said, taken aback by the question. 'The fact that you're going through a divorce, me snapping at you last night. I don't want to cause you any more grief than you're already going through.'

'That's not why I was upset, Bel.'

'Then what was it about? I'm not saying this to be difficult. Genuinely.'

She sighed. 'Bel, you're my sister and I love you. But do you know how messed up it is that you didn't call us?' She raised her palm as I opened my mouth to reply. 'No, let me finish. You didn't just not call us when you were at the hospital, you didn't call us that evening or the next day. And the reason I'm upset is because my little sister felt it was preferable to deal with trauma alone rather than speak to her own family. The fact that you thought that breaks my heart.'

'But I didn't want to worry you . . .' I said in a small voice.

'You don't get to decide that, Bel!' Devi said, exasperated. 'I know you like your life all neat and tidy, but does it occur to you that we'd maybe like to be there for you? That if it gets too much, you can say: *hey, guys, back off, it's too much*? But you didn't even give us that chance. And the fact that something could have happened to you, and the last time we spoke was . . . I can't even remember when it was or what it was about . . . I'm sad. I'm sad that our relationship is like this.'

'But I'm sad about it too,' I burst out.

'You are?' she said, sounding surprised.

'Of course I am! D, I wanted to hug you yesterday and I didn't know whether I could. That's weird, isn't it?'

'I mean, that *is* weird, but not because I made it weird. You're the one overthinking whether or not to hug me. Why didn't you just do it?'

'Because I didn't know if you wanted me to.' The more I tried to explain it, the more insane I realised it sounded. That's the problem sometimes with living alone and believing your internal monologue is fact. It's only until those words are spoken out loud that they reveal themselves to be insubstantial.

'I know I shouldn't say this,' I sighed, 'but it really sucked that I found out about your divorce from Mum and Dad. And not because of some pathetic need to be the first to know but because I wish I had been able to be there for you. And I feel guilty that I wasn't.'

'Well,' she replied, 'it really sucked that I found out days after that you were in hospital after you almost died. And not because of some pathetic need to bring you *Heat* magazine but because I wanted to be there for you – it must have been really scary.'

'See! I knew you'd bring me magazines. Stupid Gregor didn't even bring me grapes.' That made her laugh, and I hadn't realised until then how much I'd missed the sound of it. It was somewhere between a giggle and a snort, and was how she'd always laughed when we watched *The Simpsons* together after school, lying on our stomachs in the living room. But also, the reassurance of someone recognising and knowing that I might have been scared, someone who saw that little sliver of vulnerability in me and wanted to protect me, softened me towards her.

I felt the space between us shrink. Lining up all of the things I wanted to say to her, I opened my mouth then closed it quickly before anything could escape.

'What is it?' she said, a bit more gently.

My throat felt tight. 'I don't know how to say this the right way.'

'Just say it,' said Devi. 'I know you want it to be perfect, but just say whatever it is and we'll muddle through it.'

But I couldn't. My throat felt like it was stuffed with rocks. Devi looked at me and said: 'Do you feel like your throat is really tight?' I nodded.

'Okay, here's a trick I learned in therapy with Nikhil. Take your hand and put it on your throat, then just hold it there. Mentally tell yourself: *It's okay, I can let go of it*, and then just say whatever pops into your mind. And then at the end of it, I'll give you a biscuit.'

'Is the biscuit part of the therapy?'

'No,' she smiled, 'that's a Devi special.'

Okay, I could do this. I put my hand on my throat and the feeling inside surged up like a wave that was going to engulf me. But I had been treading water for a long time. Maybe it was time to stop. I closed my eyes and released the control I was clinging onto.

'I didn't mean to upset you,' I said, unable to look her in the eye. 'And I wasn't trying to punish you. But sometimes . . . this sounds so stupid . . . sometimes I feel like I don't belong in this family. Like if I wasn't here, would anyone care? I feel like you guys have everything sorted, and I'm just this person who comes in from time to time. I don't have kids, I don't have a partner, what exactly do I contribute? And with the accident . . . of course if it had been serious, I would have told you immediately. But I was fine. It's all, you know, fine.'

I regretted opening up when I saw how upset Devi looked. 'Families *are* messy, Bel. Is that why you're never around? Because you think we're better off without you here? That isn't true. I'm not perfect . . . take a look at my life for Exhibit A! My husband has been banging his receptionist. It really doesn't get more clichéd than that.'

'I'm sorry, Nikhil is WHAT?'

'Yeah, it's . . . bad. But also, what's worse is that I'm upset about my marriage ending but I'm not really upset about the affair.'

'Why is that worse?'

'Because it means our marriage got to such a bad state that I don't feel anything but indifference. And indifference is worse than anger. It means you don't love that person anymore.'

'So you being angry with me is your way of saying you love me?'

'Too soon, Bel,' she said, flicking a biscuit crumb at me. 'Mum and Dad don't know about the affair, by the way, and it's excruciating because Mum keeps saying things like "you could still make it work" because she's terrified I'll end up alone. But look, we can talk about that later. Our stuff is more important.'

I looked down at my palms as if they contained a map to figuring out my relationship with Devi again. I traced the heartline with a fingertip. 'Unless you don't want to,' she said, with a note of uncertainty I hadn't ever heard from her before.

Don't give up.

'I do,' I said quietly. 'Devi, I want our relationship to be different. I know that's a lot to ask, and I don't know what that looks like yet or how we do it. But I don't want you to go through this divorce alone. I know that in my heart and in my bones. I know you have your mum friends, but I'm your sister.'

The moment the words left my mouth, I felt as if a layer of skin had been removed. She looked at me pensively. I could see it on her face, the words already forming. *But, Bel, you're never around.* Maybe I had to take responsibility for some of that.

'I'll be around more,' I said before she could speak. 'I want to try. If you do too, that is.'

Some of the guardedness left her face and she slowly handed me a Jammie Dodger. 'I do want to try,' she said. 'But you should know that while you're wistfully looking over here as if we're Sylvanian Families, I'm looking at your life and thinking: *That could have been mine.*'

'What?' I said, through a mouthful of biscuit. 'You wish you could live in a home a third of the size of this place, dating losers and working in an environment that's like the Hunger Games?'

'Maybe not quite, but it was always my dream to move

to London, remember? And then I met Nikhil and it never happened. It was easier to be near the parentals. Now I'm just a mum, who lives in the town she grew up in and will probably never leave and it'll all be very *What's Eating Gilbert Grape?*'

I patted her arm. 'I'm sure you won't die in your own house. And if you do, we won't burn it to the ground.'

'Very reassuring.'

We hadn't spoken like this in a long time. It hadn't occurred to me that while I felt as if I was looking at my family from the other side of a bridge I couldn't cross, Devi saw a similar chasm between her life and mine. 'Listen,' I said, 'what do you need right now? Like, name one thing and I'll do it.'

'Could you make Nikhil move his stuff out faster? Kidding! Nothing could make that man move with speed.' She got up and started tidying away the plates.

'How are things with you both? Do you hate each other or are you friends?'

'Things are fairly civil. I mean, apart from me getting irritated that he's useless at finding a new place. He's staying here at the moment but is moving out as soon as he gets something sorted. But at the same time, he's not my problem anymore and that's actually a relief. But if you really mean it about helping out, I could do with Karen being out of the house for a bit. Nikhil is away, and she's been moping about her mate Jas, and I'd love an hour or two of peace.'

'I'll take her into town. Also . . .' I bit my lip. Since my former flatmate Roger had moved out, I had loved living alone. But after the accident, waves of insomnia flowed through me at night. Whenever I was aware of falling asleep and felt that darkness crowding the edges of my consciousness, it jolted me awake. I didn't know if having someone else stay with me would make a difference, but now when I reached into that gravitational pull between Devi and I, I felt her reaching out towards me too.

'Here's something to think about,' I said. 'Maybe let Karen stay with Mum and Dad for a while. And why don't you come up and stay with me in London for a bit? Take some time off work – tell them you need to sign off. They'll understand – a divorce is a big thing. I've got a spare room. The break might do you some good.'

'Are you serious?' she asked, almost sagging with relief. 'Oh, Bel, that would be amazing.' Then her face crumpled. 'But I can't. Karen needs me here.'

'Karen is sixteen. She'll be fine. If she misses you, or you miss her, she can always stay the night with us. It'll also mean that you don't have to be around when Idiot Boy moves his stuff out.' The divorce papers hadn't been signed yet but, in my mind, Nikhil had already been demoted and stripped of his name.

She looked at me, and for the first time in years there wasn't irritation or any need to correct something in her expression. Just love. And gratitude.

'By the way,' Devi said, 'if you want to get in with Karen, she loves anything woo-woo. You know, crystals, tarot, that sort of thing.'

Somewhere inside me, a tiny piece of ice melted and dreamed of becoming a river.

*

After promising Devi a few hours of peace, I'd wrestled Karen into coming out with me.

But despite my magnanimous gesture, I wasn't great with children. I'd already ignored her cries of: 'Auntie, WHERE are we going? Auntie! I've got schoolwork to do!'

Once in a while I come across a child who is great, and this child will be hilarious, make scathing jokes about their parents, won't grizzle, likes reading books and is a damn delight.

Karen was mostly that. But when she was a young child, I was still figuring out who I was. The patience I had learned and the joy I took in her now simply didn't exist in my twenties. There was a lot of ground to make up between us. I needed to take this carefully.

Although she was a bit angsty as we trudged down the wide street lined with carefully landscaped gardens, Karen wasn't like most teenagers I'd encountered. She had more common sense than the majority of the adults in her life. I also found her utterly fascinating because, from what I could tell by observing her life through Devi's social media and her own, she didn't fit in any of the boxes that existed back when I was her age.

She played football but wasn't overtly sporty. She cared about how she dressed but wasn't caked in a thousand layers of make-up learned off TikTok videos. She listened to a wide variety of bands and musicians, from her namesake Karen Carpenter to Little Mix, and didn't care what her choices said about her. In appearance, she had lost some of that cartoon cuteness that came from having naturally big eyes, but she was still a beautiful child. She carried within herself a sense of independence and self-possession that suggested she didn't need anyone much in her life, except for her mother.

As we walked, her shoulders rounded over as if she was trying to collapse in on herself like a neutron star, packing all of that emotion and uncertainty in as tightly as possible.

'Is there anything you want to talk about?' I asked.

'No,' she said grumpily, the affection she'd displayed towards me the evening before completely gone.

'Your mum mentioned you were upset about a mate named Jas, are you okay?'

'I don't want to *talk* about it,' she said, her voice rising in pitch.

'Ouch!' I said. 'I think even bats could hear that one. I'm not your mum, kiddo. And I get that it's shit – I've been your age. But trust me when I say, being moody doesn't help. And talking does.'

The awkward weight of many things unsaid pushed against the wall of silence, but I knew if I left it for a while, the pressure would ease. Eventually it did.

'Jas . . .' she said hesitantly '. . . isn't returning my texts.' She bit her lip. 'I don't know what I did wrong.'

Teenage girls never change. 'Well,' I said slowly, 'have you asked her why?'

'Yeah. She just said "I should know".'

Of course she did, the little shit. Whoever this Jas was, I already hated her.

We were starting to get nearer to the town centre and there was something about being here that jogged memories of trying to find hidden corners to smoke a cigarette in, looking longingly into pubs we weren't allowed to enter. I'd likely swerved it at first to avoid bumping into Marina and Ling, and then when the past had stopped feeling so raw and angry it became a habit to just dip in and out. At least now I had Karen as a buffer, even if she looked utterly miserable. What would I have wanted to hear when I was her age?

'Okay, I have an idea,' I said. 'Do you have a favourite song, something you both like listening to together?'

'Yeah. Doorman. Slowthai.' I had no idea whether Doorman was the band, or Slowthai. I didn't want to ask.

'Well, why don't you send her a Spotify link to the song and tell her you're thinking of her? It might help?'

'Can't get any worse, I suppose,' Karen replied gloomily. 'Where are we going by the way?'

'This sounds silly but I kind of want to get my tarot read. I remember there used to be someone in the Princes Road Centre.'

'Oh, they demolished that place,' she said tapping her phone. I thought she was texting Jas but she'd been industriously Googling.

'Okay, there's one in the Emporium,' she said.

'What's the Emporium?'

'FML, Auntie, you really haven't been here much, have you?'

*

The Emporium was a huge, light-filled, flimsy building that housed nearly a hundred little stalls. Between Pete's Pets N Stuff and Kids Kuts was Madame Zaza's Tarot and Spiritual Healing.

We both stood in front of a thick purple velvet curtain that had seen the aggressive end of a glue-stick and fistfuls of glitter. 'When I was in Year Ten, we had to do this school project of bedazzling everything,' Karen said. 'Phone covers, birthday cards, Girl Guide woggles and it looked exactly like . . . this.'

'I don't know if there is a waiting area,' I said doubtfully, 'are you safe to be on your own?'

Karen gave me a withering look. 'Auntie.'

I hadn't realised how rusty I was at this. The last time Karen and I had gone on a day out, she was around ten and I'd had no idea whether I could let her go to the loo by herself. When did stranger danger stop? Never, that's when. But she was a much more sensible teenager than I had been, and at her age I was running around all over town (admittedly with my parents not knowing about half of it) and had gone on holiday to Cornwall.

'Sorry, of course you are. You aren't a kid. Do you want to come in with me or go wandering?'

147

'Nah, I'm not in the mood. I'll just wait outside. I won't eavesdrop,' she said, sticking her AirPods in.

'I sense someone is out there!' warbled Madame Zaza in an Eastern European accent. It was safe to say she was using one of the usual senses – hearing – given that we were talking at normal volume and her door was a curtain.

Karen was already comfortably seated on the floor, her hair spilling over her phone as she swiped through god knows what. I stepped past the curtain and, in the dimly lit cubicle beyond, saw a woman in her sixties wearing a purple turban. She was seated at a small round table with candles around her. The smell of lilac drifted from an incense stick in a plant pot; it was more cosy and inviting than I'd expected.

'What can I do for you today, my dear?' she said. I couldn't quite place the accent.

'I'd like the thirty-minute tarot, please,' I said, taking a seat on what looked like a folding garden chair. 'It's been years since I've had a reading though.'

'Oooaw! Beryl Kumar?' she squawked, no longer Eastern European but in an accent more suited to Temple Hill down the road. 'It's me, June. Steven's mum! Cor, you weren't half in love with him back then, weren't you?'

*

In the long, messy timeline of our romantic histories, there are certain people who act as a whetstone for some truly defining life lessons. One of mine was Skateboard Steve.

I probably would never have acted on it, the desire eventually biodegrading in my body. But Marina had done a
tarot reading that fateful afternoon when we were discussing Ama's birthday, which opened my mind to the possibility of asking him out. And that was swiftly followed by
the summer school disco where I was sure he was about
to kiss me before he vomited on his lap.

Both of those things emboldened me to the point
where, the following week after drinking some WKD
Blue, I found myself with Ling outside his house, playing Extreme very loudly on a portable cassette player.
She'd lied to her dad and said we were at an after-school
maths event, and I remember appreciating having time
alone with her, a precious interlude when Marina wasn't
around. Ling was softer, gentler, at those times. After the
last notes of 'More Than Words', I finished with 'STEVE,
I LOVE YOU!' delivered with all the delicacy of a jilted
lover in *EastEnders*.

It turned out Steve wasn't at home. But his mother June
and her then-boyfriend Nigel were, and with his 'n' hers
cigarettes hanging off their lips, they came outside to tell
us that. And then they told Steve, who afterwards behaved
as if I was on some kind of perverts' register and refused
to get within ten yards of me.

Time had not been kind to June, correction, Madame
Zaza. On closer inspection, the turban had seen better
days, her fingers were yellowed with nicotine and she was
missing a front tooth.

'What do you want to know then? Want to find out if

my Steven is still single? He is, as it goes.' She winked. 'Just broke up with his girlfriend Shauna. He is back on the apps though, so you might have to act fast before he gets snapped up.'

'June, it's great to see you but I might . . .' I looked back desperately at the curtain. The tarot had been a spur-of-the-moment thing, to gain favour with Karen, but now I was here, the questions I wanted to ask were very personal. I wasn't sure if June had the gentle touch I needed.

'AUNTIE!' I heard Karen yell. Instantly I rushed outside, ready to claw someone's eyes out. Instead I was confronted by her beaming face.

'What?' I said, glaring now that I knew she wasn't in mortal danger.

'Jas texted back,' she said happily.

'I thought you were dying,' I huffed, but she'd already put her AirPods back in and started humming. I ducked behind the curtain.

'Sit down, girl,' June said, handing me the pack. 'While you're shuffling, think about what it is you want to know.'

We used to do tarot almost every week during our fifth year of school, with so much hanging in the balance, from GCSEs to our love lives. I'd forgotten I always found this part stressful. There was so much I wanted to know. Would I ever meet anyone decent? Would I ever be happy? Would I have kids? Did I want kids? Would Devi be okay? Would Ama love me? Would I be successful at work? I felt so much from the past swirling around me at that moment, a tangled ball of memories, hopes and fears.

June took the pack from me.

'Mind if I light a ciggie?' she said. 'They make me go to the car park otherwise.' Without waiting for my reply, she clamped a B&H between her lips and inhaled deeply.

'Okay,' she said, her voice growing a bit deeper and her eyes taking on a slightly glassy sheen. I'd bet she practised it in the mirror. 'I'm just going to talk, don't interrupt me. So . . . you've been through something major. Life-changing.'

'Erm, not exactly.'

'What did I just say about interrupting?' June glared at me through the smoke like a disgruntled genie. 'You've been through something life-changing. You've gone down into the darkness and everything has been exposed to light. And maybe you don't realise it, and you're all "I'm fine, la la la". Well, you can fool everyone else, girl, but you can't fool The Universe. Whatever it is has shaken you to the core, okay? If I was to pull a card out of that stack right now, I bet it would be the Wheel of Fortune. Let's see . . . don't believe me? There you go – what did I say?'

It was the Wheel of Fortune. I was ready to admit June was blowing my mind somewhat. Outside, an unhappy dog was whining at Pete's Pets N Stuff. Its owner started singing 'How Much Is That Doggy in the Window?' in a loud voice.

'It's going to change a lot of things but that's good. You've stayed in the same place for a long time and change is overdue. Okay, next card. Knight of Cups. That's good, that means a big love, maybe.'

"'The one with the waggly tail . . . '"

'There's a lot of stuff I'm sensing that's coming up from the past. Some things you may have to let go of. But the message I'm getting is that it's okay to let go. In fact, you *have* to let go. Otherwise you can't move forward. The Universe has your back. Don't be scared.'

"'How much is that doggy in the window . . . arf arf!'"

I had to admire June's ability to soldier on. 'Very often we live our lives in fear,' she said, gripping my hands while looking directly at me, 'and we spend so much time trying not to get hurt, that we end up living out our worst fears anyway. Being alone. Not being loved. Not being happy.'

' "I do hope that doggie's for sale . . . "'

I couldn't take it anymore. The singing combined with the thick coils of cigarette smoke inside June's booth was too much for me. 'WILL YOU PUT A SOCK IN IT!' I yelled. 'We're having a serious conversation in here!' I heard an elderly lady say, 'Well, I never . . .' but at least the singing stopped.

'Go with the flow,' June continued, 'say yes to things. Change things up. Let people in. Be happy, Beryl. If you can do that, the spirits say that your life could be so full of joy.' Her voice changed back to normal and her eyes became more focused. 'And if you want Steven's number, just ask. Wink-wink.'

After I'd paid, and yet again refused Steven's number (unwanted things come in threes), I went outside and looked for Karen who was still obediently in the same spot. She took her AirPods out when she saw me. 'I can't believe you told off Mrs Finch,' she said. 'She runs the local bakery. Her dog Rufus was about to have his balls snipped. I had to tell her that you were having marriage problems and were highly emotional.'

'Hang on, isn't that your mother?'

'Yeah, but all you brown women look the same to them so . . .'

I laughed. 'Come on, you. I fancy a Burger King. Do you want one?'

'Did I ever tell you that you are my favourite aunt?' Karen said happily.

8

The first couple of days Devi and I spent living together were awkward. I was mindful that she wasn't in her normal environment; she didn't want to be a burden. We were overly polite about how much time we spent in the bathroom and when we used the hairdryer. We bent around each other's eating habits – my over-reliance on takeaways and her preference for making everything from scratch. The television was a polite dance of *no no I'm not fussy whatever you want to watch,* and all the things we really wanted to say were pushed deep down. Eventually, after one too many teabags left on the side of the sink and what I deemed to be an unnecessary load of laundry, we both exploded. When we eventually calmed down, she said: 'We're being too polite with each other.' After that that we agreed to mention minor annoyances to the other person before things escalated into a fight.

I'd even got her hooked on *My Indian Bae.* While I didn't share her preference for serious political dramas, it was a show we loved watching together because we got to yell at the screen and feel united in that small act.

Devi the married sister was an annoying busybody who sighed at stories of my disastrous dates. Devi the soon-to-be-divorcee was a lot more fun. I had stocked up on Kleenex, but the only time she cried was when she was due to go back after the week we'd originally agreed. The prospect of returning to her old bedroom at Mum and Dad's, and the job, where she'd have to endure pitying stares and questions from her colleagues, was too much. I said she could stay for as long as she wanted.

In some ways it was a delight learning new things about Devi. Over the following week, I learned that what I'd interpreted as a brusque demeanour actually meant she was generally unfazed by most things and loved striking up conversations, even with total strangers. As a newly single woman, that made her adventurous and approachable. On the first night I took her to my local pub, a horribly young man with a wispy moustache who couldn't have been more than twenty-five, sent over drinks and then tried to chat her up. Which she declined.

In other ways, it was hard to let go of the images we'd had of each other throughout our adult lives. At first she didn't want to talk about Nikhil. I was unsure whether this was because it was too painful, but the more I overheard her talking to friends on the phone, the more I realised she too was struggling to adjust to our new relationship. But I gently pushed and said that, while I didn't need gory details, I had no idea what had actually happened. Initially she mounted a defence and I called her out on it. 'I would never make you talk about something you're not ready to,' I said, 'but it does feel like you're shielding me from things.'

'Well, yeah, you're my little sister,' she replied.

'That's true,' I said. 'Devi, don't get mad but . . . you have to stop being an extension of Mum. I know I'm your sister but it's like you never got past me being a teenager. I don't need to be parented by my own parents now, let alone my sibling.'

'Do I do that?' she said, stunned.

'Yeah,' I said, a bit more gently, 'you do. It makes sharing things with you really hard. Like if I tell you I've got a promotion, you tell me to be careful with money. If I tell you I'm dating a guy, you tell me to make sure his bathroom is clean because—'

'A dirty bathroom means he doesn't have his shit together, literally,' she finished.

'See?' I said. 'I know you're only saying it because you care about me, but it makes me not want to tell you what's going on in my life. I'm thirty-six, I don't need to be coddled.'

Although she didn't open up immediately, snippets of information trickled out as she'd chop onions for dinner, or we'd go to the pub for a cheeky wine, or do the supermarket shop and argue about which chocolate to buy. Things had been bad at home for a few years, it seemed, and she and Nikhil had found themselves leading separate lives. She knew not having sex was a bad sign, but didn't know how to change it. Despite being in a marriage that couldn't be saved, she strongly believed that if she left without a big enough reason, a part of her would always wonder if she'd tried hard enough. In desperation, she asked him to go to couples therapy with her. He agreed but by that time had already started sleeping with Priyanka, his receptionist. When he told her, during a drunken fight, Devi was relieved. Because at least now she could leave and the scales of guilt and shame were firmly balanced against him.

I liked having her in the flat. And she got to finally taste that London life she'd always wanted. A lightness had started to come into her voice.

Around a week into being flatmates, we were assembling an IKEA bedside table I'd bought to replace the one Roger had stolen when he left. Devi asked me how I was doing after my accident. Following our fight about it at Mum and Dad's, we hadn't really talked much about it. Instead of lying or brushing her off, I decided to tell her the truth. That it had unmoored me. Made me re-evaluate things. That I had taken a look at my life and hadn't liked what I'd seen. When I'd finished explaining, she said, 'I wish you had called me.'

'I know,' I replied, not able to look her in the eye.

'Have you changed your emergency contact at work?' she said, trying to sound casual though I knew there was more to it than that. I wasn't ready to have this conversation yet.

'No,' I said, 'but I will.'

'Okay,' she replied, 'just don't go falling into any more cellars.' I threw the Stanley key at her.

'Ow!'

'You are terrible at this by the way,' I said, pointing to the table. 'Didn't Dad teach you anything?' She threw the key back at me.

*

I'd told Devi that Karen could stay over whenever she liked – after all, it wasn't as if I'd be entertaining any dates at home while my sister was staying with me. The longest she'd gone without seeing Karen was five days, so after a week, when I saw Devi pining like a mother bear missing her cub, I asked Maggie to arrange for Little Mix tickets at the O2. We'd been working with the venue as a client and they managed to arrange it almost immediately. Karen screamed down the phone, especially when she found out she could bring three friends.

Although she was more than capable of catching the train from Waterloo to my place, Devi hadn't seen her for ten days so went to collect her. Apparently the noise they made when they were reunited actually made the station pigeons scatter. When she turned up, Karen poked about in literally every cupboard and drawer, amassing information about my life from the skincare products I used to the magazines on my coffee table. The plan was that she would go out with her friends after having an early dinner with us, and then spend the next day with her mother.

The smell of roast chicken filled the entire flat. Just as Devi was pouring me a glass of red wine, the doorbell rang. 'It's for me,' Karen yelled, but I got there first, skidding in my socks. I'd dreamed of this moment of being the embarrassing oldie.

I opened the door to three brown teenagers, dressed in Nike and neon mesh tops. 'Oh,' I said. I wasn't sure what I'd expected but it seemed I had imagined Karen's friends to be white.

A girl with pigtails, a tiny crop top, baggy jeans and an exquisitely made-up face, looked at me as if I was the most boring thing she'd ever seen. 'Hi,' she said in a sing-song voice, 'is Kiran here?'

I scrunched up my face in confusion. 'You mean Kar—'

'Auntie!' Karen huffed and stepped around me to hug Pigtails. 'Jas! You look amazing. Hey, guys!' she said, waving to the rest of them. 'You alright, Kiran,' they chorused.

They all stood in the doorway and said: 'Hello, Mrs K,' to Devi. She waved back. 'Hey, kids.' I coughed.

'Oh, yeah,' said Karen/Kiran, 'this is my auntie Bel. Auntie, this is Jas, Dean and Aditya. 'Bye, Mum!' Jas refused to come any closer but was peering inside the flat as far as her neck would stretch.

'Have fun!' Devi yelled. She blew her daughter a kiss and just like that they were gone. While Karen had already been fed and watered, we'd decided to have our dinner a bit later and Devi was plating up.

'That's it?' I said to her. 'No threats of "you'd better behave, make sure you get home by this time or else it's the slipper"? Nothing like that?'

Devi shrugged and handed me my plate, which was crammed with roast chicken, her special pork stuffing, roasties, carrots and gravy. 'It doesn't work. I mean, did it work with you?'

'No,' I admitted. 'Also, what was the Kiran thing about?'

'Oh, that,' she said, bringing over the bottle of wine. 'Remember how I used to call myself Dee to make my name easier to pronounce, and you once threw a massive tantrum about wearing a shalwar kameez to Deepa Auntie's wedding because you knew we'd have to stop at a service station along the way and you didn't want white people seeing you?' I nodded. 'Yeah, they're the opposite of that.'

I blinked. 'Well, that's a very unexpected but pleasant surprise.'

'Social media, Bel. They're proud to be brown, empowered by it. And also times have changed. We celebrated Diwali at home alone when we were growing up. Now they have a whole party in Dartford Park. I have neighbours named Geraldine and Bob who wish me Happy Diwali and want my recipe for lamb curry. It's mad.'

'Wow,' I said, spearing a piece of chicken onto a potato. 'I'm not sure about that Jas girl though, didn't like her.'

'Now *you* sound like Mum.'

'Fug oo,' I said with my mouth full.

*

The next morning, while Devi and Karen were running around Nike Town in Oxford Street, I found myself trying not to invent new ways to murder Tristan. We were meant to be interviewing people all day for Crispin's brand-new project, which he'd called Thunder in a cringeworthy attempt to suck up to Lightning. Our aim was to recruit a five-person team to focus on diverse talent and campaigns. Crispin's definition of diversity was questionably vague. I voiced the suggestion that if we really wanted to show willing, he could pledge to reshuffle his leadership team, but he said: 'Ha-ha, good one, Bel.'

Tristan had laughed along and said that we'd get the team set up in record time. Except he was not with me in meeting room 5. The candidate and I looked at each other, having exhausted all small talk such as 'did you have a good journey' and 'what did you get up to at the weekend'. The clock ticked and the tea Maggie had placed in front of us was too hot to drink.

Just as I was about to text an angry message to Tristan, in he walked.

'Ben Akabusi, is it? Hey, bruv,' Tristan said, but instead of shaking the interviewee's hand, he offered a fist bump. Ben looked down at his closed fist almost as if he was having an out-of-body experience. He looked at me. My eyes wide, I shook my head imperceptibly as if to say *don't do it, don't fist bump him back.*

Realising he wasn't going to get a fist-bump, Tristan lowered his hand. We were lucky to have got Ben in for the interview at all – he was already working at a competitor agency and I prayed this didn't put him off.

The rest of the interview went smoothly enough, mainly

because I asked most of the questions. But then, when Tristan expressed his surprise that Ben had gone to university and used the word 'peng', I knew we'd completely lost him as a candidate. I could see the line of his jaw tighten with the anger he kept carefully damped down.

Afterwards, I asked Maggie if she'd come with me to get coffee from the kiosk around the corner. She looked surprised but said yes and grabbed her sunglasses.

I told her about Thunder and the whole crap circus of Ben's interview, well away from any other colleague who might overhear. I was already treading on dangerous ground after my 'this company is racist' text to Ranvir. 'I know it's wrong but tell me why it's wrong. Don't worry about me being your boss, I promise there won't be any repercussions and what you tell me won't go anywhere. But tell me why it's wrong.'

She took a sip of her coffee and said: 'It's simple. You're starting a new department and you . . . don't have any Black people doing the recruitment.'

'I don't know how to fix it,' I said. She looked at me pointedly, daring me to ask for her help, to put yet more of the burden on her. 'I think we need to hire a consultant,' I said.

'Yes,' she replied evenly.

*

When I got home my empty flat felt hollow. Funny how I'd become so used to Devi being there even though it was barely over a week since she'd moved in. How quickly a person makes their mark. A smudge on the kettle handle. A jacket draped over a chair. I grabbed the post from the mat and saw a fat, embossed envelope. Ama and Bron's wedding invite.

My chest had filled with so much joy and relief when Ama had first texted asking me to come, that I had immediately shelved the worry about who else might be at the wedding. Now it snaked through my body. I thought back to when we were all in Cornwall and had drunkenly debated who would be each other's maid of honour when we got married. 'You can be mine,' Ama had said, pressing my hand. But that was before our world broke apart. Despite my worry about confronting that particular part of my past, though, I felt a rush of excitement, especially when I saw the invite came with a plus one. I'd ask Devi when she came home.

I took a photo of the invite and immediately texted Ama: **YES!!!** I loved that I could text her now without hesitation or a frisson of fear that she might not reply.

> **Ama: Ha ha! You still on for tomorrow?**
> **Me: Er, does the Pope wear a dress?**
> **Ama: I don't know, *does* the Pope wear a dress?**
> **Me: Yes, you bozo.**

We'd been texting regularly and were trying to arrange another date to meet up. But with my schedule and her shift work at the hospital, it had proved difficult. To complicate things further, she'd been looking after a friend's rescue dog named Bosco, who'd chewed his way through fifty per cent of Ama's wedding dress. She had a soft spot for animals and was the kind of person who would melt over any animal in need, including the sort who looked like they'd gnaw your arm off given half a chance, but when she found Bosco in the midst of the savaged tulle, even she couldn't stop herself from yelling 'BAD BOY!' Afterwards she cried.

While I'd already agreed to come to her wedding barbecue (a mixer for both sides to get to know each other) and hen do, the dog incident led to me being asked to go wedding-dress shopping with her in Hackney too. A close friend of hers, Teresa, who was also accompanying her, worked as a Diversity & Inclusion consultant and might have some advice to give me around Project Thunder, Ama added. And, she said, she'd be grateful for an extra pair of eyes given that Teresa only ever wore suits.

I was flattered to be asked and didn't begrudge any of the wedding commitments because I was just glad to be with Ama. But it raised more questions: why hadn't she asked Marina or Ling, and how close were they all still?

When I told Devi where I was headed the next morning, she wrinkled her forehead and said: 'I didn't know you and Ama were still friends. Didn't she stab you in the back along with the moody one and that girl who wore eyeliner like a raccoon?' Marina and Ling, respectively.

'I mean, yeah,' I spluttered, 'but Ama was different.' I had been so elated at our reconnection that I hadn't thought much about the part she'd played in the general falling out. Then I remembered that Ama and I had still only seen each other in person once recently. What if I'd overestimated the permanence of our reunion? Feeling uneasy, as a buffer I arranged a date with a guy I'd been texting, Gary.

I'd been fobbing him off because he seemed a bit short on brain, but he was eager and had a dolphin-smooth six pack. It'd give me a solid reason to head off if things got awkward between Ama and me when we met.

*

Saturday morning was underway with streams of people heading in various directions for brunch: a sea of sun dresses, tailored shorts, Wayfarer sunglasses and straw baskets. Outside Hackney station where I waited for her, Ama was immediately recognisable in her boyfriend jeans, emerald-green vest and Timberlands. In some ways, she looked exactly as I remembered her. But that daub of bright pink lipstick was a reminder that time had passed. I'd turned up in my usual uniform of black jeans and a black vest. 'Well, this look is very familiar,' she said, making me realise that perhaps I wasn't the only one drawing a comparison chart between the past and the present, 'minus the Balenciaga trainers, of course.' I blushed – the trainers were a moment of weakness after a particularly bad date since – as I'd ranted to the sales assistant – I would be 'dying alone anyway'. But they were beautiful.

'Thank you for coming with me today. I'm so bad at this kind of stuff. Teresa will be meeting us there,' Ama said after we'd hugged.

We made our way to the Wedding Cult Club, a too-cool-for-school shop with high ceilings and huge lead-paned windows. It had no actual wedding dresses on show but lots and lots of plants. Peach, a short woman with a platinum-blonde pixie cut, voluminous white dress and oversized thick, black-rimmed glasses, greeted us at the door effusively.

She showed us to the white sofa in the middle of the room and handed Ama a questionnaire, asking, 'Would you like some tea?'

'Don't you normally do champagne at these things?' I asked.

She shook her head and said: 'We have a sobriety policy at WCC, I'm afraid, but we can offer a beautiful blend of tea grown in the hothouse behind the shop? It's exquisite.'

Ama and I looked at each other. 'Sure, that sounds great,' I said. As Peach retreated to the back, I whispered: 'Remind me, why are we here again, apart from the obvious?'

'Teresa's wife Jessamine knows the owner and said she could get me a discount. Which surprised me because Jessamine is the type of person who has wheatgrass for breakfast and I'm pretty sure she sewed her own wedding dress.' Her phone pinged. 'Oh, that's Teresa,' she said. 'She's running ten minutes late. Oof . . . and she's bringing

Jessamine with her.' Ama rolled her eyes. 'I know I'm in a couple, but why the fuck do some people just assume it's okay to bring their other half without checking with their friends first?'

While we waited for Teresa and Jessamine to arrive and for Peach to re-emerge, we sat peacefully side by side in the boutique. 'Ama, can I ask you something?' I said. She nodded.

'I'm really flattered to be here, but . . . why wouldn't you ask someone like Ling or Marina to come with you? I saw the pictures of you all at your house, and I just . . . I mean, you've been friends with them all this time.' I held my breath, relieved to be finally asking the question, but also nervous of the reply.

'We've kept in touch,' she said, 'but I wouldn't say we're particularly close. And they live in Kent. It'd be a nightmare. Ling has four kids – yeah, I know, FOUR – and Marina is always running around to some client's house. I mean I love them but . . .' She squeezed my knee. 'I also want us to hang out and reconnect. This is important, you know?' I did know, but Devi's words resounded in my mind. Ama hadn't been there for me at a time when I'd needed her most. Could I trust her again or would I always have to stay on the back foot, ready to run if necessary?

Before I could reply, the door burst open revealing a very tall, bald Black woman in the most expensive-looking and beautifully cut suit I'd ever seen, and next to her a middle-aged white woman in a flowery sack dress wafting

POORNA BELL

waves of patchouli. *'Every saucepan has its lid,'* I murmured under my breath.

*

By the time we had introduced ourselves, Peach still hadn't returned. Jessamine disappeared into the back to look for her. 'Do you know Ama from GALAN?' Teresa asked me. She gave the impression of someone being terribly busy, speaking quickly while tapping at her phone.

'GALAN?'

'The gay and lesbian nurses' group at work,' Ama explained. 'No, Teresa, Bel works at Leopard, remember? I told you she might want to ask about consultancy?'

Teresa stopped typing into her phone and looked up with interest. 'We're starting a new department at work,' I explained, 'that is meant to focus on elevating diverse talent but the people doing the hiring are me and this one English guy. I'm thinking of hiring a consultant to represent the Black community.'

Teresa laughed. 'It sounds like a terrible project! Like something you might have done several years ago for worthy points. And what exactly *is* your definition of diverse?'

'It wasn't my idea,' I said, slightly defensively.

'But you work for them, right?' she said, amused. 'You're part of this project? Then you're complicit.'

'Easy, Teresa,' Ama said gently, squeezing my arm to

reassure me. It felt good to have her on my side again; I'd forgotten how safe it made me feel.

'Look,' said Teresa, 'I know this is hard stuff. And I know this feels confrontational but I'm very direct about things like this – it's why I'm good at what I do. You feel attacked, right? Like I've said you aren't a good person, and now you're thinking: *how do I show Teresa I'm a good person?*'

This was horribly accurate, as if she was peering into my brain with a flashlight. 'It's not about being a good person. It's about that feeling of knowing something isn't right and acting on it. Not staying quiet or going: "It's not my company, I didn't make the rules." People uphold them by not saying anything, even if they think they don't. My advice? No self-respecting creative is going to touch this with a barge pole. Lightning might have signed out of desperation, but no one else will. You're offering scraps. And you need a proper in-depth overhaul of your working practices.'

It was a similar feeling to having clawed my way up the side of a mountain, only to find I was back down at the bottom and the slope had become steeper. 'Anyway,' she said, 'we're not here to talk shop, we're here to get a dress!' She squeezed Ama's arm. 'Call me if you want to talk about it further,' she said, handing me a business card to signal the end of our conversation.

'Have you got everything sorted?' Teresa then asked Ama. 'And has your mother finally come round? Is she still in Sri Lanka?'

'Your mother isn't okay with everything?' I said, surprised.

'Was your mother when you came out?' Teresa asked me curiously.

'Bel is straight,' Ama said.

'Ah,' she replied, 'my condolences.'

'Thank you,' I said solemnly. The three of us laughed then, which released the tension humming between us.

Ama sighed and turned to me. 'Mum was fine when I came out – or at least, as fine as she could be – but she's been a bit strange about the wedding. She said she needed to "think about it", then that she was happy I was happy, and then she went to Sri Lanka and hasn't been back since.'

'She's retired?' I asked.

'Yeah. I think she thought she'd be looking after some grandchildren by now but . . .'

'You do want kids,' Teresa mused, 'so it'll happen but maybe not to the timeline she expected.'

I didn't know Ama wanted children, nor did it even occur to me that she'd been dealing with so much other stuff with her mother. That must have been doubly hard when she'd had one parent for longer than she'd had two, placing added emphasis on the relationship.

I kept quiet, not knowing what to say because there was so much about Ama's life that Teresa knew and I didn't. They chatted between themselves until Jessamine emerged from the back. 'I've just been talking to Peach,' she said, 'and I'm sorry, my darling,' looking at Teresa, 'we have to go. I've got a spiritual cleansing to conduct at home and completely forgot about it.' Teresa glanced ruefully at Ama and kissed her goodbye. 'Get in touch, okay?' she said to me before they both swept out of the door.

Peach had now been gone for thirty minutes and I didn't want to drink anything that had been brewing for that long. 'Ama, who do you have down as your emergency contact?' I asked out of idle curiosity. 'Is it your mum or Bron?'

'Oh, definitely Bron,' she laughed. 'She's a fire fighter – it's literally what she does. And she answers the phone, unlike Mum.'

Her answer came so quickly, so naturally. Four weeks later, despite thinking I was working through things, I still didn't know how to amend the HR form at work. Sensing the turmoil within me, emotions rising and reacting like vapours on the surface of an unhabitable planet, she asked: 'Is everything okay?'

'Oh, yeah, it's fine,' I said, waving the query away.

'Bel. Is everything okay?' she said again.

'What? Yeah, it's fine.'

'Is everything okay, Bel?'

'What's going on with you? Are you having a stroke? Do you need to be rebooted?'

'You ask someone if they're okay more than once if they don't seem okay. Because the first time, most people usually say: "I'm fine." Your brow is doing that whole gathering-storm-clouds thing by the way.'

'This is going to sound mad,' I said tentatively.

'Try me. Last week, a bigamist magician came in with a foot injury and both his families turned up. There is nothing you can say that will faze me.'

When anyone asked me anything in relation to my accident, my answer was always: *I'm fine.*

As ridiculous as it sounded, though, it *had* shaken something inside me as June/ Madame Zaza had seen. Even though I was in the corporeal world, I could feel that other reality pressing close to me. It didn't mean that I was going to sell my worldly possessions, quit my job or go live on a boat. More that I felt like I was being nudged to take a proper look at my life. But how was I meant to distil that confusion of impressions and intimations into a snappy answer?

'I . . . don't think I'm okay with what happened with the accident,' I said.

'Well, of course not,' Ama replied taking my hand. 'It was a big deal, Bel.'

It was the first time someone who wasn't a romantic partner had held my hand in years. 'Is it though?' I said. 'Physically I'm fine.'

'Yeah, but . . . look, it's different for us, okay? It has taken me a lot of therapy to realise this – I mean, a *lot* – but having immigrant parents fucks us up in ways we don't even realise.'

'I didn't know you'd been in therapy.' I blinked. Ama didn't seem like the type of person who needed it, and then I realised how stupid that sounded. People who needed therapy probably didn't advertise it on a sandwich board.

'Yeah, there was a lot of . . . stuff that came up when I came out to Mum. She's fine with it now, but the expectations of a brown mum – you know, it's a lot. All I'm saying is, what happened to you was a big deal. And I'm not saying that to freak you out or panic you, but I know from experience that if you don't sit with it, even for just a little bit, it'll express itself in a way you really don't want. And okay, so you didn't die. And physically you're fine. But you're still allowed to feel fucked up about it. As women we are expected to handle a lot, pick ourselves up and carry on. That voice – the one that wants to acknowledge and scream and say that we're sad and it's unfair? Our mothers don't ever allow that voice to be heard, they refuse to listen to it. So we learn to do the same. We inherit all of that silence and sadness, and it crushes us in ways we don't even recognise.'

'I didn't realise therapy could tackle all of that. I mean, I tried it once before but it didn't really seem to be my thing.'

'Yeah,' said Ama, 'it's pretty amazing. Like, imagine if we'd had this stuff when we were growing up, you know. We might not have been so . . .'

She trailed off and we both sat there, marinating in words that maybe didn't need to be voiced. Peach eventually returned with tea that smelled like the soiled hay of a hundred horses, and a rail of garments that resembled the combined results of a GCSE project and a BDSM shoot.

'Remind me why I'm doing this again,' Ama said.

'Because you love Bron and life would be a hollow shell without her,' I replied.

'Right.'

Usually I wouldn't offer up an opinion on this unasked but seeing how dejected she looked, it felt important that I did. 'Listen,' I said, 'I know you're doing the whole white wedding dress thing, but have a think about whether you actually want to do it the Sri Lankan way.'

'I considered it, but . . . I don't know if my family have really accepted this. Mum says she's fine with it but it still feels awkward.'

'I get that,' I said, 'but it's who you are. Whether or not other people approve is their problem. No one can take away being Sri Lankan from you.'

Peach clapped her hands and said: 'Right, Ms Bride, are we ready to try a few things on? I have this avant-garde wedding dress crafted from recycled tampons . . .'

Ama and I looked at each other. 'I think we should go,' she said.

*

I regretted my previous lack of faith in Ama. I'd had no idea just how much I would enjoy being back in her company. We'd grabbed a coffee and laughed hysterically together about the tampon dress, but date o'clock was approaching.

Grudgingly, I left to meet Gary at The Bloated Duck, a pub tucked away behind Oxford Circus. Normally I wouldn't venture anywhere near what I considered office territory at weekends, but as is the way with London dating, organising a location involves triangulating the journey home of both parties, ongoing engineering works on Tube lines, and finding a drinking establishment that isn't too dire.

While we were arranging to meet, Gary had concerned me with his replies, which were chiefly limited to 'ok, lol'. That was his response when I suggested the time, the location, and eventually, when it became clear he wasn't going to book anything, the venue.

Apart from IT Alex, I hadn't dated for a while, barring a regrettable sequence of shags sifted from the bottom of the dating barrel. I didn't expect Gary to join the Hall of Fame in terms of romantic significance; he was merely an implement on which to exercise my dating muscles. But after talking to Ama about her home life, and hearing about the time she was so hungover Bron gently washed and dried her hair for her, or when Ama sang Tamil lullabies to soothe Bron to sleep after she'd been called out to a multiple car crash, part of me yearned for a relationship like that.

I got to the pub early to prep with a glass of cold white wine, but Gary had had the same idea. He was so gelled and waxed I was surprised he didn't slide right out of his booth, but there he was, reading a newspaper. It wasn't what I'd expected after 'ok, lol' but I was pleasantly surprised. *He reads!* I silently cheered, and remembered that congratulating hetero men on the bare minimum was a habit that needed breaking. *He made toast! He calls his mum on her birthday! He puts the toilet seat down!*

We were exchanging small talk when he asked me what I'd been up to today. The moment the word 'wedding' left my mouth, his entire body froze, as if he'd been shot with a dart laced with paralysis-inducing venom. I found this fascinating. Some men reacted as if the mere mention of the word (see also: children) would cause a woman immediately to demand it of the nearest available unattached male. According to them, our ruling criterion isn't that they are kind, loving or stable, merely that they are willing. While I would possibly go so far as to sleep with Gary, depending on my wine consumption, the thought of hitching my fate in marriage to his overly waxed wagon made my stomach turn.

He then laughed nervously, as I knew he would. 'He-he, hope it didn't give you any ideas!'

'What, get married to my Tinder date whom I've met for all of five minutes? No worries there,' I said, marvelling at the blind confidence of men.

'Ah,' Gary said in an all-knowing way, 'I suppose you'll be getting one of them thingies instead . . . you know, arranged marriages.'

I really needed to have sex, and usually, in order to achieve the end goal, I had the capacity to overlook all manner of things. I could deal with a man having different politics from me, hobbies like chess-boxing (where

competitors, usually anaemic-looking nerds, play a game
of chess and then beat each other up afterwards), even
bad sartorial choices on a date like flip-flops and Disney
T-shirts. But the sex handbrake was firmly pulled over
certain things, and these ranged from dates who genuinely thought women shouldn't get paid the same as men
to those who made clumsy assumptions about me because
of the colour of my skin.

'Why? Because I'm Asian? We don't all have arranged
marriages, you know.'

There was an awkward silence, and I tried to break it by
asking him what he did for work. He talked about being a
project manager, how many people he managed, how he
had to deal with personal problems like Barbara's psoria-
sis when it wasn't his job to do so, and how he was living
with his mother while he saved money for a mortgage.
Any lingering plans of still sleeping with him went out of
the window. I wasn't bringing anyone home while Devi
was there, and I didn't fancy Gary's mum waking us up
with a cup of tea in the morning. My plans rapidly recali-
brated to leaving after this glass of wine, and I was about
two sips from the bottom. 'You know, Gary, I'd better . . .'

'Oh, shit, I'm so sorry,' he said, 'I should have noticed
your glass was empty.' He waved at the barman for another
round by twirling his finger in the air. I goggled at him.
What was happening in Gary's brain that signalled to him
this date was going well?

Our drinks refreshed, all I could hope was that he
didn't say anything else to make my soul shrivel.

'What's your proper name?' he said. 'It can't be Bel, can it?' The prospect of getting into the whole Bel/Beryl conversation with him exhausted me.

'Hold that thought,' I said. 'I just have to nip to the loo but I'll be right back.'

I stood in the murky corridor outside the toilets, staring at the generic pub art of a picture of Audrey Hepburn. What was I doing? I put my head in my hands and let out a muffled scream. *'Fuuuuuuuuckkkkkkkkk!'*

I heard someone cough and looked up.

'Fireman Sam?' Of all the pubs in the world, what could have brought Luke to this one? And what was he doing in Central London at the weekend instead of tinkering around on his boat? I barely cared for his opinion, barely knew him beyond that brief encounter in Ama and Bron's kitchen, but even I didn't want him witnessing my meltdown.

'It's Luke actually,' he said, leaning against the wall. 'My station is round the corner and this is our local. So what are *you* doing here, and why are you making a noise like an injured manatee?'

I glared at him. 'Don't you have cats to rescue?'

'Nice deflection,' he replied. 'But seriously, what's up?' He wore a band T-shirt, indeterminate trousers and a pair of Converse. I followed the ridge of his biceps, my eyes half-glazing over as I noticed how defined his arms were, until the spell broke on the shore of his dirty, muddy fingernails.

'I'm on a terrible date,' I admitted. 'I don't want to go back in there.'

'Who is it?' he asked, craning his neck at the doorway. 'Please don't tell me it's the guy who looks like a *Love Island* reject.' I let out a strangled noise.

'What is wrong with you women?' he muttered.

'EXCUSE ME,' I said. 'Are you going to shame me or help me?'

'Fine, I'll help you. But only because you asked so sweetly. That and because the guys I'm with are leaving shortly. I don't have anything better to do.'

'Charming.'

*

Normally I wouldn't take instructions from someone as grumpy as Luke, but I was desperate. He told me to go back in and sit down as if everything was okay. Gary had barely got into an anecdote about how his friend Chaz had super-glued his hand to his bum as a dare, when Luke swaggered over. 'Cuz!' he yelled. I looked up and waved.

'Cuz? As in cousin?' Gary said, confused.

'Yeah,' Luke replied, crossing his arms, daring him to ask further questions. I was both thrilled and ashamed to admit that I liked him coming to the rescue. It felt good to have someone else take the load for a bit. Gary's eyes shuttled between Luke's tanned white skin and my deep brown skin, as if trying to do the maths and failing. 'I'm sorry to do this, mate, but her mum's been trying to get hold of her,' Luke continued. 'We've got a family thing

on. Grab your stuff.' I had never been so grateful to be
ordered about.

'Thank you,' I said as we stood outside the pub. It was
early evening, but still light. I hadn't seen him in proper
daylight before and took in the extra details. The bright
blue eyes, the industrial work trousers covered in paint
and crud. 'It's strange bumping into you,' I said. 'I'm not
usually in this area at weekends.'

'Why not?' he said, pulling out a cigarette.

'My office is near here,' I gestured down the road, 'and
I don't like coming to this end of town any more than I
need to when I'm not working. You know.'

'Not really,' he said. 'I like my job. I'm here a lot, and if
I'm not here, I'm on my boat.'

'Or at Ama and Bron's,' I said lightheartedly. When he
didn't smile but blew smoke while squinting into the distance, I decided it was time for me to go. 'So, thanks, I'm
just going to head off . . .'

'Do you like music?' he said abruptly.

'Not garage or techno. Or most pop music.'

'Who likes that shit?' he said. 'Come on, there's a place
I know nearby.'

'Don't you need to get back to your boat?' Enough
about Luke intrigued me that I wanted to see where this
might go. I knew he would never be the 'let's exchange
numbers and go for cocktails' kind of guy, but I actually
found that refreshing.

'The boat doesn't currently have electricity so . . . no,'
he replied.

Although it felt strange to be going somewhere I didn't know, with a man I barely knew, I somehow trusted in Bron and Ama not to befriend someone who would harm me. Then again, I'm sure that's what many women have told themselves before something terrible happened. I chewed the inside of my lip, trying to decide whether to go home, until Luke pointed at the entrance to a bar located just around the lip of a dodgy alleyway. I could hear Nirvana's 'Lithium' floating out of it. I dropped the pin of my location to Devi just as a precaution.

*

Crusty Pete's was the kind of dive bar my fifteen-year-old self would have lost her mind over. Black walls and sticky flooring rendered atmospheric and cosy by the use of low-watt lightbulbs. Peeling posters of bands that had passed through, graffitied *Hazel loves Harry* and scrawled quotes such as: *You don't know you're born until you die.* Hieroglyphs of Instagram affirmations. At that moment, a local band were playing Nirvana covers on a small stage, the lead singer a man in his thirties with ragged jeans and scuffed trainers. An elderly man, his back shaped like a comma, was drinking whisky shots at the bar, piling them one on top of the other like a tiny leaning tower of Pisa.

'I know it's not the kind of fancy place you're used to,' Luke said before pulling a stool up at a safe distance from the sad old man.

'What do you know about the places I'm used to?' I said, sitting down next to him.

'Hmm,' he replied with the loquaciousness I'd come to expect. 'White wine?'

'Rum and Coke, please. And stop thinking I'm some character from *Sex and the City* for fuck's sake. Next you'll be asking if I do brunch,' I grumbled.

Luke raised an eyebrow. 'Yes, alright,' I rolled my eyes, 'I like brunch – who doesn't like brunch? But I still stand by my point.' This actually made him laugh, the first time I'd heard that from him. It made me relax a little bit.

'I have questions about your boat,' I said.

'Yes?' he said.

'Living there must be . . . cool.' I really was trying here.

'Cool?' he said, raising an eyebrow. 'Cool is what you say when a kid gets a bed shaped like a racing car. Living on a boat is . . . complicated. I love it, but it's not for everyone.'

'Yeah, but who chooses their living situation based on what other people like? I mean, I live in Battersea, and I bought a two-bedroom flat because I thought people would stay over and that happens maybe a handful of times a year. My sister is staying with me now but . . .' I trailed off, abruptly realising that subconsciously I'd bought my place to bring people closer to me, to give my niece a place in London to crash, but hadn't taken any steps to make that happen, until recently. How can people know that you are another home for them, a safe landing, if you don't welcome them in?

'What would you have done otherwise?' he asked.

I thought about it for a moment. 'I mean . . . maybe that's not entirely true. I think I bought it because it would be the type of place my parents would respect me for having. But if I'd really allowed myself the space to dream a bit bigger, it would have been maybe a loft, like those everything-in-one-room places.'

He snorted. 'They are overrated, trust me. It's all fun and games until the guy you invite over wants to take a poo, and then neither of you can look each other in the eye.'

'What a beautiful image.'

'Anyway, it probably wouldn't fit in with your fancy job. Bron said you work at some ad agency – do you like it there?'

'Newsflash, Luke, no one uses the word fancy anymore.' I said, picking up my rum and Coke from a sticky mat.

'You tend to avoid questions, you know that?' he said, signalling for another beer.

'Like what?'

'Like when Bron asked you if you were fine about your accident. Me asking you about your job.'

'I'm not avoiding questions, I just don't know you. Or Bron come to that.'

'Okay, so maybe that makes it easier. You don't have to put on a front for me. How are you doing?'

'Why does everyone ask me that?' I said, exasperated. There was something about this man that made me mad, but he also carried with him a depth and stillness that made me feel comfortable with being angry around him. He raised another eyebrow, as if calling me on my bullshit. *Because if you were fine,* he seemed to say, *you wouldn't be getting upset.*

I leaned into that silence and found it soft, yielding. I let out a breath.

'Do you know how shit it is, to have almost fallen to your death, and then when you wake up, the people you love most aren't there, but your shitty ex-boyfriend is? And then when he leaves, you realise that you don't even know any longer who the people you love the most *are.* Worse, the ones you suspect fit that bill, you've basically pushed out of your life?'

Luke didn't move a muscle. He sipped his beer and stared at the wooden bar top. Eventually, he spoke. 'I don't know how shit that is,' he said, 'but I do know something about anger. The kind that comes from being terrified or worrying that the bad thing might happen again, and feeling no control around that. But the reason why people are asking you if you're okay now is because, if you don't deal with what happened, it will worm itself into your life one way or another.'

I laughed. 'What about anything I just said was funny?' asked Luke through gritted teeth.

'It's not that,' I replied. 'It's just . . . I didn't know you were capable of saying that many words at once.' He looked at me deadpan.

'You should talk to someone about it,' he said. 'I did that once, it helped a lot.'

'Funny, Ama just said the same thing earlier today.' Luke didn't strike me as the kind of person who'd have therapy. More the type who'd whack heavy things in order to work through his catharsis. Then again, it was a reminder that in the same way I hated people making assumptions about me, I would do well to return the favour.

He excused himself and went outside to smoke. By the time he returned, the distance was back in his eyes and we drank in silence, listening to the band play. 'It's funny,' I said, 'I haven't heard some of these songs for years, and there was a time when Ama and I would have this on repeat on our Walkman for weeks on end. Music was such a big part of my life but . . . I haven't even been to a gig in years.'

'I'm going with her and a few others to see System of a Down in a few weeks, if that's your thing. Brunch not included, sadly.'

'It is my thing – are there still tickets?'

'I have a spare – mate dropped out. Give me your number and I'll text you the details.' He handed me his phone and I typed my number in, something shifting between us as I did it. Was this the start of a friendship or something else? I was notoriously bad at reading the signs unless a man literally said: 'Me like sex, want sex now?'

He said he'd walk me to the station and when I retorted that I was more than capable of getting there by myself, his mask of indifference slipped. 'Jesus Christ, woman, I'm trying to be nice!'

'Oh. *Oh.* Alright then,' I said uncertainly.

Just before we parted, I wondered whether to kiss him on the cheek. It felt strange, as if much more time had passed than a couple of hours. It was also unusual for me to be so open and forthright with a stranger – usually I hid what I really thought behind a blander version of myself. Luke felt *comfortable*, or rather, as if I could be myself around him and not worry whether he would think I was too much. Despite that, I decided against a cheek kiss. Mixed signals wouldn't be great at this stage given that our paths would cross again.

Luke had his hands stuffed in his pockets and seemed to be debating something as people huffed and moved around us, walking quickly into the depths of the station. 'So that wasn't terrible, was it?' he finally said.

'No.' I smiled. 'That wasn't terrible. Thank you for helping me out with Gary.'

'No problem . . . Cuz.'

'Oh, wow, Luke, was that . . . a joke?'

He smiled, his entire countenance altering, the sun appearing finally through a bank of cloud in a bright blaze. 'Yeah, don't tell anyone, alright. I'll see you at Ama and B's wedding barbecue, maybe?'

'Right,' I said. 'Thank you again.'

By the time I got to my front door, I had a text from him.

You get back safely?
Yes, you mother hen. See you next week.

'Why are you smiling?' Devi said as I came in. I didn't know how to explain it, that moment when something very small and new and fragile enters the world, a spark that could be extinguished in a breath, a something that could be a nothing, a thing that you didn't want the particles of reality to stick to, in case it became easier to see and then knock down. I murmured 'Nothing' and headed to the shower to wash the day off, losing myself in the rising steam, feeling the gentle curl of something opening inside me, and wanting to protect it.

9

My first-ever barbecue had been glorious, and every barbecue since had only ever been a letdown.

Marina was an only child not just lavished with clothes,
gadgets and albums, but also treated like a little adult.
Her bedroom was in an actual wing and her parents had
a housekeeper who'd bring us snacks and take our dishes
away. At weekends, her parents were prone to giving her
little sips of alcohol, while they sank long tumblers of G&T.
For her fifteenth birthday, they'd let her have a few friends
over. We were allowed to take whatever we wanted from a
big bucket filled with ice, beer and mini bottles of wine. I
remember sitting under Marina's cherry tree in a drunken
halo, eating what tasted like the best burger in the world,
while her parents were off in some other part of their
expansive garden, leaving us to gossip and stare at the
clouds passing overhead.

Despite wanting to be there for Ama, I knew today's
festivities wouldn't match up. Not just because most bar-
becues tended to promise much and deliver little, but

because it was one of the pre-wedding events and therefore some sense of decorum was required.

Wanting a buffer, I debated asking Devi to come with me. I couldn't take Katrina; even the imagined conversation between her and Ama made me wince. I realised with some satisfaction that I *wanted* Devi there, a gentle reminder of how much our relationship had grown in the last few weeks. Eventually I took a deep breath and asked. She hadn't taken much convincing because she wanted an excuse to be outdoors on a beautiful day with clear blue skies and a light breeze to take the edge off the heat.

'Will any of your old crew be there?' she asked as we picked our way across Streatham Common, which was turning yellow from days of unrelenting heat. I froze. 'Do you know,' I said, 'I didn't even think of that. I assumed they were invited to the wedding but I thought this would be for her London lot.'

'What would you do if they were there? Didn't you have a massive falling out with one of them?'

'Ling,' I said absently. 'Her name was . . . is Ling.' I had been thinking about her a lot in the lead-up to the barbecue, and the possible scenarios I sketched out ranged from awkward silence to a yelling match. I'd never been one for fighting, but it didn't seem beyond the realm of possibility given how Ling and I had ended things.

'Don't panic,' Devi said. 'I'm here. And Ama. It'll be fine.'

But that sense of creeping dread followed me to their front door. Hosts were disqualified from being added to the body count of people you knew at a party because at best you had a few minutes of face time before they disappeared to get more ice, drinks, buy the veggie sausages they forgot in the big shop or greet tardy guests. Luke didn't count either because we'd only had one and a half meetings.

Time shifted and wavered, the boundary line between then and now smudged by the faint strains of 'Wonderwall' drifting from the back garden. Ama greeted us at the door, looking beautiful in a ruffled white summer dress. 'I decided to take your advice and go Sri Lankan for the wedding, so I thought I might as well wear white today,' she said conspiratorially, before giving Devi a big, enthusiastic hello.

'Congratulations, Ama,' my sister said, pulling her into a hug, 'you haven't changed a bit.'

'Devi!' she said admiringly, pulling a lock of my sister's curly hair between her fingers in a familiar way, the kind that comes from sharing a skin colour, language, cuisine and womanhood. 'You have only got more beautiful with time.' My sister beamed and handed her the two bottles of Prosecco that we'd brought with us.

The garden was filled with people from two distinct tribes. The first had clean, earnest faces and were wearing freshly ironed shirts and floral sun dresses. They looked like the kind of people who made responsible choices like paying into fixed-term ISAs and going for morning runs.

I assumed this was mainly Bron's family, who originally hailed from Norfolk. The rest were distinctively London; perfectly aware of who they were and unwilling to bow to conformity. A small group eyeing the barbecue hungrily while drinking Pimm's made me realise why I loved living in London. Where else would you get a man sporting a full set of acrylics and eyeliner, standing next to a sixty-something blonde woman in a Tilda Swinton hairdo and bright red lipstick?

I waved at Teresa, who was wearing a pink shorts suit as a concession to the occasion. She waved back with a cursory smile and continued talking to a muscular woman who looked as if she might be one of Bron's firefighter friends. I couldn't see Marina or Ling. What would I say to them if we met? Social fakery such as: *It's been a while? You look great?* Or worse: *Do you remember how you were an absolute arsehole, and stabbed me in the back?* I looked around for Luke, but I couldn't see him either.

Despite the crowded garden, the smell of charcoal in the air, the pop of Prosecco corks and the low hum of chatter, I missed one presence. Mrs Sendhil's. According to Ama she couldn't get back in time from Sri Lanka due to a third cousin taking ill. Bron had rolled her eyes ever so slightly at this. Bron's parents Andy and Sue were instantly identifiable because they looked exactly like her; her mother sporting a dyed blonde bob and kind eyes, while her father looked sturdy, pink-faced, and had neatly trimmed white hair.

Before I had the chance to ask Ama if any of our old

school friends would be there, she and Bron bustled off. Devi had gone in search of the toilet, leaving me in the worst possible position: making conversation with people I didn't know. Even more awkwardly, how was I to explain I'd known Ama for years when they'd never seen me around? But what if Marina and/or Ling were to come across me and I was standing all alone and sad like a loser? It would hardly be the reunion I'd imagined, which was some iteration of me being wildly successful, surrounded by friends and a gorgeous boyfriend, dressed in Stella McCartney. Just as I was about to pull my phone out, wondering for the millionth time how we used to navigate pockets of social awkwardness before the invention of the smartphone, a familiar cough behind me made me jump.

'Hello there,' Luke said, significantly less dour than when we'd first met. I was both relieved and nervous to see him. Interesting how the moment you started to care about someone's opinion of you, the pressure of presenting your best side, the uncertainty and angst, took you further away from your true self. 'Aren't you jumpy?' he observed.

'I'm not,' I said, lowering my voice to a loud whisper, 'I'm just a normal person, doing normal things.'

'Yeah,' he said, 'that's exactly how a "normal" person talks.'

'It's just . . . have you ever met Ama's friends Marina and Ling?'

'No.' He frowned. 'But then again, why would I? I work with Bron, remember. Who are they?'

I sighed. 'We all went to school together but had a massive falling out.'

'Let me guess: some kind of girlie thing, like one of them fancied a guy you liked?' he replied. I glared at him.

'You know, the way you sometimes talk? It's like you've never been around women.'

'Ah, I see Luke has discovered full sentences and isn't being quite so silent,' Ama said, creeping up on us. I prayed he wouldn't mention Marina or Ling.

'Silence isn't such a bad thing sometimes,' I said.

'Oh, really?' Luke replied dryly, and I tried not to smile. Our non-verbal language gave away too much. Ama looked at both of us, amused yet enquiring, knowing she'd missed something: the defining moment when we'd shifted from the silence of our first meeting to this slightly gladiatorial way of talking.

'We actually bumped into each other the day you and I went wedding shopping,' I explained to Ama. 'I was on a terrible date with Gary and . . . Luke happened to be in the same pub. He pretended to be my cousin and whisked me away.'

'Cousin?' she squeaked. 'He may be tanned but he's whiter than a baguette!'

'Oy!' said Luke in an injured tone. Before she could ask further questions, Bron pulled her away towards the kitchen, muttering something about vegan burgers.

She was replaced almost immediately by Devi, who came over with two glasses of Prosecco and as many sausage rolls and mini quiches as her tiny paws could hold.

'Barbecue will be a while,' she said, 'better line your stomach with this. Don't want you barfing into the bushes.'

Luke looked at me meaningfully, then silently left to join another group. I glared at my sister. 'What?' she said. 'I'm not mothering you! I just don't want to be the one mopping up puke later. Remember when you threw up after Mum and Dad's Christmas party when you were fifteen?'

'Did you have to say that in front of Luke?' I groaned.

Devi's eyes grew big. 'Ohhhh, do you like him? He is cute.'

'No. I mean, maybe. Probably not. Also, I don't puke anymore,' I said indignantly.

'Is that actually true?'

'No,' I grumbled, snatching a mini quiche from her outstretched hand.

*

Devi had no problem making conversation with people. 'Tell me how you are able to do this,' I demanded.

'Years of taking Karen to football games and kids' parties,' she replied. 'Once you learn to make conversation with the human equivalent of paint drying, you can basically chat to anyone.'

'I don't have the patience,' I replied. 'How long do you think we have to stay before it's considered rude to leave?' Ama was deep in conversation with her future in-laws and Bron was sorting out yet another crisis in the kitchen, this time regarding halloumi. Devi looked at me. 'We're not leaving, Bel. Also, haven't you noticed, Ama doesn't have any family here? There are zero other Asians?'

Devi was right – there weren't any. She didn't need to explain further. I knew us being here mattered. I thought Ama had allowed me back into her life because she'd taken pity on me, but I hadn't stopped to question whether *she* needed *me*.

'Also,' Devi said, 'I have some intel.'

'Intel?'

'Your friend Ling isn't going to be here – she's had some kind of kid-related emergency, babysitter cancelled or something.'

'Oh, thank god,' I said, relief washing through me. Until Devi added: 'But your friend Marina, she'll be here at some point.' The unease returned.

'What happened between you all anyway?' she asked, stuffing a sausage roll into her mouth. It had been her last year of university when things had changed, and she'd been immersed in planning her wedding to Nikhil. The falling out of teenagers didn't even feature on her radar. If I explained to her what happened back then, I knew how hollow and stupid and anti-climactic it would sound.

Fortunately, Ama came over then to borrow Devi to introduce her to their friends Alex and Erica. 'They're thinking of starting a football team for their kids,' Ama explained, 'and I know you've had a lot of experience with your daughter . . .'

I used the distraction to escape to the upstairs bathroom.

A social no-no as most hosts passionately steered people towards the downstairs toilet for a reason, but I didn't care. I needed space to breathe.

In the light and airy bathroom, there were numerous signs of Ama and Bron's life together. The bottle of shower gel with beads of water still glistening on it. A smiling rubber duck. A brief insight into the type of shampoo and conditioner they used. Head and Shoulders for Bron, the expensive organic stuff was clearly Ama's.

I sat in the dry bathtub and checked my phone messages. No texts from Katrina, but a string of Instagram stories that showed she'd had quite the night at Petrol, a new club in Stoke Newington, with a friend of hers, Tasty. I'd met Tasty and wasn't a fan.

I had held off from looking up Ling and Marina on social media, but now swiped over to Instagram and typed in Marina's name – I was going to be seeing her today after all. She worked as an interior designer, apparently. She had no children, but a dog named Worzel and a horse named Buffy. Judging by the size of her house – a Jacobean-style mansion in Wrotham, framed by acres of countryside – she hadn't needed to worry about money either.

I remembered Marina as a creature of sharp edges. She was capable of softness but her jokes were often like a cake with razor blades hidden inside. Her thoughts ran deep, suppressed under a thick layer of ice, and when she was upset about something, it was often hard to tell where that emotion came from. It made things like forgiveness and contrition impossible, because her reaction to you buying her the wrong kind of Coke could be as extreme as finding out her boyfriend had cheated on her.

My phone buzzed.

Mum: Bel can u talk
Me: Is everything ok?
Mum: I'm worried about Devi – call me pls.

Ever since Devi had moved in with me, my mother had increased her texts and calls as if I'd been awarded guardianship. If she couldn't get hold of Devi, she'd call me and ask where she was. Very often this would happen when I was at work, and rather than getting myself a cup of tea or having some breathing space in between meetings, I'd have to try and track down my sister, who would most likely be on the Tube or have turned her phone off to give her a break from Nikhil asking questions like: 'Are you planning to keep the toaster?'

'What's up, Mum?'

'I haven't heard from Devi – I'm worried sick. Is she okay? She hasn't replied to my message.'

'When did you send the message?' I said flatly.

'This morning!'

'Right. To recap, Devi is a forty-two-year-old woman with her own daughter. She is not a child anymore. If she doesn't reply, it doesn't mean she's dead or ignoring you, but that she's busy.'

'Bel. Can you please get her to call me?'

'Why?'

'What do you mean, why?'

'I mean, what's the reason you need her to call you?' I had now been down this road with my mother many times and knew it wasn't an emergency.

'Because I want to speak to her! I think she needs to come home or else Nikhil is going to take all of her nice things. She's been gallivanting in London for far too long.'

'I don't agree.'

'What do you mean, you don't agree?'

'She's not "gallivanting", Mum. She's taking a break from her life, and that's okay because she's going through this enormous thing.' My parents still didn't know about Nikhil's affair and I'd promised Devi I wouldn't say anything. 'You spoke to her yesterday, I'm pretty sure you spoke or texted the day before that – just give her some space.'

'Oho!' my mother said angrily. I knew that when her Indianisms like 'oho' came out, she was pissed off. 'She's a mother, Bel! You don't know what that's like. She can't just dump her daughter and go off like this.'

I propped my arms against the sides of the bathtub. 'Well, you did, didn't you?'

'EXCUSE me?' The frost from her voice was icing up my screen.

'When I was a kid, didn't you go to India for the whole summer while Dad and I stayed in England?'

'That's different and you know it,' my mother said, but there was something new in her voice. Not anger but upset. And a dash of shame.

'Is it? I know I'm *"not a parent"*, but I also know Karen is a sensible and loving child, and she understands that her mother needs a bit of time to regroup. She doesn't need to be hassled continually about what she should be doing, when she's been the perfect daughter and wife for her entire life.'

Mum's silence on the other end of the phone was unnerving, but I had to admit, it also felt good being Devi's security guard.

'Just tell her to call me, Beryl. I'm her mother and I need to speak to her.' Beryl. The use of my proper name conveyed exactly how mad she was.

'Sure thing. Gotta go, 'bye.'

I clambered out of the bathtub. Fuck hiding from Marina! I was Beryl goddamn Kumar! If I could stand up to my mother, then a rich thirty-something businesswoman who owned a horse named after a vampire slayer would be no problem.

*

I walked back into the garden like a triumphant Amazon. Only to have my confidence punctured like a helium balloon wheezing skywards the moment I saw Marina talking to Ama and Devi. The sight of her wrinkles triggered a dark schadenfreude – facial lines wouldn't be a problem for me for a while since brown skin ages in a different way. We tend to sag like a Bassett hound rather than wrinkle like a Shar Pei. But Marina still had that unreal glossy healthiness that distinguishes rich people, from her shiny blonde hair to her dark blue manicured nails.

How easily they stood together, Marina's arm draped around Ama's shoulder. The way they both laughed at some joke Devi had just told, heads tipping back. The sight of them together brought so much back to me, I didn't know how my body would contain the emotion. But also, Ama and I hadn't properly spoken yet about what happened in Cornwall, the final days of our friendship as a gang of four. It was a painful reminder that there were events in the past I was still not alright with; that however sunny things seemed between us now, however grateful I was to be back in her life, Ama owed me an apology for what happened then. But I'd made a vow not to bring any of this up until after the wedding.

For now, my biggest problem was Marina. She wore that smile, the one that doesn't meet the eyes, and said hello in the sort of high pitch women summon like a shield to conceal their discomfort. 'It's been years!' she exclaimed on first seeing me, her green eyes assessing me inch by inch. I was so glad Devi and I'd had our nails done the day before, and that I'd decided to wash my hair rather than pull it into a greasy bun. 'I love your jumpsuit,' she said, and I volleyed back with: 'I love your hair.'

The Marina I knew gave small talk short shrift; this was unfamiliar ground. I almost wished for her former directness, the way her thoughts would sit so transparently behind her eyes. For a moment, I missed that. Only for a moment, mind.

'I was just saying to your sister that I remember her from your sixteenth birthday – you had it at Pizza Hut, which was *so* cute.'

The inflection on *so cute* wasn't lost on me. Marina had held her sixteenth birthday at Claridge's, to which I wasn't invited because we had stopped being friends by then. But I wasn't ashamed because back then Pizza Hut was the place to be. All-you-can-eat pizza and a salad bar filled with ranch dressing, potato salad and bacon croutons, was *the* height of adolescent sophistication in nineties suburbia.

Devi may have been absent during our big falling out, but it turned out she was well versed in the politics of teenage girls. She watched my face fall. More at the memory of missing Marina's sixteenth birthday than the Pizza Hut put down, but she didn't know that. All she saw was Marina being a classic Mean Girl and hurting my feelings.

'I remember someone had an epic case of the shits and backed up the toilet,' Devi said, 'because they ate a ton of Blue Cheese dressing that had gone a bit rancid. Was that you, Marina?'

I'd completely forgotten about that. It definitely was her. But she replied quickly, 'No, I don't eat cheese,' seeming flustered by how exposed the memory of it made her feel in her adult body.

I felt slightly sorry for her, despite everything. While Marina made me feel childish, some acknowledgement had to be made that I was no longer a teenager. I tempered my response with kindness and changed the subject.

'Congratulations by the way – your interior design business seems incredible. I was stalking you a little on Instagram and you seem to have some pretty high-profile
clients.'

'That's so kind,' she said. 'It was a real struggle getting it off the ground. My parents were the only ones who
wanted to invest, but luckily now I've investors biting off
my hand!

'And what about you, Devi?' she asked, pronouncing
it *Davey*.

'I work as an office manager back in Dartford,' she said
nonchalantly. Marina sniffed and said: 'Oh, right.' Again,
I'd forgotten how much disdain she could convey with
such economy. It truly was an art form. But she hadn't
reckoned on Devi.

'You know, Marina,' my sister said, 'I remembered
something else. Before the designer suit and the Chanel
bag . . .' she waved at the sophisticated outfit '. . . you came
to our house once wearing stockings, suspenders and a
mini-skirt.'

Marina smiled faintly. 'Yeah,' said Devi cheerily, 'Mum
thought you were a prostitute.'

*

About an hour later, everyone apart from Bron's parents were entering the phase of day drinking where shots
seemed like a great idea. Through a filter of Jägermeister,
the sky took on a beautiful texture of crushed blueberries,

the flowers melted into smudged watercolours around us. The food was yet to be served and some people were getting perilously drunk.

'How's it going? All okay with Marina?' Ama had asked me when I managed to grab her for a few moments in the kitchen.

'She seems . . . the same,' I said.

'Very diplomatic, Bel,' Ama laughed, 'I'm impressed.' She pulled out a tray of croquettes. 'Also . . . thank you. I know this can't be easy, you haven't seen her for years. But it means a lot that you're both here.'

My biggest fear was that Marina would want to talk about what had happened back then. But it was clear this was not going to happen. When I headed back out, leaving Ama to finish off things in the kitchen, I found myself in an odd group with a couple named Linda and Ian, one of whom was Bron's cousin, who were avidly listening to Marina talking about interior design. She still liked to come across as an authority on things, tended to steer the conversation towards herself and referred to people and things that we would have no way of knowing, just so she could say 'Oh, don't you know who that is?' or 'That's a special type of marble found in a quarry in southern Italy'.

People say alcohol brings out the buried truth but I don't think that's what pours out. I think all of us have rage reservoirs buried deep down, and *that* is what the alcohol releases. The more Prosecco I vacuumed into my body, the harder it was to make polite appreciative noises to Marina's monologues. I was relieved when Luke came over.

'Where've you been?' I asked.

'Getting ice,' he said, and introduced himself to her.

'How do you two know each other then?' Marina asked with interest. Something about her admiration made me finally look at Luke through a different lens. Rather than a cranky, boat hermit, I saw the man. Call it societal conditioning but his verbal reticence made him mysterious, allowing the other person to fill the gap with their fantasy of him. He was in great shape because of his job, and that rugged outdoors air made him just the kind of person you wanted on your side in case of the apocalypse.

'Um,' I began, 'we met when I came over to Ama's for dinner – Luke works with Bron.'

'I didn't know you and Ama were in touch, to be honest,' Marina said looking at me sideways, playing with the straw in her drink. I could feel us starting to circle each other and the stinker that was our shared history.

'We haven't been,' I replied. 'I reached out to her recently and she seemed to want to meet up. Several weeks later . . . here we are.'

'What made you want to reach out?' she said, no longer looking askance, but directly, with a flash of the old Marina. We were no longer in small-talk-ville, but two fighters facing each other.

My instinct was to lie, fudge the facts. But to what end? And what was the worst that could happen if I told her the truth? She held no power over me now. She wasn't in my life, and she was no longer my friend to lose.

'It might sound hard to believe, but a few weeks ago I

fell into a beer cellar – you know, underneath a pub – and it's made me reassess some things.' Luke nodded and clinked my glass with his.

Marina laughed and it hit something raw and empty inside me. I hadn't factored that into my 'what's the worst that can happen' internal debate. 'Oh, Bel, I have to say, that is very on brand for you.'

'What do you mean?' I said, frowning.

'Well, you know.'

'No, I don't.'

'We should probably just leave it,' she said evenly. Switching back to being the calm one, making me look mad and emotional after riling me up.

'*Please,*' I said, 'I work for an ad agency. I'd love to know what my "brand" is.'

'Well, you were so high-drama when we were at school,' she said. 'It'd always be "I need this boy to like me or I'll die". Or what about that time you got trapped in the art closet for a few hours and ate some of the wood shavings because you thought you'd starve to death?'

The rest of the group laughed and that made me even more upset. I was surprised by how close beneath my skin the rage lived. I could see it arriving down a long, empty highway, like a bus with the brakes cut. I'd always been slightly scared of Marina and how rich and self-assured she was – but I was angry. It felt old, an anger that hadn't seen the surface for a very long time and was swimming furiously upwards.

'What a weird, shitty thing to say,' I told her flatly.

'You're comparing me having an actual near-death experience to being trapped in an art cupboard?'

'I was only joking, Bel,' she replied, rolling her eyes at the group. 'Can't you take a joke these days?'

'But you did say it was on brand for me, right? Like high drama is my brand?'

Another fun thing alcohol does: while you might think you're speaking quietly and with control, you're probably bellowing and behaving like a character in a soap opera. Ama and Bron were far enough away that the music drowned out what we were saying, but some of the other guests nearby were looking over curiously.

Marina looked at me like I was a piece of chewing gum she'd found at the bottom of a handbag. 'Can we just leave it? This is Ama's wedding barbecue, it's about her, not us.'

'Well, that'd be a first for you, wouldn't it? Actually making something not about yourself,' I said sarcastically, unable to stop myself, the autonomic tracks of our relationship brightly lit and drawing me in.

'Bel,' said Luke, his voice gentle in a way I hadn't heard it before, put his hand on my arm. I knew he meant well, but he wasn't part of this. I brushed him off.

'You know what, Marina? Here's some advice. I know you're a robot but when someone says they've had an accident, the humane response is to say: "I'm sorry that happened, are you okay?" Even if you want to make a joke – which by the way is not what I'm saying you did, because a joke is funny. And has a punchline.'

I'd spent long enough at the barbecue that it would be

fine for me to leave now, without raising Ama's suspicions. I had to hope she wouldn't hear about this. I couldn't bear her being mad at me. 'Linda, Ian, it was a pleasure. Luke, see you around.'

I walked off in search of Devi, already feeling sick at the thought of what they'd be saying about me behind my back, hot shame replacing my anger.

10

'Why do you think you are here?' said Kendra, my new therapist.

'Because Luke, who lives on a boat and has a questionable sense of cleanliness, told me it was a good idea,' I replied, staring out of the window of the small room, designed in soothing shades of taupe and grey. A collection of healthy-looking succulents clustered on her desk. 'You must be amazingly green-fingered, looking after those plants,' I said. 'I find them impossible to keep alive.'

'Truthfully,' she sighed, 'I kill them about every six to eight weeks and have to replace the lot. I follow all the instructions but . . .' She shrugged, shaking out her long braids, and I knew what she meant all too well. My desk succulents at Leopard contemplated staying alive in a toxic corporate environment with recycled air . . . and chose death.

'I don't know why I'm here, if I'm honest,' I said. 'I have a thousand things going on in my head, and none of them seem important enough to talk to a therapist about. It's not like I can't get out of bed or am unable to function.'

'And is that when you think people should see a therapist?'

'That's what I've always assumed. I mean, I had two friends who recently told me they were in therapy, which made me think about it. And I have insurance through work so . . . why not? I suppose. But no one else in my family has ever visited one. And I . . . have some problems, but who doesn't? I'm sure you don't want to listen to my problems!' I laughed.

I expected Kendra to laugh too, but she didn't. 'Bel, that's my job. I'm not a friend or a colleague that you happen to be chatting to. My entire purpose in this moment is to listen to you. And you'd be surprised how many people feel like you – that they shouldn't burden others, so instead they bottle things up. This is your moment perhaps to open up in a safe space.'

I felt ridiculous because simply hearing Kendra say that made me emotional, my throat getting tight like it did that day in Devi's kitchen. I didn't say anything for a couple of minutes. We sat there, the bergamot diffuser making a soft hissing noise and the distant clank of workmen putting scaffolding together audible in the background. 'What are you thinking?' she said gently.

I'm thinking that if I start talking, I won't be able to stop. I'm thinking that I'm scared. I'm thinking that I might start crying and then I'd be crying in front of a stranger, which barring walking down the street with my knickers accidentally tucked into my tights, is one of the most mortifying things I could do. I'm thinking that my worries are unimportant because I have a job and a home and I should be grateful . . . and my mother would laugh herself silly if she knew I was having therapy.

'A lot,' I said. 'What my mum would think of me having therapy, for instance.'

'Ah,' Kendra said, leaning forward. 'That's a good place to start.'

'I really don't want to talk about my mother,' I said tightly.

'We don't have to talk about your mother,' she said. The unspoken words 'we can talk about anything else' hung between us, but still I couldn't speak.

'Here's something that might help,' Kendra said, realising I wasn't going to say anything. 'I'm half Indian and half West Indian. My parents are both immigrants, like yours. If our parents are immigrants, there's a lot we inherit from them about gratitude. Some of it good, some of it bad. The bad stuff might be that you should be grateful to have enough money to pay your bills. That as long as you can do that, you don't have any problems. If you think you do, then you're being self-pitying. But that just isn't true. What we then inherit from them is this sense that we should keep carrying on, even at the cost of our own sanity. We don't feel that our voices have any value. We believe no one else would want to hear about our problems.'

This reminded me of what Ama had said that day in the wedding shop of horrors, and I was taken aback by how true it was. The first time anyone had really articulated this for me.

'We don't have to have the perfect session,' she said.

'Don't think of what I might want to hear, and how I might want to hear it. Just tell me what is at the top of your mind.'

I fiddled with the cushion on my lap. 'I feel like I'm losing control. I had an accident a few weeks ago, a bad one. It made me realise something bad could happen at any time, any place. It made me . . . look at my life and I didn't like what I saw. So I started making changes.'

Kendra looked at me, silently encouraging me to continue.

'A couple of days ago, I went to a friend's barbecue – she's an old school friend I've just reconnected with. It was an important occasion – she's getting married. And I saw another old friend there, someone I haven't seen for years, and lost my temper. I'm not usually the kind of person to do that in public. And what's ironic is that the whole reason we fought is, she thinks I'm a drama queen based on some version of me she remembers from twenty years ago. But it made me feel like I was unravelling. I couldn't stop myself from getting angry – it just happened – and I want to make sure it doesn't happen again.'

Kendra was writing things down on the lined pad propped on her crossed knee.

'Okay,' she said, 'and how do you feel now that you've told me this?'

'I feel like I just wasted your time. Like I could've texted that to a number of friends.'

'Okay, and did you do that?'

'What?'

'Text it to a number of friends?'

'No.'

'Why not?'

'Because . . . I don't know. I was busy with a hangover and then work?'

Kendra looked straight at me. 'When we text our friends information like this, we're not really doing it to get an insight into our behaviour. We're not looking for an unbiased perspective. We want them to tell us that we were right to behave the way we did, and that the other person is a arsehole.'

'Are you allowed to say the word "arsehole"?'

'Yes,' she said, putting her pen down. 'The reason why you're here, I suspect, isn't because you want me to tell you that you are a terrible person. It's because you're reacting to things in ways that might be unsettling you. That maybe seem out of character. That maybe lack *control*. People who want to control things might do so for a number of reasons. Alcoholic parents. Bullied at school. Never felt like they fitted in. Traumatic relationships . . . and so on. My job isn't to tell you that your friend is an arsehole. Maybe she is, maybe she isn't. My job is to help you understand *why* you feel the need to control everything. Because when you figure that out, then you might see that the fear of things going wrong, and all of the energy you expend trying to keep everything under control, is far worse than the chaos you fear so much.'

'So,' she said, picking up her pen, 'does finding out why you feel the way you do, sound like something you want to do?'

Never had I ever felt like someone was peering into

my actual soul and telling me what I needed to hear. Of course, I didn't tell Kendra that. Instead I looked at her like a stunned hamster. 'How far back will we need to go?' I squeaked.

'It's your timeline, Bel. As far backwards or forwards as you want and need to go.'

1999

This is the list of things I had to agree to so as to be allowed to go to Cornwall, because my parents are unbearable control freaks:

- Allow them to speak to Marina's uncle and aunt, Jasper and Tiggy, before leaving for the trip
- Let them drop me off at the train station (I wasn't allowed to stay over at Marina's the night before like Ling was – Ama actually wanted to spend the last night with her mum, go figure)
- Call home every day without fail
- Visit Padmini Auntie and Rakesh Uncle for lunch during the trip
- Promise not to do anything naughty like drink alcohol
- No talking to boys
- Keep my wits about me and take the screwdriver from Dad's workshop for self-protection

It was all worth it, though, when we finally took our seats on the train, holding packs of Marks and Spencer's sandwiches and bags of Percy Pigs. I'd forbidden my parents from giving me a packed lunch and had a little bit of money put aside from my Saturday job at Superdrug. Just when I was about to scream from the number of last-minute dos and don'ts, Mum gave me a little card just before we said goodbye. It had a £50 note in it.

'Spend it on something fun,' she said, my dad smiling as he squeezed my shoulder.

'SHOTGUN WINDOW!' Marina yelled, scooting into a window seat around the table we'd been assigned. She had been grumpy ever since her parents dropped off her and Ling. Ama, Ling and I were just so excited to be on a train, on an adventure, without parental supervision, that we would have sat in the toilet if necessary. Marina put her headphones on, pulled her hood over her eyes and burrowed into her corner.

I looked at Ling, who shrugged. 'She's been in a weird mood since last night,' she whispered. We didn't need to ask why; Marina was prone to moods that seemed to arrive like unexpected storms. In a way, it was really nice that it was just the three of us. We joked and laughed, drank horrible amounts of fizzy drink and pored over *Kerrang!* Periodically we'd put our empty sweet wrappers onto Marina's head as she slept.

Something eased in my chest as the grey steel and glass of London was left behind and countryside softened our surroundings. We were moving away from Skateboard Steve. Away from Devi and Nikhil. Away from Mum and Dad's suffocating rules. I felt lighter. I had no idea what was going to happen, only that *something* would, and that made my skin tingle with excitement.

'I hope we finally meet some decent boys,' Ling said. 'B, I hope you're not still pining over Steve.'

After serenading him outside his house and being ignored, I was now even more obsessed with him. Seeing my lovesick expression, she said in a low voice: 'I've got something that'll make you forget about him. I nicked it off my parents.' She looked around to check there wasn't anyone around and reached into her bag, pulling out a battered book.

The Joy of Sex: A Gourmet Guide to Love Making had a picture on the cover of a man with a moustache leaning in to kiss a woman. 'Oh, you beautiful pervert,' I said, before grabbing it off her with shiny eyes and flicking through the pages. I'd never seen images like this before – breasts, penis, pubes – the works.

'Oh my GOD,' said Ama, yanking it out of my hands. 'Ling, do your parents use this to, you know?' She mimed her finger going into a circle she made with her other hand.

'Ugh, shut up!' she said. For the next ten minutes there was just a cacophony of 'Gross!', 'Ew!' and 'Why is there so much hair down there?' until we woke up Marina.

As she lifted her head, a shower of Opal Fruit wrappers cascaded around her. 'You bastards,' she said, shaking herself free.

'Oh, come on, GRUMPS,' Ama said, and scooped her into a big hug.

'Let me go,' she griped.

But Ama just held on tighter and started singing '"We're all going on a summer holiday!"', really loudly, until Marina couldn't help but laugh.

*

Even the air smelled different here. Sharper, cleaner, cut through with salt from countless waves, the boom of the sea so close by we could feel its endless movement. Piercing cries of seagulls tore through the air as a dilapidated people carrier wheezed into Newquay station car park.

'Uncle Jasper!' Marina cried, and a man who looked like he was wearing the patched-together remains of several suits, unfolded himself from the driver's seat. Marina's mother Delilah came from 'good stock' but had no money to speak of, and although her own finances had improved after marrying Marina's father James, her brother Jasper's hadn't. He had the accent, the family home, and that was about it.

'Marina, my darling! I almost drove past you.' Jasper looked at the rest of us with a strained smile. I had a sneaky suspicion that he was expecting to see at least one more white person in our group and trying to comprehend where Ling sat within that. 'Girls,' he said, grabbing our bags, 'welcome to Newquay!'

The car was worse on the inside because, in addition to being grubby, it absolutely reeked.

A ten-minute drive took us to their home and Ama whispered: 'Now this is more like it!' It was a grand dame, a real beauty of a building, three storeys high. Though it was set back behind hedges for privacy, we could see the glitter of the sea from the front doorstep. We clapped our hands excitedly. But that enthusiasm quickly faded once we'd stepped through the front door. Even at first glance, we could see there were missing floorboards and the curtains were tatty and moth-eaten. Was that a bucket in a corner, catching a drip?

'MARINA!' bellowed a voice so posh and high it could command armies. A tall, tanned girl in cut-off jeans, her extremely long blonde hair the same shade as Marina's, thundered down the stairs on bare feet.

'India!' yelled a woman's voice from the back of the house, jolting me for a second. Were they calling out our home countries? 'WHAT HAVE I SAID ABOUT RUN-NING LIKE A FARKING LUMMOX DOWN THE STAIRS!'

'She said fuck!' Ling whispered, clutching her Green Day satchel a bit more tightly.

'Yeah, posh people swear loads, apparently!' I whispered back.

'Girls, this is my cousin India,' Marina said, once they'd disentangled themselves from each other's arms. She'd switched from the Kent accent she used with us to her old private-school tones. I almost laughed to see how different they looked. Marina had on Black Cherry lipstick, purple-and-black-striped tights, a leather mini-skirt and

217

a high-necked black velvet top. Whereas India looked as if she had been communing with nature – there were the actual remnants of a flower crown in her hair, she sported a toe ring and wore a vague, dreamy expression, in marked contrast to Marina's intense scowl.

We all said shy hellos and then an older woman, best described as rangy and heron-like with a strong nose, emerged from the kitchen. She looked at us with the same slight jerk of surprise that Jasper had. 'Hello, girls! I'm Marina's aunt Tiggy. I'm just making dinner, won't be long,' she said.

Before we left Kent, my parents made Ama promise that she'd make sure I called them every day and the moment we arrived. The little do-gooder took her role seriously.

'Er, auntie?' Ama said, looking at Tiggy, who looked back at her in surprise. Marina laughed until she was doubled over, while India giggled. Usually when Ama reverted to being a boaty – the term we used to describe native-born brown folk, as in 'off the boat' – I wanted the ground to swallow me up. A swift glance at Ling told me she was feeling something similar.

Tiggy laughed as well. 'I'm not your auntie, my girl!'

'Oh, I'm Sri Lankan,' Ama said, unperturbed. 'We call any older woman "auntie", or if you're a man, "uncle". It's a sign of respect where I come from.'

'Tiggy will be fine,' she replied.

'Can we please use your phone as we need to call our parents to let them know we arrived safely?'

'India will show you,' she replied, still chuckling as

she walked into the kitchen. I admired the way Ama had refused to rise to the unpleasantness but felt insulted on her behalf as her ethnic-adjacent neighbour.

India took us to where the telephone was located. The decay had spread throughout the entire house, we saw. Piles of paperwork stood on ruined antique furniture ringed with white teacup marks; some of the chairs had stuffing weeping out of holes. The gloom deepened the further we went.

After initially making an impression as enticing as a sack of boiled eggs, India put her hand on Ama's arm and apologised for laughing. 'I'm trying to learn a lot about other cultures,' she said earnestly. 'I'm just so appalled by what's happening in the rainforest at the moment. And I was named after your country so I feel I should honour the name more.'

'I'm from Sri Lanka. Bel is the one who's from India.'

India blushed. 'Oh, yes, of course. Sorry, I didn't mean to . . . of course, it's a different country. I just mean that I care about what's happening all over the world, you know?'

'Sure,' Ama said in such a deadpan voice that I tried not to laugh. I looked over at Ling to signal 'Is this girl even for real?' but recognised the look in Ling's eyes. She was already on her way to thinking India was The Coolest Person Ever; she was prone to doing this whenever we started hanging out with someone new. She wouldn't hear a bad thing about them and would start to take on the characteristics of that person, from being upset about the

Kosovan War to changing music genre allegiances. This magpie characteristic was something Ling and Marina had in common and probably explained why they got on so well. Sometimes it was hard not to take it personally, but she always returned to us eventually.

And there could have been worse choices than India. Even though she was an earnest hippie, India was still what we'd call a cool girl. She was naturally beautiful with long legs, and her cascading hair looked like it required minimal effort. Although normally girls who looked like this got my back up because of the ease with which they moved about in the world, I grudgingly admired the rebellious little dolphin tattoo she had on her left ankle.

We passed a hallway with framed black-and-white photographs hanging on the wall. In one, a white family stood in front of a house fringed by coconut trees. A row of Indians stood behind them, dressed in saris and dhotis. 'Where was that?' I asked India.

'Oh,' she replied, 'Mummy was born in India. That was her house and those were her servants.' She saw the look on my face and said quickly, 'They had a close relationship, like one big family.'

Something dark and ugly rose in my throat. I wanted to take that photo and smash it on the ground.

I felt Ama squeeze my hand, reminding me that a secondary planet shared the same orbit as mine, and something inside me eased.

*

'Baloo!' my dad said as he picked up the phone. I had been so concerned with escaping my parents that I hadn't even considered I might miss them. But the sound of his voice, so warm and safe, made me want to cry. I couldn't let him know I was upset, so I stapled a happy voice onto my real one and told him how much fun we were having.

Marina and India had disappeared leaving us to it, and while Ama was chatting to her mother, I told Ling how weird I found all of this. 'Like, she's called India because her Mum lived as a colonial in India,' I said. 'And I feel like they don't really want us here.'

'Don't be such a baby!' she said, pulling a face. 'India is amazing – she didn't choose her name, did she? We're staying in a house just off the beach. And most importantly, we're not at home bored shitless.'

Embarrassingly, Ling's hard-nosed response made me feel even more homesick. I just wanted to be on the sofa, watching *Moesha* and eating potato waffles. She must have caught the slightly teary look on my face because she said, a bit more softly: 'Look, I know it's weird being somewhere new, but enjoy it while you can. We won't be here for long and I could really use a break from my parents. My dad is talking about signing me up for summer tutoring when we get back.'

'Oh, man, I had no idea,' I replied. Studying for our GCSEs had almost broken us; the last thing any of us wanted was more studying before beginning our A-levels, which we'd been warned were intense. I was lucky my parents hadn't gone all alpha-Asian on me and made me do extra classes too. 'It's just this house is so . . . I know this sounds mad, but I feel like because we aren't white, it's a bit of an issue?'

'Honestly, Bel – why do you always have to make it about that? I mean Tiggy seems like a bitch but most mums are. Maybe she's going through the menopause or something.'

'DINNER IS READY!' Tiggy yelled in the distance like an irate town crier.

'Maybe you're right,' I said. But I didn't think that was it at all.

I required no medal but it turned out I was right. Dinner was a terrible affair that left me seriously considering going home the following day. The dining room was as shabby as the rest of the house, but it was clear they had some money, judging by the talk of India's private school and a holiday to Malaysia they had planned. India talked excitedly about going to an elephant sanctuary. This was a phenomenon I'd heard of: posh folks who were *rich* rich but gave the appearance of being poor. As we sat down, Tiggy announced she was serving beef. Ama apologised and said she didn't eat beef but would be fine with vegetables.

'Is that for religious reasons?' Tiggy asked.

'No,' said Ama. 'I don't want to get mad cow disease.'

Then Tiggy huffed at Marina and said that she wished she'd been told about everyone's dietary requirements, and had she known, she would have ordered takeaway. To which I said: 'Oh, don't worry, my mother would rather

die than order takeaway.' And earned myself a glare from
the entire table apart from Ama.

The focus then moved to Ling. 'Tiggy and I went to the
Mekong Delta,' Jasper said, looking meaningfully at her.
'It was a magical place.'

Finally catching his meaning, Ling said: 'Oh, I'm not
Vietnamese. My dad is Chinese and my mum is English.'

'You know,' said Jasper, 'I was saying to Tiggy that I
thought you were mixed-race.' Witnessing this entire conversation was like sitting on a bed of nails, waiting agon-
isingly for it to go horribly wrong. 'But we weren't sure
because . . . you know.' He pointed to his eyes.

Ling said: 'Ha-ha, thanks!' as if it was no big deal, as if
she wouldn't remember that comment until the day she
died. For a brief moment I felt sorry for her. I knew what
it was like. That uncomfortable prickle, the bitter tang of
words that required swallowing, that you couldn't spit
back. Marina said nothing, just concentrated on cutting
up her beef.

The best thing to come out of dinner was the announcement that Jasper and Tiggy would be fucking off to the Lake
District for a few days, meaning we had the run of the house.
As a treat, they said, they'd left us a few bottles of Jasper's
homemade wine to have a little party with. That and not
wanting to ruin Ama's birthday were the only reasons I
didn't call my parents and tell them I was coming home.

We were given a choice of who to share rooms with, and
it was now an unspoken thing that Ama and I would stick to
each other like glue. I didn't know what alien had taken over

Ling, and Marina hadn't been on our side once, this whole time, from the moment we'd walked through the door.

About an hour after lights out, I whispered: 'Ama, are you awake?'

'Yes. Of course I'm awake. I'm concerned we're going to be hunted by Tiggy reliving her colonial days and our skins will be displayed on the wall,' she said in the darkness.

I snorted with laughter. 'I'm so hungry, dude.'

'At least you had the beef. The vegetables tasted like the solidified version of a fart.'

'Er, the beef tasted like a cooked shoe. And they did that thing of making just enough food for everyone only there wasn't actually enough to go round.' This wasn't the same as not being able to afford to buy enough food. It was a habit I'd noticed in English households, which were so different from Indian ones. In those, food was always made in excess amounts, because the worst thing was for someone to go hungry. If you made too much, you could always have it as leftovers.

We listened to the sound of a house asleep, quiet but for the odd creak and the soft whoosh of water. Ama's stomach growled loudly, like a cat being stepped on, and we both laughed with hands cupped over our mouths.

'I've got an idea,' she said. 'It's not that late. Maybe there's a fast-food van open?'

After getting dressed and creeping through the house, we found ourselves on the beach. We saw the twinkly lights of a food truck in the distance and, soon enough, were sitting on a wall with hot chips in our hands. The North Atlantic stretched out before our feet, streetlights illuminating the white flecks of waves reaching their destination before being pulled back into a shifting surface of liquid black, shining silver where it met the moon.

'Do you think you have enough vinegar on your chips, Ama? My eyebrows are about to turn white from the smell.'

'I'm Sri Lankan,' she said, shrugging.

'That's your answer to everything, mate,' I said, laughing, and it made her laugh too.

'Hang on,' she said. She pulled out her Walkman, pressed Play and handed me an earphone. Oasis's 'Champagne Supernova' filled our small universe. I felt like I could sit there forever. It made the whole Jasper/Tiggy experience bearable. Just to be side by side with my friend, the smell of sea and salt in our hair, on the verge of everything. Overhead an inky bowl filled with stars promised us something new.

'Marina is acting weird, so is Ling, and I'm not sure about India,' I said, unable to keep it inside any longer.

Ama sighed. 'Yeah, it's unfortunate that India's a bit of a flake. But beautiful people always are.'

'But you're beautiful, and you're not a flake,' I replied through a mouthful of chips.

'Babybel, please never change,' Ama said, putting her arm around me. For a brief moment, it felt like home.

*

The sun was high in the sky by the time we surfaced, scouring away any residual traces of Jasper and Tiggy. They'd left before we woke up, leaving behind a note and five yogurts for our breakfast. There was no other food in the house apart from dry goods and tins of beans, so we headed to the supermarket for our first-ever food shop without our parents. Tipping out bread, milk, slices of ham and cheese onto the kitchen counter, we realised we'd bought no vegetables or fruit. And there was no one to nag us about it either.

Giddy with our newfound freedom, we swiped two bottles of Jasper's homemade wine, decanted it into empty 7Up bottles and headed to the beach. It was the first day of the Newquay Surfing Festival, and although we had no interest in the waves, we were definitely interested in the bands who'd be playing as part of the entertainment.

'Mud Flaps . . . Hysterical Jane . . . Tide Breath . . . I haven't heard of any of these,' grumbled Marina.

'The bands that play here are pretty small,' India replied. 'Most people won't have heard of them. The point is the vibe. The people who come to watch them, the cool surfy types. You know.'

We didn't know, but we'd seen enough of surfer dudes on TV to be excited by the prospect and had spent ages getting ready.

Ling was beginning phase one of her Make India Love Me plan, by borrowing a pair of her jean shorts and a tie-dye shirt – with long sleeves because she tanned horribly.

'I made it myself,' India told us. 'It looks like it,' I replied, and she beamed proudly.

Her preference for walking barefoot extended to outside the house – 'It helps me to have a conversation with the earth,' she said. She wore a tiny white crop top with her shorts. Meanwhile the rest of us looked like we usually did. Marina was thankfully still Marina. The only concessions she'd made were swapping her long-sleeved Korn T-shirt for a vest top and removing her tights. Ama paired a strappy military green vest with her black jeans but took a huge hat and a chiffon shrug to cover up with on the beach. 'We don't mess about with the sun in Sri Lanka,' she said. I paired a short black skirt and a see-through black top with my big DMs.

When we found our spot, a middle-aged man with tiny stick legs and a tight, round belly, pointed and laughed at my boots. 'Gonna be a bit hot, ain't ya, girls?' His wife laughed along so hard with him that her hat fell off, revealing the dark roots beneath the peroxide.

We were a bit too early for the bands, but India offered to stay with our things, so we could mooch around the little stalls that sold T-shirts and shell necklaces we couldn't afford. As we walked from one canvas booth to another, we were amazed by the indie music blaring from the speakers versus the eighties pop that usually played in Dartford shopping centre. As Ling and Ama were admiring a rack filled with Vans sneakers, I saw a beautiful boy with dyed black hair looking at silver necklaces a few stalls over. As I stopped to stare at him, a stream of young women with chiselled abs and muscled arms walked by us, holding surfboards. They looked so confident, strong and Amazonian, I felt like a kid next to them and intently studied a table of hand-painted lamps. By the time I looked up, he was gone.

Back at our little camp, we spread out on the beach according to our varying relationships with the sun. Ama, Ling and I sat in the shade, while Marina and India lay down on beach blankets on their front. The sand was everywhere; stuck to little smears of sun lotion on our legs, trickling into our bags. Music from the festival drifted over once the bands started playing (none of them vaguely decent or memorable enough to warrant us buying a CD or going to watch them play) and the warm, fuzzy feeling of Jasper's horrible wine spread through our bodies.

'Do you think we should tell them they're turning lobster red?' Ling whispered, pointing at the middle-aged man and his wife, now sound asleep. We peered over to look at them. The man in particular looked radioactive.

'No. Let The Universe have its revenge,' I replied, and popped my sunglasses back on.

After a while, Ling started to get fidgety. 'I want to meet some boys,' she said. 'Should we go back to the bands area?'

Ama and Marina groaned. 'I don't want to move,' Marina said, her mouth smushed against the blanket.

I didn't want to move either, but I wanted to be helpful. 'I can come if you want?'

Ling wrinkled her nose. 'No, it doesn't work unless at least three of us go. Forget it,' she said grumpily.

Two things had driven a wedge between Ling and me recently. The first was her repeated rejection of any help from me. Every time I offered to do something nice for her, she'd get irritated. And the more irritated she grew, the more I kept offering because I felt as if I'd done something wrong and needed to make up for it. The second thing was her discovery of boys. It made her single-minded and utterly ruthless if she felt someone was messing with her territory. She had gone from the little girl being reduced to tears to the big girl reducing someone else to tears, if she suspected them of looking at a boy she liked. The three of us were mostly safe if we had someone we already liked, but even then, Ling's jealousy could be daunting and unpredictable.

But the prospects here were bleak. There were either groups of surfers in their early twenties who didn't register our existence because we looked like children, trendies – boys with gelled spiked hair carrying Unity bags – or shirtless old men.

We were so busy staring at the parade of people in front of us, at first we didn't notice two boys come over. When I did, my heart stopped. One of them was the black-haired boy I'd seen at the stalls, and the other had blond hair in an undercut. They both wore baggy skater jeans and band T-shirts. 'Sorry to bother you, girls,' said Blondie, 'but have you got a light?'

We all stared at him until Ling elbowed Ama, who had been designated keeper of the cigarettes. I had the kitty and Ling had the wine; Marina and India had carried the blankets. When Ama got drunk, her brain slowed to the consistency and speed of mashed potato. She patted around for her bag, which she didn't realise she was sitting on.

'Are you alright?' Blondie said, laughing.

Ama liberated the bag from a butt cheek, rummaged around in it and handed over the lighter.

'Ignore her,' Ling said, giggling, 'she's been drinking homemade wine.' She could be a good wing woman if there was a specific boy you were trying to hunt down. But if it was a group of boys, Ling's tactic when charming them always involved making fun of us, as if we were some sad community project she'd taken on to enhance her Record of Achievement. It had never been a problem in the early years when boys weren't much of a feature in our lives but increasingly it was starting to irritate. Ama remained oblivious, however.

'Lucky you,' he laughed. 'My friends and I have been trying to get hold of some booze but the local offy asked for ID. I'm Ben, by the way, and this is Brandon,' he said, pointing to the boy with the black hair.

'I think I saw you guys at the stalls earlier,' Brandon said.

As I looked closer, I realised he had green eyes, and was definitely the most beautiful boy I had ever seen. Hasta la vista, Skateboard Steve. I could feel the same shift in Ling's body language too, his presence drawing a sharp focus from both of us like the lens on a camera.

'I'm Ling,' she giggled, trying to get Brandon's attention, 'and this is Beryl, Ama, and those two over there . . .' she pointed to Marina and India, who had passed out from the wine '. . . are also with us.'

'It's Bel,' I said firmly, furious at Ling for using my real name when she knew I hated it. Brandon raised an eyebrow.

'Where are you guys from?' he asked, and we all stiffened because that could be such a loaded question. It was never about where you were from geographically, more about where your parents were from.

'Well, I'm half-Chinese,' Ling began.

'No,' Brandon laughed. 'I mean where do you all live? We're from Manchester.'

'Oh,' Ling said, blushing furiously, 'we're from Kent. We're just visiting for a few days.'

'But China is very cool,' Ben said enthusiastically, 'I eat Chinese food all the time.'

'And what about you,' Brandon said, looking at me, 'have you been on the homemade wine as well?'

If I had been sober, I wouldn't even have been able to speak to him because I would've been so consumed with shyness. But I'll say this for Jasper's moonshine, it gave me a (false) sense of confidence. I put on an exaggerated accent. 'Yes, good sir, I too have been on the homemade beverages.' He laughed and Ling frowned.

'We probably need to find Kev and Derek,' Ben said to Brandon, who nodded.

'You're welcome to join us,' I said. They looked at each

other. 'Sure,' Brandon said slowly, 'we might do that. We wanted to check out the bands but we'll see you around.'

After they had gone, Ling hissed: 'What was *that?*'

'What do you mean?'

'That lame joke! *Hello, sir, I've been on the homemade beverages,*' she mimicked. It was beginning. This was the first overt demonstration of her jealousy. I didn't know if it was the wine, the fact that we were on holiday, the turncoat behaviour she'd displayed the night before, but this time I was less inclined to roll over and indulge her.

'What was so bad about that?!'

'Your jokes are terrible.' Ling looked really cross. 'They're not coming back. Thanks a lot, Bel.' I felt as if I'd been slapped.

Ling was the kind of person who, when she was in a happy mood and you were in her good books, made you feel like you were directly inside a sunbeam. And when you weren't in favour with her, a cold slurry of fear poured over you. Although Marina could also be moody, she was like lightning in a stoppered bottle; she contained it within herself. The unspoken pact was that when she indicated to us that she needed to be left alone, we did, and in doing so dodged the storm. But with Ling, although she was funny, cool, and often a joy to be around, her unpredictable and often acerbic moods kept me in a constant state of uncertainty.

'What's going on?' a sleepy Marina said. India was groaning next to her, clutching her head – a combination of wine and too much sun.

'Bel just scared off a couple of skater boys. They were gorgeous,' Ling grumbled.

India sat up. 'Don't worry,' she said, 'we'll find them again. Marina and I need to go and buy some Cokes anyway. We'll bring them back with us. Promise.' A part of me felt grateful to her for her kindness in trying to smooth things over.

An hour later (a very awkward hour, during which Ling and I didn't talk, except to Ama who woke up towards the end), India and Marina returned, with four boys in tow. My jaw dropped in disbelief. Ling looked delighted. 'India is the best,' she said. Ben sat down next to her with a thump, spraying sand all over her and making her yell. Derek and Kevin were non-descript and introduced themselves in a mumble, keeping a slight distance from us like boys at a school disco worried about female contagion.

Despite the fact that she could have had any of them, India showed no interest in the boys. She plopped down in front of Ama and asked for help applying some after-sun to her back. Marina meanwhile was handing out a fresh bottle of wine-disguised-as-Coke and Derek retched as he foolishly took a greedy swig.

'What kind of music do you like?' asked Brandon. I squinted at him in the sun. Why was this boy talking to me? He looked like a Jared Leto type, albeit a bit shorter. He could get any girl he wanted, I was sure, and my friends were all better-looking than me.

'Alternative, mostly,' I said warily. 'A bit of industrial, some grunge. I love Alice in Chains.' I pointed at his T-shirt.

'I'm into this new band at the moment, Fever Pitch. Want to listen?' I could feel my friends going a bit quieter, which meant they were paying attention to us. He handed me one of his earphones and pressed play.

'Oh! I said. 'They sound a bit . . .'

'. . . Soundgarden,' we both said at the same time. He laughed and took a sip of wine, before handing the bottle to me. A warm feeling spread through me that had nothing to do with the alcohol. I felt the sea bouncing every inch of blue back into the sky, and all that vast expanse of radiance reflected how happy I was. I didn't know what might happen next, only that I wanted to stay in this moment forever.

'Bel?' Marina called after we'd listened to a couple of songs, breaking me out of my reverie. 'Can I borrow you for a moment? I need to get some extra wine from the house.'

I looked up at her reluctantly and handed back the earphone to Brandon, our fingers brushing as I did so. Even that fleeting touch made me feel like a circuit board that had just lit up. Marina and I walked back up the trodden path to the house, picking our way through the long grass.

'You know Ling likes Brandon, right?' she said rather abruptly, as we shook the sand off our feet on the kitchen mat.

'I didn't know,' I replied, my heart sinking, 'but . . . I like him too.'

'I can tell. It's just that she asked me to say something to you.'

Marina had a way of bringing my anger and irritation to the surface faster than anyone else I knew. Ama frequently had to intervene when we started bickering and sometimes we'd spend days not talking to each other. But we were on holiday together and we couldn't afford the luxury of getting mad. I tried to stay calm. 'Then she should've said something to me rather than asking you,' I said. 'We're not kids. I mean we're sixteen, after all.'

'I agree – I told her to talk to you – but you know Ling, sometimes she's a bit shy.' A treacherous part of me wondered if Ling was really shy, or manipulative enough to get me out of the picture so she could chat to Brandon. Marina looked at me sideways and said: 'So are you going to back off and give her a shot?'

'Why shouldn't she be the one to back off?'

'Ling's going through a bit of a hard time,' Marina said. 'She could really do with feeling good about herself.'

'And I couldn't?' I sensed my self-control slipping, anger yanking at me like a disobedient dog.

Marina sighed. 'I don't want this to turn into some big drama, Bel,' she said. 'I'm just asking you to maybe let Ling have a win.'

'Marina, you're my friend, and I know we don't always agree on things. But it's not my fault I like him, in the same way it's not Ling's fault if she likes him too. I'm also pretty sure Ben likes her, so why don't we spend a bit more time with all of them and then suss it out? I don't want to fight about it.'

'I don't want to fight either,' she replied. 'I'm just trying to do right by Ling, but I don't want you to think I don't care about you. Okay? Skin?'

I hesitated. 'Skin' was our shorthand for saying everything was okay again after a fight. I'd felt ambushed and my anger was still cooling. I wasn't ready to reciprocate. But if I didn't, it would turn into a whole thing and I didn't want to have Ling and Marina whispering together about me. 'Skin,' I replied. We swiped our right hands together palm to palm.

'You know what we should do?' Marina said as we locked the door behind us. 'We should invite them to Ama's birthday party. We'll have a bonfire. It'll be great.'

'Good idea,' I replied. 'We'll have the best time.' But my words sounded flat to me. This felt like playing a board game where I didn't know the rules.

11

After therapy with Kendra, my head felt so full, I had to walk around the block for a bit. I wove into and around Harley Street, wondering how many others had done the same, lost in their own world, their thoughts louder than the construction noise on the streets.

When I'd tried to talk to Devi about everything that had happened on that holiday in Cornwall, she hadn't listened to me. I remember her telling me that girls fighting was normal, and that we'd make up in no time. But the rest of that summer had gone by, the loneliest I'd ever spent, and we hadn't.

As the new school year approached, I became more panicked about starting my A-levels with none of my friends talking to me. I started humming to calm myself down, biting my nails until they were raw. The weekend before the start of term, I was left with only my parents to ask for advice. Dad was the one I'd usually approach but he was at another dentists' conference. Out of sheer desperation, I asked my mother for advice, fully expecting to be told I was being silly. Instead she made me sit with her and roll the *pundi* for a dish called *yetti pundi*, a coconut-based prawn curry accompanied by rice dumplings. It was a very labour-intensive dish and was being made as a treat for Dad's return. I groaned at having to do chores, but rolling the rice into little balls was unexpectedly soothing.

I didn't tell her about why my friends and I had fallen out – I wasn't that stupid – but as we prepared the dish, I remember her saying that she'd grown up in a big family, and what she'd learned was that you couldn't avoid conflict. You couldn't control someone else's actions and reactions, and the best you could do was to learn how to handle disagreements in a way that you felt comfortable with. I don't think I fully understood her advice then, because I was so consumed with feeling betrayed and angry at the girls, but I remember thinking, *I'm so glad I came to you.* But then the next time I came to her with a problem, she told me I was overreacting, and we went back to not talking about things.

Something about the parallels between then and now resonated enough for me to call her. We hadn't spoken since our abrupt conversation at Ama's barbecue.

'Bel,' she said, her voice immediately tight and upset. My mother held onto hurt feelings in the same way that camels can retain water for long periods of time. We exchanged small talk about Dad, how Karen was doing ('she's on her phone ALL the time'). Then: 'Well, I have to go. Dinner won't cook itself,' Mum said. That, along with 'this isn't a hotel', was one of her favourite phrases.

'Mum,' I said gently, 'I'm sorry. I didn't mean to snap at you when we last spoke.'

'You really hurt my feelings,' she said, not without justification. It was hard not to spring onto the defensive when faced with her disappointment, but I tried.

'I know. I think we're all just worried about Devi and want what's best for her, and you're her mother, of course you're worrying the most.'

Mum almost didn't know how to respond to this. The new Bel who didn't snap back at her and then ring off in exasperation. 'I *am* worried,' she said, sounding more mollified. 'But she said she's happy staying with you, and I'm glad the two of you are getting along.'

'She said that?' I asked, eager for every sweet crumb of validation.

'Yes, of course she's happy to be with you, Bel. You're her sister.' But with family, there was always that crucial difference between love and like. I couldn't gauge Devi's feelings purely by her physical proximity to me.

'Thanks, Mum. I've got to go, but I'll see you soon, yeah?' I had noticed Ranvir walking towards me on the street.

'Yes, darling,' she said, and under the warmth of that little epithet, the wall that had been between us at the start of the call, broke into rubble.

I waved at Ranvir to attract her attention. She'd had been away on holiday in Spain, and after I'd turned down her suggestion of after-work drinks a few weeks ago, things between us had lost momentum. But in the spirit of trying anew, after we'd exchanged our hellos and I'd said, 'Oh, wow your tan looks amazing!' I asked if she'd get coffee with me.

'Let me check my diary,' she said.

'No, I mean now. If you don't have any meetings, that is?' She looked at me in surprise then said she'd love to.

As we walked to the coffee shop, she asked me how I was. I replied that everything at work was fine. 'No, Bel, I mean post-accident. Are you feeling okay? Quite well?' In the last few weeks she'd sent a few messages to check in, which was more than Katrina had.

'I'm fine, honest. And I have my sister staying with me for a bit.'

'I think if my sister and I lived together, we'd murder each other,' she laughed.

'You have a sister?'

'Five of them. Each more annoying than the last. Apart from the little one, and she's only a darling because she hasn't had time to turn into a little shit.' There was so much I didn't know about Ranvir but I found myself wanting to learn more.

'My sister and I are getting on surprisingly well at the moment,' I told her. 'She's going through a divorce, which is shit obviously. But it feels like we're becoming friends, and that's precious to me because we didn't get along that well when we were younger. Sorry, I know that sounds weird.'

'No, I don't think so. I mean, it happens the other way around too. I was so close to my oldest sister – I was the fourth of six girls – but when we grew up, we just . . .

drifted apart. And I don't think either of us wants to fix that now,' she said with a shrug.

As we crossed the road, a man in his twenties with excruciatingly tight jeans and a blond mullet tipped his sunglasses down his nose so that he could stare at me appreciatively. I rolled my eyes and Ranvir laughed.

As we waited for our coffees from a fancy new café, Thimbles, I told her how terribly work was going. Tristan had been a no-show at yet another interview. Crispin had then FaceTimed me from his treadmill desk to get a progress report but I'd had nothing new to tell him. Thankfully, he'd been called away by his assistant. The coffee shop was so hipster, one of the attractions was that you could get rare varieties of beans. Little wooden signs peeped out through glass display jars, promising things like: *Hush: harvested from beans grown in the grounds of a Trappist monastery.*

Family talk had segued into telling Ranvir about the sorry state of my love life, and Luke and the barbecue, and wondering whether I should ask him out for a drink. She called me out for being snobby about him living on a boat – her third sister Radhika had done it for about ten years before she had a baby.

'What would you prefer: that he lives with three flatmates who don't clean up after themselves properly? I think life on a boat sounds romantic,' she said. 'And shows he's independent, self-sufficient, all that.'

'And what's stopping you from living on one then?'

She laughed. 'On-demand hot water. And I quite like solid walls.'

'I don't know,' I said. 'He rescued me from that terrible date with Gary the human dolphin, but he may just have been doing that as a friend.'

'Okay,' she said slowly. 'Well, what's your type? I might know someone.'

'I don't really have a type. I mean, I like guys who take care of themselves. Have a decent body. Decent job. I don't really date Asian guys though.'

Ranvir went quiet. 'Why's that?'

'I went to a school that didn't have a lot of Asian pupils. My parents don't really have a big community here. But I went to a fairly Asian uni – Westminster – and when they'd chat me up, it felt a bit claustrophobic. Like if we were in a club and another guy would talk to me, especially a white guy, they'd get all territorial and weird about it.'

'I mean, they *can* get like that,' said Ranvir, 'but they're not *all* like that.'

'I guess I've never really given it a chance. I don't know if I'm attracted to them, you know?'

'No, I don't,' said Ranvir, laughing. 'Racial bias is still bias, we don't have a type programmed into our DNA. Though we do have different experiences. I mean, my community and extended family is huge. It's a big part of my life. The music, the clothes, the food. I'm not a coconut . . . unlike some.' She winked at me.

'Oy! I'm not a coconut,' I said. The waiter signalled our iced coffees were ready.

'You've heard that word a lot, I bet,' she said.

'Well, yeah, but it's not my fault. My parents could

have taught me more about where we come from, but they didn't. They stopped taking us to India with them when we were teenagers. And most of the Asian community here isn't representative of where we're from. The amount of shit I get for not listening to *bhangra,* and I'm like . . . I'm not Punjabi, what's the big deal?'

'Fair enough,' Ranvir said, taking a long slurp of her coffee, 'but you don't think you're attracted to Asian men. And that *is* a problem because it says that you don't find your own kind attractive. To be super Freudian about it, I'd say there's something about your own brown-ness that you don't find attractive.'

'You know,' I said, 'I think I liked you better when I thought you were just another Asian chick gunning for my job.'

'*Maadherchod,*' she said, laughing. 'You don't have to speak Punjabi to understand that, I hope?' I laughed because Punjabi or not, every South Asian understood the word for 'motherfucker'.

'In all seriousness,' she continued, 'I'm engaged to an amazing Asian guy. I've had the whole territorial male bullshit and, believe me, it's not my thing. But Sunil, he's not like that. He supports the fact that I do martial arts. We both go on mates holidays without each other. He's loving, kind, and we let each other do our own things.'

'You do martial arts?' I said with surprise.

'Yeah, BJJ,' she said. 'See? Bet you thought I did Zumba or some shit.' To be honest, Ranvir had skin the colour of buttermilk and a streamlined frame I'd assumed she

POORNA BELL

attained by not eating bread. But when I looked closer, I could see some well-defined muscles.

We were nearing the office and passed one of the Indian IT guys who worked on the third floor. The two of them did an almost imperceptible nod and smiled at each other.

'What was that?' I asked. 'The nod?'

'You don't do the nod when you pass other Asians in the street?' I shook my head.

'Bloody hell, man. I think I'm going to downgrade you from a coconut to a lychee!'

*

'Quick question,' I said to Ama on the phone as I navigated the air bridge connecting a million platforms at Clapham Junction station, where swarms of people carrying bicycles, briefcases, netted bags filled with food for after-work picnics, all streamed past me. 'Am I a coconut?'

She laughed. 'What makes you say that?'

'I got called a coconut today and I haven't heard that for a while. Am I?'

'I can't vouch for any Indian-based activities you may have taken up over the years, but I'd say yes. You're a beautiful little Bounty Bar.'

'But why? What makes me a coconut?'

'Off the top of my head? You don't really wear Indian clothes, I'm fairly sure you don't listen to the music, you don't have that many Asian mates apart from yours truly, you don't go home that often, your parents don't interfere

244

much in your life. Your Indianness is probably evident in your skin colour more than it is in other things.'

'Hang on, doesn't that make *you* a coconut? Aren't these your boxes too?'

'Nope,' she said cheerily. 'You forget that I was in Sri Lanka for the first decade of my life, so I'm Sri Lankan. It's always been a part of my identity and I don't hide it because I'm trying to fit in. Not,' she said hastily, 'that I'm saying you do that. But I had the experience of knowing my home country whereas most of you guys here haven't. It's like the difference between loving someone in real life and loving them only through a photo.'

I was so lost in thought, I only narrowly avoided being whacked by the back wheel of a scooter. 'Bel?' she said worriedly. 'Have I upset you?'

'Not at all. Thank you. It's all food for thought.' I had been so relieved and surprised that Marina hadn't told her about our argument at the barbecue that it would have taken a lot for Ama to upset me. I don't think I realised until that moment that she'd been the first person I'd wanted to consult about Ranvir's teasing. That even though she'd only been back in my life for a brief period of time, I couldn't imagine navigating the rest of my life without Ama.

*

When I got home, Devi had a cookery book open and was wearing her wide polka dot hairband, which meant she was trying something new. 'Bear with me,' she said, 'I'm going to experiment with making buttermilk chicken, but baked and not fried. I saw it on Leilani's TikTok – you know, the one on *My Indian Bae* who dated the Jain guy and had to walk down the street sweeping away insects in front of her?'

I stifled a laugh at how anyone overhearing our conversation might react to the framing of her last sentence. I knew I should shower the day off, but instead I flopped on the sofa. There was a point at which the romance of hot sunny days melted into annoyance as you sat in airless rooms praying for your sweat glands to cease production. 'Devi, can I ask you something?'

'As long as it's not: *Devi, are you sure you're making the right decision?*' she said mimicking our mother.

'Ah, Mum's still trying to get you to reconcile with Fuck Pants then?'

'Don't call him that. But, yes, it's doing my head in. She's the last person I'd go to for marriage advice. Want a beer?' she asked before I could ask her what she meant by that. Mum could be irritating, like a dog with a bone when she had a point to make, but she did have years of a long and successful marriage behind her. I nodded and Devi handed me a cold Peroni. 'OK, what's up?' she said, going back to measuring out spices.

'I'm a coconut, aren't I?'

She laughed. 'What makes you say that?'

'I was chatting to a workmate about it. But – whose fault is that? Is it the fault of Mum and Dad, who didn't bring us up with our own culture much? Or is it the fault of white society, because I feel like I have to fit in and so I've stifled my Indian side?'

'Two things,' she said. 'First, is your mate Asian?'

'She's properly Asian – she can speak Punjabi, does stuff with her community all the time. She's not the dutiful type you and I saw around town when we were kids, though. She's pretty independent, with some unusual hobbies.'

'But Asians aren't homogeneous,' Devi replied. 'She may find it easier to be part of a community if she grew up within it. We didn't. We had no family around us at all. We had only Padmini Auntie in Plymouth and we barely saw her and Rakesh Uncle. Depending on where you are, what colour your skin is – for instance, we're darker-skinned – you might feel more pressure to assimilate than someone whose skin colour is more cream than it is chocolate.'

'What's the second thing?'

'Second thing – is it really important to work out whose fault the situation is, or will it be more useful to you to figure out which parts of yourself you've been suppressing and start being reconciled with them?'

'When did you get so disgustingly perceptive?' I said, draining my beer.

'I can't take all the credit, I've been reading and watching these videos on training to be a psychotherapist,' Devi said, putting down the chicken. She looked at me and took a deep breath. 'I've decided I can't stand being an office manager anymore. It's basically like being a parent to adult children, and it's shit. I'm thinking of changing careers and this might be something I want to do.'

'That's incredible, Devi!' I was delighted for her.

'Thanks.' She smiled. 'But back to you. Mum and Dad didn't really bring us up in line with our own culture, that's true. They didn't teach us the language. Plus we lived in a pretty racist part of the country, so it's no wonder you learned to code-switch.'

'Huh? What's code-switching?'

'Karen was telling me about it,' she said. 'It's when you feel you have to present yourself in a certain way so as to assimilate and be accepted. For people like us that might mean altering our accent, how we dress, the things we talk about – especially around white folks.'

'But I don't really feel like I do that. Is that bad?'

'You might not realise you do it because maybe you have been for so long. But here's something else Karen told me – and I know it's ridiculous we're being schooled by my sixteen-year-old. Look at your life and ask yourself how great a part of it reflects your culture. I'm not talking about flying the Indian flag and chanting the National Anthem every morning, but the people you date, your mates, even how you talk at work. Are there people you feel more "yourself" with and others who are hard work? When you see something overtly Asian, do you feel an instinctive need to hide it or move away from it?'

When I was a teenager, Mum tried to make me wear dainty Indian clothes to weddings. I'd refuse, she'd yell at me, and I'd always concede. But once I rebelled and wore my Doc Martens. She was furious when she realised that we were halfway to Slough and I hadn't brought a pair of sandals to change into, but she had also run out of energy to fight me on it.

'I would say that my first instinct is to move away from it,' I said. 'But I also think a big part of that comes from my school days. I don't think I felt confident enough then just to be who I was. It was harder for me with boys because I wasn't white, and didn't have a model's body like Ama. And with others . . . it felt like if I was properly Indian, that would give them more of an excuse to make fun of me, and I think I just wanted to avoid that.'

'Well, yeah, there you go. I made friends with a lot of Asian people at uni,' Devi said, coating the chicken in breadcrumbs. 'That made a massive difference. And even though I moved back to Dartford, I married Nikhil and he comes with a huge extended family. That gives you the breathing room to figure out who you are and how you want to be. I don't think you've ever had that.'

This new information felt like a different type of code. Not to hide behind but to help me understand myself better. It made me realise that perhaps there were ideas I'd been carrying around, about myself, about the world, that were too restrictive and served no purpose anymore.

'I have another important question for you,' I said, getting up to go to the shower as Devi put some more beers in the fridge and started wiping down the kitchen counter. She nodded at me to continue.

'Why are you using the oven during a heatwave?'
She threw a tea towel at my head.

*

The temperature had lowered by the time Karen came over to stay for the weekend. All that accumulated rain massed into dark clouds just as we decided to go to Tate Modern.

After my conversation with Devi and Ranvir, I had decided to go back on Tinder with renewed enthusiasm. Luke hadn't texted after last week's encounter and I was too embarrassed to message him given my outburst at Marina.

Besides, as handsome and mysterious as Luke was, I'd decided to do the mature thing and let things lie. Ama told me the reason he lived on the boat was because of a painful break-up six months previously. He didn't strike me as the type who was looking for stability or commitment and I didn't much fancy having to deal with his emotional baggage. So I decided to try something less complicated. The goal was to arrange a date with a South Asian man. I hadn't realised until now how instinctive it had become for me automatically to swipe left, consigning them straight to the digital dustbin.

I woke up on the morning of what my niece dubbed 'Karen Day' to find three matches and started a conversation with a financial adviser named Arjun. I tended not to date men who worked in finance based on terrible experiences in the past – I found it jarring to talk to someone whose entire life pivoted around money, because usually it led to other conversations I couldn't give two shits about, like the size of their TV or what kind of car they drove. The hypocrisy was not lost on me, given that I was prone to buying the odd piece of designer clothing and liked the members' club lunches we were invited to through work. But I saw these as little flourishes of gold dust in an otherwise down-to-earth existence, versus aspiring solely to make money and show it off.

We'd arranged to meet for a drink at The Ned the following day, a place I normally couldn't stand. It seemed to be *the* place for rich, entitled men to show off the escorts they'd paid for, and for twenty-somethings to acquire a brief taste of a world they couldn't afford to live in full-time. But he'd suggested the place, and I hadn't wanted to seem fussy. Why do the first steps in dating always seem to involve inflicting a million little deaths on the self, tucking away what we really want behind an acceptable shopfront?

Karen turned up at the flat wearing the mint-green Nikes I'd bought her, along with an oversized T-shirt with a screenprint of the Bollywood star Rekha on the front of it, black leggings and sunglasses. 'What?' she said at my look of surprise. 'Rekha is the OG. My friends and I are obsessed with her.'

'How does your daughter get to look more cool than we ever did or ever will?' I grumbled to Devi, who looked at her proudly.

'Some of us are just born with it,' Karen said smugly.

'Remind me again,' I said stuffing an umbrella into my backpack, 'are you Karen today or Kiran?'

'AUNTIE!'

*

Tate Modern on the Southbank was one of my favourite places to wander aimlessly. It stood in a strange, set apart pocket of the urban landscape, located in one of the busiest cities in the world yet still almost magically managing to keep it at a distance. I loved that Karen seemed to like it too. Being here made me feel like an explorer, as if at any moment, I could step into yet another room and find myself passing through to another dimension.

A step to the left might lead to a dim room illuminated only by red lightbulbs wired to switch on and off. A plush curtain might swish open to reveal a rocky cavern beyond; a vast room turn out to be filled with oversized hand-painted globes. Another few steps and you could enter a space the size of a cupboard filled with Polaroids taken of the same person, every day, for the past ten years. The cumulative effect of seeing works that had taken immense amounts of time, and often focused on a single small aspect of life, was to make me wonder at the certainty of the artists' choices. How could they be sure that this was the right detail? The right project? I wondered.

But it was something my niece seemed to understand instinctively. She didn't ask: *why did they do this?* She said: *they did this and it is amazing.*

After an hour of walking around, we decided on our favourite room. It was pitch black except for three wall-to-ceiling screens that played a film of the ocean on a loop. It was shot from the viewpoint of someone standing on the shore, knee-deep in saltwater, facing the oncoming waves. It was called *Grief*.

'I need to pee,' said Devi. 'Don't move.'

Then it was just Karen and myself, sitting on a bench in the middle of the room, watching the ocean that was not an ocean break into a spray of foam at our feet.

'Auntie,' Karen said, 'can we do this again sometime?'

'Yes, of course,' I said, pleased and surprised. 'I'm here whenever you need me.'

Karen didn't say anything for a moment, just bit her lip. 'Yeah, but you haven't always been. I don't mean that in a horrible way but I didn't know if this was a one-off.'

'Aw, that's not true, is it? I've always come to your birthday. Well, not the last two after you said it was embarrassing to have us there.'

'Yeah, but . . .' She hesitated. 'I've seen you more in the last few weeks that I have in the last two years. And it's good. It's really good for Mum too. I know you're busy but . . .'

I stared at the screen, the sound of waves around us. I had long suppressed the guilt I felt about my behaviour towards Karen. I had told Devi that I'd stayed away from the family because I worried I didn't fit in, felt they seemed to have their lives sorted without me, and that was true so far as it went. But it was also easier to stay away. It meant

I didn't have to answer my parents' questions about my lifestyle or undertake family obligations, spend time with Nikhil or deal with Devi's problems. But by evading all of that, I'd missed out on doing so much with Karen.

I cleared my throat to try and stop myself from crying. 'I'm never too busy for you,' I said. 'I know it might take time but I hope you'll come to understand that. I haven't been around much, I know. I'm sorry for that. But . . .' I hesitated, not knowing whether or not to continue. 'I didn't know you were bothered about having me there. You always seemed so glued to your mum, you know?'

'Auntie,' she replied, 'you're a really intelligent lady, but that is the dumbest thing I've heard.'

'You sound just like your mother.'

'Mum is the best,' Karen replied, 'but we can drive each other crazy. She's in my life ALL the time. And isn't that when aunts are meant to step in? To help out when our parents act batshit?'

'Yeah,' I sighed, 'that is what aunts are for.' We both sat in silence for a bit, contemplating the screen. 'Where is your mother?' I asked finally.

'Oh, she's gone for a poo,' Karen said matter-of-factly.

'How do you know?'

'She told us not to move, which means she knew it'd take longer than a pee takes. Do you want some of my Nik Naks?' I was impressed by her mental gymnastics. And her choice of crisps.

'Do you mind if I hug you?'

Karen leaned in. 'I'm sorry,' I said, putting my arms around her. 'I didn't know you needed me. I'm here now, okay?'

'Don't make it weird,' she said into my sweatshirt.

*

Something had shifted between me and Karen. I wanted to know what kind of music she liked, where she shopped for clothes, who her friends were, what kind of TV programmes she watched, why she liked football. I also knew that when I got like this about a person, I had a bad habit of overwhelming them with my attention and love.

Rather than doing that with my niece, I asked her to send me a few recommendations of Asian Gen Y Instagram accounts to follow. She sent them, plus a few suggestions for Spotify: 'Because I know your taste in music is terrible without even needing to look at your playlist, Auntie.'

I lost myself in the profiles of these confident, incredible girls and women, and also South Asians who felt proud and safe enough to declare themselves trans, non-binary or gay. The LGBTQ+ community being non-existent when I grew up. Seeing them now all happy and out there, looking at the sheer talent they had grown in their own bedrooms and then shared with the world, blew my mind. I passed on so many to Ama.

Imagine if we'd had this growing up.

There were South Asian clothes, but not as I knew them. Rather than being carbon copies of the traditional outfits I'd seen my aunts and cousins wear, these were clothes that were ancient and new, different and yet familiar. I saw young girls with body hair, plus-size women lifting weights, girls talking about their bodies, sex and dating, and I was so proud and thankful things were easier for them now but, at the same time, filled with enormous sadness for the insecure girl I had been. For what Ama had struggled with. Did our mothers feel like this when they looked at us? Did Mum look at Devi and me and wonder about the choices she had made for herself?

If I was a coconut, then they were dragon fruit. Beautiful, colourful, multi-faceted.

*

The next day, I stopped scrolling and emerged from the tunnels under Bank station into daylight, to meet Arjun the banker for our first date in the City. The last time I'd had a date in the financial district, it was with Gregor. Every time I came here, fighting my way through a sea of navy and grey suits, it reminded me of the set from a dystopian film.

Just as I walked up the steps into The Ned, my phone pinged. Luke. Yet another example to convince me that hetero men have access to some subterranean database that shows them exactly the right time to text a woman and fuck with her chance at happiness.

Luke: Got those System of a Down tix. Let me know when you want to pick them up.

Was he asking me to come to his bloody boat? As a friend? More than a friend? I had too much going on right now and lacked the brain-space for a full enquiry. Plus, Operation Brown Boy was already underway.

I locked my phone as I entered the palatial ground floor, my heels clicking against the marble. I hated high heels. But this was not the kind of place where one wore trainers or ballet pumps, and I wasn't in the mood to be stared at. It was early but the place was already filling up fast. People in velvet booths drank Old Fashioneds and Martinis while the resident pianist played an instrumental version of 'Bad Romance'. Below my feet was The Vault, an airless underground bar in a converted bank vault accessible to members only, an even worse iteration of upstairs.

Arjun looked exactly like his photo, if a bit smaller, and had pre-booked a table. I liked the forward planning, but I preferred guys with a bigger build. Not necessarily muscled, but while we slept, I wanted to feel like a mouse that had been invited to cuddle up next to a hibernating bear. We said our hellos and, in those first moments, that quick sequence of dating alchemy took place. He seemed relieved I looked like my photo; I reserved judgement. He had a good hairline and decent teeth. But that didn't tell me much – only that I could sleep with this guy and not need ten drinks to find him attractive.

We exchanged small talk, first about our respective journeys. He'd only had a five-minute walk while I'd had to sweat for twenty minutes on the Central line. Somewhere on my mental dating scoreboard, a mark against Arjun appeared. Then we talked about family. He had two elder sisters and his parents had married young. He raised his eyebrows when I said my sister was getting a divorce but then he told me he wished one of his sisters would do the same. She was in a bad marriage, profoundly unhappy, and didn't want to leave because of her children.

'Have you been on dating apps for long?' he asked.

I never knew how to answer this. If you said 'a while', it made you sound like a supermarket chicken that had passed its sell-by date, and if you said 'recently', it led to questions about your previous boyfriend and why it ended. I had slept with a lot of people, gone on a few consecutive dates – like IT Alex from the office – but I hadn't had a serious boyfriend since Gregor.

Arjun been single for about nine months, he said, and was looking to meet someone 'normal' and settle down. I remarked that it was a bold choice, choosing Tinder as a place to meet his future wife. He barked a laugh but I wasn't convinced he got my sense of humour.

'What are you looking for then? What do you want your life to look like?' he asked me.

Another question I never knew how to answer. If you brought Five Year Plan energy into a first date, it put so much pressure on what questions to ask, how to present yourself. I had a tier system when it came to dating expectations. At the bottom was the hope that, at the very least, I'd get a shag out of it. Moving upwards, it ranged from second date to regular shag to long-term prospects. Since Gregor, no one I'd met came anywhere near the long-term tier.

As he talked about what he did in his spare time – he liked to cycle on Box Hill and was passionate about IPA beer – I became aware of a pattern I'd fallen into. Barely had a sentence left Arjun's lips than my brain had already worked out and processed what he was going to say next, exactly how he was going to think.

His hair carried a curl that was just about tamed by his short haircut, but I couldn't imagine what it would look like mussed, while he slept next to me. I looked at the deep chestnut brown skin of his hands and imagined them entwined with mine, but I couldn't picture them exploring anywhere else on my body. His shirt was immaculately pressed, his shoes shiny. He was a well-presented man, and I wasn't attracted to any part of him. There was something about him that was familiar while at the same time leading me down a path I wasn't yet ready to take. There was still too much here to decode, to learn about myself.

I must have looked distracted because he asked: 'What are you thinking about?'

Some people are terrible liars, but not me. I tell myself I'm an actor playing a part. I need to be convincing for only a brief period and then it's over. But something about

Arjun, and the fact that my head was already overcrowded with challenging thoughts, made me say: 'I was thinking about how this is the first date I've ever been on with an Asian guy. I don't usually date fellow browns.'

I'd said it to be witty but the moment the words were out, I realised they sounded supercilious and vain. The sort of thing I'd heard too many times when a white guy would turn up to a date saying it was the first time he'd dated an Asian woman – to make you feel like you were the exception, and the rest of your race were gargoyles.

His jet-black eyes widened. 'What, *ever*?'

I nodded.

'I don't even know what to say to that,' he said. 'I mean, why not? Actually, no, don't answer that. How about: why now?'

I shrugged. 'Some things happened recently that made me question the choices I've made, and . . . this is one of them.'

'So I'm some kind of social experiment in your *Eat, Pray, Love* journey?' He looked really pissed off. 'Let me guess: you don't date Asian guys because you think we're all going to make you give up your career and peel potatoes? Or that we won't let you wear what you want?'

'No, I—'

'If I were to look at you and assume that all you want is marriage and babies, or for me to buy you expensive handbags, that would not be okay, would it?'

'Look, I'm sorry.'

'You seem like a catch,' Arjun barrelled on. 'You have

a lot going for you. But this sense of superiority you gain by distancing yourself from your own kind? White people are never going to accept or respect you for it. They don't understand the cost and they don't understand the sacrifice.'

He was right. Not the bit about white people – I had been loved and loved several who had accepted and respected me for who I was. And not everyone made stupid assumptions about arranged marriage and whether I only ate curry. But he was right about me distancing myself from others like me. He took a few sips of his drink and looked at me sideways as I stayed quiet. 'What are you thinking?'

'You seem like a great guy. You're clever and perceptive, which is not what I expected from a finance guy. And I don't mean that in a patronising way . . . it's just the last banker I dated got drunk and then windmilled his penis to the entire pub.'

Despite obviously being furious, Arjun laughed. 'Yeah, I can't argue with that. My colleagues do like their drunken nudity.'

'I am sorry,' I said sincerely. 'I know I've blown it and I don't think I came on this date for the right reasons, but it was good meeting you.'

'Well,' he said, finishing his drink, 'while we won't be arranging our wedding anytime soon, that doesn't mean we can't have a bit of fun. You know, I live quite close to here if you wanted to come back to mine. We could mess about a bit?'

Then I realised that while it wasn't fair to judge Arjun

by the colour of his skin, it also didn't mean he was exempt from being a creep.

'Gross,' I said, grabbing my handbag.

'Oh, *now* you're frigid?' he said, laughing.

I unmatched him on Tinder before my heels passed over the threshold of the front door.

12

The day before Ama's hen do, I went to pick up the gig tickets from Luke. I was on the fence about going but after the encounter with Arjun I wanted to be around a man who didn't make me want to shed my skin like a snake. Luke had taken the week off, he said, and had decided to spend the time doing maintenance on his boat. He was docked at Teddington Lock, which wasn't that far from Battersea.

In this quiet, leafy suburb of south-west London, pretty wedding dress shops sat alongside nail salons; independent coffee shops with hand-stamped paper cups displayed homemade cakes. A little local pub already had people sitting out at wooden tables enjoying a pint in the morning sun. In the distance, I saw the glint of the river.

Boats lined the moorings, all shapes and sizes of them, some decrepit and peeling, others pristine in fresh paint. I was keeping an eye out for Luke's – *Serenity* – when the world's ugliest dog loped towards me, happy and drooling. As I stooped to pet it, half-grimacing but feeling I'd go to hell if I didn't, a deep voice intoned: 'Bosco!' I looked up and saw Luke's silhouette outlined against the blue sky, with a hammer in one hand. 'Well done then, you found it.'

'Is this the famous Bosco, eater of wedding dresses?'

Luke laughed. 'Yes, his owner is still away and Bron begged me to take him. Come aboard.' I stepped up a short gangplank and down onto the deck.

I'd planned to turn up, ask for the tickets and leave almost straight away, but something about this place made time move slower. I could feel the swell of the river in the varnished boards beneath my feet, regular, soothing. 'Cup of tea?' he asked, and I said yes. He took some steep steps down below deck. As I followed, so did Bosco. Luke's boat was surprisingly clean and tidy. Everything had its proper place in the ranks of cupboards and drawers that sprouted off every available surface.

'Shoo,' he said, 'get back upstairs.' And with firm hands steered me towards the ladder. He smelled of soap. The pressure of his skin against mine, and being that close to him, almost made me unravel. He looked at me as if catching the quickening in my body. Before it could turn into anything, I cleared my throat.

'Why does *he* get to stay?' I said, pointing a finger at Bosco.

'Because *he* is not conducting a silent survey like a bailiff. Go on, enjoy the view. I'll bring the tea up.'

A few minutes later, we were sitting in canvas chairs on the deck. I closed my eyes against the sun, letting the sweet, beautiful warmth pass through me. Feeling the tiniest but most powerful pleasure there is: just being alive.

'You look peaceful,' said Luke, breaking the silence. 'Maybe you aren't as ill-suited to boats as you think.'

I snorted and kept my eyes closed. 'Why, are you looking for a boat wife?'

He laughed. 'Not a chance. I moved here to be away from wives and women, thank you very much.'

'And yet, here sits a female human,' I smiled lazily. 'But seriously, is that true?'

'Yes,' he said after a long pause. 'Bad break-up. Found that being surrounded by concrete and steel made me feel terrible in here,' he tapped the side of his head, 'so I moved to the water. I was brought up on a farm, which I know isn't the same, but it makes me feel peaceful.'

'Dating is *hard*,' I said. He didn't reply.

We sat in peaceful silence. 'Are you dating anyone?' he asked after a while. For the first time, I heard the faintest note of vulnerability in his voice.

'No,' I murmured. 'It's not just because the dating scene is trash. I don't know what I want. I feel like I'm supposed to want to meet someone to settle down with, but I can't begin to imagine what that person would be like. My sister is going through a divorce and that has shaken my belief in marriage a bit. And I don't even know if I want a forever love. I mean, what is forever these days anyway?'

'Don't ask me,' he said and tipped out a packet of Hobnobs. 'There are many ways to love. It's weird that we only seem to pursue and prioritise one type.' I was pleasantly surprised by our chat; I hadn't expected Luke to have such depth to him, I realised.

'Like me and Ama, for instance,' I said. He raised an eyebrow. 'No, not like that. We're reconnecting after a long time apart and I've never stopped loving her. After all this time. That friendship didn't end, it just got put on hold.'

'What about your other friends,' he asked, 'the ones you don't talk to any longer?'

I had already decided I would apologise to Marina if I saw her at the hen do. It didn't take much to apologise to someone when you were mostly indifferent to the outcome. But Ling . . . the love between us had been deeper. That hurt cut through all that shared history like a laser through rock.

'Probably not,' I replied. 'It takes two to repair something that is utterly fucked, and with those two, I'd have to do all the work myself.' I didn't really want to keep talking about my feelings, so I did what my dad tended to do and deflected the conversation.

'So what's this maintenance work you're doing?' I asked. 'It must be significant if you're taking the week off.'

Luke looked at me wryly, as if he knew exactly what I was doing. But he played along.

'Remember when we met and I told you the electricity wasn't working?' I nodded. 'I've had to overhaul the electrics, and that's meant taking up some of the decking.' He pointed to one end where planks of wood were neatly stacked. 'I need to get that nailed down. But it's a two-person job and I'm struggling to get any of my mates to come over. Normally I'd ask Bron but she's busy with wedding prep.'

'I can help you,' I said. Seeing his shocked expression, I continued: 'Seriously. I know how to do this type of stuff, my dad taught me a few things. Just tell me what you need doing.'

As I held the planks steady for Luke to hammer nails into, I had the answer to my question as to whether we were meant to be mates or something more. He couldn't stop sneaking sidelong glances at me, and as was always the way when I knew someone liked me, I kept avoiding them. I never knew how to cross that bridge between platonic and romantic without it becoming embarrassing. After an hour of sweaty work, I checked the time and realised I had to go. Devi was cooking dinner and Yorkshire puddings waited for nobody.

As Luke headed downstairs, I wiped my hands on a cloth I'd found slung over the side. I was glad I'd come but I was leaving with more questions than I'd arrived with. Bosco had loped up to sunbathe on the deck and looked at me with his head cocked to one side as if to say: *What now?*

'Don't ask me, dog,' I said.

'Are you talking to the dog?' Luke said, trying not to laugh.

'You should laugh more often,' I told him, throwing the cloth at his face, 'it suits you.'

And then began a world story. 'Come here,' he said, wiping his freshly washed hands on his jeans. And hesitantly I moved forward. He cupped one callused hand around my face. I nearly stopped breathing. With the other, he wiped away a smudge of grease from my cheek and picked a wood shaving from my hair. 'There,' he said, 'much better. Although grease and wood shavings suit you.'

I blushed right down to my toenails, the latent energy of our withheld kiss pinning my feet in place.

'Right, well, I'll see you,' I said.

'Hang on, here's your ticket.' He gave me the thing I'd come for and as I took the ticket, he grabbed my hand and pulled me tightly to him. Then he kissed me. A good kiss, one that felt soft, intuitive, knowing. My legs curled around him as he lifted me up and set me down on the side of the boat without taking his lips off mine. Bosco was embarrassed and slunk off. A choice hovered in the air – go below with Luke and give in to the desire running through my body. Or pull away and leave, and hope that if this was meant to turn into something, pressing pause now was not going to prevent it.

'I can't,' I said, holding his face in my hands. 'Not because I don't want to, but . . . I need time.'

'No stress,' Luke said, kissing my neck and pulling away. 'It's not a big deal.'

Not a big deal, I thought. People seemed to believe that throwaway words and displays of indifference were to be expected in casual intimacy. I disagreed. It didn't have to lead to marriage or a long-term relationship, but I believed the connection itself mattered, however briefly it lasted. If I had gone downstairs with him, what started out in passion and fire, would have felt hollow with regret and emptiness afterwards.

'Not a big deal,' I repeated, and looked at him, already swallowing that disappointment behind a small smile.

'I didn't mean it like . . .'

'No, understood. Not a problem, I get it. I'd better be going anyway,' I said. 'Thanks for the ticket.' And hurried off the boat and down the path before he could say anything more.

I wanted to text Ama and then realised I couldn't, that I didn't know enough about her present day to be sure my romantic entanglement with Luke wouldn't upset her or piss her off. Maybe I shouldn't have left. Maybe by leaving, I had blown things with Luke. Wasn't that what the old me did – just leave? But every step I took forward made it harder for me to turn back, and on the train home, the regret around Luke came anyway, just not in the way I expected.

*

The next day, Devi and I were on the train back to Kent for Ama's hen do. My sister had very generously been offered a place as my plus one to that too, and was also overdue a visit to check up on Nikhil and the house.

'You know, Anju is going to lose her shit when she realises that I'm not going to be staying at theirs, right?' I said to Devi as the train pulled away from Crayford station. It was nice having company for once on the way to Mum and Dad's.

'Don't call Mum "Anju",' she groaned.

'Why?'

'Because if one day Karen calls me Devi, I would hate it. She carried you for nine months and fed you for however long.' My sister pinched the bridge of her nose. 'Sorry,' she said, 'I don't mean to nag but going back home is stressing me out. It's been nice having a holiday from my life.'

'We're only back for the weekend,' I said reassuringly, while peering out of the window at a group of teenagers with their hair gelled back and pulled into high buns. Their microbladed eyebrows looked terrifying, as if they'd gone rogue with a Sharpie.

'I know,' Devi replied morosely, 'but at some point, I do need to return for good.' We both sat in silence, contemplating the prospect. We'd got used to each other. Caring for each other. Issuing reminders about the next episode of *My Indian Bae*. Making sure dinner was in the fridge; Post-Its with little smiley faces stuck to the handle of the kettle. Tiny ways we'd knitted our lives together, forgetting we'd have to unravel them at some point. 'I hate being a grown-up,' my sister said.

'Me too,' I told her.

*

Dad picked us up from the station. After dropping Devi at her place, he handed me the house key. 'How late do you think you'll be?' he asked.

'Actually I'm going to stay at Devi's, Dad. You know you and Mum will have a heart attack if I'm back later than eleven.'

When I was a teenager, Dad would sit in his favourite armchair in near darkness, waiting for me to come home. The first time it happened, I almost had an out-of-body experience. It was unfortunate timing that this was also the first time I decided to try a weed brownie. After that, when I knew we'd be drinking or taking drugs, I'd stay over at Ama's whose mother would either be working or asleep like a normal person. Or if I knew I had to come home, I made sure I was sober.

'Well, you'll always be my baby, Bel,' Dad said, his bushy moustache twitching with the effort of trying not to laugh. 'Get it? Baby . . .'

I groaned. 'Where's Mum?'

'She's at the shops but said she wants you to sort through the rest of your things, I'm afraid.'

'Ugh. You sure there's nothing you need help with in the garage?'

'Nice try, but she'll be cross if it doesn't get done before you leave. Also keep the key. You should have our key in case of emergency.'

I took it and worked it around my keyring until it nestled against my flat's keys and Devi's. I looked at him. 'She knows that Devi isn't going to move in with you guys, doesn't she?'

'Bel,' sighed my father. 'You know your mother prefers to operate within her own reality.'

*

My *Badass Rock Tunes Mix Tape* was midway through Garbage's 'Stupid Girl' and I was trying to detangle a nest of friendship bracelets. 'Hi, darling, sorry I missed you getting here. Tea?' Mum said, popping her head around the door.

She came up a few minutes later with two steaming mugs and took a seat on the worn ottoman. 'I really need to re-upholster this,' she said, frowning at the fabric.

'Mum,' I said, quickly gathering some letters so she couldn't see the medley of cocks scrawled on top of them. 'I've been thinking about a few things. Why weren't Devi and I brought up with much Indian stuff around?'

'I don't think that was the case,' she said, a touch defensively. 'We always made Indian food at home. We have a Gods shrine. We celebrate Diwali, don't we?'

'I'm not blaming you – I'm just saying that other Asians learned their language, even went to a special school to do it. They hung out with their cousins . . . other people in their community. We didn't really do any of that.'

'Would you have wanted to go to a special school just to learn Kannada or Bengali?' she said. 'I'm pretty sure both you and your sister would have screamed blue murder.'

'Yeah, I guess so.' She was right. If she had made me go to a Sunday School or anything that wasn't strictly mandatory, I would have kicked up such a stink. 'But what about community events?'

'Again, would you have wanted to go to those? Dr Patel and his wife would drive all the way to some Gujarati community centre – no non-veg food, by the way – with no games or entertainment apart from kids singing songs and reciting poetry.'

She was right. It sounded like hell.

'I know we probably didn't get it right with everything we did,' she continued, 'and maybe we should have introduced you to a bit more, but your dad and I didn't share the same mother tongue, and we didn't want to push both languages down your throat. We thought you'd learn what you needed to because you were our children, living in an Indian household, and that you'd make your own choices.'

'I get it but . . . why didn't you take us to India with you more? I can remember you going or Dad going, but I don't remember us being out there as a family very much.'

She sighed. 'You may have a point there. But being an adult is hard, Bel. I know you remember things from your teenage years and question why we did this or that, but at the time we were only a bit older than you are now, still trying to figure things out. You think you know how it was for us, but you don't. Your father and I went through a lot at that time. We did take you both back to India at the beginning but it was such hard work. With his family in Bangalore and mine in Kolkata, it was a lot. And perhaps it was selfish of us, but your dad and I really needed to spend that time in India together and not have to worry about you girls all the time.'

I'd never really thought of my parents as they had been when they were young. All I saw, when I looked at the past, was my own history. It didn't occur to me that I was judging their parenting choices, expecting them to have been fully formed, infallible adults at an age when I could barely sustain a second date.

'Is there anything for lunch?' I said, shovelling the last

of the letters back into the sack. A silly question. There was always something for lunch.

'Come,' my mother said, 'I'll show you what's in the fridge. Dad said you're staying at Devi's tonight. Are you heading there in a bit?'

'Yeah. Mum?'

'Yes?'

'I don't want to get into a fight about it like last time, but could you ease off her about working things out with Nikhil? She's finding things hard enough.'

My mother pursed her lips. 'I know you're doing it with the best of intentions,' I continued, 'but to quote what you said – you think you know, but you don't know. She needs our support, Mum, that's it.'

A flicker of sadness came into Mum's eyes, as she nodded and left the room.

*

As much as I loved Ama, the pre-club drinks at her mum's place sounded like the stuff of nightmares. One of her nurse friends, a highly enthusiastic lady named Laura, told us all to be there promptly for some 'games' and lots of 'Secco'.

I much preferred the alternative Devi proposed, which was getting ready round hers while listening to Rihanna. Karen was old enough to look after herself and was spending an evening in with Jas.

To avoid the jitters I'd felt before the barbecue, I'd

asked Ama whether Ling might be there. She had been noticeably absent so far from the wedding preparations. She worked as a lawyer, Ama said, and was married to a property developer who often left her to deal with child-care on her own. She was supposed to come to the hen party, but he'd just announced he was going away for a weekend of golfing with his buddies, so it was unlikely she'd make it. Babysitting for one or two kids could be sorted at short notice, but four children required a military operation.

Imagining Ling as a mother required some suspension of disbelief. I remembered her as someone who was fun to be around but fundamentally fragile. Devi and I may have had our problems, but growing up with a sibling was better than growing up as an only child in a house where no one was on her side. I knew, despite all of our family dysfunction, that somewhere in my life there was a unit if I wanted and needed it. But Ling, I was starting to realise, had never had that. In her own home, she had been lonely, given that both her parents made her feel as if she never lived up to their expectations.

The recalibration of my relationships with Ama and Devi had already shown me what I was capable of. I might never forgive Ling for her behaviour in the past, and I would never be friends again with her, but I could try to understand her. The news she might be there didn't fill me with the abyss of terror I'd expected, but I still felt that cord of anxiety knotting somewhere deep inside.

Upstairs, while drinking a horribly strong vodka and

soda, I vetoed Devi's outfit. 'This is a hen do, not drinks at the local Wetherspoons. No jeans and top – find a dress.'

My phone pinged.

I groaned. It was just Katrina sending me photos of her holiday. I'd hoped it might be Luke, but I hadn't heard from him since we'd kissed and left things a bit awkwardly.

I put my phone on silent and turned my attention back to Devi. I was pleased Ama had invited her, but concerned about how tacky the night might be. Ama had decided to go down the 'let's pick somewhere so shit that it will be funny' route and had chosen the nightclub of our younger days: Zen's. Now called Snaps, it also held the lofty accolade of 'Kent's Most Dangerous Nightclub' according to the local newspaper.

'Who was that?' Devi asked while pulling on a dress that looked insanely good on her – like liquid night.

'My friend Katrina. I thought it was Luke. Where has *this* been hiding?' I breathed.

'It's new. And don't change the subject. Luke – the hot firefighter guy from the barbecue, right? Moody and brooding?'

I almost held back from telling her what had happened. Previously, any stories about my love life would have met with disapproval. But things had changed lately. I'd give her a chance. 'We kissed yesterday when I went to go pick up the tickets.'

'WHAT?' Devi said, throwing her mascara at me. 'You came back home and ate two goddamn' Yorkshire puddings and didn't say a SINGLE word to me about this!'

I groaned. 'I know, I know, but not because I didn't want to. I'm still figuring out what to do here. If I'd told you, you'd either have told me off or said I should give him a chance – and I need to make my own choices.'

'Why would I tell you off?' said Dev, her brow wrinkling in confusion.

'Well, that's what you used to do,' I reminded her.

She sniffed, deciding between getting mad or satisfying her curiosity. 'Do *you* like him?'

'I do, but I can't tell if it's a 'I just really want to shag you' thing or something more. And he's mates with Bron, so the shag-without-consequences isn't an option. But neither do I know if I want something more significant.'

'Baby sister,' Devi said, 'it sounds to me like you're overthinking this. So what if he's not The One? Just have fun.'

*

When I was seventeen, there were dazzling neon lights outside Snaps, and inside plush carpet and a long bar that stretched into the distance, with bottles of exotic and rare alcohol lining the back wall. Riding high on the euphoria of making it past the bouncers without being ID-ed, I was always awed by the glamorous people I saw in the club, wafting around in clouds of hairspray and Lynx. Now it was apparent that as nightclubs went, it was the equivalent of a petrol station sandwich: girls smoothing down ill-fitting dresses, boys in flowery shirts and hair wax, eyes darting in the hope of being noticed. When we were younger, we'd always laugh at the older people we'd see dancing around ice buckets holding bottles of champagne, avoiding them and their diminished collagen levels as if ageing was contagious. And now, that was us.

After the flurry of introductions to Ama's friends, some of whom I'd seen at the barbecue, Devi offered to get us drinks at the bar. Some of our old school lot would be coming later, Ama said, looking absolutely devastating in a tiny black snakeskin dress and a Bride-To-Be sash. Marina, who'd gone for 'Secco' at Ama's place, was standing next to her alongside Claire Forster, a girl we went to school with. I remembered how she'd loved horses. She still had the same haircut – a long brown bob and a fringe, now streaked with grey. On the other side of Ama, her weasel face unforget-table, was Bethany Barratt, of 'you've got BO' fame. I said hello to Claire, ignored Bethany and debated whether to talk to Marina, but she looked straight through me as if I were made of glass. No sign of Ling, I noted with some relief. Excusing myself, I went in search of Devi.

'Well, well,' I heard a familiar voice drawl. My sixteen-year-old self would have fainted. My thirty-six-year-old self longed to be swallowed up by the ground or, failing that, at home watching TV. I turned around to see Skate-board Steve. This was starting to feel like a version of *A Christmas Carol*, where the Ghosts of Pre-Accident Beryl were coming to pass. How many more termites were due to crawl out of the woodwork?

A polite way to describe Steve would be that his face

looked 'lived in'. Crow's feet furrowed the skin towards his temples, and his eyes were watery and dilated, speaking of nights of bad sleep on sofa beds, missed dinners, grifting and grafting. His two semi-redeeming features were his hair, which was still thick and lush with a surprisingly well-maintained undercut (perhaps June's handiwork), and the fact that he was covered in tattoos, which I liked on a man even though I didn't have any myself.

'Beryl Kumar,' he said with a smile that was toothier than I remembered. 'Don't you look stunning. Mum said she saw you the other week. Apparently you turned her down on taking my number. Naughty . . .'

I laughed despite the awkwardness of the situation. 'Steve. What are you doing here?' I asked, surprised he even remembered who I was.

'Ama sent out a Facebook invite to the old school lot. I wasn't going to come, I mean . . . look at this dump. But you know Ama. She does a lot for other people and that, so I thought I'd make an appearance. I'm glad I did.' Ama and I had done our A-levels at different schools, and I had forgotten that classes between her school and the boys' sixth-form college down the road had merged. Hence, Steve.

He looked me up and down, grinning. 'Can I buy you a drink?' While my submerged teenage self said 'YES SAY YES', my adult self noted the way he slurred his words.

'Actually,' I said, 'my sister has just bought drinks. But maybe later?'

*

Devi and I decided the only way we could get through the evening was by committing to getting drunk. After lining our stomachs with vodka while getting ready, we started our Snaps journey with Sambuca shots, and then moved on to Prosecco. I saw flashes of Marina through the crowd and part of me longed to tell her about my encounter with Steve, regretting I couldn't. Devi didn't understand the nuances because she hadn't been part of that period in history. When I pointed out Steve, she just said: 'Ew.'

Time grew elastic the more I drank. It felt as if we had been there both hours and mere minutes. I was entering the dangerous territory of Attempting To Make My Own Fun. While sitting on the toilet, I debated whether to text Luke and ask him to meet for a drink. It seemed like a great idea, but before I could tap out a message, I heard raised voices. I craned my ear towards the 'Sharon Woz Ere' graffiti on the door.

'You nudged me and made me drop my Mac eye-shadow. That's twelve pounds!' I heard a woman yell.

'I didn't do it on purpose!' someone replied, defensively but also sounding scared. Oh, no. I recognised that voice. Either I could bide my time and pretend I was having a poop, or do the right thing and help her out.

I took a deep breath and squared my shoulders, puffing myself up like a pigeon entering battle over a piece of bread.

'Hey, Marina,' I said as I came out of the cubicle. 'Everything alright?' I looked at the two young women who had

her backed into a corner. It was strange to see Marina looking so small within herself. One bully had a gelled pony-
tail scraped up to the top of her head and was wearing a
cut-out pink jumpsuit. The other had an Adidas tracksuit
top over a neon green mini-skirt.

'Who the fuck are you?' the girl in the pink jumpsuit
said to me. She was in her late teens, at best, twenty. The
older I grew, the more I realised that age was a super-
power. It made me not give a shit about certain things,
and one of them was being intimidated by a girl barely
old enough to vote. Plus I had the element of surprise on
my side. White folk don't know how to handle aggressive Asian women. To them it's like being confronted by
a savage poodle. Never mind that I couldn't fight and all I
could hope was that they'd leave us alone, I had to give the
appearance of being mad enough to do and say anything.

'I'm her fucking friend!' I said and stared at Pink
Jumpsuit, praying she wouldn't stab me with a hair clip.
I couldn't believe I was putting myself out like this for
Marina.

'Your *friend* owes me a MAC eyeshadow,' she snapped,
but backed off imperceptibly. The other thing about being
older and solvent is that you can always buy your way
out of situations.

I crossed my arms. 'Maybe rather than us all yelling
about it, why not let my friend buy you ladies a bottle of
wine to make up for the inconvenience?'

Pink Jumpsuit had already taken a deep breath to argue
back, like a dragon sucking in oxygen before spouting out

a huge flame. 'Oh,' she said, holding fire mid-way. She looked at her friend who shrugged. 'I *suppose* that might be alright,' she sniffed. 'But none of that house shit. Something decent.'

Once the ladies were ushered out of the toilet and settled with their bottle at a table far away from us, Marina and I stood against the bar, facing the crowd. She looked at me sideways. 'Thanks,' she said. 'You didn't have to do that.' She handed me a shot of tequila, and although I was certain that it would tip me over from drunk to very drunk, I felt I couldn't say no.

Ranvir once gave me the best advice when it came to talking to someone after a fight, which was: think about how you'd like to feel at the end of the conversation. I didn't want to be best mates with Marina, but nor did I want my skin to prickle whenever I was around her. I had worked a lot over the years on managing my temper and not flaring up, and felt as if being around these people I hadn't seen in years made me regress to the person I no longer was or wanted to be.

'I'm sorry,' I said looking at her. 'About how I was at the barbecue. It wasn't okay to talk to you like that.'

I don't think I'd ever apologised to Marina, ever. Back then we just ignored each other until we forgot what we were fighting about. 'No, I'm sorry,' she said, turning to face me. It was the first time she'd ever apologised to me. 'I shouldn't have laughed at you. It must have been awful. The accident.'

'It was,' I said truthfully. I was tired of saying it was

fine and 'not that bad'. 'But I am better now. Also Ama's barbecue was a good reminder of why I don't day drink anymore.'

'Tell me about it,' she said. 'My hangover was insane. And it lasted two days. Why did no one warn us about two-day hangovers?' I laughed, relieved that we were having a normal conversation. I think she felt the same. We weren't the same people, and maybe we didn't have to ruin an entire evening by simmering with rage as we'd done in the past. 'Do you remember that day in Cornwall,' she said slowly as if testing the water with me, 'when we spent the whole day drinking on the beach? Wasted on my uncle's terrible bathtub wine. And my cousin India sunburned her feet and had to walk around wearing two supermarket bags filled with ice strapped to them?'

'Ah, India,' I laughed. 'How is she? Still wearing flower crowns?'

'You won't believe this but she works for an oil company,' Marina said, giggling. The thought of India – she who had a flower-power keyring and only bathed once a week to conserve bathwater – working in such an environmentally brutal industry was so ridiculous, it made me throw my head back and laugh with her.

When we finally stopped, the lightness we'd felt was quickly replaced by that familiar constraint. I didn't see how it could ever be lifted unless we talked about things.

'Marina . . .' I began.

'We don't have to,' she said abruptly, guessing what I was going to say. 'We can, if you want to. But I want you

283

to know, I'm not holding onto it. Things can be as light or as heavy as we want to make them.'

What was I holding onto? I wanted an apology. I wanted her and Ling to say they had fucked up, and they were sorry, and they shouldn't have cut me out. I wanted to tell her how much it had hurt me, how it had meant I never properly trusted people again, that I found it easy to make friends but hard to keep them. That groups of women still made my breath hitch uncomfortably because being in them didn't feel safe. But I also knew that I didn't get to write the story of how it went. That even if she apologised, and I got to say all of that, it didn't change the past. All I could control was the future and decide the type of person I wanted to be.

'I don't want to hold onto it,' I said. 'We don't have to be mates but we can be . . . decent to each other.' She nodded. We stood next to each other. Earlier in our history, we might have reached out and said: 'Skin?' And all would have been forgiven. But we were grown-ups now, and our hearts had been knocked about too much for us to believe in easy endings. We stood in silence until Marina's face lit up and I saw who had entered the club.

Ling.

*

Devi was of no use. She was talking to a well-built bald white man in his late forties, who wore a short-sleeved blue shirt and actually looked fairly decent. For Snaps, anyway. His name was Tony and he was the single dad of a girl Karen went to school with. While Tony fetched drinks, my sister said she was fine but please could I bugger off for a bit so she could talk to him? 'If I need rescuing I'll holler, but I'm not a child, B. I can handle myself,' she said firmly and steered me away.

Seeing Ling made me regret not having eaten properly before we left. Usually I favoured a minimum of two slices of bread to act as a booze mattress but we'd run out of time. The sensation of something pressing down on my chest was accompanied by feeling as if my blood had been replaced with jet fuel. The sight of Ling was the lit match.

As I saw Marina hug her, and then Ama, it was my worst nightmare realised. Every friendship group has its unique shape and history. I realised that they had been friends with each other far longer than they had with me, and the shift that knowledge brought felt horribly similar to the moment when my feet met empty air before I plunged into the cellar.

Ling saw me and reflected in her gaze was mild curiosity but also something worse: indifference. What had mattered so much to me, had not mattered to her at all, it seemed. I stood outside the group, looking in. The dread that opened within me wasn't about what I'd say to Ling. It was facing the prospect that I might lose Ama to her all over again.

The best thing I could do was to remove myself and go home, I thought, but Devi was nowhere to be seen. As I sat in a corner gloomily nursing an Espresso Martini, I attempted to text Luke but couldn't quite see the screen – the letters were swimming in front of my eyes.

'There you are!' Ama said brightly. 'What are you doing over here? You know who's come, don't you? Skateboard Steve.' She waggled her eyebrows. 'I wanted to keep it a surprise.' But I didn't smile back.

I looked over to where Marina and Ling were doing shots and said: 'I can't.' I wanted to be there for Ama, and have fun, and do all the things a friend was supposed to, but I couldn't.

'Oh, that?' she said, looking over at them. 'It's all fine now, surely. Water under the bridge. Ling doesn't care.' *Ling doesn't care. But I do. So what does that say about me?*

'It's not fine for me,' I said morosely. 'Ama, I don't want to be that one friend who fucks up your hen do and makes it about me. But it's . . . hard seeing everyone together again.'

'I don't know what to do with that, Bel,' she said exasperatedly. 'I want everyone to have a good time. Do we have to talk about this now?'

'No!' I said, 'I don't want to talk about this now, that's what I'm trying to say. This isn't coming out right. I'm drunk, you're drunk.'

'I'm not drunk,' she said in the high pitch of someone who was fairly drunk. 'Look, just come and dance with us and it will be fine.'

I stared at her. Ama wanted everyone to get along and have a good time, and sometimes that wasn't possible. She had chosen a side back then, and she was choosing a side now. At least that's what it felt like.

'You know what? I'm good here,' I said. 'I'm just waiting for Devi and then we might head home. Go out there, dance, have a good time – I'm sure Ling and Marina will make it the best night for you.' The bitterness I placed on their names stuck in her throat.

Ama looked at me, eyes creased in disbelief. 'I can't believe we're back here again,' she said.

'Ama, I don't want to . . .'

'This isn't a big deal, Bel, so much time has passed. Can't you let it go?' When I didn't say anything, she said: 'Fine.' Holding her hands up to end the conversation. She tottered back to her friends, adjusting her hen do sash. I felt sick. I drained my drink; wanting the alcohol to epilate every ounce of upset from my body, until I didn't want to feel or think anymore.

'Enjoying yourself?' Steve said, sitting down next to me with epically bad timing.

'What do you think?' I replied, willing him to go away.

'I did mean what I said earlier, by the way,' he said wistfully. 'I know I was an idiot at school – but you are beautiful. I regret not making a move.'

I wasn't sure if it was the nostalgia that billowed around us like dry ice, the pre-game vodka, the shots of Sambuca earlier or the Martini, but I looked at Steve and something in me yearned to feel better about myself. I leaned in and kissed him, hoping to breathe in something of my past, the innocence of that time before decisions were made and things that couldn't be taken back. Steve was a surprisingly good kisser – not too much tongue and soft lips. But then I pulled away and remembered that I was at Snaps, kissing the guy I'd liked when I was sixteen. Everything seemed smaller and sadder.

A wolf whistle cut through the room, and I saw Ling whisper in Marina's ear while looking over at me in Steve's embrace, with some of our other school friends cheering. Ama was the only one not laughing.

I looked at Steve and thought: *I will actually DIE if Ling thought I was still pining after this man, who I'm pretty sure still gets his mother to buy his underwear.* Before I could say or do anything, as a great philosopher once said: sometimes what goes in must come out. I felt a great swell of emotion, a tidal wave of memories and pieces of the present trying to come together. And then, as is the way with the circle of life, I vomited on Steve's lap.

13

On first meeting Ben, Brandon, Derek and Kevin, Marina missed her chance to ask them to Ama's birthday because the birthday girl had puked up the lion's share of Jasper's wine, and we had to take her home. We hadn't exchanged numbers or MSN messenger IDs, and Ling had been beside herself. Until she realised she was being a selfish arse. Mainly because I'd said to her: 'You're being a selfish arse.'

Since then, the tension hung between us like a boat taking on water. It grew heavier and heavier until at some point, I knew it would capsize.

We'd spent the day after nursing our first-ever hangovers, feeling as if we would die. Until India brought us pizza and Coke. It's not that we hadn't drunk alcohol before but we'd never really suffered its after-effects so severely. After passing out in front of the TV watching videos of *The Lost Boys* and *Heathers*, we woke up the next morning feeling brand new. Having wisely swerved any more of Uncle Jasper's wine, we were all in a much better mood and decided to go and watch some of the bands at the festival. After a couple of hours, the four boys from before spotted us and came over.

'We're having a party,' Ama said. 'It's my sweet sixteen, you have to come.' She didn't fancy any of them, but she also wanted to be a good wing woman to us.

'Are you going to be there?' Brandon said, playfully elbowing me.

'Duh, where else would I be?' I replied, trying not to smile because I didn't want to rub the extra bit of attention in Ling's face.

Unfortunately, she caught our little exchange and said: 'Well, normally you're at home with your parents because they won't let you out, aren't you?'

Even Ama, who usually prided herself on operating neutrally like Switzerland, frowned.

'Yeah,' I said trying to laugh it off, 'they usually keep me chained in a basement like Sloth from *The Goonies*.' Everyone laughed but the heavy, dull feeling in my chest wouldn't disappear.

After we said goodbye to them, I went to the house without saying a word. I could hear Ama saying to Ling: 'Dude, that was messed up,' and Ling replying in a bored voice: 'Whatever, it was just a joke.'

In the gloom of the house and its decaying connecting rooms, I called home and felt that rising feeling of homesickness as I punched in the last number. It tasted bitter; a loneliness that couldn't be quelled even by Ama and her softness.

'Bel, are you okay?' my dad asked, concern flooding down the line.

'Yeah, Dad, I'm fine. I just miss you and Mum.'

'Maybe we shouldn't have let you go away at such a young age,' he said, clicking his tongue.

'Didn't you and Mum meet when she wasn't much older than I am now?'

'Yes, exactly,' he said. 'Are you going to Padmini Auntie's tomorrow?'

'Yes,' I said, the feeling of homesickness quickly dissipating with the nagging.

'You're taking the girls with you, nah?'

'Just Ama, I think.'

'Why, what has happened to the other girls?' he said.

'They're fine, I just don't think they want to waste a day of their holiday coming to visit my aunt. It's not exactly exciting, is it?'

'Bel, this isn't what we agreed.' Dad sounded annoyed and he *never* sounded annoyed. 'I'd like you to take at least one of the other girls with you. I'm not happy about just the two of you going to Plymouth alone. Okay?'

'Okay, Dad,' I said, the familiar sensation of bile rising in me. Having any friends other than Ama near my family brought on the sweats, and given her current behaviour, I'd rather die than take Ling, which meant . . . Oh, god. I'd have to ask Marina.

I knocked on her door. 'Come in!' she yelled and took off her headphones.

'Where's Ling?' I said.

Marina crossed her eyes. 'Doing some tie-dye shit with India. I know she's my cousin and I love her, but this hippie Captain Planet stuff is just sad. What's up?'

I forced myself to ask. 'So . . . I need a big favour. I spoke to my dad and he wants me to go and see my aunt in Plymouth tomorrow. But he's not okay with me just taking Ama. Would you . . .' I couldn't do it. I couldn't ask Marina to do something I knew she'd complain about for the next ten years.

'Come with you?' she said. I nodded.

'Sure.'

I hadn't expected it to be that easy, and my surprise must have shown. 'The beach is fine and all but I'm getting bored of it,' she said, shrugging. 'Ling is being a bit of a head case and I'm pretty sure Plymouth has an indie record shop we can visit afterwards.'

'You know we'll have to eat lunch there, right? At my aunt and uncle's?'

'I actually like Indian food,' Marina said as if it was something I should have known despite never hearing about it before this. 'My parents and I went to Kerala two summers ago.' Of course they did.

*

I hadn't seen Padmini Auntie for about three years. The last time was a tense overnight stay at our house, and then she'd moved with her husband Rakesh to Plymouth. In telling Ama and Marina about her, I realised that I didn't know much. Maybe if they'd had children we would all have been closer, spending holidays together and having sleepovers, but they didn't. Although Asian families never discussed things openly, it was assumed that every couple wanted children. If they didn't have them, it meant something was wrong with their ability to.

My aunt and uncle lived in an area called The Hoe. We dissolved into contagious giggles when I told Ama and Marina this. Every time one of us stopped, the other would start doing a Muttley laugh, wheeze the word 'hoe', and that would set us all off again. Plymouth was much busier than Newquay; people bustling to their offices, and tourists streaming towards the harbour to catch a ferry. My aunt had a new puppy and couldn't pick us up from the station, she said, but instead would send a taxi. Seeing my name written on a little board delighted me, and even Marina looked impressed.

The taxi pulled up at a small townhouse with an unruly garden in front. My heart sank lower and lower. If the outside wasn't particularly well-tended, what did that mean for the inside? And would my aunt be appropriately attired or in the same type of shapeless gardening clothes my mother had started wearing even when she wasn't gardening? She greeted me at the door, opening it just a crack so as not to let the puppy escape. 'Beryl,' she said warmly and gave me a big hug. 'Hi, girls, nice to meet you. Come on through.' I breathed a sigh of relief: she was in a loose linen shirt and jeans.

A long corridor cut through the house downstairs.

They were in the middle of redecorating, judging by the paint swatches on the walls and the stripped-back floorboards. Cardboard boxes were neatly stacked to one side with books poking out and dustsheets lay over the sofa in the living room. I bit my lip. What would Marina and Ama think? But it was still in better condition than Jasper and Tiggy's house, and my aunt apologised for the disruption. 'I'm not sure it was the best project to take on while also training a new puppy.'

We were introduced immediately to Arthur the Golden Retriever, and he was the best thing for breaking any awkwardness. While my friends bounded around with him in the living room, I went to the kitchen to help Padmini Auntie with lunch. If I could cut down the amount of time they were all in the same room together, it would pare back the potential for embarrassment. 'Your uncle isn't home, unfortunately,' she said. 'He's on call. Sick parrot.'

Rakesh Uncle was a veterinarian and it was his job that had brought them to Plymouth. 'That's okay. Do you want me to tell Mum and Dad he was here?'

Auntie looked at me sideways while spooning hot lamb curry into a bowl. 'You're very sharp for your age, aren't you, Bel?'

'I am sixteen,' I said. 'Practically a grown-up.' I offered to lie because my parents would see Rakesh Uncle's absence during my visit as a slight, even if Noah's entire ark had been taken ill.

She laughed. 'Yes, that's true. I think I forget that sometimes. You've grown up so much.'

'Thanks,' I said, puffing out my chest with pride.

'Sometimes that's not always a good thing,' she said sadly, like she was remembering something long ago and out of reach. 'I remember when you were just a baby and you'd fit right here, in the crook of my arm.'

I didn't want to dwell on me being a baby, so I asked her if there was anything I could take out to the dining room. I look dubiously at the curry and hoped Marina's digestive system was up to the task. She shook her head. 'Go and see if your friends are okay. Maybe take them out some cola or something?'

Ama and Marina were rolling around on the floor with Arthur. They stopped when I walked in. 'You okay?' Ama asked. 'Something smells amazing.'

'I'm not really sure what I expected,' I said, scratching the side of my neck. 'But . . . my aunt seems alright.'

'Your aunt and uncle are cool, man,' Marina said. Those were words I'd thought I'd die before hearing. 'Check out their vinyl.' They had LPs in one of the boxes, placed high above the reach of a curious pup. Don McClean, Neil Young, Womack, Nirvana – *Nirvana?!*

When I'd played 'Lithium', my mother asked me to 'turn down that noise'. I know that was just her being a parent, but as much as I loved my family, I sometimes felt like I didn't fit in with them. But this made me feel like I fitted in here, and I almost felt sorry we were only staying for an afternoon.

As soon as we sat down at the dining table, I realised with cold dread that I didn't know if Padmini Auntie would eat with her hands. I could always coerce Mum and Dad into using a knife and fork, but I couldn't be that rude to my aunt. I held my breath until I saw her reaching for a fork. All I needed now was for my friends not to mention anything about boys or other behaviour that could land me in trouble. Ama knew the deal, but Marina was unknown territory. She'd eaten at my house before – always oven food like Bird's Eye Potato Waffles and chicken nuggets that I threw together while my mother was out, as we watched the latest episode of *Headbanger's Ball* or one of the B-movies on Bravo.

'I've been to India,' Marina said confidently to my aunt.

'Have you now?' she said, picking up a samosa in her fingers. Samosas were fine, curry was not. 'What did you learn?'

Marina paused and looked thoughtful. 'There are lots of people,' she said. 'The toilets weren't as bad as I thought. But they were bad. Some people bathe in a bucket. The food was wonderful, and I got sunburned.'

Padmini laughed. 'Apart from the bucket, the rest could be said of a lot of places,' she said. 'We like to travel too.' She pointed at the photos on the sideboard. They'd been to New Zealand, Thailand, Canada. There was Rakesh Uncle ice fishing in British Columbia, here was Padmini Auntie drinking a mug of beer under a frangipani tree.

'You've travelled a lot,' I said with wonder. My parents didn't go anywhere apart from India.

'Yes, well,' she said, reaching for the bowl of steaming rice, 'we don't have children.'

'Was that on purpose?' Marina asked. 'My mum wanted a second child after me, but she couldn't.'

'MARINA!' I hissed at her. 'You don't ask that!'

'It's okay,' laughed Padmini Auntie. 'It was on purpose.' I goggled at her. I'd never heard a brown woman say they didn't want kids. 'It's not that we disliked children,' she said looking reassuringly at me, 'but . . . we're both the youngest in our families. And we saw how much it takes over your life and there were things we both wanted to do. And yes, travel was one of those things. We didn't want to do all of that stuff when we were old, and kids are a big commitment.'

'What do you do as your job?' Marina asked. Man, what was with her and the questions?

'I work as a counsellor,' my aunt replied, 'and I do some outreach work with people who struggle with addiction. It shows me a lot about what can . . . happen in a person's life and that you never stop worrying about your kids no matter how old they are. We just didn't feel that was a commitment we were able to make. Your mother didn't agree with that decision though, Bel,' she said wryly.

Mum felt that if someone wasn't in a relationship, they must be deeply unhappy. About any woman who wasn't married by the time they turned thirty, she'd say: '*That poor girl, what a shame, what a waste.*'

'What's it like – your job?' I asked my aunt.

'It's hard,' she said. 'Complicated. But also hugely rewarding. I think it changes you. It reminds you that everyone deserves love and dignity, no matter how they might sometimes behave.'

We ate the rest of the meal while Ama talked about Sri Lanka, and what her dad was like. She swapped stories with my aunt who'd spent a year living in Colombo when she was younger. Seeing her had eased some of my home-sickness. After lunch, we took a bus to Plymouth Vintage Vinyl, where we lost our minds at the second-hand cloth-ing, records, and the sheer joy of being surrounded by other alternative-looking people. When we were back on the bus clutching our precious cargo (including Ama's secret birthday present – a copy of David Bowie's *Aladdin Sane* album), I was deep in thought about my aunt and the kind of life she had. I hadn't known not having kids was even an option until that point. I was also still shocked that nothing embarrassing had happened. Marina had been pleasant. Had actually said the words: 'I had a lovely time.'

Two of my worlds had collided, and nothing had exploded. In fact, it opened a door to the possibility that perhaps they could co-exist.

*

We walked along the beach, trying to protect our chips from overzealous seagulls by eating them as fast as we could. 'Ow!' I said, opening my mouth like a chimney to release the steam from a fat piece of potato.

To our left, the sky was steeped in marshmallow col-ours against a background of deep orange, shot through with wisps of white cloud. The sea was a still, dark mirror, holding onto the warmth of the day until the sun returned. We entered the house still laughing about Ama and the seagull that had divebombed her, making her scream and drop her last few chips.

Everything was quiet. 'India! Ling!' Marina yelled. No one answered and there was no note near the kettle – the designated spot to leave messages for each other. Sometimes it would be 'Ama your mother called' or 'A & M have popped out to get milk' or 'If you're reading this, you're a dick'.

We went upstairs and found Ling lying on her bed staring at the ceiling. 'What's wrong, dude?' Marina said, sitting next to her. But Ling just turned over and faced the wall. Ama and I looked at each other. We didn't know if something was actually wrong or if this was dramatics.

'I can't believe you all left me,' she said in a muffled voice. Ah, dramatics.

'I didn't think you'd want to go, L,' I said as gently as I could. 'I mean, it was going to visit my saddo relatives. And I thought you'd have a much nicer time with India.'

Technically a lie. I'd felt like things were weird between us and, truth be told, I was still mad at her for making me out to be such a mega nerd in front of Brandon. But I wasn't above spinning it to sound magnanimous.

'She left me here!' Ling wailed. 'One of her friends called, and she said she'd be right back and that was about eight hours ago!' She put her arm over her face and started crying. Marina gestured at us to go.

'What should we do?' I whispered as I shut the door behind us.

Ama rubbed her eyes. 'I'm pretty tired. I'm going to head to bed. Maybe tomorrow will be better?'

We had two days before Ama's birthday to set things right. I'd wait until Marina came out and then I'd go and smooth things over with Ling. It was beyond stupid that we were fighting over a boy. Wasn't there a saying . . . sisters before misters?

I sat on the carpet and waited outside but couldn't help overhearing Ling and Marina talking. They hadn't lowered their voices, probably thinking Ama and I had returned to our room on the other side of the top floor, which was bisected by the central staircase.

'Did you have a good time?' Ling sniffed, her crying mysteriously abating the moment we'd left.

'Nah,' Marina said. 'I wish you'd been there. I was *so* bored without you.' Either Marina was putting on the greatest act when she was with us in Plymouth, or she was saying this to make Ling feel better. Either way, it didn't make me feel great . 'Did you see the boys?'

'That's the worst bit,' Ling said. 'I went out on the beach to see if I could find India, and I bumped into Ben. No sign of Brandon. Ben then tells me he likes me. Like what the fuck?'

'Okay, but why is that a bad thing?'

'Because I like Brandon? I don't want Ben and his blond undercut!'

'He's cute though,' said Marina. 'I know you like

Brandon but, you know . . . so does Bel. The whole thing is messy. Meanwhile you have this hot guy who says he likes you – what's the harm in seeing what happens?'

'Because what if Brandon likes me?'

'Did he say he liked you?'

'Well . . . no. But what are you saying, that he likes *Bel*?' The disdain with which Ling said my name made me feel like a bag of garbage.

'I'm not saying that,' Marina protested. 'I don't know Brandon. Who knows what he wants? What I'm saying is that I don't think some guy is worth falling out with your mate over. And definitely not if there is an equally cute person who says he likes you.' I didn't know if Marina was saying all of this to help me out, or to restore some sanity and perspective to Ling, but I was grateful.

'Yeah, maybe,' Ling said. 'But I might just ask Brandon who he likes more.'

Marina groaned. 'And what if he says Bel? It'll make you feel like shit. It'll happen if it's supposed to happen.'

'*No fate but what we make,* remember?' Ling quoted Eddie Furlong's line from *Terminator 2*, which we were all obsessed with and watched repeatedly. 'I'm going to ask him.'

I pulled away from the door, not wanting to hear anything further. Anything that could take our friendship to the point of no return. I didn't know how to feel about what I'd just heard. Even during times of peace, we talked about each other behind our backs. But it was one thing to vaguely know it, and another to listen to it. It brought me a small amount of comfort that, for all her prickliness, Marina at least tried to be fair, but that was dwarfed by the awful words that had come out of Ling's mouth.

When a friendship breaks, everyone looks at the big event that caused the final rupture. But more attention should be paid to the fault lines, the little stress fractures that form over time. That perhaps could have been reinforced or repaired with a loving conversation, but instead just grew wider.

If Ling had spoken to me about Brandon, I would have backed off. But there was a sense of entitlement in her exchange with Marina that even my threadbare sense of self-esteem took offence at. That somehow *of course* Brandon would like her more, because why would he like someone like me?

That felt like the real betrayal here, the sense that Ling assumed she was better than me. And it hardened in my heart something cold and ugly: the resolution to prove, no matter what it took, that she was not.

14

The Fear is a nightmare demon, invoked by vast quantities of alcohol, that uses your most embarrassing moments and worst anxieties to mentally whip you for a minimum of twenty-four hours. I was familiar with it, but the morning after Ama's hen do was so painful and upsetting I had no idea how I was going to make it through the day, let alone fast forward to Ama's actual wedding in three weeks.

If the embarrassment of kissing my childhood crush and then vomiting on him wasn't enough, the fact that I'd done it in front of Ling made me scream loudly into my pillow. Even worse than that was the realisation I had upset Ama after working so hard to reconnect with her.

The past was being stirred up in a way that made me feel as if I was standing in quicksand. How the fuck was I going to fix this? It was one thing to mess things up as a kid, another thing as a thirty-six-year-old adult.

Then there was Luke. I'd sent him a drunken text asking if he wanted to meet for a drink. He hadn't replied. *Why would he?* I thought. *I'm a fucking mess.* The only bright spot was that things with Marina had been smoothed over, and Devi hadn't minded looking after me when we got back to hers.

I took the train back to London just before lunch, while Devi and Karen went for pizza. Despite my own mixed feelings I texted Ama an apology, saying I hoped she'd still had a great time, but this was met with silence. I needed to talk to Kendra about it, but I wouldn't be able to see her for another few days. It was both a blessing and a curse that it was a bank holiday weekend. The extra day gave me more time to recover from my hangover, but it also gave me more time to think. Especially since Devi wasn't there to distract me and wasn't due back till Monday evening. I spent most of the day at the gym and trying to send emails, but sometime in the late afternoon, the emotion swirling through my head, made me lie down on the floor and cry.

I was there for what felt like hours. I didn't hear the front door open. I only noticed Devi's return when she came and put her arms around me, and that made me cry even more. She kept stroking my back and making soothing noises.

'I'm not a baby,' I sniffled through my sobs.

'It's not just babies who need comfort.'

When I had finally stopped crying long enough to form a sentence, I said: 'I'm sorry, I'm just being silly. '

'What's going on?' she said gently. 'Why are you crying? Is this about your friends? You know they're the dickheads, right?'

I hadn't realised how much I'd needed that. How much I had needed someone just to say *I'm on your side*.

'It's so hard to explain, D.'

I cried because I deserved more than being with men because they liked me, without considering whether they were good for me. I cried because at some point, missing my family had been an actual physical ache I had numbed out. I cried because I felt like I would never live up to what my mum really wanted of me. I cried because I *almost fucking died in that cellar*, and the reminder of my own mortality and how closely my world had brushed against the realm of death, made me feel grateful, scared and regretful for all the time I'd wasted. I cried because every time someone asked me if I was okay and I replied *I'm fine*, another part of me wanted to howl: I'M NOT FINE. I cried because the loneliness of my life hurt, and I wanted to be taken care of for once.

'Try,' Devi said.

'I just . . . I'm scared I've lost Ama all over again. And I don't know what I want from my life, but at the same time, I know I want that special someone I can rely on and lean on. And there's a part of me that worries that I'm never going to meet that person, and if I do, I'll just push them away. Fucking Luke hasn't replied to my text about going for a drink. Work is a bag of shit . . .' I trailed off crying again.

'Okay, okay,' she said, pulling my head into her lap. 'Listen. Are you listening? Good. Bel, I like Ama. But if you lose her because of some disagreement you had while

you were drunk, then she wasn't worth it. I know you will
be able to work things out but you *have* to tell her what's
going on. And as for meeting this special person . . . where
is all this coming from? You can meet this person but it still
doesn't mean they are going to act the way you want them
to. Trust me, I was married, remember? Sometimes you can
be in a situation like that and STILL be completely alone.
Support doesn't have to come from just one person, it can
come from a lot of different people, okay? And Luke . . .
don't worry about him. You're trying to see the whole picture, and that can be so overwhelming. Sometimes we just
need to focus on a part of it.'

'Like a thousand-piece puzzle?' I sniffed.

'Exactly,' she said. And we stayed on the floor together
for a while, Devi stroking my hair. I could never have
imagined how comforting it felt.

*

The next morning, something in me had eased. The ground
felt more solid beneath my feet. As I was buttering some
toast, Devi came back from a run, red-faced and wheezing.
'Running is horrible,' she panted. 'Why do people do it?'

I shrugged.

'Don't ask me, the only time I run is for a bus or to
escape danger.'

'Listen,' she said, filling a glass with water, 'there's
something I need to talk to you about. I was going to tell
you yesterday, but it didn't seem to be the right time.'

I held my breath.

'I'm really grateful you've let me stay this long,' she continued, 'but I think I need to move back, and deal with Nikhil and the house. If I'm not there to harass him, nothing will happen. He hasn't done anything apart from remove some saucepans from the kitchen.' My heart sank. Even though I'd always known Devi would have to move back, I'd got used to having her around. But I couldn't let her see that, and so I gave her a smile and said: 'Totally understand. I've got to get to work though, so . . .'

'Shall we talk about it later tonight?' she asked. I nodded and grabbed my bag, trying not to let her see my face crumple as I headed out the door.

*

I knew it was unreasonable to feel upset about Devi leaving, but it was hard to shake the raincloud hanging over me. Fittingly for the When It Shits It Pours week I was having, Tristan decided to call a meeting to discuss how our project was going.

'Crispin's concerned we aren't making enough headway with putting together the team,' he'd said, looking at me as if I bore sole responsibility for this. I realised, looking at him, that he was a more grown-up, polished version of Brandon, the first boy I ever kissed – at least in looks. That was why I was attracted to him despite his obnoxious personality, and the realisation made me shudder.

'We aren't making enough headway because you don't show up to half the interviews you're supposed to,' I said. He smiled blandly and replied: 'I've been busy with clients.' The inference being: *unlike you.*

'We need to double down on it,' he said, frowning, 'or both our arses will be on the line. Crispin wants a call next week. I think we should spend a couple of hours before then brainstorming and coming up with an action plan. What do you think?'

'Sounds like a good idea.'

'Great, I'll get Oliver to email you with a time.' Oliver was Tristan's assistant.

'Maggie,' I said.

'Sorry, what?'

'Get Oliver to email Maggie – she's my assistant.'

'Yes, of course, that's what I meant,' he said. It wasn't what he'd meant. But I was interested to see the faint blush blooming on his throat.

Later that day, Mum called. I ignored it. Then I received a ping.

Mum: Bel – do you know where your sister is?

I wasn't sure I could withstand a talking conversation so I texted her back.

Me: No, I'm at work but I'm sure she's fine.
**Mum: If you don't know where your sister is, how do
    you know she's fine?**

I sighed.

Me: Do you have any message you want me to pass on?

Mum: Yes, tell her it's about the house. We need to sort out the equity so Nikhil can repay us.

Me: I don't understand any of this. I'll get Devi to call you when I see her.

Mum: Okay, but tell her it's important!

*

I took the long way home that night, walking along the riverbank to allow my thoughts to unspool with the tide. By the time I reached my building, I'd decided I had to focus on the good things that had come out of Devi and me living together, the most important of which was that we had a much better relationship. Even if it would feel lonely without her, it would be fine, and we would still see each other. I had to be supportive.

The smell of chicken curry greeted me when I turned the key in the lock and I exhaled a sigh of gratitude for having someone who loved me enough to cook dinner and be there when I got home. *I could do this*, I thought. *I could be loving and kind.*

When I saw my sister with her hair tied back in her polka dot I'm Cooking headband, I felt a slight pang. She was singing away while stirring. 'Ah! You're home!'

'Have you checked your phone?' I said, dumping my bags by the sofa.

'No, why?'

'Mum has been trying to call you.'

'Ah. I've put her on a filtered list, so if she calls it goes to do not disturb. She's driving me mad.'

'Well, she is mad,' I said, trying to be breezy. 'She said it's something about Nikhil and your mortgage. Are you selling the house?'

Devi emitted a long and gargled groan.

'Why does Mum have to be so intense?' she said, washing some basmati rice in a pan before placing it on the cooker. 'We've just been talking about it. Nothing definite.'

'What is she stressing about?'

'We borrowed money from them when we bought the house about ten years ago. And rather than paying it back regularly – because we had Karen's school fees and a lot of other bills – they just told us to repay the loan when we eventually sold the house and released the equity. That's probably what Mum was referring to. She wants to make sure Nikhil doesn't weasel out of paying them back.'

'Wait, Mum and Dad lent you money for that house?'

'Yeah, why do you ask?'

'No reason,' I said, my previous upset coalescing into something a lot more volatile: anger. I needed to be in a different part of the flat. 'I'm going for a shower.'

'Dinner in ten,' she called after me.

One of the main reasons I took a job at Leopard wasn't the potential for promotion, or the free drinks. It was because they offered to help first-time home buyers through a company loan scheme. That and the rise in my salary when I went there, meant I was finally able to scrape together a down-payment on a flat. Regardless of whether you were married or not, the ultimate sign of success for boomers was ownership of property. Mum and Dad had passed this on to their offspring.

I had exhausted all previous avenues to raise the money for a deposit, including my parents. I'd asked them for help but they said they didn't have the money, what with them trying to reduce their hours in the dental practice. I'd never asked them for anything like that before and it was a big deal. I'd never borrowed money, never showed any sign that I had mismanaged or fucked things up and needed them to bail me out. So being told no . . . that had stung. I had fully expected them to say yes. Brown parents could be unrelentingly harsh in their expectations of their children but the unspoken trade-off was that, whatever that child needed, when it came to housing or education, they'd find a way of providing.

Finding out that my sister had been given the help I had been refused . . . rankled. I felt it in my chest, sour and seething. Despite the steps I had taken to becoming closer to my family lately, I felt as if I'd been duped. How could Devi not have considered how this would affect me? Resentment wrapped itself around my chest like a mangrove root.

I didn't trust myself to get through dinner with her. However angry I was, though, I didn't want to lash out. So with great restraint, I asked her if she minded if I had dinner in my room because I had a ton of emails to get through. She looked a bit hurt but said: 'No, of course not.'

'So we'll talk about the moving out stuff tomorrow?' I said. She nodded.

*

Over the next two days, I made excuses and worked late to avoid any one-to-one time with Devi. On Friday morning I stomped into work having slept badly. Maggie placed coffee and a doughnut on my desk and departed as quickly as she could. I threw it in the bin. No more dough-nuts. New regime.

I texted Katrina.

Me: You free for drinks after work? I've had a shitter of a week.

It took her three hours to reply.

Katrina: Would love to babes — it's been ages. But I've got a work do. Text you tomoz to arrange.

I knew she wouldn't text me. Katrina was slowly disap-pearing into the ether, as my friends often did. It'd start with a volley of dates to arrange a meet-up, which mys-teriously one of us couldn't do, then we'd finally settle on something only for the other person to cancel last-minute. Several weeks would pass and eventually we'd meet up for the equivalent of a break-up dinner where you're going through the motions to keep things polite. It was strange how you could share so much intimacy, from late-night kebabs to peeing in a park, and then drift into becoming near strangers.

I debated about texting Ama again but held off.

And now I had to spend the afternoon with Tristan working on plans for the new department. It was taking up too much brain space and the rest of my work was falling behind. When he first suggested meeting off-site, I had almost said no. Off-sites took more time, they involved working quite intensely together and our working relationship was already at such an all-time low. But Crispin was getting impatient.

As I walked into the lobby of the drippy hipster co-working office in Soho, I knew he'd made the right choice. There was something about being in neutral territory, away from the old fiefdoms of the office, that made me relax slightly. He was already waiting when the receptionist showed me to our base for the next few hours – a room with a table big enough for six people, and an industrial-looking bookcase with decorative glass pears and books on architecture carefully displayed.

Away from his office Tristan looked different. Less sure of himself. I swore I saw his hands shake slightly.

'I know we haven't always seen eye to eye,' he began, 'but I'm hoping this is a chance for us to have an honest and open conversation about Thunder. I don't think it's quite working. In the spirit of doing the right thing, I wanted to ask if you could tell me why you think that is. And it'll stay in this room, I promise.'

This was unexpected. But I wasn't going to be won over easily.

'I appreciate the olive branch,' I said, 'but that's the problem. I don't know you or trust you enough to believe you when you say this conversation will be just between us.'

'What can I do to show you I mean it?'

'Hmm. Who's the most important person in your life?'

'My mother,' he answered without missing a beat. I was surprised. Tristan was the kind of person who behaved so obnoxiously that at times it seemed like he'd been hatched from an egg.

I pressed record on my iPhone. 'Right. I want you to swear on your mother's life that you'll keep your word.'

He looked at me like I'd gone mad. In response, I pointed at the phone.

'I swear on my mother's life that I will keep my word. I will not discuss what happens today outside of this meeting.'

'Good.'

'And also, for the record, I'm not a racist,' he said.

'What?'

'You know, what you texted in that directors' meeting. To your friend Barry.'

'Great to have that cleared up,' I said. 'So, getting down to it. This isn't working for a number of reasons. First, you seem to turn up or not turn up as you please. I know you're busy but so am I – I'm your peer. It's unprofessional and it makes me think I can't rely on you.'

'Okay—'

'Second, I don't like being undermined and I feel you do that because you're trying to gain favour with Crispin. It makes me feel like I can't trust you. Third, when you do show up to interviews, you turn into a trustafarian and attempt to use slang – what is that? Is it because you went to private school and encountered literally no Black or brown people?'

'But—'

'Fourth, this scheme isn't going to work because we aren't the right people to run it. And it's a terrible idea. A special "diversity department" segregates people. It's actually mad when you think about it. If it has to go ahead, we need outside consultancy. It can't just be you and me running it.'

'You finished?' he said finally.

'Yes,' I said, crossing my arms.

'One, I didn't go to private school. I got a scholarship to Oxford but my family is working class and I've had to earn everything I have.' I'd had no idea and felt a bit embarrassed. Only a bit, however.

'Second, because of that, I have to do everything I can to survive in this place. I didn't go to Eton like Dan or have a trust fund like that idiot intern on the Oseni account. And, yes, that means I can sometimes act like a dick but it doesn't mean I don't respect you.' I was pleasantly surprised but still not won over.

'Third, you're right about the interviews – both points. I'm sorry. And maybe you're right about us not being the right people to run this initiative. But my concern is that if we don't do it, it'll be given to someone else who still won't be the right person.'

'But that's why things never change,' I replied. 'We have to be bold and think differently about it. We can't be self-serving, only worrying about giving up personal power because someone else might take it. We have to make sure that it's given to the right person. And to do that, we need to build up a proper presentation for Crispin about how we'd like to take this forward. I think I even have the right external hire in mind for the leadership role.'

A knock on the door signalled the return of the receptionist. 'Coffee?' she asked, looking at Tristan adoringly. 'You're an angel,' he said. 'A cappuccino for me . . . and Bel?'

'Americano, please.'

After she had shut the door, I said: 'You can charm people when you want to, you know. Why is it that you're so hard on me?'

He looked as if he was about to disagree and then settled for the truth. 'When you've spent most of your life in survival mode . . . it's hard to switch it off.'

'There's something about me that makes you feel like that?'

He laughed. A proper laugh. Not a sneer or a scoff. 'Stop fishing for compliments. You know you're good at your job.'

I felt a small glow of pride. It wasn't enough to make me forget or overlook how Tristan had behaved, but something in me softened.

We spent several hours hashing out two options. One was to dissolve the department and set out a new plan of accountability goals around diversity across the company. The second was to plan out how the department might run if it had to go ahead. But we were reaching the end of the day and were nowhere near done. The choice was to continue tomorrow or try to get it all done in one go. Given that we'd managed not to argue once (apart from a heated debate over budget allocation), we felt optimistic enough to take advantage of the brief peace brokered between us and continue.

While Tristan stepped out to vape and make some calls, I sat in the open-plan lounge checking my phone. I'd had several messages including one from Devi asking if I was okay. Part of me wanted to be abrupt and give her cause to worry, but even though I was mad at her, Nikhil and our parents, she didn't deserve to be left hanging. In the end, I texted back to say I was fine and working late. The next message was from Luke and infuriated me with its nonchalance.

Sorry I haven't been in touch – busy week. U ok?

He had completely ignored my suggestion to go for a drink, and after several days deigned to text me . . . ten words.

'Ready?' Tristan said and I put my phone on silent.

Four hours later we'd finally finished. We had our presentation, our budget breakdown and a good case for how more integrated diversity could strengthen Leopard's brand. I was taken aback by how focused and competent Tristan had been. I had always thought of him as someone who had coasted to get to where he was, and perhaps that was his fault due to the rakish persona he cultivated at work, but I should have known that Crispin wouldn't have hired someone as filler on his team. He rewarded us financially but he also demanded a lot of us.

Tristan's hair was ruffled and he had damp patches under his arms from the warm room we'd been holed up in. I'd never seen him look anything less than pristine, and perhaps it was this flash of normality that made me say yes when he asked if I fancied having a drink. Normally any suggestion of socialising with Tristan would have met with a hard no, but he hadn't been overbearing once, and I didn't want to go home and risk having a conversation with Devi about the whole house thing. At least until I'd calmed down a bit.

'There's a place I know nearby,' he said.

While I was freshening up, I got a text from Katrina.

Plans just got cancelled. Could meet you for that drink if you wanted?

Just as I was about to reply, the cleaning lady came in. I switched my phone off and made a note to text Katrina later. A five-minute walk took us to a roof bar, a tiny pop-up speakeasy that had small tables with candles already flickering on them despite the soft blue sky. 'A friend supplies the wine here,' Tristan said.

'Of course he does,' I said dryly.

He laughed. 'I'm not the posh twonk you think I am, you know.'

'I'll be the judge of that,' I said, smiling. I was smiling. At Tristan. Why? The waiter came over. 'Two Old Fashioneds,' Tristan said.

'Hey! How do you know that's what I want to drink?' I whacked him with the menu.

'Because you drink whisky and bourbon – I've seen you chugging down Crispin's twelve-year-old Yamazaki. This bar currently serves the best cocktails in the city. If you don't like it, I'll get you a different drink.' I caught myself basking a little in that slightly proprietorial *I'll*, then hated myself for it.

Our drinks arrived and he looked at me out of the corner of his eye as I sipped. 'And?' he said with a raised eyebrow.

'Yes, it's the best goddamn' Old Fashioned I've had. As if the orange peel has been curled between the thighs of goddesses, etc., etc.'

He laughed, and in the silence that followed grew a bit pensive. 'I'm sorry by the way.'

'For what?' I asked.

'For not really asking if you were okay after your accident. Are you?'

'Yeah. I mean no. But also yeah. Like physically I'm fine. Mentally . . .' I took a sip of my drink. 'I don't know why I'm telling you of all people.'

'What's so bad about me?' he said in mock outrage.

'Come on, you must know,' I replied. 'You're a bro. You

hang out with your other bros. You all beat your chests and howl at the moon and then wank on a communal biscuit.'

'Wow,' he said, raising an eyebrow. 'Well, first you're referencing at least two separate animals in there, and second . . . that might be how it comes across, but that's not really what we're like. There's something about guys – when we hang out in a group we become, I don't know, different. We're not like that around our partners.'

'I'm impressed you have one.'

'I don't right now, but I mean when I do. When we do,' he said.

'But then who's the real you? Is it the person in the group? Or the person outside of the group?'

Tristan grew more thoughtful. 'That is a good point. I think there's a part of us that needs that validation, or maybe I should say the ability to be base and gross in a group. But there's also a part of us that needs to be wanted by a partner.'

'But,' I observed, 'it seems like in both scenarios, you're never really yourself? And that sounds exhausting.'

'Have you never felt like that?' he asked.

'Yeah, but mostly when I'm at work, and for different reasons.' We were reaching the end of our drinks. He looked at me and I nodded. He signalled the waiter for another round. It felt delicious to communicate with someone without using words.

'What reasons?'

I let out a big sigh. I didn't want to have this conversation because nine times out of ten, it led to me having to explain structural racism. And usually the other person didn't quite understand, and without realising what they were doing, often dismissed it. Or, worse, made a joke out of it – like being racially profiled at the airport. You felt like a child, trying to explain to your parents why it wasn't your fault you'd been given detention, and they didn't believe you.

'If I tell you, you have to listen properly,' I said. 'I don't have time for *why*s and *is it really*s. You have to accept that this is reality for me. It doesn't matter whether you're struggling to understand because that's not the point of this conversation.'

'What *is* the point then?' he said, but in a tone that was genuinely enquiring rather than defensive. On that basis, I explained.

'The point is that I'm telling you something that is true to me, that matters to me. I don't need or want to debate whether what I'm saying is true. It's something that has happened to me over and over again, enough that I *know* it as a truth.'

'I understand,' he said. 'I think.'

'At work . . . I have to be someone else in order to get ahead. I'm a brown woman, and there are not many like me in our company above a certain level. Plenty at junior and middle-management levels but only one director. I have to code-switch all the time. I didn't even realise I was doing it until recently or that other people did it too. But I have to dress a certain way, laugh along to certain jokes– even if I don't find them funny – so that people don't think I'm a prude. I distance myself from the IT guys in case their brand of brownness – which incidentally is biriyani and Gaviscon – rubs off on me.' I looked at him to see if he was bored but he seemed to be listening, so I continued.

'Sometimes people will ask me if I eat pork because they assume I'm Muslim, and being Muslim has certain connotations, so I go for the fucking bacon sarnie even if I don't want it because I want to show how well I fit in. My success at work depends on not being myself as much as possible. And when confronted with myself out of that . . . it feels like lying next to someone who has cheated on you, and it's hard to love what remains.'

I looked at him, daring him to laugh, or mock, or tell me I was imagining it. I'd already pictured leaving my drink untouched and grabbing my bag.

'I can't understand what that must be like,' he said carefully. 'I mean, I don't have to deal with any of that. The only thing I can say is, I'm sorry. It's shit. It's unfair.'

I could feel him weighing up what to say next. 'Tristan, I know we're having a nice time and I appreciate the apology but . . . you were such a dick about that whole Oseni thing. Do you get why that was messed up?'

'I think so. I mean, yeah, I do,' he said sheepishly. 'I don't think I realised what I was insinuating and why it was wrong. I think I was just trying to score points against you because Crispin favours you so much – I didn't think about how it actually came across.'

We drank in silence for a bit. Finally, I said: 'Okay, so I

told you a lot about myself. Now you tell me something. Why aren't you like this at work?'

'Well,' he said, smiling, 'now you'll have to swear on your mother's life that this stays between us.'

'Yeah, yeah, I swear.'

'Remember I told you I'm working class?'

'Yeah?'

'No one else in the office knows that,' he said simply. 'I don't lie about it but I don't tell them about it either. They know I went to Oxford and, based on that, they make assumptions and . . . I don't correct them. They don't know my mother is a single mum, or that I helped her clean offices while I was at school, or that I had a scholarship. I worked every hour I wasn't studying to make ends meet, and then when I moved into advertising, I kind of reinvented myself. People here know I go to Soho Farmhouse for weekends. They see the clothes I wear. The bars I go to. The Rolex,' he said, flicking his wrist. 'Beyond that our chat never gets too deep. It's easier for men to pretend because most people just see the armour; they have no interest in seeing what holds it together.'

The candle glowed more brightly as the sky darkened to ink. Around us, people pressed together more closely. A young woman in a white jumpsuit tucked her hair behind her ear self-consciously as her handsome date, in a tight T-shirt and jeans barely containing his muscles, spread himself more expansively over their table. Two men in their fifties, whose gestures spoke of old familiarity and love, from arranging each other's napkin to the ease of their laughter, were debating whether to move on to Martinis.

It was dawning on me with terrible certainty that this was the most connected I'd felt to a man in a long time. I liked Luke, but it wasn't like this. This was unexpected, unbelievable. How intoxicating, how dazzling, the truth about a person could be. It could burn through a litany of grievances in a flash. This was dangerous territory.

'I should go,' I said suddenly. The hurt that blossomed on Tristan's face was difficult to witness. I immediately regretted my abruptness. He didn't know that I was starting to find him attractive, pre-empting something happening between us by trying to shut it down. He thought I was leaving because of something I'd seen, the vulnerability he'd revealed.

'I'm not leaving because of that – because of what you've just shared. I mean . . . thank you for sharing your background with me. I'm just not sure it's a good idea for us to get drunk together.'

Something in his face shifted and eased, relieved that it wasn't about him. 'Are you feeling drunk already? Lightweight.'

'Oh, really? I'll show you lightweight!'

Several drinks later, we'd talked about a lot. Mostly work, but also ex-partners and families. While he was in the bathroom, I tipped my head back and looked at the night sky, my heart soaring at the sight of a million stars cupped in the cosmos above me. 'What are you doing?' he said, and I told him.

'You can't experience the full effect while we're still surrounded by so much light,' he scoffed.

'How do you know?'

'I grew up in the countryside. Let me pay the bill and then let's go where we can see them properly.'

We walked for what seemed like a hundred years until I realised it was barely five minutes from the bar and we had reached a square. 'Didn't they teach you how to read directions in the country?' I said.

'Quiet, you,' he replied while squinting at his phone. Just then, two streetlamps above us sputtered out. 'Well, would you look at that?' I said. I peered up until my eyes adjusted to the darkness and there was so much beauty beaming down, I wondered why I didn't look at the night sky more often. 'Isn't it out of this world?' I breathed. I turned to look at Tristan and saw him gazing at me, not the stars. 'Yes, it really is,' he replied, and as he bent down to kiss me so softly, I felt the galaxy out there, spinning its light through me, and my heart felt as if it would burst from trying to hold it all.

15

You could tell a lot about a man had from his reaction to the morning after. There was relief and gratitude on Gregor's face when he saw me still there the next day; his pilgrimage to get proper coffee and pastries was a bid to make me stay longer.

Other men, whose names are lost in a haze of Dans, Steves and Marks – whose faces I'd struggle to recognise if I passed them by in the street – would sit up awkwardly in bed and cough me into wakefulness. Others would want to talk about their problems. But the worst were the men who had been emotionally damaged in some way, either in childhood or else previous relationships, to the point where words weren't accessible to them and silence was weaponised.

I cracked open one gluey, hungover eye to see Tristan fully dressed, trying to pick up his shoes quietly. Witnessing someone in stealth mode was actually worse than waking up to birdsong and emptiness. 'Hey,' I said, and watched with satisfaction as he jumped.

Anyone neurotic about their sexual prowess might think: *Holy shit! Was I that bad in bed this person is now running away from me?*

But this wasn't my first time on the merry-go-round. I knew this was about him, not me. Nothing had taken place that was so bad it merited this behaviour. What I was witnessing was a coward in his natural habitat.

'I didn't want to wake you up,' he said, as if he'd been doing me a favour. What a humanitarian. 'But I've got to get to the golf club. Are you okay to let yourself out?'

I murmured a yes and shortly after, heard the front door close. Sifting true thoughts from hungover thoughts was hard in the first hour of the day, but I felt like an orange newly cut open. Tristan had pressed my flesh between his hands, had tasted how sweet I could be. But then he had left. What did that mean?

I couldn't be in this apartment any longer. Although, *damn*, was it incredible. Spotless and modern, with huge windows in the lounge that overlooked the London Eye. We were well paid but given everything he'd told me last night, how could he afford this? I knew he sometimes had the guys in the office over to watch sports. Perhaps it was to impress them.

I shook the thought away, showered and pulled myself together as quickly as I could. Even though I was still upset about the whole mortgage thing, I saw several increasingly worried texts from Devi and sent her a short message:

Didn't mean to worry you but ended up staying at a friend's last night. Be home soon. X

*

The glorious smell of bacon wafted through the front door as I let myself in. Devi had her Admonishment face on. 'I won't lecture you,' she said, 'but you gave me such a scare, Bel! I've made bacon sarnies – thought you could do with one.'

I was thankful, but the avalanche of upset caused by Tristan's premature exit was making me feel sour and hateful. 'Coffee?' she said, placing a fresh mug in front of me. 'What happened last night? I want to hear everything. Were you with Luke?'

What happened last night?

I went for drinks with my work nemesis, who as it turns out is quite charming and wields his vulnerability like a butter knife, making cuts so soft you don't realise he's doing it. I then fell for the oldest trick in the book: stargazing, before melting into one of the best kisses of my life. I went back to his place. We drank more wine. I looked around his apartment. I pictured us on the sofa snaked in each other's arms like a pretzel watching Netflix and moaning that there was nothing on. I imagined the dinner I would make for him on a Friday night, while we'd share a bottle of red wine and talk about our day. After we'd had sex and I'd showered, I came to bed to find him half asleep, and I smiled. And he'd put his arm out for me to tuck myself beneath, and pulled me closer before he drifted off into proper sleep. Then I woke up, and all the beauty of our brief intimacy was burned away by the morning sun. He found me lying there and whatever he saw made him think he should get as far away from me as possible.

'I slept with Tristan,' I said in a hollow voice.

'That guy from work? The one you hate?' Devi said incredulously.

'I don't have to explain myself,' I said, and turned my back on her, walking over to the sofa. I regretted the words the moment they came out of my mouth, but I didn't know how to stop.

'Bel, what is going on with you?' Devi said, looking upset. 'You've been weird the last couple of days, and I'm trying here. Have I done something wrong?'

I huffed in silence and she rolled her eyes. 'No, don't huff at me. That's what my sixteen-year-old does. You're *thirty-six*. You don't want me to mother you, as you're always saying. So come on, tell me what's going on.'

'I don't want to talk about it, Devi,' I said, picking at my sandwich. 'Not because I'm being a child but because we'll only end up in a fight.'

'Then we'll agree to try and not fight about it,' she replied reasonably. But I wasn't feeling reasonable. My sister was leaving and I was angry at her, though I knew I didn't have the right to be. But she'd become my safety wheels after the accident, and I was filled with fear of what life would be back to once I was on my own. She would move out and never come back and we'd return to how we'd been. Distant, cold, strangers in each other's lives. I couldn't bear it.

'You have to tell me, Bel,' she said. 'You can't just pretend this isn't happening.'

I told her about the mortgage and Mum and Dad. I left out the part about wanting her to stay.

'That's really shit,' she said. 'But maybe it was because they genuinely didn't have the money?'

'They *did* have the money, Devi,' I snapped. 'But I guess I'm not considered a priority because I don't have a husband or kids.'

'Oh, come *on*. Mum and Dad love you, Bel!' she said, exasperated.

'What has that got to do with it? Why do people always say that when it's so deeply unhelpful? Of *course* they love me! But they don't respect my choices in the same way that they respect yours, Devi. They *had* the money, but it was more important for them to support the child whose lifestyle matched theirs. And let's say they didn't have the money – why didn't they? Because they'd already spent it on you and Nikhil!'

'That's not fair, Bel. What were we supposed to do – not take the money or buy the house?'

'I don't know. Maybe not send your child to private school if you can't afford to pay your parents back the loan you took from them?' I was yelling now. I hadn't yelled at someone I loved in a long time.

'That is so low! I can't believe you'd say that. She's your

niece, for god's sake! Why wouldn't you want the best for her? But then again I'm not surprised given that you never bothered to spend time with her until now.'

'I'm sorry, what *I* said was low? You were such a helicopter parent that you never let me near Karen when she was little. I always felt like I was intruding. And you wonder why I find it hard to be around now she's a bit older? She's an amazing kid and I know I missed out on a lot.'

'That's on you, not me, and you know it.'

I rubbed my eyes, horrified by the way this had escalated so quickly. 'I'm not saying that I don't want the best for Karen. I'm not even saying that you and Nikhil shouldn't have got that house or whatever. And I'm not entitled to Mum and Dad's money – that's *their* money, I get that. But you all . . . you all make these choices for yourselves because it's best for you, and none of you seem to realise or even factor in how it might impact me. I love Karen, alright, Devi? I *love* that girl to my bones. And I know it's not exactly as clear-cut as this, but your decision to send her to private school ultimately meant I wasn't given the same help to buy my own home as you were. I don't have a partner to rely on for these things. So could you *maybe* see how this whole thing might be making me feel like shit and not sure my family loves me? Like maybe I can't depend on any of you when things get tough?'

'I can see that,' Devi said abruptly, 'but I also think you're feeling sorry for yourself. Bel, families are hard and they are messy, but they work things out. You very rarely ask for help, and when it's offered, often you don't take it because of some obstinate need to be self-sufficient. You can't have it both ways! You don't just fuck off and then, when your family learns to cope without you, get upset about it.'

'And that's what you think I've done?'

'How would you say you've handled things this week? You've been angry with me about that loan, but rather than talking about it, you've just avoided me. How's that working for you?'

'You think you're so perfect?' I snapped. 'Wasting your life married to some arsehole who never cared about you or your dreams, and needing to start over again in your forties? Taking care of everyone but yourself? Having your mother call you every five minutes because she's worried you're going to collapse without her?'

Devi looked at me, not even angry anymore, just sad and disappointed.

'It's not a weakness to love and need people, Bel,' she said, getting up from the table. 'I'm going to pack my things.'

*

After Devi left, even the apartment seemed reproachful. *I can't believe you let her leave like that. She kept us really clean, always did the dishwasher, AND made you proper meals. Before she arrived, you ate like an absolute dumpster, and your laundry was so sporadic you wore bikini bottoms as underwear, you ungrateful oaf.*

The only bright spot was that it was Saturday and I could wallow at home under a blanket on the sofa. The hours passed by uneventfully apart from my Deliveroo of a Korean chicken burger. Usually I received at least a text a day from Karen, but nothing had arrived so far. Nothing from Tristan, though I half expected that. My fingers hovered over Ama's name several times, but I couldn't think what to say.

I hated myself in that moment. I didn't know how I'd managed to fuck things up so badly. In the end, tired and strung out, I took a Valium that Roger had left behind in the bathroom cabinet and fell into the sleep of the dead.

*

I had made the journey to my office countless times over the last few years. I'd stopped at the same coffee place, made small talk with the security guard – *good weekend how was yours not bad Mondays are the worst* – and headed towards the lift. But it was funny how, burdened with the consequences of certain actions from sleeping with a colleague to embarrassing yourself at the office party, that familiar, well-worn journey today seemed fraught with landmines.

My first mission of getting to my desk went well. After texting Katrina asking if she'd meet me for lunch, I called Maggie in and asked her to close the door. She came in hesitantly, unsure of what mood I'd be in. I had been an ogre of late and silently made a note to make it up to her.

She clocked that I was wearing my power dress – a heavily structured black mini-dress from Cos, like a strange piece of architecture made from cloth. I had worn it with a platform pair of DMs, something I hadn't worn in years. If I was going to encounter Tristan, I wanted him to think of me as one of those highly unapproachable sea urchins with long black spikes that the diving instructor warns you not to touch under any circumstances.

'Maggie, please sit.' She smoothed down the skirt of her crisp white dress as she lowered herself into a chair, eyes wide. 'Nothing's wrong,' I said to reassure her. It did not reassure her.

'Are you happy being an assistant?' I asked her. 'Your job isn't in jeopardy,' I said quickly as her eyes widened again, 'but I'm wondering if you want to do something else. You know that new department I told you about – the one I'm setting up with Tristan McClean? I'm recruiting and I wanted to know if you'd like to be part of the team. We're devolving the recruitment to a senior consultant we're hoping to bring in, but I could recommend you, if it's something you'd want? We'll have a list of roles available in a couple of days.'

'I'll certainly think about it, thank you,' she said, still slightly wary.

After she left, I found myself fiddling with my phone. How could Devi not have called or texted? Was she okay? I could call my mother, but I wasn't that desperate yet. I opened Instagram. A new story popped up: Devi and Karen having breakfast.

With my best girl, read the caption. I felt irrationally jealous. Of whom? Not Karen – not really. It was more about no longer being in the full beam of Devi's affection. We'd fought before and sometimes spent weeks not talking, but this felt different. Something had changed. Unwilling to sit with my thoughts like a grown-up, I decided to go and make a cup of tea, then hesitated. *What if I bumped into Tristan?*

So fucking what? Are you going to let that chump make you feel like you can't walk around your own office? I stood up with purpose, the sorrow I felt at Devi's Instagram converted into anger that I was going to lay at Tristan's door.

As I stomped over to Tristan's office, his assistant Oliver glanced at me and went back to what he was doing. He pretended to adjust some papers, a stapler, before finally he looked straight at me. 'Where's Tristan?' I asked.

'Good morning, *Oliver*. How are you doing today, *Oliver*?' he said.

I rolled my eyes. In any corporation, one important rule is that you should always be polite to the EAs – the executive assistants – because a) they talk among themselves, and b) they could make your life easy or very, very hard. But Oliver was beyond redemption because he was a sarcastic little goblin no matter how nice I was to him. 'Good *morning*, Oliver,' I said, my voice dripping with sugar, 'is Tristan around?'

'No,' he said, smiling sweetly back.

'I can see him moving about behind the glass,' I pointed out.

'He's not seeing anyone at the moment.' Oliver stood up as if his reedy frame could prevent me from barrelling through. My ancestors were fishermen; I'd inherited their sturdy forearms. He stood no chance as I barged past and knocked on Tristan's door in a cursory nod to politeness before entering immediately. 'It's fine, Oliver,' he said, and I closed the door.

'Bel,' Tristan said tightly. Gone was the disarming smile, the glimpse of the actual person beneath the cool, emotionless mask. 'Everything okay?'

Everything was not okay. He was behaving as if what happened between us hadn't happened, and now I found myself in the land of ghosts, a limbo of not knowing what to feel, how to feel. Only the numbing shame and horror of having exposed my softest side to a wolf, who had taken what he wanted and left. *Don't show you're bothered, don't show you care. Behave as if he is nothing, an insect you happened to gift with your presence.* But I couldn't. Sometimes the cost of feigned indifference is too high.

'Are we okay? I hadn't heard from you and things seemed a bit awkward on Saturday,' I said.

'Yeah. Why wouldn't we be? It was just hanging out together, not a marriage proposal,' Tristan laughed.

'What does that even *mean*?'

'It means it's not a big deal. So maybe we shouldn't make it one?' He looked pointedly at me. Something inside me cracked. I hadn't expected dinner or a date, but I'd expected at least a baseline of respect. I saw ahead into the future, how our story would be retold with us playing different characters. Me, the desperate single woman lusting after her co-worker; him the dashing playboy who decided to engage in a pity shag, like the final pat on the head of a sick dog before the forever sleep. I wanted to get away from him; every passing second spent in his company only gave added credence to his false narrative. I shouldn't have come here. I couldn't afford to give him any more ammo.

'It's not a big deal,' I said, in the manner of someone brushing off a speck of dust, even though inside I felt disappointed and rejected. Which was mad because I didn't want to date Tristan, but briefly I had allowed myself to get lost in a picture I had created in my mind of our lives coming together. 'I just wanted to check that we're still on to present our new plan to Crispin. Jane has scheduled a conference call later this week. We have an hour, which is generous.'

He took a sip of his coffee. 'Yeah, I've been thinking about that over the weekend and I'm not sure it's the best option. We've done so much work already on the recruitment side, maybe we should just keep going. Not bother with outside consultancy. We don't want to piss off Crispin.'

At work, I was known for being calm. For being able to deal with extraordinary amounts of pressure when other people erupted into tears and anger. I could sort of handle the romantic rejection, but his reneging on our work agreement was too much. When enough cracks have formed, a volcano has to blow.

'No, I don't think we should do that at all,' I said slowly.

He looked at me with that carefully schooled, bored expression on his face, which I now knew was complete artifice. Part of an act designed to make me think he was superior. It wasn't just because I had got Maggie's hopes up that I refused to be swayed; it was because for the Tristans of this world, the stakes were always lower than they were for the rest of us. Regardless of his upbringing, he had the luxury of wallpapering over it a new identity. Some of us did not. And there would be other opportunities for him because there always had been.

'Why are you being weird about this?' he said, leaning back in his chair. 'You just agreed what happened between us wasn't a big deal.'

Molten lava flows so slowly that generally it's easy to move out of the way. It destroys as it goes, but most living things can see it coming and escape. But sometimes lava that has been confined to a small space, a channel or a tube, can flow much more quickly and overnight lay waste to homes that have seen generations of families being born, living, dying. I didn't know Tristan well but I recognised what he was doing, and knew that he would continue to do it to every woman who came after me, leaving her stricken by the belief that she hadn't been enough for him.

'You fucking asshole,' I said.

'Excuse me?'

'You heard me, you're a FUCKING ASSHOLE.' It was loud enough for Oliver to pop up on the other side of the glazed door, looking concerned. 'I don't give a shit that we slept together,' I told Tristan. 'In a year, I won't even remember your name. What, you think you've got a Midas dick – made of gold? I'm sorry to be the one to break it to you, but you don't. I'm doing that presentation, with or without you.'

Tristan spluttered: 'You can't talk to me like this.'

There was so much blood rushing to my head, a tidal wave of rage, that I didn't notice Oliver open the door as the entire office heard me saying: 'Go fuck yourself, you arrogant prick.'

*

The temperature outside had dropped by lunchtime, enough to make me pull on a jacket as I stormed out to meet Katrina.

Although I was not in the mood after the weekend I'd just had, she'd texted and wheedled a bit about missing me. I knew if I stayed in the office I'd unfairly take out my anger on my unsuspecting colleagues, so I agreed. She'd chosen Neptune, a high-end restaurant that people usually selected for business lunches, on account of the fact that no sane person would pay £30 for a postage-stamp-sized piece of lemon sole. *If she is late,* I raged, *I am never going to talk to her again.*

She was dressed in white jeans and a peach silk camisole, sporting a deep, healthy tan. There were two glasses of Champagne on the table and she got up to kiss me on the cheek. 'Apology Champers, my love,' she said, and stuck out her bottom lip in an attempt to look disarming. 'I'm sorry I haven't been around much recently. I only just came back from Mykonos.'

'The pictures looked great,' I said. 'Who did you go with?'

I could see the fear in Katrina's eyes now. Weighing up exactly how much to tell me, turning the dials of jealousy down by throwing in a few *it was very last minute* and *I could only use my BA points for one person*. 'Tasty,' she replied. 'But—' As she made the predictable excuses, I knew our friendship was pretty much over. Not because we'd argued or said unforgivable things, but because I felt indifferent to her. I just wanted to get through this lunch as quickly as possible.

'Anyway, what's going on with you?' she asked, picking at a bowl of olives. I didn't touch the Champagne.

'A complete shitshow at work.'

'But it's always a shitshow, isn't it?'

'Not like this. I broke my number one rule of not sleeping with anyone at work. Again.'

Katrina's eyes sparkled. I finally had something of interest to tell her. 'Ooh, I want to hear everything!'

'Don't get excited, it's not a good story. You know that guy in my team that I hate? Tristan? Him. We spent the whole afternoon working together and I finally thought I'd seen the real him, you know? Like the person behind this mask of arrogance. And I'm sure what I saw was real, but he's so concerned about what people think of him that he's gone right back into arsehole mode.'

Her air of pleased anticipation at the prospect of gossip

was replaced by a curdled expression. 'What day was this?' Katrina said.

'Friday. Why do you ask?'

'Un-fucking-believable,' she said under her breath.

'What's wrong?'

Katrina normally exuded an easy-breezy, friendly demeanour. She was the type of person who'd always make you feel welcome at a party, find something to talk about, and came across as someone who'd never had a negative thought. But her mouth was now pinched into an expression I'd never seen on it before. 'Remember I matched with him, Bel? The Tristan you said you weren't interested in? We had a third date on Friday. Except he cancelled a couple of hours before we were due to meet. Now I know who he was with instead.'

My mouth fell open. I'd had no idea. How could I? Right swiping and matching on someone wasn't a claim in the same way as putting dibs on a co-worker or someone in a group of mutual friends. If that were the case, half of London would be off limits.

'I'm so sorry,' I said in a strained voice, 'I had no idea. Honestly, Kat, if I'd known you were genuinely interested in him and going on a date, of course I wouldn't have slept with him.'

'Yeah, but I don't know that, do I?'

'You *should* know it, we're supposed to be friends!'

'You haven't been around at all! Hanging out with your sister and that nurse friend of yours. If you'd been there for me lately, you would have known.'

'Katrina,' I said, refusing to rise to her snide tone, 'you literally date two new guys a week. I can't remember who you slept with yesterday, let alone who you might have matched with a few weeks ago.'

'Oh, *nice*, Bel. Way to slut shame me!'

'No! I don't mean it like that.' Nothing I said was coming out right. 'I just . . . look, it was literally a spur-of-the-moment thing. And for what it's worth, he didn't know anything was going to happen either. We *were* working late – I'm sure that's why he cancelled, not because he was trying to get in my pants.' I'm not sure why I was trying to make Tristan seem like a decent human being. I think I was just desperate for the situation to be okay. 'Look, if you really like him, why not suggest rearranging?'

She snorted. 'Have your sloppy seconds? No, thanks.'

Then I realised that this wasn't about Katrina's cancelled date, or even the fact that Tristan and I had slept together. I could apologise over and over, even squeeze out a few tears, and she would still never accept it. This wasn't about contrition. This was fucking Ling all over again. In Katrina's world, she expected to be the most desired, and now she had been presented with proof that perhaps she wasn't. And worst of all, that the person who had beaten her to a prize was someone she didn't consider her equal, at least not looks-wise.

'You're being really unfair, Katrina.' I felt as if I was shrinking under the glare of her anger, and if one of us didn't leave soon I'd be the size of a mouse.

'Life's not fair, Bel,' she said, getting up. 'Especially when one of your best mates fucks a guy you think has boyfriend potential. Which in London is like finding gold in a sewer.' She walked away without paying the bill, and the fact that all I felt was relief, told me everything.

16

Bel, we need to talk. 8 a.m. meeting. Jane will schedule.

Crispin liked to email at odd times and expected an answer within the hour, which did little for the mental wellbeing of his direct reports. He'd sent this at 9 p.m. Afterwards I'd barely slept, wondering what it was about, but I was grateful for the distraction from the trash fire that was my personal life. We were still due to present our update on the project, and I started to worry about whether this summons was to do with Tristan, or my overall performance.

To add another layer to the turd Viennetta that was now my life, Devi still hadn't texted. But then again, I suppose, neither had I contacted her. It was strange how not long ago, whole days and weeks could go by without us speaking. But now, especially with Ama's continued silence, I felt her absence keenly. As for Katrina, it was unnerving how okay I felt about never speaking to her again.

Although I'd expected the meeting to be virtual, I wanted to do it from the office in case of any technical difficulties. I'd texted Maggie in the morning as I knew she liked to get to the office ahead of when I'd be arriving.

> Me: Will be there in 10 mins, can I have a double espresso please? No doughnut. Honestly. Has Jane emailed which meeting room the conference call is in?
>
> Maggie: Meeting is in his office, he's here. Flew in last night.

Less than thirty minutes later, I found myself sitting outside Crispin's office, anxiety gnawing at my stomach. *Stop chomping, there's nothing left to eat,* I said to it. I could hear the murmur of his voice, the clink of a cup on a saucer. It reminded me of being outside the head teacher's office when Ling and I had accidentally set fire to our classmate Rebecca's hair while experimenting with deodorant cans and lighters.

Finally, I was ushered in, Jane's expression unreadable. Crispin sat at his marble-topped desk and gestured for me to sit down. His tan was even more intense against the crisp pink shirt he wore. He looked like a raisin that had gobbled up the sun.

'Bel, you know I've always been fond of you,' he began. 'I saw your potential early on, promoted you to director and gave you this new project because I thought you were the best person for the job.' Uh-oh. This was not going to be good. When someone starts listing what they've done for you, get ready to upload your CV to LinkedIn.

'But I'm starting to get a bit concerned,' he continued,

'that maybe it's too much. Is there anything you want to talk about?'

Now this was the tricky thing. I recognised a management tactic, but I didn't know what *exactly* Crispin knew, and if I wasn't careful, I might end up giving away more than I needed. Better treat it like a game of tennis and volley a bit.

'Is this about Tristan?' I asked, trying to keep my voice calm even though the blood was thundering past my eardrums like white-water rapids.

'Yes,' he replied.

Crispin and I had a special relationship, but I had to balance this skilfully. I had to be professional while also leveraging our familiarity.

'What did he say?' I let out a sigh, just enough to indicate that I felt Tristan was overreacting. He'd probably already made me out to be the typical hysterical woman, and I had to try and flip that narrative.

'He said that you were being obstructive. That you'd come into his office and caused a scene. Apparently, Oliver felt threatened.'

'*What?!*'

'I told them,' Crispin said firmly, 'that they didn't need to raise it with HR. But I said I would speak to you about it.' Then I understood that we were having this conversation *because* we had that special relationship, and that any partiality Crispin felt towards me had already been expended on this chat. He loathed being dragged into office politics, and so trying to implicate or take down Tristan would only incense him further.

'Crispin, I'm sorry. You shouldn't need to be pulled into this kind of stuff. I'll work things out with Tristan. It's just . . .' I knew it wasn't the right time, but I also felt I might not have another opportunity, especially if Tristan was already undermining me. 'He and I had agreed on a new proposal for you, and then he backed out of it.'

'What's the proposal?'

I laid out the new plan, explained why it was the right thing to do, and finished by saying we had a presentation ready to go.

He looked mystified. 'The right thing to do?' he said. 'Bel, I don't give a fuck about *how* it gets done, just *get it done*. We don't have the budget to hire an external consultant. Lightning have a campaign they need us to run for their autumn-winter collection, and we need them to attract other brands. Make the hires within the week, and I want the new team ready to start ASAP.'

*

The longer you work in an office, the more aware you become that it isn't just hot desking and watercooler chat, there's a whole sub-level of things going on there, from the favoured toilets to take a dump in to the best spot to smoke a covert spliff. The quietest place to cry was currently the third-floor toilet because that entire level was being renovated.

It was here that I retreated for a cry and to hyperventilate. Crispin, Tristan, Devi, Ling, Luke, Katrina . . . how and why was it all such a mess? How did one person manage to fuck everything up at the same time? I pressed my hands against my eyes as if trying to force the tears back in. *'Oh god oh god oh god,'* I said, trying to release some of the pressure.

'Bel?'

No. Just no. I couldn't deal with talking to anyone right now. And definitely not Ranvir because I wanted her to think I was professional and calm.

'Bel, it's me, Ranvir.' I tried to blub as quietly as I could. Unfortunately, I had reached the stage where I needed to take in big gulps of air.

'Bel, you don't have to talk to me,' she continued, 'but I want you to listen to me. Okay? Just take a deep breath. Or take the biggest breath you can. And then take another one. And then another. Okay? And just slow it down. Think of something slow and solid, like a tree. Think about the roots of that tree, going into the ground, and it's cool and dark and quiet, and everything is growing slowly. And then take a deep breath . . .'

It was mad how something like breathing, that really was just the simple act of keeping alive, could be so powerful in calming you down. Like a bucket of water thrown over my overheated brain.

*

Ranvir refused to leave until she could see I'd be okay alone. When I eventually came out, she said: 'Oh, mate,' and handed me a tissue. She didn't hug me because she knew on some level that bodily contact might set me off all over again, the intimacy of it too much.

'What are you doing here?' I said through a stuffy nose.

She fidgeted uncomfortably. 'It's the best toilet to, ah, you know.'

'Understood.'

'We don't have to talk about it,' she said after a while, 'but if you trust me, I have something that might take your mind off things. Let's get you cleaned up and then we'll go.'

I nodded, tired and likely to say yes to anything and anyone who would help me feel better.

I began to regret that when I saw where Ranvir had taken me. A ten-minute walk from the office had landed us at the doorway to a martial arts gym that also looked like it moonlighted as a venue for AA meetings. 'Oh, no,' I groaned, 'is this your BJ thing?'

'BJJ,' she said firmly, 'Brazilian Jiu-Jitsu. Try one class. If you hate it, you never have to come back again.' As we walked into the gym and I saw people wriggling around on the floor in the cotton kimono or *Gi*, I realised I'd seen people post about this increasingly on Instagram with photos of their sweaty, smiling faces.

The warm-ups made me want to die. I was gasping for breath. But before I had a chance to think about it, our instructor, a young guy named Miguel, started talking to us about submission holds and body leverages. I was grateful for the brief pause to suck some oxygen into my lungs, and then we moved on to sparring. Ranvir was a blue belt, and as I fumbled with my arms, feeling self-conscious about being that close to someone bodily, she patiently explained what I should do. A gentle nudge here, a tap to indicate where to put my hand. While listening to her and working out my range of movement, I realised I hadn't been thinking about any of my other problems. I hadn't been worrying or agonising about Devi or Tristan. Before I had too long to dwell on it, Ranvir and I started practising holds again.

During a brief respite, after she'd pinned me down, she said: 'Do you know why I love this?' I wheezed out a 'why'.

'Because I can't think about anything else when I'm on the mat. It's all about the here and now, and what I'm doing to progress. There have been plenty of times I've felt stuck in my life, but this helps me to move forward. Plus, there are some pretty sweet self-defence moves.'

'Like what?'

'Say you're at a bar,' she said, 'and there's a guy wearing a suit and he's being aggressive. You could literally use the lapels of his suit to choke him.'

'Really?' I said.

'Yeah. I mean, I wouldn't advise it,' she winked at me, 'but you never know when it might come in handy. Let me show you how.'

'Right,' I said, grateful for the distraction but vowing never to return.

'Do you want to talk about it?' she asked on the walk back. I didn't want to, but I knew that if I didn't, I'd go back to my flat and be alone with thoughts that would just spin around and around. I told her everything that had happened in the last week, even the stuff with Ama and Ling, and Marina. The only part I left out was Tristan.

'Oh, wow,' she said.

'Yeah, I know.'

'You know what this reminds me of? When I was a kid, I always remember there being at least one uncle or aunt who didn't come very often to family gatherings. Like people would gossip about them or just not mention them very much. Did you have someone like that?'

'Yeah, actually,' I said, remembering Padmini Auntie and Rakesh Uncle, and how much I had liked them but never seen much of them.

'And I think they lived their lives in a non-traditional way and so staying at a distance made them happier, but I also think that must have been a lonely way to live. And I don't think we need to live like that anymore, do you know what I mean?'

'Yeah, I guess,' I replied. 'But it's not just the family stuff. Everything about my life seems like a mess. When I die alone, in my hut, clutching a pair of knitting needles, and they go *wasn't it sad, no one loved her*, my ghost will know that's not true. Because I *have* a lot of people who love me,' I broke off, trying not to cry. 'But I push them away. And then, when they go, I think, *See, they don't love you*. I test their love in impossible ways and I don't try to fix it when it breaks. And, Ranvir, it always breaks.'

'I know it might feel like that,' she replied, 'but that's because it feels big and overwhelming. What's the easiest thing you can fix? Just text that guy Luke back. And then once you do that, you can move onto the next thing. It sounds to me like you want to fix things with your friend Ama. It might be hard, she might not react well, but is that really going to be worse than not talking anyway and then missing out on her wedding? That would be a lot harder to recover from.'

She had a point.

*

That evening, I finally texted Luke. The session with Ranvir had settled my thoughts a bit more, like sediment on a riverbed, but I wasn't ready to text Ama yet. Luke was the easier task. I had to stop overthinking it.

> **Me: All okay, sorry it's taken so long to get back to you. It's been a mad week.**

He texted back almost immediately.

> **Luke: No probs. Things mad at this end too, but if you're free Friday night, why don't you swing by the boat and we can have beers on the deck?**

I checked the weather forecast and it was 28°C. There were worse ways to spend my time.

> **Me: Sounds good.**

Buoyed by our little exchange, I decided to call Mum to surreptitiously find out how Devi was doing. While I was still angry at Tristan, and worried about my job after that meeting with Crispin, Devi was the most important person. Mum sounded irritated, but when I offered to call at another time, it only made her more exasperated.

'No, now is fine. Your father and your sister are both driving me up the wall,' she said. 'He's in his workshop all the time, and Devi is just not listening to anything I say. She thinks she knows best, as always.' I knew eventually her irritation would rub off on me and we'd both say words we didn't mean and end the call feeling upset. I took a moment and tried to put myself in Mum's shoes rather than going down the same, well-worn path.

'Are you okay, Mum?'

She was startled into silence for a moment. As if no one had asked her how she was doing in a while and she was considering how to respond.

'I think so,' she said, before sighing. 'I'm just worried about your sister. I don't want her to end up alone.'

Again, I had to measure my response to avoid being pulled into that rich vein of irritation. 'Mum . . . can I give you some advice?'

That made her snort a laugh but then again, she'd always had fixed ideas of parenting. No matter how old Devi and I were, we'd always be the 'kids' and they'd always be the adults.

'I'm being serious,' I said.

'Okay, continue,' she replied, trying to indulge me.

'Consider that maybe we don't know everything that's going on between Devi and Nikhil, and why they broke up.'

'But—'

'Let me finish, please. I don't know the whole story, but maybe consider that it's not up to Devi whether or not they reconcile. So if you're saying that kind of stuff to her, it's just going to make her feel worse.' I could tell by the silence on the other line that this hadn't occurred to Mum. 'I know you love her,' I said a bit more gently, 'and that's all she needs. Just to know we love her.' I felt like such a hypocrite given that she and I weren't even talking.

Then I heard a big sigh at the other end of the line. 'You know,' she said slightly defensively, 'we tried to do our best for both of you.'

'I know,' I said, 'but that doesn't mean that sad or unexpected things aren't going to happen to us. You must have had your fair share of things to deal with when you were our age, didn't you? Things you weren't sure about?'

'No,' she said abruptly. 'I was always sure. We didn't have the luxury of doing anything other than what our families wanted us to do. Anyway, I've got to get the dinner on, Bel. Call soon.'

Something about the quickness with which she shut the conversation down, made me suspicious. It reminded me of some of the things Devi said, about Mum not being the right person to comment on other people's marriages. But that realisation was like a creature of the deep, poking its head momentarily above the waterline and being burned by the sun, before diving straight back down to the bottom.

*

By Friday, one hundred and forty-four hours since our fight, I received a message from Devi. I saw her name flash up on my phone during an extremely dry meeting with Ben the accountant, who was talking me through profit and loss on the new project. A special punishment cooked up by Crispin. I was excited and nervous, but it was merely a terse text to ask if I was still okay to have Karen come and stay with me at the weekend. I texted back 'Sure' and added the most aggressive of emojis, the thumbs-up.

When I came out, I saw that Tristan had put in a meeting right at the end of the day. I poked my head out of my office. 'Maggie, cancel with Tristan McClean, please. I have to leave early.' While there would be zero repercussions for all the times Tristan had bailed on interviews and meetings with me, I would likely be ripped to shreds or complained about (loudly) for cancelling one meeting. But I didn't care.

Control, I was starting to realise, only got you so far. Because you couldn't control the narrative other people created about you. And that if Crispin, someone who knew me so well, who I'd worked countless hours for, done untold things for, could reprimand me on the basis of another man's word, without caring about mine, then there was no point to any of this farce.

*

I arrived at Luke's with a stormfront on my face, but even I couldn't help laughing as Bosco humped my leg so enthusiastically by way of greeting that I fell over on the grassy bank.

'BOSCO!' he yelled. 'This dog . . . I swear, I can't wait until his owner comes to get him.'

For a moment, I couldn't speak. Luke had his shirt off yet again and was only wearing a pair of cargo shorts. 'Sorry,' he said, blushing, catching my gaze, which snagged on every one of his six pack. 'You're a bit early. I'll just put a shirt on.' He disappeared below deck and came back up with two beers.

I could debate every little thing about Luke, do a pros and cons list, and talk myself through why I shouldn't meet up with him, but it was dawning on me that the scenarios I sketched out in my head weren't reality at all. They were forecasts. I wouldn't know until I tried.

'It looks like thunderclouds might be rolling in,' I said, as we sat on beanbags on the deck. In the distance, the *whomph* of a swan's wings filled the silence, getting louder as it approached and skated alongside the boats. I wanted to ask him how Ama was, but I couldn't without telling him why I hadn't spoken to her. 'How've you been?' I asked. 'You seem busy.' He shrugged. It was going to be a painful couple of hours if this was as chatty as he got. I decided to skip the small talk. I had nothing to lose.

'So you said you switched to living on a boat because of a bad break-up. What happened?'

The line of his jaw hardened. 'I don't know if I want to be talking about that now.'

'Because it's painful or because we kissed?'

'Jesus, you really get to the point, don't you?'

I laughed. 'Actually, I usually don't get to the point. It takes me a while to say what I really think.'

'And I just happen to be the lucky exception?'

'What happened?'

He sighed. 'It's not as dramatic as it sounds. We were together for five years. Nothing I did was good enough for her. She worked as a lawyer and it drove her mad that I didn't make anywhere near what she did. We lived in a fancy – yes, I said fancy – high-rise building in Canary Wharf. I caught her fucking one of her colleagues. The rest is history.'

'And the boat?'

'The boat is because I've always loved the river. There is nothing quite like that feeling of falling asleep and the water just rocking you back and forth. The first thing I see is the water, and the first thing I hear is birdsong. It also weeds out women who are superficial about this kind of thing. Normally people hear the word "boat" and make all sorts of judgements.'

'I don't know if you can just blame the boat. Your personality, I'm sure, goes some way towards painting the picture.' He flicked a beer cap at me. 'Honestly, I thought you hated me when we first met.'

'Far from it,' he said with a smile. 'I tend to get quiet around new people. Especially people who look the way you do.'

'Extremely cheesy, but I will take it.'

He looked at me sideways. 'What's been going on with you?' he asked.

Unexpectedly and to my deep embarrassment, I started welling up. Again. I knew that if I cried, it would make things awkward. But Luke surprised me by getting me some tissues and putting his hand on my shoulder. Physical touch. That was mostly all I needed.

'It's been a shitter of a week,' I said. 'Everyone hates me, even Ama. Even my sister.'

'I'm sure that's not true,' he said.

I felt it was true, in that moment. 'I can't believe I'm crying on a date.'

'I mean, technically this isn't a date, we're just hanging out . . .' he said a bit sheepishly.

'Seriously?' I said staring at him. What was *wrong* with men?

'Well, I'm seeing other people.'

'Yeah, Luke, I didn't think this was a series of events leading to matrimony. It can still be a date even if we're dating other people. Hanging out . . . what are you, fifteen?'

'Why are you so mad?' Our raised voices were beginning to attract the attention of people on neighbouring boats who were craning their necks at this unscheduled bit of evening entertainment.

'I'm not mad, I'm just disappointed. Because you men . . . you assume women want more. You assume we're going into this thinking you'll be The One. What if we just want a shag? Or what if we're assessing whether you're good enough for us and have no intention of taking it further?'

I could feel Luke shutting down, his fists tightening, his lips thinning. Why was I fighting with the entire world? I took a deep breath and tried to calm down.

'I'm sorry, Luke, that wasn't fair. I'm taking my anger out on you and you didn't cause it. Okay? It's some guy at work that behaved badly, and that's who I should be yelling at, not you.'

He got up and headed below deck without saying a word. I felt miserable. *I deserved that.* I checked my phone – no messages. I got up, ready to leave. 'Where are you going?' he said, sticking his head out of the hatch. 'I just went to get more beer.'

'I'm being a bad guest. I should go.'

'Don't be an idiot.'

I looked out at that beautiful scene, water rippling with the movement of leaves and tiny birds. There was so much turmoil in my heart, but I knew the answer to one thing at least: I wasn't going to sleep with Luke. As nice as that kiss had been, he wasn't able to give me what I needed or wanted.

Something had emerged from the darkness of the accident, a voice that said: *Live fully, Bel.* The fireworks, the pain, the love, the peace, the home of other people – none of that came neatly packaged. I wanted big love, the kind of love that consumed me. I liked Luke, but he was never going to be that for me.

'Luke, I think we should just be friends,' I said. He stared out across the water, his expression unreadable. 'It's not that you aren't gorgeous – I mean, look at you. But if we have sex, we'll end up not being friends, and I don't think it's worth it. Sex is easy to come by, friends aren't.' Luke would never be The One, but he could be one of the several people I relied on, who could literally fight through flames to get there.

We sat in comfortable silence for a good while. 'My ego is bruised,' he said, 'but you make a fair point.'

His phone pinged. 'It's Ama,' he said, and all that raw hurt flooded back. That strange sensation of knowing a loved one had closed their door to you, yet you saw flashes of them through the windows of someone else's home. 'She's got a burst pipe. Plumber can't get there till tomorrow and Bron isn't at home. I've got to go,' he said, getting up. 'Why don't you come with me? You can help – I've seen your handyman skills. Then you can sort out whatever it is you need to sort out with her?'

'I don't think she'd like that.'

'Look, I don't know what happened between you both, but she's got a lot of shit going on at the moment. Bron is out of town, she has a ton of wedding prep and her mother is now saying she doesn't know if she'll make it back in time from Sri Lanka for the wedding. Which is an obvious lie. However mad she is, I am sure Ama would rather you were there.

'And we have to go now. Her kitchen is flooding.'

17

We turned up at her door, and I was shocked to see Ama looking dishevelled and tired, in a dressing gown. I'd never seen her look bad; looking good was always so effortless for her. She was surprised to see me hiding behind Luke's big frame. 'We were just hanging out,' he said. 'I brought her because she knows how to fix things.'

'Fine,' Ama said, in a voice so tired that it worried me. 'Thanks for coming.' We took stock of the flooding in the kitchen and upstairs bathroom and divided our tasks. Luke would take the kitchen while I headed upstairs. We turned the water off at the mains, while Ama made us tea.

I could hear Luke and her talking while I still wondered how to broach things. Working away at the pipes felt calming, a puzzle I could actually solve.

'I'll just pop it down here, shall I?' Ama stood by the door holding a mug of tea.

'That'd be great,' I said, not looking up. 'Why don't you grab a chair and stay for a bit?' I could feel the pause before I heard the scrape of wood against tile.

'Luke said your mum might not be coming to the wedding. How are you doing?'

She laughed mirthlessly. 'I didn't expect her to walk me down the aisle,' she said, 'but I thought she'd at least be there.'

'Spanner, please.' She handed it to me.

'I'm sorry, Ams. I can't imagine how it must be. She does love you, you know.'

'People in my life have a funny way of showing it.' Ah, the first shot fired.

I pulled my head from under the sink and looked at her. There would be time to respond to that, things I needed to say, but for now, simply words of softness. 'I know you want her there. I can't imagine how much you must miss your dad at the moment. But, Ama, we don't get to choose our family. They are often difficult, don't accept our choices. What you have with Bron is beautiful. And you have so many people who support that choice and want to celebrate it with you. She'll come around.'

Ama started crying then; I'd forgotten what a comedically ugly crier she was.

I got up and shuffled over on my knees to give her a hug. 'I know we're in a fight,' I said into her stomach, 'but I'm here for you, okay?'

'It's been so shit,' she said. 'Bron has been away, and there hasn't been anyone to chat to. And we've been . . .'

We both knew what we'd been.

'Bel, what the fuck are you doing?' yelled Luke. 'There's still a drip coming through.'

'OH, FUCK OFF!' I yelled back. 'Give me a second, would you?' Ama stopped crying and stared at me. 'Yeah, we're friends now,' I said. 'Not friends with benefits, just friends.'

Although it had barely been an hour since our conversation on his boat, I knew the decision for Luke and me to remain friends was the right one. Things had immediately felt comfortable between us once we were no longer trying to impress the other or dance around what certain things meant, like sleeping together or simply sharing a beer. With sex and romance off the table, I was able to enjoy his company.

'Impressive,' Ama said, raising her eyebrows. 'Usually Luke doesn't make friends with anyone he doesn't work with.'

We sat in silence as I worked underneath the sink. 'IS THAT BETTER?' I yelled.

'YES.'

I wiped my hands with a rag and picked up my tea. 'Ama, when I first reached out to you after my accident, why did you message back?'

'Why are you asking?' she said warily.

'Because we still have stuff to sort out. I've been too afraid to ask you before but I think, if we want to be in each other's lives properly, we have to be honest with each other.'

Her mouth twisted. 'Because . . . because things with Mum are hard. And they've been hard for a long time, and . . . there aren't really many people in my life who knew me from before. Marina and Ling . . . they don't quite get it, and you have always just *got it*. I couldn't talk to Bron about how lonely it made me feel because I didn't want her to feel rejected, but then you came along. This bright, wonderful reminder of the past but also the future . . . and I didn't want to ruin it by talking about what happened. I was just glad to have you back.'

I hadn't considered what I'd given to Ama's life, only what she'd given to mine. But that still didn't explain why, if I was such a cherished friend, she'd behaved the way she had at the club. And I had to say it.

'Ama, your hen do – I know it wasn't the time or place and I am sorry for what happened. But that conversation we had then hurt my feelings.'

'It was my hen do, Bel,' she said, that familiar note of exasperation returning to her voice.

'I know,' I said. 'But you understand why I find it so hard to let go of that stuff, right?'

'It happened so long ago, what does it matter now?'

'It matters because of what happened between you and me,' I said quietly.

'What do you mean? We chatted about that.'

'I'm not talking about that day in the bar with my workmates or the months after. We've *never* spoken about Cornwall. I've never told you how hurt I was because I didn't want to lose you too. But I can't let go of what happened between us. If trust is a pillar of friendship, I don't see how we can move forward until I understand why you did what you did.'

'What did I do?' Ama looked genuinely mystified and, now, unnerved. 'What happened?'

I wrapped my arms around myself and stared at the ceiling. I knew that this was the moment to say something. If I didn't, our second chance at friendship wouldn't last much longer.

I felt the blackness of that cellar swirl around me. I had survived it once. I could do it again. I started to tell Ama about our last day in Cornwall.

1999

The morning of Ama's sixteenth birthday, I decided to clear the air with Ling. Or give the impression of clearing the air. 'Come in,' she said as I knocked on her door, then her face dropped when she saw it was me. I rallied despite that.

'Mate, can we talk?' I said, sitting on her bed.

'Sure, whatever.' I'd given her space the whole day previously, trying not to irritate her or draw attention to myself. I'd taken myself to a nook in the house and read my books.

'I know things are weird between us, but I just wanted to say I'm sorry. You're my friend, and I love you, and no boy should come between that. I don't know what I was thinking.' The words felt like hot ash coming out of my mouth because they weren't true, but I didn't want Ling to be mad at me anymore.

She looked at me as if measuring something I couldn't see. 'You mean that?'

'Yeah, of course.'

It was extraordinary. Her entire countenance altered, as if this wasn't actually about Brandon at all, but some test of dominance and friendship. That I had somehow passed.

'Skin?' she said, holding out her hand.

'Skin,' I replied, and as our hands touched, I felt repelled by the action. By lying and prioritising my needs below hers, the gesture had now become meaningless for me. A Band-Aid for how we truly felt, a peace treaty signed with our fingers crossed behind our backs.

'Where's the birthday girl?' she asked.

'I think we should go in and wake her up. Marina has the cake, and I have the silly string.'

She smiled impishly, and for a moment actually looked like her old self. Sweet and carefree. 'Let's go terrorise her.'

*

While the garden was as dilapidated as the main house, India had somehow managed to tame part of it into a beautiful dell fit for a sixteen-year-old queen. Fairy lights were strung up around the trees, and she'd made a makeshift firepit from bricks and stacked wood inside it. Little tealights were dotted around the place. No one wanted to touch Jasper's wine with a barge pole, so she'd even managed to ask a friend with ID to buy beers with the money we'd pooled together and cooled them in a tin tub filled with water and ice.

I was sorting out the music while Ling and Marina

pulled together the snacks – carrots for India, cocktail sausages for us, and what seemed like a hundred bags of crisps. The first song I chose was 'Otherside' from the Red Hot Chili Peppers' new album *Californication*. Upstairs, India was doing a few braids in Ama's hair, and when she finally emerged, we were all speechless. Under her crown of braids, her long limbs were dark bronze from spending the day out on the beach, made more luminous by the contrast with her white lace dress. She fleetingly looked like the adult she might turn into one day, apart from her feet stuffed into scruffy Doc Martens with charms hanging from the laces.

Peace reigned between Ling and me, and Ama seemed genuinely happy about it. I didn't roll my eyes when Ling kept fretting about whether the boys would turn up, even though I wanted to yell at her to stop making it about herself. I was secretly relieved we'd be going home tomorrow; I had completely run out of undies and was now wearing my swimsuit as a replacement underneath my short satin mini-dress. I wanted to light the candles but couldn't find any matches, so I sought out India. Usually she was like a mountain stream, calm, zen and collected. But she was flustered – red-cheeked and pulling out clothes from her wardrobe.

'Yes?' she snapped. 'Sorry,' she said, seeing my face fall. 'I can't figure out what to wear. Help me.'

I scanned the clothes on the bed and pulled out a white slip. It would go perfectly with her tan. 'What about this one?'

She blushed. 'Ama's wearing white – I can't wear the same colour as her.'

'It's not her wedding,' I laughed. 'Anyway, Ama's not like that – she won't mind.'

'I can't,' she snapped again. Clearly not the time for jokes.

'Do we have matches? For the candles?' I asked.

'Shit. We've run out. And I'm not even ready. Oh, no . . .' she wailed.

'Don't worry, I can pop out and get them,' I said backing away towards the door. 'We've only just started and the guys aren't here yet.'

'Bel,' India said hesitantly, 'does Ama . . . like any of them?'

'I don't think so,' I replied. 'Ben likes Ling, we both like Brandon and the other two are pretty ratty. Why do you ask?'

'No reason,' she replied. 'See you later.'

*

I decided to walk along the seashore on my way to the little corner shop. Although walking on the tarmac was quicker, I wanted to feel that final lick of salt air on my face before we went home. Tiny crabs were darting towards their dark little tunnels. Although I had been homesick for most of my trip, with the end in sight, I looked at the sea with a slight pang. I took my boots off, rolled up the socks and stuffed the fiver in my pocket deep inside the toe.

The beach was mercifully empty as the surfing festival had wrapped up and it was that short interlude before people would start arriving to look at the sunset. Something about that vast expanse of water reached into me and quietened everything down. I slipped my dress over my head and draped it over my boots. I tied my hair tight into a bun.

I got to my knees under the water and dipped myself in, right to my chin, making a wish. *I wish that Brandon turns up to the party. I wish that he likes me. I wish that everything will be okay with my friends and that'll we'll remain close forever.* I wasn't expecting a talking lobster or anything, but the water kept sloshing around me, getting on with the business of being a wave, an ocean. *Be like that then.* I stuck my tongue out at it.

'Are you sticking your tongue out at anything in particular or just the sea in general?' a familiar voice said.

I bobbed around slowly. 'Hi, Brandon.' *Kill me now,* I whispered to the sea. *Just a little tidal wave.* There was no way I was getting out in front of him.

'I'm headed to your party. Want to come with me?'

'I do but—'

'If you want to swim longer, I'm happy to wait,' he said. He wore long black shorts and a black vest, with a little silver dog chain. A rucksack and a towel were slung over his shoulder. 'But, in fairness, you don't look like you're swimming. More like you're having some sort of existential crisis.' He grinned. He was so beautiful when he spoke/laughed/breathed. Ling was going to kill me.

I squinted at him. 'This is going to sound weird.'

'You've pooped in the sea?'

'No! Ew! Not that. I need your towel,' I said.

'That's fine – why is that weird?'

'I need you to close your eyes when I get out of the sea and just hold the towel out.'

'Okay, that *is* weird. You have a swimsuit on, right? You're not a secret nudist?'

'Get that hopeful look off your face. I have a swimsuit on but – look, just do it, alright?'

'You're very bossy for someone who needs my towel, you know that?' I glared at him. 'Okay, fine, closing my eyes now.'

I scrambled out of the water as fast as I could and grabbed the towel from his hands. As I wrapped it around myself, he said: 'You know you don't have anything to worry about, right? You look great.' I punched him on the arm.

'Ow! What was that for?'

'For looking. But thanks,' I said a bit shyly. 'What's in the rucksack?' I tried to dry myself while covering my body with as much towel as possible.

'Beers. Want one?'

Drinking a beer with Brandon, while watching the sunset, was the exact opposite of what I'd intended to do. But I hadn't planned this, and I was going to be in trouble anyway when I turned up with him to the house. The sand clung stickily to my legs as we flopped down on a dune. I felt everything in that moment. The cold beer running in a bitter stream down my throat. The sea in front of us, speaking only in the movement of wind and froth as it hit the shore. Sitting next to a boy who made me feel as if my skin was on fire despite the breeze carrying across the water. We didn't say anything, but I could feel the air growing heavier between us.

This was the point in the movie where the boy would lean in. But despite the soft, sugary pink beginnings of sunset, I descended into a dark tunnel of panic. I had never kissed a boy before. What did you do with your tongue? What if you used too much saliva? What if I had bad beer breath? If Brandon had been about to make a move I would never know because, jittery and nervous, I suddenly got up. 'We should head to the house,' I said, 'they'll be wondering where I've got to.' Maybe I'd imagined the whole thing and was making this something it wasn't.

I loved my friends but they were gossip-hungry arseholes who looked at Brandon and me and smirked. Except for Ling, who looked furious. Brandon said a short hello and headed to the back garden to catch up with Ben, Kevin and Derek who had already arrived. 'We bumped into each other by accident,' I said, hoping this wouldn't be a big deal.

'And you're in his towel because . . .' Marina said.

'I decided to go for a swim, it was all very spontaneous,' I replied, aware that every word coming out of my mouth only made me sound more guilty. I could feel every grain of sand rubbing into my legs, the saltwater sticky on my skin.

'You never swim though,' Ling said flatly.

'I know how it sounds,' I replied miserably, 'but the sea was there, it just seemed like the right moment, and then Brandon came along.'

'I'm sure he did.' Ama winked. 'Have fun, B,' she said before floating serenely into the garden.

After I'd showered and changed, the atmosphere outside was different with the boys there. Brandon was deep in conversation with India, which made sense given that she looked like a goddess – why wouldn't he choose someone like her over me? But the strangest sight was Ling, who was wrapped around Ben like a pretzel, sitting in his lap while he circled his arm around her. Derek and Kevin were talking mainly to each other, with snippets of their conversation drifting over ranging from video games to comparing the smell of their own farts. I had made a paper fortune teller for Ama and we were messing about with that, laughing at the answers.

When I went to grab another case of beers as the tin tub was looking a bit bare, Marina followed me in. I wasn't in the mood for yet another lecture, but she surprised me by saying: 'Are you okay?' She looked really pretty, like a young Courtney Love in a pale pink slip dress.

I'd felt strangely down since my swim on the beach. 'I don't know,' I said, 'I feel a bit weird out there. I tried . . . talking to Ling about Brandon, you know? I didn't want things to be horrible between us so I said I wouldn't do anything with him, but now it seems like she's into Ben, so what was the point with all of that? I can't figure her out.'

Marina was silent, as if figuring out whether to tell me something and wondering if it might come back later to bite her in the bum. 'I asked Ling if she liked Ben,' she said, 'and apparently now she does. Maybe don't worry about this too much. Just enjoy hanging out with us. Boys aren't important anyway. Like I've said to Ling a thousand times.' She rolled her eyes, which was reassuringly familiar.

'Thanks, Marina, you're a good friend,' I said, and actually meant it for once.

*

When we came back out, Ling and Ben were gone. India was curled up at Ama's feet attempting to read her palm, their arms a tangle of warm white and rich brown. Brandon helped me unload the rest of the beers into the tub while Kevin and Derek were trying to set fire to some ants emerging from their home. We sat and watched them. 'You've been friends with them for long, yeah?'

'Since primary school,' he said resignedly.

Night was starting to pour in quickly after the sun set and already the air was getting chilly as the sky turned a deeper shade of blue. 'We should light the fire,' India said, and soon warmth spread from the pit. She drew a blanket over her and Ama, which was odd given that while Ama didn't dislike India, she had made a fair number of scathing jokes about her vegetarianism and love of the environment.

After a while, Ben finally came back from the direction of the house, but no Ling. He had a big grin on his face. Something had obviously happened between the two of them. When he saw that I was sitting next to Brandon, he changed course and made a beeline for the other two boys. He held his finger out and they sniffed it, laughing raucously. *Boys are so* gross, I thought. Marina had been reading a copy of *Kerrang*, but after eyeing them over the top of the magazine, scowled and went inside to find Ling.

'You know what I wish we had?' said Ama. 'A guitar. We'd be able to have a sing-song.'

'I think we have one somewhere,' replied India, snuggling closer. 'But I'm too comfy to go and get it.'

'Tell me where it is, and I'll go,' I said. As India gave directions to the outdoor shed where she thought the guitar might be, Brandon offered to come with me. 'It's getting dark,' he said, 'I don't want you falling in a ditch.'

When we reached it, he flicked on the switch, which flooded the small space with dim warm lighting. There were heaps of blankets and an old dog bed, belonging to some dearly departed pet. The guitar was easy to find among the gardening equipment, which had clearly sat there rusty and unused for some time. He twanged a string that was slack with disuse. As he tuned the guitar, he asked me what song I'd like him to play, saying that I could only choose from Metallica's 'Nothing Else Matters', Oasis's 'Wonderwall' or Radiohead's 'Creep'.

'"Creep",' I said softly, feeling as if I had stepped into a dream. As he started playing, I sat next to him and closed my eyes. His voice wasn't perfect but it was true and authentic and heartfelt. I was so lost in it, I almost missed him singing: *'You're so fucking special, Bel. I wish I was special.'* I opened my eyes with a start, to find him looking at me. And this time, I didn't think about whether or not he was going to kiss me, I leaned in and kissed him. I didn't know what I was doing, but I felt the place where his mouth fitted mine and moved into that non-verbal slipstream where only thought and feeling guided me. He pulled away abruptly, and I instantly thought it was because I was a crap kisser. But it was so that he could put the guitar down and slide his hands behind my head to pull me closer.

Music from the garden drifted over the summer air; the first few notes of Smashing Pumpkins' 'Today' were carried with it. I wrapped my legs around him, as if I was an anemone and he a beautiful sea creature that happened to float past my soft, blue world.

I didn't know how long we were kissing for. Eventually we broke apart. 'Shall I go get us some drinks?' I said.

'Yes, please,' he said, smiling, and kissed me full on the mouth. When I returned to the bonfire, Marina had decided to liven things up with a makeshift shots table. '"Today is the greatest day I've ever known",' she was singing loudly, stopping when she saw me. Drunk Marina was actually fun. She whooped at the sight of my pale, chapped lips, a sign that I'd kissed everything I had into Brandon. The rest of them did wolf whistles. 'Bastards,' I laughed. Ling had returned but was now sitting next to

Ama wrapped under the same blanket. She looked at me with an unreadable expression.

'The beer bucket is empty,' India said, 'would you mind bringing a few out from the kitchen?'

By the time I returned Ling had disappeared again, but I picked up two beers and headed back to the shed. I saw the light shining through the wooden slats, reminding me of who and what was waiting for me. A slow warmth spread through me. I felt like a jellyfish lighting up in the dark. Just as I was about to open the door, I heard Ling's voice.

'You and Bel got together, I take it?' I could hear her saying to Brandon. Her words were slurred; she was drunk.

'Yeah, why do you ask?' he said, confused as to why she was there and not me.

'I'm just surprised,' she said, 'she didn't seem your type.' My face burned in shock. *What was Ling doing?*

'I'll treat her with respect, you know,' he said, not realising why Ling was ambushing him. 'I promise. I really like her.'

Ling laughed bitterly. 'What does that mean? You're going to come down from Manchester to visit her? Two of you going to get married?'

'No, this is just a holiday thing. Why are you being so nuts about this?' he said, irritated. My heart sank at *holiday thing.*

'You know what,' she said, 'I should just go.'

'Yeah, maybe you should,' he said, starting to play a few chords. I ducked around the side and could see through a gap that she was turning to leave. But before she did, she said the words that would be hammered into my heart for ever afterwards. 'I don't know what you see in her. She's just like all those other coloured girls, you know. Her house *stinks* of curry.'

I could see Brandon's jaw clenching but he didn't say anything.

When she realised he wasn't going to reply, she said, laughing: 'I'm *joking*, Brandon, lighten up.' She opened the door and walked back to the house. I froze against the side of the shed, shock and rage blossoming in my heart.

He didn't say anything, I thought, over and over again, as I sagged against the wall for support. But Ling – Ling had said everything. My head felt like it was about to burst. I would never, ever talk to her again. There was nothing she could say to me that would change that. I stayed there for what felt like an eon, until eventually I heard the door of the shed open and Brandon leave. Presumably to go and find me.

The cold night air was starting to make my teeth chatter. I headed back to the bonfire and saw Ling surrounded by our friends. The boys were nowhere to be seen.

'What the FUCK is your problem?' I shouted. Everyone went quiet.

'Excuse me?' Ling said with a look on her face that I wanted to smack off with a plank of wood.

'I heard what you said to Brandon.'

She had the grace to look embarrassed for a fraction of a second before defensiveness kicked in. 'Yeah, and?'

'"Yeah, and?"' I mimicked. 'It's not enough that you hook up with Ben, you just can't bear the thought of me actually getting together with someone?'

'Bel, what happened?' Marina said firmly.

'This mad bitch goes over to Brandon and starts talking shit about me,' I yelled. I couldn't bring myself to mention the coloured word or the curry bit, because I hadn't yet been able to overcome the shame I'd felt on hearing those words. I couldn't believe Ling had said them. The few times people had been racist towards me, it had made me feel as if I wanted to unzip the skin I was in, find a rock and crawl under it. I certainly didn't have the courage to confront them or to tell my parents. It was a feeling that was simultaneously so loud and deafening it made the blood in your body waterfall through your head, while at the same time rendering speech impossible. Ling herself had received plenty of racist comments – where was the solidarity? And did it mean she had thought this way all the time we were 'friends'? And that she thought the same about Ama?

But then Ling started crying. Marina immediately rushed over to comfort her. It only made me angrier. Ama hadn't moved or opened her mouth. 'Aren't you going to say anything?' I asked her.

'Bel,' she said finally, 'maybe Ling didn't mean it like that. Maybe we don't know everything.' Why did no one believe me? Why was no one on my side?

'I can't believe you,' I said, by now crying myself. 'She said some of the worst things. She did! I'm not imagining it. She's been an absolute bitch this entire week. And now she sheds a few tears and none of you give a fuck.'

'Bel,' India said gently, 'that's not true.'

'Oh, fuck *off*, India,' I said through snot and tears. 'Go and light some fucking incense or chant at the moon.'

I ran into the house, so angry, so upset at every single one of them, and even more furious that none of them followed me to see if I was okay. I would never forgive them.

18

'That is awful,' said Ama, the colour draining from her face. 'I am so sorry you went through that, and what she said . . . it's unforgivable. I didn't know.'

'I needed someone on my side, Ama,' I said, without anger. 'I always thought I could rely on you to be that person. It felt like such a massive betrayal. I had no one I could count on.'

She had put her head in her hands, the sleeves of her dressing gown pressed over her eyes.

'BEL, WHAT'S THE HOLD UP . . .'

'SHUT UP, LUKE,' we both yelled. There was silence from downstairs.

'I'd better apologise to him,' Ama groaned, getting up. I started sorting out the screws in the toolbox, wondering if I was doing the right thing with her. I could stop talking now and things would be fine. But then it wouldn't be the type of friendship I wanted, which was based on honesty and love without resentment. Ama came back up. 'Luke's gone to the local pub to get a drink and give us some space,' she explained. I went back to fiddling with the toolbox.

'Bel, I'm sorry,' she said, sitting on the floor with her knees pulled to her chest. 'If I could change the past I would.'

'I don't want that. But I needed to say how I felt, and how badly it affected me back then. *Why* weren't you on my side?'

'It wasn't that I wasn't on your side,' she said, fiddling with a screw. 'I can see that's how it looked. But . . . I'm going to say something about that holiday and all I ask is that you listen to me before you say anything.' She looked at me pleadingly and I nodded.

'There's a big thing and a small thing,' she said, 'and I'm going to start with the small thing. I know it was a big deal that you kissed that boy. I know that first kisses are a big deal. But that was also *my* first kiss.' She saw my frown because Ama had kissed boys before. 'With a girl. India was the first girl I'd ever kissed. On my sixteenth birthday. I'd known for a while but that moment crystallised it for me. I couldn't talk to any of you about it because I was scared. I was ashamed – not of who I was, but what you all might think of me. I didn't know how you might react. I had this beautiful, magical moment where this missing part of me finally slotted into place, and I couldn't tell anyone. Can you imagine what that felt like?'

'I can't,' I admitted. When I'd kissed Brandon, I'd wanted to announce it to everyone. I knew the reaction would be nothing but high fives.

'When all of this kicked off, my head was in a strange space. I wasn't thinking about you, or Ling, if I'm being honest. I kept thinking about my mum and how she might never talk to me again. There was this wonderful thing I knew about myself yet I couldn't tell the person I loved most, because it might make her love me less, or not at all.'

I went to hold her hand but she shook her head, as if being touched would make her cry. 'I'm sorry,' I said.

'For what? You don't have to apologise about that at all. That's *my* stuff, my issues, is what I'm trying to tell you. But I'm also trying to explain that what you thought was me not caring was not that at all. Anyway – Ling. You remember how weird she was acting during that holiday? And how moody she got in that last year of our GCSEs, like nothing we did or said was ever right?'

I couldn't forget it even if I wanted to.

'It'd probably be helpful for you to know that she has ongoing mental health problems. It's not for me to share all the details but it explains a lot and it started when she was young. I think fifteen or sixteen . . . it was a particularly bad time. The intense feelings that might change a few hours later. The neediness. Impulsive behaviour, paranoia. I only know about it because I'm a nurse and she told me a few years ago. You don't know her as an adult but . . . it's a lot. She hasn't been able to hold onto any of her older friends apart from me. And Marina. But even they aren't as close as they used to be. And I'm not as close to either of them as I was.'

I shifted uncomfortably, trying to recalibrate who I thought Ling was.

'Shall we go downstairs?' Ama said. I tidied up the toolbox as best I could and followed her.

Once we were settled on the couch, we both instinctively grabbed cushions and placed them on our laps, as if we were in couples counselling.

'I'm not telling you this to make you feel bad or to say you aren't justified in being upset, but to explain why she behaved that way in Cornwall. But the big thing is what happened with her and Ben.'

I tried to remember the details of that evening. All I recalled was Ling disappearing with him. But, funnily enough, I didn't remember them being lovey-dovey when they returned. Ben had done that gross sniff-my-finger thing with his friends while Ling had gone straight to Ama. I was starting to feel slightly sick because now I knew more about the world, and had a feeling where this was going.

'There's no way of sugar-coating this,' Ama continued, 'Ben sexually assaulted Ling. We wouldn't have called it that back then, but that's what it was. They'd gone to her room, and she thought they'd do a bit of kissing and fumbling. And they did, but then he said he wanted to you know, put his hand inside her. She wasn't comfortable with that and said no, but he forced himself on her anyway.'

'Oh my god,' I said, the colour draining out of my face.

'I know. He said all of that manipulative shit to get her to do it when she first refused – *you led me on, I thought you were cool, you owe me after all the beers I bought*. But we were young. She was young. She didn't know, not really. She did it but she didn't consent and she felt awful. Even after it, she wasn't going to blame him but then she saw him bragging to those other two little idiots. He didn't even seem to think what he'd done was bad, and it made her go crazy.'

'That is horrible, Ama.' I felt so bad for Ling, who had deserved love and protection and ended up in the hands of a predator. But as awful as that was, I hadn't deserved the way she'd treated me either. And my anger deserved to be recognised too.

'But . . . that stuff she said to Brandon, I still remember it. Clearly.'

'I know. I'm not excusing it. But she felt that we all abandoned her, that we weren't looking out for her.' Ama sighed. 'In her head, I think she thought that if she'd been with Brandon then that awful thing wouldn't have happened with Ben. So that's why everything converged on you. And when you came out yelling at her, she'd just told us what had happened with Ben. We'd already asked the boys to leave.'

'But, Ama,' I said, trying not to get upset. 'That stuff she said has stayed with me for twenty years. You asked me to let it go at your hen do, and I can't. Any self-loathing I feel has her words at the heart of it. And she felt we all abandoned *her* . . . I get why, but where do I feature in that? And why didn't you talk to me about it at the time? I felt like you just gave up on me.'

'I honestly thought you knew I would never do that.

That even if we disagree, it doesn't mean I'm not there for you. And it breaks my heart that you thought I didn't love you, and that's why you pulled away.'

Love is grief, Kendra had said in our first therapy session. Every moment that you spend loving someone, you have to live with the knowledge that one day you'll be without them. Ama and I both started crying then, and as if sent by the God of Bad Timing, Luke poked his head around the door. 'Forgot my wall . . .' He trailed off when he saw us. 'Never mind.' The front door banged shut.

'Bel, can we fix this?' she said, wiping her nose on her dressing gown.

'That's GROSS. Here, take a tissue.'

Second chances. That's what the accident had given me, and that's what it was trying to tell me. Sometimes you can fly through a chasm where by rights you should break your neck against the rockface. And sometimes life offers you an opportunity to make a different choice.

'I want to fix it,' I said. 'I mean, even just talking about it helps.' It didn't mean things would be perfect or that we would never fight, but if we could talk about things and not silently store up resentment, we had a chance.

'I never, ever meant to make you feel alone,' she said. 'And I didn't mean to hurt you.'

'It hurts because it matters,' I said simply. 'That's a good place to start, I think.'

'I think we need more tea.'

We moved to the kitchen, which was now an absolute bomb site thanks to Luke, and while Ama put teabags into mugs and fussed about with milk and sugar, I started tidying up some of the mess he'd made.

'Does knowing any of this stuff make you feel differently towards Ling?' Ama asked.

I sighed. 'It makes me feel desperately sad for her. I wish I could go back in time and hug her and tell her it will be okay. But even if we'd patched things up, the stuff she said . . . that would have been burned in my brain.'

Ama nodded. 'I had no right to tell you to let it go. I forget that I have a different history with them.'

'You're a better person than I am,' I said, thinking about Ama's softness and kindness and how I wished I was capable of that.

'I'm not, Bel, honestly. It just means that I take on other people's crap, and you have less tolerance for doing that. I kind of admire it, actually.'

Was it less a matter of tolerating other people's crap, though, and more about avoiding it? I didn't know the answer to that and it troubled me.

*

Ama texted Luke when it was safe for him to return, and after finishing off the rest of the work, we wolfed down two giant pizzas. I then gave Ama the world's longest hug and said *I love you* into the crook of her neck. Luke offered to drop me back to Battersea, as a thank you for helping. 'This isn't how I thought the evening would end,' he said as we crawled through the traffic on Battersea Rise.

In Case of Emergency

'I know,' I said, 'but I think it's for the best.'

Although the flat still felt horribly empty, I decided not to fill the void with alcohol. I cleaned it from top to bottom in preparation for Karen coming over and staying for the weekend. Waking up hangover-free and full of energy on the Saturday morning made me realise just how much time I had wasted as a tithe to drinking. I texted Ranvir asking if I could join her for an early morning BJJ class, which was marginally less daunting than the first but still left me gasping and pouring sweat. Freshly showered, the flat tidy and smelling of lemons, sunshine pouring through in cleansing waves, I felt clear-headed for the first time in ages.

Just as I was finally about to catch up on *My Indian Bae*, my phone rang. There were only three people approved for calls when my 'do not disturb' mode was switched on: my parents, Karen and Devi.

My heart almost stopped when I saw it was my sister. Something told me that this was important. That Devi wouldn't call me at the moment unless it was an emergency.

'Bel,' she said in a panicked voice, 'is Karen with you?'

'No,' I said, bewildered, 'she isn't due to come to mine until later today. Is everything okay?'

I could hear Devi saying, *'Oh my god oh my fucking god oh my god.'*

'DEVI,' I said loudly to try and snap her out of it. 'What has happened?'

'Karen said she was coming to yours last night, that you'd asked her to come a day early. But I just checked

387

your Insta stories and saw your dinner for one and your class this morning and realised she isn't with you.'

'Okay, listen, don't panic. Remember we used to do shit like this all the time and we were always fine. Okay? We'll find her. Let me try her and I'll call you right back.'

I immediately dialled Karen's number, but it went straight to voicemail. I checked her Instagram, even the private one that her mother wasn't allowed to see, but there was nothing – no stories, no posts. I then checked her Snapchat and TikTok and they were silent.

Devi picked up before the first ring completed. 'She's not answering and I've checked all her social media accounts. Is there anything else I should know?' I asked.

Apparently Karen and her friend Jas had been dropped off at the station by Jas's mother. Bilquis, or Billie, was an odd character who wanted to be Jas's friend more than she wanted to be her mother – making up for lost time as she was married off quite young and was now divorced. Billie's mothering tended towards the sloppy side, said Devi. Jas had told her mother they were going to some sort of football hang out, but didn't say exactly where and Billie hadn't pushed. It all seemed above board. She hadn't heard from Jas since then but that was normal, she said. When Devi asked her to call Jas's phone, like Karen's it was going to voicemail.

'Wait,' I said, 'I follow Jas's private account. Let me check if she's posted anything.'

My heart jumped as I saw there was one recent video

story – of her, Karen and a few older people playing with a football in a park, drinking beer and listening to music. Jas had her arms around an older guy, and Karen made a peace sign at the camera and stuck her tongue out. In the background I could see a part of the skyline along the Thames – they were in London.

'What do I do, Bel? She's my entire world,' Devi said, her voice cracking with worry after I told her what I'd found.

I needed to be the mama for once. 'Devi, listen to me, okay? I've got you. It doesn't matter if her phone is switched off, Find My Phone can still take me to her last location. Text me the address and I'll go there right now and find her, okay? And call the police, tell them what has happened.'

'Should I drive up?' she asked tearfully. 'Nikhil is out of the country – I don't know what to do.'

'No, stay at home just in case Karen comes back or calls for whatever reason. I'll handle it this end. I promise I'll let you know what happens as soon as I can.'

I was in an Uber within five minutes. The last location Karen's phone recorded was on a street near London Bridge station. I knew the area a little bit and my heart sank when Devi named it, though I didn't tell her that. It was in a blighted pocket of land that stretched towards Bermondsey; dead spaces of concrete, scrubby patches that overlooked the river, and stack after stack of high-rise council flats. The area was so expensive to live in that now it was inhabited by an uneasy mix of people who worked as financiers, drank Champagne and shopped in Selfridges, alongside others who had been given government housing but nothing to get by on.

The police told Devi they'd look into it and call her back. I had no faith in their abilities to locate a paperclip, let alone a brown teenager, so I called Luke. He didn't hesitate, didn't tell me to leave it in the hands of the Met or advise me to calm down. He just said: 'Text me the location, I'll meet you there.'

The Uber dropped me off at a high-rise council building that soared forty floors skywards. My heart sank – how on earth were we going to find her in there? And what if we were already too late and some predator had already done his worst?

Karen wasn't my child, but I couldn't bear the thought of anyone hurting her. I would reach into this guy's chest and tear his organs out if he harmed her.

Just as I was about to lose my mind, Luke's battered van pulled up on the side of the road. I almost cried at the sight of him. He hurried over and hugged me.

'Any update?' he asked.

'Her phone says she's in this building, I think, but there must be a hundred flats here at least. I have no idea how we'll find her. It seems utterly hopeless.'

'No, it's not,' he said cupping my face. 'Bel, look at me, it's not hopeless. Okay, so there's a hundred flats? We'll knock on a hundred doors.'

'We might not find her,' I whispered.

'True,' he said, 'but on the other hand, maybe we will.

Get a photo of her up on your phone and text it to me. We split the number of flats per floor. Get it done faster.'

I nodded. We waited until someone exited the building and then snuck in.

After what seemed like an incredibly long time, we had worked our way up nine flights of stairs. Most people wanted to chat and ask questions, but at least only one person told Luke to fuck off. We had a system that when we finished a floor, we'd meet at the stairs and walk up to the next level together. 'That way I can be sure you don't get kidnapped,' he said.

'That's not funny.'

'It's not a joke,' he replied.

On the tenth floor, a slim young Asian woman in her early twenties walked past me. Wearing Nikes with a mint-green tick and red soles. My chest hammered at the sight of them. Unless she also knew someone who had access to limited-edition trainers, those were my niece's shoes.

'Hey, love,' I said, smiling, while suppressing every urge to shake her, 'those are amazing trainers.'

Her face was encased in such a thick rind of foundation it seemed to levitate off her skin. 'What's it to you?' she said sullenly.

'I'm just wondering where you got them.' She tried to snake past me but I blocked her way. I didn't know what the fuck I was doing, but I knew this might be my only chance to find out where Karen was.

'What the fuck are you doing?' She scowled. 'Let me pass, you mad bitch.'

I stared at her. 'You know what? I am mad. Because those trainers don't fucking belong to you.'

She looked nervous and her eyes started darting sideways. 'Yes, they do.'

'No, they don't. They belong to my niece. Karen. So I'm going to ask you nicely. Where is she?'

'I don't know what you're talking about,' she said.

If this was a Guy Ritchie film, I'd tell her I was going to tip her over the side of the balcony. Cut her face up with my nails. Boil her bones in acid. Sadly this was real life and you could go to prison for that shit. So I took my phone out and snapped a picture of her. 'Oy – what the fuck . . .'

'If you tell me, you can keep those trainers and I'll give you . . .' I fished about in my pocket '. . . thirty quid. If you don't, I'm going to show your picture to the police, who are out looking for Karen, and tell them you also nicked her trainers.'

She stared at me and sucked her teeth. 'FINE, man, such a headache. She's with that little bitch friend of hers in my cousin's flat. 12B.'

'If I find out you're lying, I will come after you.' Now I was channelling Liam Neeson.

'Whatever,' she said and grabbed the £30. I didn't wait for Luke. I raced up two flights of stairs and stood outside the door.

12B was one of five flats accessed off an unremarkable concrete balcony with a metal safety grille, overlooking scaffolding and glass-and-steel high-rise buildings on the riverbank. One resident had tried to beautify their outdoor space with a pretty hanging basket of red geraniums and pink petunias, but the other flats looked indistinguishable. I knocked on the door.

'Who is it?' a man's voice answered from inside. Now that I was here, I had no idea what I was actually going to do. I knew I should call for Luke, but it was too late and I didn't want to spook the guy on the other side of the door. Adrenaline coursed through me like lightning and made me feel as if I could do anything. What would make him open the door?

'Delivery,' I said in a cheery voice. I didn't want to risk him opening the door with a chain on it, and a delivery seemed harmless and innocuous. 'I'm not expecting anything,' he barked. 'I don't know, mate,' I said as brightly as I could. 'It says 12B, and I'll get in trouble if I don't deliver it.' He opened the door fully. I saw an Asian man, short and stocky, in his early twenties, with a shaved head. The guy from Jas's Instagram stories. His eyes were pinpricks and he had a faint trace of body odour and old takeaway food. He looked down at my empty hands and said: 'Where is it then?'

I hadn't thought that far ahead. So I did the only thing I could and wedged my foot in the door (god bless steel toecaps), yelling: 'KAREN KAREN KAREN!'

'Are you mad?' he said, trying to shove me backwards, but I braced my arms against the doorframe.

From what I could see behind him, his flat was similar to a student home. It was filled with a collection of inherited furniture and cheap plywood, with a few naff touches such as a furry rug and CDs glued to the wall. The curtains were closed and a video game had been paused on the screen. Oh, god, what if Karen wasn't here, and Luke was right, and I was going to get kidnapped?

Then I heard a small voice say: 'Auntie!' and I almost passed out from relief. How many girls were not so lucky? There they were, huddled on the brown leather sofa – Jas and Karen. They didn't move or say anything – maybe too scared to. No shoes on Karen's feet – just Adidas sliders, which meant that shithead downstairs had taken them off her. 'Girls, are you okay?' I said, moving towards them. I didn't hear the snick of the front door closing behind me.

'Of course they're okay, I'm not some pervert,' the guy said, coming round to block my way. 'They're here because they want to be. You need to leave. You're trespassing. *Auntie.*'

'Who the fuck are you?' I snarled.

'Who the fuck am *I*? Who are YOU?' he said.

'That's Mark,' Jas said in a small voice. 'I know his cousin Dina.'

'Shut up, Jas,' he said. I didn't like Jas, but I liked Mark even less. And I was willing to bet that in his own household, his dad had been a bully. Because no normal South Asian boy would ever think of tussling with an auntie. He grabbed me by the arm and started forcing me to the door.

I knew why Jas and Karen hadn't moved or run away – they were in shock. Without even thinking about it, I grabbed Mark by the lapels of his shitty tracksuit top and tried to choke him.

The good news was that my grappling finally spurred Karen into action. She opened the front door to escape and found Luke just outside. The bad news was that choking someone with their lapels is actually harder to do than I'd realised, and Mark was not going quietly. He whacked his elbow into my left eye but I held on despite the searing pain. Thankfully Luke took over almost immediately and pinned Mark's hands behind his back.

'I've called the police,' he said.

'How did you know where I was?'

'When you didn't meet me at the stairs I got worried, then I heard you yell Karen's name like you were in *Candyman*.'

'Smart boy. And thank you.'

'This isn't what you think,' Mark protested as his face was pressed into the floor. 'I'm just babysitting them for Dina.'

I grabbed Karen and hugged her tightly. 'He took our phones, Auntie,' she whispered.

'WHERE IS HER PHONE, YOU ASSHOLE?' I yelled at him. 'TELL ME BEFORE I KICK YOUR BALLS INTO DUST.'

'Kitchen drawer,' he wheezed. 'I was going to give them back.'

'SHUT UP,' I said and retrieved two iPhones. Karen's had a cute Hello Kitty phone cover, and the sight of that tiny piece of sweetness and innocence in the midst of this nightmare almost broke me. I swallowed the lump in my throat and handed them to the girls.

Five minutes later, two policewomen came to take away Mark, who was still protesting his innocence. 'They're friends with my cousin Dina,' he said. 'I'M NOT A PERVERT!'

I asked Luke if Jas and Karen's statements could be taken in my flat rather than at Mark's Peter Pan hellhole, and he went over to ask one of the policewomen, Constable Marta. The other constable waited for the return of Dina. I called Devi immediately and handed the phone to Karen. From what was discernible through the tears and the thousand *I'm sorrys*, Devi was going to drive to my apartment and meet us there. Jas's mother Billie said it was fine to send her back on the train. After her statement was taken, I did as she asked, but seeing how shaken Jas looked after the whole ordeal, felt guilty.

That feeling quickly vanished, however, when I found out Jas was the reason Karen got into this whole mess in the first place. But I wanted to tell Devi in person.

When she arrived, she looked upset and angry but she swept Karen into a hug for a long time. Then she saw my black eye and burst into tears. 'I don't know how I can ever repay you,' she whispered, hugging me tight.

'There's nothing to repay,' I said, my voice breaking.

Luke left soon after, and was bear-hugged by each of us. After Karen gave her statement to Constable Marta with Devi holding her hand, she inhaled a bowl of Singapore noodles and barbecue pork, she fell asleep in the guest bedroom, earphones dangling on her pillow. I poured a big glass of red wine for Devi and we sat on the sofa, alone for the first time that day. Devi had agreed to stay the night because she didn't want to wake Karen up, and shakily talked me through Karen's statement.

'The summary is that they weren't physically harmed or assaulted. Jas was friends with Dina, Mark's cousin, who is all kinds of trouble, known to the police. Jas wanted to spend the night partying at Mark's and asked Karen to come with her. When it was clear there wasn't a party, just the four of them, Karen felt uncomfortable and wanted to leave. Jas wanted to stay and smoke weed, and when Karen kept trying to get her to leave, Dina nicked her shoes.'

'That fucking asshole,' I breathed. Devi nodded and continued. 'Mark took their phones and said he'd give them back when they were better behaved, which he now says was a joke. He is having a blood test done, but they suspect he'd been using a mixture of different drugs which made him erratic. He says he didn't prevent them from leaving, and was always going to let them go.'

'Why didn't they leave when it was clear he was dodgy?' I exclaimed.

'The constable said it happens all the time,' she said. I could tell how hard she was trying to keep it together. 'Usually girls and women in a situation like that don't want it to escalate. Even if a man hasn't yet been violent, they are scared witless that he might be. Fear paralyses people. If there's another woman there, like Dina, they think they might be okay, which we obviously know isn't the case. I think the girls didn't know what to do without their phones and felt bullied, so they just stayed quiet and did what they were told, which was to play video games while Dina and Mark drank.'

I didn't know what to say. I couldn't imagine how Devi must be feeling. Or Karen. Devi said she was going to talk to Billie about the whole incident, but was undecided whether to press charges. Even though Jas was clearly shaken up by how the whole thing turned out, she was implicated in the way Karen got stuck there in the first place. It was a mess, but Devi didn't need to figure it out immediately.

The mountain of unresolved things loomed between us but we were still too exhausted from the day's events to talk. We had inherited from our mother a flawless ability to brush things under the carpet, and so I said: 'Have you seen the *My Indian Bae* finale?'

I put it on, and we chatted about how Clare had made the most deranged-looking *jalebis*, and how it seemed weird that she looked a lot like her husband's mother. When the credits rolled, I realised we couldn't avoid talking forever.

'What are you thinking?' I asked as she took a big sip of wine. She took her time answering.

'I'm thinking how glad I am that my kid is okay and alive,' she said. 'I'm thinking how lucky she is that she doesn't just have one mum, but two. An aunt who will fly into the face of danger and try to strangle someone with their own tracksuit top. I'm thinking that a big reason we had that fight is because you think I don't respect you or your choices, when I do. And if you feel like that, then maybe I need to tell you more often.'

This was all I needed to hear, and more. 'What are *you* thinking?' she asked.

'I know I said some awful things before you left, but I was angry. Not at you, but I took it out on you. I respect your choices too, you know. You made this incredible child. Devi, I would die for that kid. You made a tough choice to leave what you know because you believe something better is out there for you. I believe that too.'

'Thank you,' she whispered. 'I hated that we fell out. I felt like I had just got you back and then we fought and it was awful.' I knew then that we would be okay. Because she wanted to try as much as I did.

She paused as if summoning the nerve to continue. 'I did a lot of thinking while I was keeping away though, Bel, and there is something we should probably talk about.'

My heart skittered with dread. I was clueless as to what this could be. 'Sure, whatever it is, I'll understand.'

'It's not that simple,' she said sadly. 'Look, I've protected you from this for a really long time, but now I don't think it's fair to keep this a secret any longer. I didn't realise how much it had affected our relationship until we started living together. I love you, you're my sister. But I don't know that I really understood or knew you before now. You're this amazing person and you deserve to know.'

'Good god, Devi, please just tell me whatever it is.' My nerves were completely fried from Karen, I couldn't take much more.

'Do you remember just before you started secondary school – the summer you broke your leg?'

'Yeah, of course,' I said. 'Mum was in India visiting relatives and you looked after me that whole summer.'

'She wasn't visiting relatives,' Devi said, closing her eyes. 'She went to India and told Dad she wasn't sure if she was coming back.'

'What? No! I would've remembered that.'

'Dad and I went to great lengths to keep it from you, and when Mum eventually came back, we all just . . . pretended like it never happened. But I was angry with her for a long time afterwards. And I think that's why I always smothered you. It wasn't because I thought you were incapable of looking after yourself. I just couldn't shake the feeling that she might leave us – you – again.'

I lay back on the sofa. 'What. The. Fuck?'

If I concentrated, events from that time came into closer focus. Mum was in India but normally she went for three weeks and this was . . . three months. Devi was Mum. No. Devi was being Mum. She did the grocery shop, she gave me money to go out with my mates. She didn't shout at me for getting up late and watching TV. Where was Dad? Dad was working but when he wasn't working, he was . . . sad. He sometimes went to his workshop but didn't go in there to make anything. I remember thinking, *That's weird, it's so quiet in here.* And I went inside and saw him crying, head buried in his hands. I remember thinking, *But it's summer, why is he so sad? Mum is away and finally there's no one to nag us.* Then I retreated quietly and didn't say a word.

In Case of Emergency

Mum would call but she would speak to me and then hang up. At first, it was great. Like being at work when the boss is on holiday. There was no one to shout at me or make me do chores. But after a while I missed her, and that grew into a gnawing emptiness. Her toothbrush gathered dust and the kitchen looked like a cess pit no matter how hard Devi tried to keep on top of it. *When are you coming home?* I'd ask with a slight whine to my voice when I spoke to her on the phone and heard the monsoon in the background. Every time I'd mention Mum's name to Devi, she'd become angry and start muttering under her breath. And then I broke my leg while cycling to the shop after a car rushed by me and the slipstream knocked me over. Everyone was really upset.

When Mum came back she was being nicer than usual and couldn't stop hugging me. Devi had left the night before Mum's flight was due to arrive, but it was as if her anger had been transferred to Dad. He worked a lot and spent most of the weekend in his workshop, drinking beer, hammering things and listening to The Pretenders. Mealtimes became even more fractured and I only ate dinner with one parent at the table for a while. Things with Devi were different. She was always nagging and haranguing me. School started and I was busy hating being there and not making friends apart from Ling. Then Ama arrived and I forgot about that whole summer. Apart from a scar on my leg, it was like it never happened.

'Why was she not sure if she was coming back?'

'It wasn't because she didn't love us,' Devi said, trying

401

not to cry. 'She just . . . she'd spent so much of her life doing what she thought she was supposed to do, I think she reached this breaking point where everything felt too hard.'

'Do you forgive her for it?'

'I didn't for a long time,' Devi said. 'But then I had Karen and that just took over everything. And now that I'm the same age more or less as she was at that time, I get it. I get why people want to blow their lives up. When you spend so long not articulating what you want . . . it feels like if you don't get out, you literally might die.'

'I don't know what to do with any of this.'

'It's as big or small as you want to make it,' she said, reminding me of Marina's words at the club. 'You can punish her for something that you can't change, that she can't change either. Or you use it for something useful. Like understanding why I was the way I was with you, or why she sometimes overcompensates.'

'I think maybe I've known,' I said slowly. 'Somewhere deep down, I've known. I think that's why I never put her name down as an emergency contact, or the person to fetch my body if I die on a mountain.'

'Maybe,' Devi said. 'I know we haven't been close the last few years,' she said hesitantly, 'but I've never stopped worrying about you, thinking about you. And I don't mean whether you have a boyfriend or any of that dumb shit. I mean whether you're happy.'

'How do you do it with Mum?' I asked. 'You two seem to have such a good relationship now.'

She sighed. 'The way most Asians do it, Bel. We don't talk about it, ever. There are times when I find that really difficult, like when I see how hard Dad tries and she's dismissive of all the small things he does. Or right now, when she's lecturing me about marriage and I think, *You have no right*. But I also know why she wants me to reconcile with Nikhil because she did it with Dad and whatever happened in the past, they're in a relationship and they love each other. A lot of people their age can't say the same.' She paused. 'Does it made you think about Mum differently?'

There was a lot I wanted to say but I was conscious of damaging Devi's relationship with her further.

'I've always felt like she had this unreachable place in her, you know? The weird childhood she had, how young she was when she married Dad and so on. Maybe that distance is what I've somehow emulated.'

'And does it hurt less, now that you know?'

'No, of course not. It just hurts in different ways. There are things Mum should have done differently, but I still made my own choices. I can't be sad that no one is around when I've made that happen. The whole thing with the accident and Gregor turning up as my emergency contact . . . it was a wake-up call.'

'And what about Ama – have you sorted things out with her?' Devi said.

'Reconnecting with Ama brought up a lot of stuff,' I replied honestly. 'I missed out on many years with her because I was too concerned about being right and punishing them for the way they behaved on that holiday.'

403

'You're being quite hard on yourself though,' she said, reaching for the bottle and filling her glass, then mine. So much for quitting drinking. 'Sometimes we don't know all the facts.'

'Yes, but I have to learn that loving people and having people around is not a weakness. Today with Karen . . . there is no universe in which I wouldn't have behaved in exactly the same way, done anything I could to find her. I would do the same for you. And if I can give to other people, if I can be there for them, *why* can't I accept people doing the same for me?'

Devi's face crumpled as the day's events came back to haunt her, as I knew they would do for the months and years to come. 'I don't know what I would have done without you today.'

I leaned over and hugged her like a bear. 'But I was there. I was. And I always will be.'

19

The next morning, Devi and Karen left soon after break-fast. Mum and Dad had tearfully demanded to see their granddaughter. That was the difference with grandparents and parents. If we'd pulled something like that, we'd likely have been shipped off to India. Karen would probably receive a light telling off, and then be swamped with kisses, cuddles and a mountain of food.

I'd woken up early to see them off, and in doing so caught a fraught email from Crispin sent the night before.

Crispin had CC'd Tristan.

Team, conference call tomorrow at 9 a.m. C

The next morning was the first cold snap of the season. A slight drop in temperature set the flowers smelling of sweet rot, starting their slow decline into death.

I got to the conference room early and checked messages on my phone. Crispin would be dialling in from Monaco but wanted Tristan and me in the same room for the meeting.

While I was midway through typing a text to Devi, Tristan came in and sat as far away from me as possible. It was the first time we'd been alone together since I'd called him an arrogant prick. It was incredible, once you saw how insecure and shallow a person was, how quickly any attraction you'd felt to them turned rancid. 'Hey,' he said as he came in. I looked at him and wordlessly went back to texting Devi. I was done giving my energy to people who didn't care about me and being dismissive to those who did.

Crispin's face loomed on-screen, large and sunburned. He was wearing a linen shirt unbuttoned to a horribly low point on his chest. 'We're cancelling Thunder,' he said.

'What?' I said, dismayed. 'We've made nearly three-quarters of the hires!' Most of them had already started handing in their notice and I was already interviewing for a new assistant.

'Have any of them signed contracts yet?'

'Well, no, but . . .'

'Then tell them it's off. Lightning have gone with a different agency, and we don't have the budget to waste.'

'Okay, Crispin, I'll let them know,' said Tristan. I knew that weasel would make Oliver do it.

'Crispin,' I said, in a final attempt to appeal to some scrap of humanity remaining in him, 'other agencies are already putting into place their Diversity and Inclusion plans. Without this, we don't have anything. It'll make us look like we aren't progressive.'

He was already turning away from the camera to yell at someone: 'I *told* you I don't like the chef using vinegar when poaching my eggs. How hard is that to comprehend?'

We waited patiently until he turned to face us. 'Bel, I know this isn't PC but I don't care. We haven't the budget. There are other more pressing areas of growth. I know you don't like it, and I know the profit and loss of the company is something you're not interested in, but this is how real life works.'

There was no point explaining or trying to do the right thing when the people running the show didn't care. And as long as people like Tristan and Crispin were in charge, things would stay the same. There would always be some excuse to worm out of making systemic change; some aspect of their own fragility that would need propping up in preference. As Tristan and Crispin carried on talking, I realised that, for at least a year, I hadn't liked being at work. Though it pained me to say it, Katrina was right – I complained about it constantly. The only thing keeping me here was the pay cheque and I didn't want to be one of those sad creatures like Bernard in Analytics, grumbling for years but never making any plans to improve things for themself. Like most other people I needed money so as to eat and to pay my mortgage, but I'd also saved up enough to give myself room to breathe – to change and grow and take some chances.

'Great chat, guys,' Crispin said. 'Let me know how it

all goes. Anything else before I leave you?' But he was already distracted by someone placing a plate in front of him. 'Take away the fucking bread!' he yelled.

'Yes,' I said. 'I'm handing in my notice.'

*

The following weekend, I'd wanted to see how Karen was doing. But before I went over to Devi's, I needed to chat to my parents. I was under strict instructions not to tell them about everything that had happened with Dina, Mark and the police. As far as they were concerned, Karen had been naughty by going to stay with a friend without telling me or Devi.

My mother, who always grew uneasy whenever one of us said we needed to talk, tried to delay it with a number of tasks, from asking me to help her move a nest of coffee tables, to making the filling for samosas. Instead I firmly steered her into the living room.

'I need to ask you both something,' I said.

I could see them running through their inner tombola of disappointment – was I accidentally pregnant, broke, going to ask to move back in with them?

'I have decided to set up my own agency,' I said. Their eyes popped in surprise. 'I'm really good at my job and I know I can make a success of it. But in order to do that, I need some seed money. I've got savings, but it would help a lot if I could borrow some investment capital from you. I can give you a business plan so you'll see how quickly you'll get a return.' I took a deep breath. 'Do you think you might be able to help?'

Mum looked at Dad. 'The short answer is yes,' she said. 'We're still sorting out the house stuff with Nikhil and Devi but it won't be a problem. We can move some other things around.'

'Okay, thanks. I'll get the business plan to you as soon as it's finalised.'

'We don't need to see the business plan. If you need our help, you have it. And you know what you're doing. You're a successful businesswoman.'

I was unexpectedly overcome by a wave of emotion. This was one of the nicest things my mother had ever said to me. One of the first times she'd acknowledged I was good at my job. (At least that's how I interpreted it.) But even as I said my thank yous, I knew I had to ask them about them turning me down before. I wasn't angry anymore, but I had to clear the air. 'Mum, why did you and Dad help Devi with her mortgage and not me? Is it because I'm not married?'

'Don't be silly,' she said. 'Gosh, look at how high the grass has grown in the garden. Das, can you take the mower out?' A classic tactic of hers in avoiding uncomfortable conversations. Create a list of things that need doing immediately.

'Mum, I'm not mad about it, I promise, I'd just like to know why.'

'I've got to get the lunch on, Bel . . .'

'We weren't the only ones who helped them,' Dad said,

seeing how much I needed a proper answer and knowing Mum would just keep listing things. 'Nikhil's parents did too. But it was partly the timing. We had made a plan to cut down our hours before retirement and it was already in motion when you asked. It wasn't because we didn't want to help you, Bel. You're our daughter, of course we want to help.'

I didn't know what to do with that, or how to feel about it. 'We didn't mean no forever,' he said gently, 'we just meant no at that point in time. We could've done it for you later on, but by then you were insistent on going it alone.'

It wasn't quite enough, but it made me feel better.

*

Karen had moved out of Mum and Dad's and back to her own home with Devi, who had finally managed to evict Nikhil. The plan was that she'd stay in the house until it sold. Nikhil was given an hour to pack everything he wanted to take – which wasn't a lot – so the place looked pretty much the same. The moment I rang the doorbell, Karen barrelled down the stairs and almost knocked me down with the velocity of her hug.

After checking she was okay, asking lots of questions and arranging a date for her to come over, I'd taken the train back to London. I rushed to meet Ranvir who'd wanted to hear all about the encounter with Mark and had just finished with a hospital appointment. We were sitting outside her favourite café in Soho, and the waitress was giving me dirty looks as I broke off bits of a sausage roll I'd grabbed from Greggs.

She screamed when I got to the part about choking Mark with his tracksuit top. 'You did *what*? Are you insane? It takes a long time to master that move. And also, you have to try and get him on the ground first.'

I flicked a bit of pastry at her. 'I'll make a note of that next time I'm emancipating my niece from the clutches of a creep.'

'So things are okay? Getting better on the home front?'

'Yes. I took your advice, decided to chip away at that mountain bit by bit. To ask for help. Stop stressing so much. Stop thinking everything needs to be planned.'

I liked Ranvir a lot, and realised, if I made the effort, this could be the start of a proper friendship.

'Ranvir, I know this is a big ask,' I said, 'but would you ever consider leaving Leopard and trying something new?'

'Funny you should mention that,' she said, growing a bit more serious. 'I was actually thinking about it.' She fiddled with her engagement ring. 'Why do you ask?'

'I've got an idea. Let's swap these for some stronger drinks and talk about it further?'

'I like the way you think,' she said, signalling for the bill.

20

I'd always felt like an odd bod when it came to weddings. I knew I should like them. After all, other girls seemed to. Monica on *Friends* had a wedding book, and a whole genre of movies evolved around women who were the bridesmaid-never-the-bride, whose unhappiness was resolved by finally attaining that status.

I found heteronormative love exhausting and narrow. The expectations, the judgements, the confinement. I knew with growing certainty that I wanted to meet someone who mattered, who would be there for me and be my partner in all things, but I didn't know if I wanted marriage or children. And I was starting to realise that was fine.

'Things might change,' Devi said after I confided all of this to her. We were pulling up to Marina's lovely old country house. She'd let Ama and Bron hold their wedding ceremony there in among the trees and it was a beautiful act of generosity.

'Maybe,' I replied. 'Did you end up going on a date with Tony from Snaps?'

'Once. But I'm not seeing him again. It made me think

about what I really want and I don't want to go straight into another relationship,' she said, picking up the hem of her chiffon maxi-dress. I had chosen to wear a beaded jumpsuit. Both of us were wearing trainers, and only planned to change into heels for the actual ceremony. We were unwilling and too old to sacrifice our feet yet again to the bunion gods. 'I want to see what's out there. I want to date, I want to have sex, lots of sex.'

'Devil!'

'Shut it, Grandma,' she said, laughing. 'And what do you want?'

Ahead of us, the trees opened out into a high wall of blooms: purple, red and pink. We were surrounded by the fragrance of lemons. There was a big board welcoming us to Ama and Bron's wedding, along with another crammed with pictures of their life together.

'I want this,' I said.

'What, to get married?'

'No, not that part,' I said. 'I want to meet someone, and I want to share my life with them. But I want it to be about this. About love, and joy and growing together. To need and be needed. I think I want that.'

She looked thoughtful. 'It can be the most amazing thing,' she said. 'That connection and that bond. It's also sacrifice and work and compromise. People think betrayal is your partner cheating on you, but it isn't. It's the small, slow betrayals of not being there for each other, forgetting to champion and cheer each other on. Whoever this person is, just . . . don't forget that.'

I squeezed her hand. I had been instructed to make my way to Ama's dressing room, but there was something I needed to do first.

*

She was standing against a trellis of honeysuckle, wearing a pale blue jumpsuit and huge Christian Dior sunglasses, tapping away at her phone. 'Hi,' I said softly.

'Hi,' Ling replied with a small smile. She was as nervous about this as I was. I felt the possible topics of conversation open up before me like a highway: her kids, husband, making a joke about Ama's hen do. But I was paralysed by anxiety at the thought of it all going wrong and finding myself on the sharp end of her tongue. 'You look incredible,' she added, 'but then again, you always did.'

'Thank you,' I said with some surprise. I don't think we had ever complimented each other as girls. 'So do you. But then again, you always did.' It was a safe joke, a gentle repartee that didn't risk much.

'MUMMY!' the sound of several voices screeching in unison carried across the garden.

'They'll be upon us soon,' she groaned, just as the smallest child barrelled into her legs and pulled at her leg for attention. I saw her face change. Despite her sardonic comment, she grew brighter the minute they arrived, pieces of her finally coming back into alignment. We didn't have to have a big conversation about things. She was happy, and it was enough.

'Ling,' I said, before going to find Ama.

'Mmmph?' she said, looking up from her toddler who was trying to put his hand over her mouth.

'It's good to see you,' I said, turning away before she could see the sadness in my smile, because life isn't about sunsets and happy endings. It's about realising, despite your ego convincing you that you are the sun in everyone's solar system, sometimes the people you once loved are happier without you.

*

'Bel, it's a disaster,' said Ama. She was usually the most beautiful person in the room on a normal day. But in her wedding clothes – a regal red *lengha* covered in crystals, and a diamond tika – she looked like a queen. Not a *yaas queen*, but a ruler of lands and seas. A conqueror of kingdoms. By some miracle her mother had managed to come back in time from Sri Lanka, but apparently was now refusing to do her speech.

'I am going to help you with this, don't panic,' I said. 'But you *cannot* cry. Yes, I see your big Bambi eyes filling up with water, and the make-up artist has already left, and I don't have her skills, okay?'

'Say something to make me laugh then, you asshole!'

'First, that is a lot of pressure. Just imagine if the only joke I have is a knock-knock one. Second, jokes are not going to help this situation. Cold, calm logic will.'

'What's the logic?'

I took her elegant, *mehndi*-covered hands in mine and kneeled down. 'Ama, this is your wedding day. You are marrying the love of your life, pal! That's what this is about. Your mum is here. That's what matters. Maybe the speech is too much for her. That's okay too. You don't have to think about it today, you don't have to worry about any of it yet. The only thing we need to decide is if you want to cut the speech altogether or ask someone else to do it.'

'But there isn't anyone else,' she said, tilting her head back to keep the tears from falling. 'It needs to be a family member and there's no other family here but her. None of my relatives from Sri Lanka came.' I hadn't realised just how much Ama had been affected by them not being there. She'd told me it was all fine, that she'd sorted things out with her mother, but it sounded like the kind of temporary peace brokered without any meaningful change. They said they supported and loved her – but not enough to get on an aeroplane and show it.

'She's not the only family you have here,' I said soothingly. 'I'm here. I know I already have a sister but there's room for one more, okay?'

'Oh, fuck,' she said.

'What?'

'I think a fake eyelash is coming off.' And with that, Ama couldn't hold it back any longer. She burst into tears, and I gave her a big hug, which was a nice gesture but an epic mistake that had us trying to extricate crystals from the beading on my jumpsuit for about five minutes.

It would have been longer had Marina not walked in

and seen us fused together. She did her trademark eye-roll but still helped disentangle us, and then got to work repairing Ama's runaway mascara.

*

I don't think I had ever seen Devi cry as much as she did during the ceremony, especially when Bron and Ama exchanged their vows under a canopy made from saris donated by her aunts back home. At first, I thought it was because Devi was sad about her own marriage, but she said: 'Not at all. It's because love goes on, it continues in different ways we often don't imagine. True love is so rare. How lucky are we, little sister, that we get to witness it?'

The celebration meal was being served in a beautiful glass conservatory that overlooked the rest of the garden. Jessamine had done most of the decorating, and despite Ama's worries that it would be sprigs of kale and bits of hessian sack, she'd done well with white flowers as a base, shot through with bright pinks and oranges. We'd all been given little stone elephants as wedding favours. I spoke to Mrs Sendhil, who was so nervous and out of her comfort zone it was hard to be mad at her for backing out of the speech. Love was a complicated thing.

Luke hadn't been on our table initially, but after all he'd done to help with Karen, Devi dragged him over. She'd begged one of the other guests to move and had gone to get them a glass of Champagne to smooth things over.

Whatever doubts Luke might have had about us becoming friends had eased. Although it would have been very easy for me to see him as a knight in shining armour and go all moon-eyed, I knew my ability to call on him in a crisis had *only* been possible because we were friends. 'Not drinking?' he asked, pointing at my water glass.

'Not until I've given my little speech,' I said. 'The last thing I need is a repeat of Ama's hen do.' Luke looked mystified. 'I kissed the guy I'd had a crush on when I was sixteen. Then vomited on his lap.' In response to his horrified expression, I said: 'Oh, like you haven't been a gremlin at some point.'

Bron's father stood up to give his speech, which started off with an anecdote about her as a baby. I had a while to go yet. 'Listen, I feel I need to clear the air about something,' Luke whispered. 'I'm glad we get to be friends. It's better than . . . you know.' He made the noise of bedsprings squeaking.

'Gross,' I said, trying not to laugh. It was so freeing to be able to say anything to each other without worrying about whether or not it diminished our levels of attractiveness, or second-guessing how cool it sounded. 'Now shut up, it's time for my speech.'

*

In Hollywood films, there's a trope where the main character, for dramatic effect, goes on stage and decides not to do their stuffy, boring speech. Instead, they throw the prompt cards away and pull off something so spectacular it rivals Barack Obama's inaugural address.

Now if that were me, I would have stuck to the boring speech. The problem was, I didn't have the luxury of doing so, given that I'd volunteered to stand in at the last minute for the mother-of-the-bride in front of a room of mostly strangers plus a few school friends and frenemies I hadn't seen in years.

Beads don't absorb sweat so the nervous perspiration ran straight down my back. I walked on stage actually praying something might happen so I wouldn't have to go through with it. Where was an open cellar door when you needed one?

As I took the microphone, I smiled over at Mrs and Mrs Sendhil-Harman who had the glow of newlyweds, eyes mad with tiredness but also shining with happiness. I looked out at the crowd and glanced over to Marina sitting on the same table as Ling, both of them looking at me. My heart sank as they whispered something to each other, but they both looked up then and gave me a supportive thumbs-up. *Do it for our girl,* the look seemed to say, and Marina actually smiled.

'Hi, everyone, I'm Beryl Kumar and Ama is one of my oldest friends. But I'm here not just as a friend – I'm also representing her as family, because that's what she is to me. That's what she's always been.' I looked over at Ama's mother and nodded, not in reproach but to reassure her that it was okay; family sometimes shared the load.

'Some of us spend our whole lives looking for a certain

type of love, not realising that we've had it for a long time. We don't always take care of it the way we should. Sometimes we think love is something that just *is* – that we don't have to sustain it or work for it, and we do. But Ama has always known what love is, and what love should feel like, because she is one of the most loving people I know. Love isn't just fireworks and desire. It's mostly in the small gestures. It's friendship. It's being understood. Knowing that, no matter what, there won't be judgement but safety and comfort whenever you are in need.

'Some of our school friends are here with us today, and they know that this is who Ama is. Years ago, I sat with her on a beach and we spent ages staring out to sea. I thought she was passing time like I was, and didn't realise she was dealing with something much bigger: figuring out who she was, and how that might affect the way people loved her, and who she loved.

'I was whingeing on about some boy, and I said to her that love isn't love if it's not unconditional. And she said that while love shouldn't come with conditions because that would be like trying to tame the ocean, you still had to take care of it if you wanted something that lasted, something that was beautiful. She was sixteen when she said this, by the way. She knew, even back then. And now she's met someone who feels the same way about love as she does.

'Bron and Ama are incredible individuals, but together they are a force field. They remind us that love is worth fighting for, that it sustains you, that it comes in many different forms, and that if you can let it in, my god, it is powerful.

'We are here to celebrate two people and their bond of love for each other. But, Bron and Ama, you are not alone in this new chapter. We are with you. We are with you.' I looked at everyone in the audience and gestured with my hands for them to join me.

As one, the whole room erupted: 'WE ARE WITH YOU.'

Epilogue

Autumn was in the air, a welcome relief after such a long, hot summer.

Maggie was getting the computer system set up when I walked in with coffees.

'Shouldn't I be doing that?' she murmured. The slow, staid surroundings of Richmond didn't exactly match my dream of an independent ad agency in a too-cool-for-school East London warehouse by the canal. But we'd been given a reduced rate by an old client of mine, and at least we had a view of the Thames, the most enduring of London's waterways, which seemed a fitting metaphor for a newly evolving business.

'Perhaps, if I was more computer literate,' I said, 'which I'm not. For now, me getting the coffees balances it out. And the DIY.'

Although I'd stolen a lot of stationery from Leopard, and exported my entire client database, I missed some of the things I had taken for granted there, such as the IT department. Thankfully, Maggie had studied computing at college. While she got the systems set up, much to her surprise I'd installed shelving, checked all the electrics and laid down some carpeting.

I was just waiting for Ranvir to turn up so we could go through the phase one organisational chart of what our team would look like.

Her nephew Vishal, an unusually quiet young man wearing jeans, a beanie and a green T-shirt, was already working away in one corner. He was studying accounting at university and had offered to help us with some of the finances. I was agreeable to most of his suggestions apart from slashing the coffee budget, and I swore he brought his own thermos in to make a point. Karen was helping me out with office admin for the two weeks before she started her A-levels, but unlike Vishal, her relationship with time-keeping was terrible.

'AUNTIE,' she said, erupting through the door, 'I'm so sorry I'm late.' She looked shyly at Vishal, on whom she had a massive crush, and heaved her bag onto her desk. She hadn't yet figured out that he was gay, and peacocked *hard* whenever she thought he'd be in, but I felt that sometimes teenagers needed to work life out for themselves.

'It's okay,' I said, 'you can make the time up later.' I couldn't let her off the hook just because she was my niece. She was being paid (minimum wage), more than my window tele-sales job had paid me when I was her age. She also had no excuse given that her new home was now only a fifteen-minute walk away. Devi, to my utter delight, had finally decided to move to the London sub-urbs to give herself and Karen a new start.

'Where did you get up to yesterday?' I asked.

'I've onboarded everyone into the system,' she said. 'Well, almost everyone.' She looked at me accusingly. 'I gave you the form last week, Auntie.'

I looked at her, mystified. 'I'm the director, why do I need to be onboarded into the system?'

'You're an employee,' Vishal piped up, his first words aside from 'hello' that morning. 'You still have to have your details recorded.'

'Ugh, fine. Give me the form.'

I took my coffee outside onto the little deck and started filling it out. (Another template ripped off from Leopard, given to me by Jane who had thoroughly disapproved of the childish way Crispin ignored me until my leaving date.)

My pen jerked as I saw the words: *In Case Of Emergency*. I knew who I was going to put down, but I wanted to check it was okay with her.

She answered on the third ring. 'Yes, stalker? You just called me ten minutes ago.'

'This is going to sound like a weird question, but . . . can I put you down as my emergency contact?'

'Really?' Devi answered. 'You mean you don't want to put down Gregor again? Or someone you met on Tinder last year? Or perhaps the Deliveroo driver who delivers your Korean chicken burger every weekend?'

'HAR HAR. Don't make me regret asking. It's fine, isn't it?'

'Baby sister,' she said, 'you would be in real trouble – literally and metaphorically – if you didn't.'

Acknowledgements

Writing a book was something I knew I wanted to do when I was seven. And I would never have thought I could do it without the right encouragement. Without a mother who would take us to the library every weekend and fill our world with books. The first acknowledgement always goes to my parents Jaya and Ashok, who built and created ground solid enough for me to stand on. Who never got in my way, who never suggested I do anything other than the thing that gave me purest joy: to write.

The second, goes to my big sister Priya. You and I are cut from the same star cloth, and there is nowhere I wouldn't go, nothing I wouldn't do, for you. We have saved each other countless times, from ourselves, from others.

Then, I must thank Mal, my best friend. For always being by my side, being one of my biggest cheerleaders and being able to see my potential and ambition when I couldn't. My incredible friend Martin who would periodically ask, 'How's Beryl?', as well as my brother-in-law Shabby. My other amazing network of friends who've checked in and encouraged me, including Aga, Jack, Niaz, Kumaran, Ahmed, Yumi, Lindsay, Poonam, Anita B, Karen, Zekra, Zehra, Shabana, Kudsia. My precious school friends Alice and Sonia. I also want to thank my incredible in-laws in New Zealand, Prue and David, as well as Gaby and Felicity. And my family in India – the Shettys – who are so supportive and proud and blow up Mum's WhatsApp with their loving messages.

But also, this book would not exist without my agent Rowan. I dreamed up Beryl during the first 2020 UK lockdown, and creating her gave me something to hold on to. (And something to do besides watching Netflix.) Rowan loved her too, and encouraged me to write the first sample chapters. I wrote these when I was still ill with long covid, so I'm incredibly proud of this achievement that led to the book you hold in your hands. (I'm now fully recovered.) But also, thank you to Sonny Marr for believing in a book that was still in fragments, and to my brilliant editor Emily Griffin who helped shape it. Thank you to the rest of the PRH team for all your support. Last but definitely not least, thank you to my managers Sarah and Grainne at Siren, who make it possible for me to do everything I do.